A GALAXY UNKNOWN

VALOR AT VAUZLEE

Book 2

BY

THOMAS DEPRIMA

Vinnia Publishing - U.S.A.

Valor at Vauzlee

ISBN-10: 1-61931-001-5

ISBN-13: 978-1-61931-001-8

2nd Edition

Amazon Distribution

Cover art by: Martin J. Cannon

Appendices containing political and technical data highly pertinent to this series are included at the back of this book.

To contact the author, or see additional information about this and his other novels, visit:

http://www.deprima.com

I wish to express my deep appreciation to L. S. for her invaluable insights and suggestions during the original creation of this novel, to Ted King for his technical expertise and encouragement during the creation of this series, and to Michael A. Norcutt for his suggestions and proofreading, and for acting as military advisor on this series.

This series of Jenetta Carver novels includes:

A Galaxy Unknown
Valor at Vauzlee
The Clones of Mawcett
Trader Vyx
Milor!
Castle Vroman
Against All Odds
Return To Dakistee

Other novels by the author:

AGU: Border Patrol - Citizen X

When the Spirit Moves You
When the Spirit Calls

A World Without Secrets

Table of Contents

Chapter One

"Eighteen thousand!" Chairman Andrei Gagarin snarled loudly and viciously at the fifteen council members seated around the orotund table. The violent life of a smuggler, slaver, and drug lord had given him a permanent sneer, and he exuded a sinister presence that the most expensive suits and assiduous grooming could never completely disguise. His vitriolic delivery, expelled with the force of a solar flare, rebounded off the smooth, unadorned walls of the spacious elliptical chamber and returned to again assault the eardrums of his fellow council members. A short man, standing no more than five feet, five inches, Gagarin was nevertheless powerfully built. His barrel chest, short coconut-brown hair, and dark beady eyes were in no small part responsible for the nickname 'Pit Bull,' conferred upon him by intimidated subordinates. An obvious reference to the vicious and deadly canine species on Earth, it was frequently whispered but wisely never spoken aloud by anyone who placed value upon his or her life.

"Eighteen thousand!" Gagarin reprised just as loudly and vehemently. "Do you know how long it takes to recruit eighteen thousand employees? Do you know how long it takes to screen them? Do you know how much it costs to train them?" With each shouted question, his anger and vocal pitch seemed to escalate.

The massive Raider organization, created through the merger of a dozen large, independent smuggling operations more than a decade earlier and growing steadily since its inception, had just suffered its first major setback. And that reversal of fortunes had been perpetrated by, of all people, a lone female ensign in the Galactic Space Command— one operating without the knowledge or involvement of her superiors.

The meeting hall where the eighty-year-old pirate was again giving voice to unremitting anger toward the responsible Spacc ensign was as secure as the headquarters of any nation's intelligence service. Located in the sheltered industrial complex of a legitimate business conglomerate, a combination of the most advanced electronic jamming equipment and sound-deadening building materials available made eaves-dropping on conversations, celebrations, and tirades that took place within the room impossible. Each of the council members was believed to be a respected member of the conglomerate's executive pool, and in fact, they were. The Raider organization, universally accepted as the scourge of the galaxy, had long ago begun wrapping itself in a cocoon of legitimacy to hide its activities and give it a means to easily move large concentrations of currency. It even hijacked its own shipments occasionally, but never so much that bona fide insurers became overly suspicious.

No one suspected that each of the council members was also a key figure in the Raider hierarchy. As members of the powerful Lower Council, they spent their days planning and coordinating nefarious deeds that would be perpetrated throughout the known galaxy.

"Plus," Gagarin continued, thick blue veins in his massive neck standing out like lengths of nylon cord, "fifty-four of our warships were utterly destroyed, and dozens of snared and repaired passenger liners, cargo ships, shuttles, and space tugs were reduced to so much worthless scrap. I'm not even taking into account the two warships, along with another two thousand employees, which she destroyed during ship-to-ship engagements, nor the two battleships she appropriated. Most significantly, our only base in that deca-sector of space was obliterated. *Obliterated*, people. Now, I want to know what you intend to do about it."

"Andrei, since the base, ships, and people have been either destroyed, captured, or killed," Councilwoman Erika Overgaard said, carefully pushing aside a small lock of platinum blond hair that had slipped down over her eyes from her expensively coiffed hairdo, "there's nothing that can be done about it except write it off as a business expense. We certainly can't recover anything of value from the detritus. As you've said, the assets are gone." At sixty-four, Overgaard was one of the younger members of the council. Her area of expertise was drug manufacture and smuggling.

Gagarin glared intently at Overgaard, long enough for her to begin squirming in her impeccable ten-thousand-credit, two-piece business suit. Gagarin could make one feel like a small child being taken to task by an angry parent, even when innocent of any wrongdoing. Personal warmth was a descriptive term that would never be used in the same sentence as Gagarin's name, unless it was to aver that he had none.

"I agree," Councilman Bentley Blosworth said calmly as he stared somberly into his tea mug. "There's nothing to be gained here. You should be concentrating on your two upcoming operations." The seventy-two-year-old councilman finally looked up to gaze at Gagarin over the edge of his large cup as he took a noisy sip of deep brown beverage. The introverted, hirsute-challenged little man, whose specialty was bank fraud and money laundering, didn't fear Gagarin half as much as he probably should have. Over the years, a number of Lower Council members had passed away from rare diseases after brief illnesses or from deadly accidents which occurred under unusual circumstances.

"No!" Chairman Gagarin screamed. "I'm not going to simply write this off the books. Our losses exceed a trillion credits. I want the Spacc responsible to feel our wrath."

"I, too, am of the opinion that we should simply drop this matter," Councilman Arthur Strauss said calmly. Unlike Gagarin, Strauss had the slick, polished look of a true business executive or perhaps even a successful politician. Of mainly Slavic ancestry, he was tall and handsome, with a smile that could melt the hearts of most women. At sixty-six, his thick, wavy hair was still a dark, chocolate brown. His association with, and support from, certain members of the Upper Council made him the second most powerful member of the Lower Council. His words carried as much weight as any five of the lesser members combined, so Gagarin couldn't simply dismiss Strauss's viewpoint as he had that of the others.

"Her death would be a *cause célèbre*," Strauss continued. We certainly wouldn't want Space Command to learn that we were responsible; she would become a martyr in their eyes and have every Space seeking retribution."

"What do we know about her, Councilman Strauss?" Gagarin demanded.

"We've only just begun to develop a file on her. Although we begin collecting information on Space Command cadets who choose to follow a career in political science or intelligence while still at the Academy and for officers selected to attend the Warship Command Institute as soon as such selection is made, we normally don't begin collecting information on other officers until they at least attain the rank of Lieutenant. And we almost never pay attention to Engineering, Economics, Science, Medical, or JAG officers until they attain the rank of Lieutenant Commander. Anything our people might have gathered at Raider-One while she was being— 'adjusted,' is gone. We know she's an ensign, comes from a prominent military family, and is highly intelligent. Although she consistently placed at the apex of her classes in mathematics and science, she was ranked near the bottom of her class at the Academy due to reported indecisiveness. For that reason, she was judged to be totally unsuitable for command. Apparently, even their intelligence people didn't feel she was worth a recruitment effort. While she was our slave, she received our age prolongation process and a substantial DNA rewrite. Although attractive to begin with, by the time the DNA changes have finished altering her body, she'll look like a goddess. No *normal* man will be able to resist her charms. We had expected to reap considerable profit from offering her sexual services at one of our resorts, and if the modification process was later found to be without— side-effects, we intended to administer such modification to all future pleasure slave acquisitions."

"Don't remind me about that fool Arneu. He should have sent copies of his research documentation to headquarters at periodic intervals. If he had, the billions we invested in developing that science wouldn't have been lost when Raider-One was destroyed."

Gagarin had been looking forward to receiving the age prolongation and recombinant DNA processes himself soon, and had been working with genetic researchers to develop a model for his new body. He would be tall and handsome, like Strauss, and his new appearance would finally make him an acceptable candidate for investiture on the Upper Council. His cherished dream had died with the entire scientific group at Raider-One, and he couldn't let go of his desire for retaliation against the individual responsible.

"Where is this woman now?" Gagarin demanded.

"Our people on Higgins report that Ensign Carver has been posted to an insignificant position in an obscure area of their Science Section, assigned to study recently gathered data on a globular cluster. She presents no further threat to us."

"It doesn't matter. I want you to continue your investigation. I want to know everything about her."

"How deep do you wish us to go?"

"I want to know how old she was when she cut her first tooth."

Strauss grimaced ever so slightly and nodded. "Maximum depth then. But if you must have your pound of flesh, I suggest you wait for a while. Wait six months or a year until the public eye is completely off this young girl and then arrange a simple accident. I'm a firm believer in that old saying about revenge being a dish best served cold."

"Very well," Chairman Gagarin said. "I can be patient for a while since she represents no further threat. You have your six months."

"*My* six months?"

"It's your idea to wait," Gagarin said. "And in six month's time I'll either be reading about the unfortunate death of one Ensign Jenetta Carver, or we'll *all* be reading about the untimely demise of one Arthur Stephen Strauss, Deputy-Comptroller of MedZip Electronics.

Strauss effectively masked the loathing he felt towards the man. He certainly didn't underestimate the ability of Gagarin to make good on his threats and decided it was time to make some arrangements of his own.

Chapter Two
~ February 20th, 2268 ~

~ February 20th, 2268 ~

"It's about damn time they acknowledged what you did out here," Lt. Commander Gloria Sabella, first officer aboard the freighter *Vordoth*, said from the comfort of her comparatively spacious quarters aboard ship. The *Vordoth* was presently floating, sans cargo, in a parking orbit around Higgins Space Command Base, which was in turn floating in geosynchronous orbit around the planet Vinnia. After a harrowing and nearly disastrous trip through an area of space dominated by Raiders, the freighter's crew was enjoying a well-deserved liberty while its next cargo load was assembled. "Especially after putting you through hell with that ridiculous general court-martial for destroying an enormous enemy base without permission," the thirty-two-year-old Merchant Services officer added.

"One of the best parts of my day was when I told off my supervisor in the Science Section," Lt. Commander Jenetta Alicia Carver said gleefully to the bedside com unit image of her best friend in this part of space. There was a definite twinkle in her azure eyes. "You should have seen the positively ridiculous look on her face. It was all I could do to keep a straight face."

"I can picture it. I don't know why she's in the service to begin with if she's opposed to killing these murdering pirates. Doesn't she know we're at war?"

"I think her only interest is her astrophysics work and Space Command offers the best opportunity to study in space."

"Maybe. Hey, we have to celebrate!"

"Okay, but not tonight."

"Why not tonight?"

"I have a date, sorta."

"What's a *sorta* date?"

"A few days ago, Commander Spence asked me to have dinner with him tonight."

"At the mess hall?" Gloria asked jokingly.

"*No-o-o.* At a restaurant on the shopping concourse."

"So, stepping out with the handsome lawyer?" Gloria asked rhetorically in a teasing voice.

"Well, I have to eat dinner anyway."

"Of course you do, dear. You know I'll want a full report afterwards?"

"Yes ma'am. Written or oral?"

"Oral will be sufficient."

"Want to go shopping tomorrow? I'll give you a full report then."

"Okay. What time?"

"I'll meet you at the shuttle dock at 1000 hours."

"I'll be there. And afterwards you'll come back here to the *Vordoth* for dinner and a little celebration with your friends."

"Okay, I look forward to it."

"Have a good time tonight, Jen."

"Thanks, Gloria. See you tomorrow."

Jenetta stabbed her right index finger lightly at the disconnect switch and then immediately recorded messages to her mom and dad, and each of her four brothers. She told them about her promotion, the medal awards, and about her new posting. She added that she hoped they would all be able to get together when she got back to Earth.

With her messages sent, Jenetta turned her attention to preparations for her date. As a result of the DNA manipulation performed on her by the Raiders while she was their captive, she continued to grow, and the dress uniform provided by Commander Spence for the court-martial had already been tailored twice to conform to strict SC regulations on length. Until a few months ago, she'd been five-foot-four, but since then she'd grown almost two inches. According to the doctors at the base hospital, her body was working overtime to complete the modifications programmed into her DNA by the Raider scientists. The genetic diagnosticians at the hospital lab predicted that she would eventually be just over five feet, eleven inches tall.

Fifteen seconds in the InstaPress cabinet left the skirt and tunic of her dress uniform crisp and wrinkle free. She then excitedly attached her new insignia of rank to the epaulets and her new command insignia to the collar. She took a step backward and smiled proudly at the gold inverted 'V' that sat above a flame design of blood-red garnet on each side of her collar. All command officers wore an inverted golden 'V' insignia, symbolic of an early spaceship blasting off from a planet, but only currently serving or former line officers could wear the insignia that included the scarlet flame at the base. The posting was more than she could ever have hoped for given her dismal graduation ranking at the Academy, and it meant even more to her than the new rank. A single golden pip was attached beside the left collar insignia.

A pip proclaims that the officer has been the officially appointed commanding officer of an active duty warship. Although many different configurations exist for combat operations and support, only Space Command destroyers, frigates, cruisers, and battleships fall under the umbrella term of warship. As far as Jenetta knew, no other currently serving line officer has been permitted to wear a pip before attaining the official Space Command rank of Captain, the rank normally required for appointment to warship command. A red pip is indicative of current warship command, while each golden pip represents a past command.

After affixing the two ribbons from her medal cases onto the ribbon bar holder she'd picked up at Central Stores on her way back to her quarters, she attached the holder to the uniform and again stepped back to admire the tunic as it hung from the hook on the closet door. "Perfect," she murmured to herself as she smiled.

With her uniform ready, the thirty-two-year-old blonde, who would for most of an extended lifetime not look a day older than twenty-one, took a leisurely bath. As she relaxed in the tub, she snacked on first an apple, then an orange, then a pear. Hunger was gnawing at her stomach and if she didn't take the edge off she'd be nibbling on the napkin or tablecloth while they waited for their food at the restaurant. Besides, a normal restaurant portion of food wouldn't sate her. The DNA changes that were modifying her body had given her the appetite of a teenager, or perhaps more accurately, the combined appetite of several teenagers. She hoped that once the changes were complete she wouldn't feel so ravenously hungry all the time.

After finishing her bath and polishing off two more pieces of fruit, she fixed her hair and then worked on applying her makeup. The pigmentation changes programmed into her DNA were starting to make their appearance, so it took surprisingly little makeup to achieve the subdued look she desired. As time passed, it would take even less, and then none unless she wished to either highlight a facial feature or make her natural coloration appear more subdued. When she was satisfied, she finished getting dressed, applied a hint of fragrance, and left for the lobby in the Bachelor Officer Quarters. The chronometer on the wall opposite the elevator showed two minutes before 1900 hours.

Lt. Commander Spence entered the lobby just as Jenetta stepped from the lift car. The handsome six-foot-one-inch JAG officer spotted her, smiled, then stopped in his tracks. The smile disappeared and he hesitated for a few seconds before continuing on to greet her.

"What's going on, Ensign?" he asked as he reached her, concern clearly evident on his face. "Why are you wearing Lieutentant Commander's bars and medal ribbons?"

Jenetta looked up into his trenchant, cobalt-blue eyes and smiled innocently. "I was promoted today," she said simply.

Spence's first response was to run his right hand lightly over his short blond hair. Jenetta had observed the mannerism previously and knew it evinced a feeling of discomfort. "Promoted three grades? That's a bit— unusual."

"That's essentially what I said to Admiral Holt, but he and Admiral Margolan put the rank insignia on me anyway— personally. Admiral Holt said that since advancement from ensign to lieutenant(jg) is not really a promotion in the usual sense, but simply an upgrade at the discretion of a commanding officer when the new officer is considered deserving, it's really only a two-grade promotion. He said that by promoting me two grades, Space Command was just making up for the years the Promotions Selection Board had skipped over my name because they believed me to be deceased."

"And the two ribbons?"

"As you know, I was awarded the SC Star posthumously following the explosion of the *Hokyuu*. The award was suspended when I was found alive, so I wasn't permitted to wear the ribbon on my uniform during the trial, but the record has now been amended and I'm entitled to wear it in recognition of the almost eleven years I spent asleep in the escape pod. The Purple Heart was awarded for the broken arm I suffered during the retaking of the *Prometheus*."

"And the gold collar pip?"

"For recovering the *Prometheus* from the Raiders and returning it to Space Command, I'm being recognized as the ship's first commanding officer. Although largely an honorary appointment, it's nevertheless official, so I received the pip as de jure recognition of being the commanding officer of an active duty warship."

Lt. Commander Spence had dropped his arm to his side as she explained. "Congratulations, Commander," he said smiling, when she was done. "I'm sure the pip will only be the first of many in a long and distinguished career."

"Thank you, Commander," she said, smiling widely. "I hope you're right."

"You look wonderful, by the way."

"Thank you."

"I'm surprised by your choice of uniform. I thought you didn't wear skirts and stockings?"

"I've had a change of heart. Lately I find them more comfortable than I used to."

"Shall we go?" Lt. Commander Spence asked, extending his left elbow.

"I'm ready," Jenetta said, as she slipped her right hand beneath his crooked arm.

Exiting the BOQ lobby, they turned left in the wide walkway and headed for the lifts which would deliver them to the concourse level.

"What else did they have to say?" Lt. Commander Spence asked as they strolled.

"Who, the admirals?"

"Yes."

"Oh, there were a few other things. I'll tell you over dinner," Jenetta said demurely.

"Alright. I've made reservations at a little place named Gregory's for 1930. The food is always excellent and the service is without peer on the station."

"Wonderful. But what'll we do until then?"

"Let's go down and see how busy they are. Perhaps they can fit us in early."

Gregory's, located on the shopping concourse in the civilian section of the base, was only a ten-minute walk from the BOQ.

"How long have you been in the service, Commander?" Jenetta asked as they walked towards the restaurant.

"Now that we're technically in a civilian area, may I suggest we use first names?"

Jenetta smiled. "Okay, Zane."

"Do you prefer Jenetta, or something else?"

"My friends call me Jen."

"Jen it is. I have seventeen years of commissioned service, Jen. I graduated from NHSA in May of 2250."

"2250? Then you must know my brother Richie. He was in the NHSA class of 2250."

Commander Spence stopped walking and turned to face Jenetta. The look of unbridled surprise on his face made her giggle. "I don't believe it. Richie Carver is your brother? We roomed on the same floor in Wilcox Hall. I didn't even know he had a younger sister. I only knew about his older brother, Billy, who was an upper classman while we were there, and about Andy and Jimmy who were two years behind us."

"It's understandable that he never mentioned me. Lots of older brothers would prefer to forget all about their kid sisters, and my brothers are no exception to the rule. As the baby of the family, and the only girl, I spent most of my childhood years trying to prove myself and be accepted as an equal. It was an uphill battle all the way, and I never really succeeded."

"I can appreciate that, somewhat. I have an older brother and I followed him around like a little lost puppy dog, always hoping he'd allow me to play with him and his friends. They rarely did." Commander Spence turned to continue walking and Jenetta followed his lead. "So you're one of *those* Carvers? I think I understand you a bit better now. Your brothers never do things halfway. I'm sure you know they were all linebackers on the football team at the Academy, but did you know the coach at the Academy even named a play after them? It was a defensive blitz designed for situations where we expected the other team's offense to execute a pass play. It was called the Carver Charge. Your brothers are all so tall and strong that they could penetrate almost any offensive line as if it wasn't there. If they couldn't go through it, they went over it. If the opposing team's quarterback was the least bit slow in getting the ball off, he either had to eat it or lose it. You take after them."

"I rather think we all take after my father. He's retired now, but he was a frigate captain when he was separated from service at the mandatory space retirement age. Actually— we come from a long line of Space Command officers. My great-great-grandfather was a lieutenant on the Severance, the first ship to break the light speed barrier, during its space trials and first several years of FTL service. We're just following along in the family tradition. Andy and Jimmy are lieutenants, but both are on the selection list for lieutenant commander promotions. Richie's a lieutenant commander, and Billy's just recently made commander."

"That's great. I hope to make commander myself within the next few years. The exposure from your court-martial defense should put me in good stead with the Promotions Selection Board."

"I hope so; you did a wonderful job. I was very impressed, and I appreciate everything you did for me."

"It was my pleasure. Ah, here's the restaurant. I think you'll like this place."

The retro appearance of the restaurant compared favorably to the other dining establishments lining the promenade. Instead of the usual collection of floating 'oh-gee' geometric lights, glitzy chrome, and flashing fluorescent colors currently in vogue, Gregory's had the subdued but elegant look of expensive restaurants from Earth's twentieth century. Real wood veneer had been brought to the station for the construction of the interior and then stained to a red walnut color. The earth tones of red, yellow, and brown were pervasive throughout the establishment. One of the few visible concessions to modernity was the opposed gravity seating, but the upper assembles of the floating chairs still retained a traditional twentieth-century appearance.

Upon entering the establishment, Jenetta and Zane observed that a couple of dozen people were waiting to be seated. Judging from their bored expressions, it appeared they had been waiting for some time.

"It looks like we're not going to get seated early," Zane lamented. "In fact, we'll probably have to wait for quite a while beyond our reservation time. Would you like to go somewhere else?"

"Where else could we go?"

"I'll find out," he said as he extended his left hand towards the Space Command ring on his right. When an SC officer touches his or her ring, it signals the station's computer to establish a voice transmission carrier wave. "Commander Jerrod Tomlins," he said, looking at Jenetta. After another several seconds, he said, "Jer, do me a favor. Check the current availability of seating at restaurants on the concourse."

"He's checking," Zane said to Jenetta, then, "Yeah, that's great. Thanks, Jer. Talk to you later. Spence out."

To Jenetta, he said, "Constantine's, the Greek restaurant just down the concourse, is seating patrons immediately. The food's not quite as good as Gregory's, but they give you a good meal for your credits."

Jenetta thought for a second before responding. "Let's wait for a few minutes and see how the queue moves here. It's not our reservation time yet."

"Okay."

"You employ your cranial transducer for personal use?"

"Not for extended communications, but in certain instances, like finding sustenance, no one's going to fault you. The computer will break in if another caller is attempting to contact you and priority messages will always override any call."

Jenetta nodded. "When my CT was implanted at the Academy, I was told never to use it except for important Space Command business."

"Yes, I know, but that's mainly to keep twelve-hundred-plus kids from overtaxing the system at the Academy. They also have to monitor the communications there pretty closely to ensure no one uses it for cheating on exams."

"Tell me about it! During my freshman year, they caught two students from my dorm. They were summoned to the commandant's office and we never saw them again. I heard that a central stores clerk came to pack up their things because they had been sent home immediately, with emphasis on the immediately. We heard later that the pair had initiated a carrier before entering the test center and were in constant communication during an exam, passing answers back and forth in Morse code by lightly tapping a pencil behind their left ear where the CT would pick up the sounds."

Jenetta had been studying the striking interior décor of the restaurant as they stood talking in the foyer and was musing about the effect of furnishings on the appetite when Gregory spotted them and hurried over. The short, dark-haired restaurateur was always on the alert for the presence of important visitors in his reception area and at all times kept one or more tables in reserved status so that important persons, even those without the foresight to make reservations, would not have to be turned away.

"Commander Carver, congratulations on your promotion," Gregory said effusively as he approached Jenetta and Zane. "I just heard about it this afternoon. I was hoping you'd come in tonight to celebrate, but I wasn't aware you would be in Commander Spence's party. Come in, please. I have your table all ready for you."

"Thank you, Gregory," she said as they followed him to an empty table with a reserved sign.

"Here you are, Commanders," Gregory said as he picked up the reserved sign and slipped it beneath his arm. "Your waiter will be with you in just a minute. Enjoy your meal."

They both thanked him and Gregory quickly hurried off to greet someone else as Zane seated Jenetta.

"Gregory always seems to know what the grapevine is saying, even before the grapevine is saying it," Zane said, as he sat down. "If he knows about your promotion, then I guess it's official."

Jenetta looked at him uneasily. "You didn't believe me when I told you?"

A pained expression immediately shrouded Zane's face and he said, ruefully, "Yes, I did. I'm sorry. I was just trying to be witty."

Jenetta, feeling guilty for being so quick to challenge, said contritely, "It's okay, Zane. I guess I'm just a little too sensitive after what I've been through the past month with so many people appearing to doubt my every word."

Uneasy after committing the solecism, Zane groped for a new topic of conversation. "I, ah, had no idea you and Gregory were friends. I feel foolish for assuming I was bringing you someplace new."

"We've only met once. I came here for lunch with my friends from the *Vordoth* after the verdict was announced last Friday."

The waiter assigned to their table arrived then and stayed while they selected from the menu, answering questions about the offerings and taking their order. He hurried into the kitchen to place their orders but returned quickly with a bottle of wine.

"Complements of Gregory, Commanders," he said, as he made a flamboyant production of pulling the cork before pouring a small sample for Commander Spence to taste. The semi-dry Maulon wine from the Sebastian Colony was an excellent vintage, and Zane nodded after taking a sip and swirling it around in his mouth. The waiter then filled Zane's glass halfway before pouring Jenetta's wine. With that, he gently settled the wine bottle into the wine bucket beside the table, bowed deeply, and left.

Zane lifted his glass. "I propose a toast to your promotion, Commander."

"Thank you, Zane."

After they had sipped from their glasses, Zane asked, "What else did the admirals have to say today?"

"I've received a new posting. I'm to be the second officer aboard the *Prometheus*. We'll be returning to Earth shortly."

"Oh," Zane said forlornly, disappointment written across his face. "Congratulations. I knew you had received a shipboard posting when I noticed the line officer insignia on your collar, but I had hoped it might be to a ship assigned to this deca-sector."

"But it is," Jenetta said. "Following the ship's official launching and my medal ceremony, the *Prometheus* will call Higgins its home port."

"Medal ceremony? Haven't they already awarded you the medals? You're wearing the ribbons."

"I'm talking about the other one."

"Other one?"

"Yes, the Medal of Honor for infiltration of a Raider base, recovering the two stolen battleships, and then destroying their base of operations in this deca-sector."

Zane's eyes grew wide. He had been swirling his wine gently in his glass, but upon hearing Jenetta's news he put the wineglass down and sat back in his chair. "Medal of Honor! Why didn't you tell me about that?"

Smiling coyly, Jenetta said, "I wanted to save something to talk about over dinner."

"Now I'm really confused. They went to all the trouble to court-martial you, and then they promote you three grades and decorate you with the Galactic Alliance's highest honor. I'm beginning to wonder if I did such a marvelous job after all."

"Of course you did. Can you imagine the repercussions on morale if they just shunted me off into a corner after making such a production of my activities during the past year? You brought so much support my way from the Space Command personnel who saw the live vid broadcast that Supreme HQ didn't dare *not* reward me. They had to show my contribution was appreciated."

"Perhaps," he said halfheartedly. "Did they say why they even court-martialed you in the first place?"

"It's not important. I'm so happy that I don't care anymore. I've been posted to the best ship in the fleet, and as second officer, I'll have the watch during part of each day."

"I'm happy for you. You seem to be getting everything you've wanted. The medal ceremony will be held as soon as you reach Earth?"

"I imagine so. It's to be held preceding the official launching of the *Prometheus*. Then we go to Nordakia because *they* want to give me something called the— the Too-da-loo Medal, or something."

"Too-da-loo Medal?" Zane said, chortling. "You mean the Tawroolee Medal of Valor?"

"I guess that could be it. I've never heard of it before and my head was already swimming from the news of my promotion and new posting when Admiral Holt informed me."

"You probably haven't heard of it before because you were in stasis sleep when we made first contact with the Nordakians. Their home planet is quite remote and they stay pretty much to themselves. We'd never encountered them until one of our patrol ships observed a spacecraft entering their home world's solar system and followed along to investigate. They've only colonized the one planet, Obotymot, as a possible hedge against future food shortages as their population grows. It seems that their priesthood actively works to dissuade anyone from pursuing a career in space. You really should take some time to study their history, especially since they're going to be honoring you. Jen, the Tawroolee Medal of Valor is a *great* honor. It's *their* top military tribute. Like our Space Command Cross, it's second only to the Medal of Honor awarded by the Galactic Alliance Council." Scrunching up his face slightly, Zane said, "I can't recall ever hearing of any Terran military people being honored by the Nordakians before."

"I guess I'm to be the first, according to one of my friends. I do intend to study up on the Nordakian culture, though. I'll have three months to read about it on the way to Earth and then almost four more before we reach Nordakia. That should be adequate time to learn about their society in reasonable depth."

The meal was superb and the couple continued to talk about the medals and the Nordakians as they dined. When they had finished their food and requested the bill, Gregory returned to the table.

"Did you enjoy your meal, Commanders?" he asked.

"It was simply wonderful, Gregory," Jenetta said. "Please extend my compliments to your kitchen staff."

"Thank you, Commander. Your meals are compliments of the restaurant tonight in honor of your promotion and the Medal of Honor you will soon receive on Earth."

"Thank you, Gregory. That's very nice of you."

"I was wondering if I might ask a favor. Could you pose for a picture for display here in the restaurant in celebration of you having visited us on this memorable occasion?"

"Of course."

"Wonderful. Just come over here please. You also, Commander Spence, please."

A photographer was waiting and the image recording took only a few minutes. Each officer received a framed copy of the animated picture before they left.

The couple walked along the concourse for a while, talking and looking in shop windows but not entering any of the still-open stores, and it was almost midnight when they arrived back in the lobby of the BOQ.

"I guess I won't be seeing you again for a while," Zane said.

"We should be back in about twelve months. As I said, this is to be the homeport for *Prometheus*, so I expect we'll be returning here after our trip to Nordakia. I hope you'll still be posted here."

In an area of the lobby where they'd be unseen by passersby outside the BOQ, Zane put his hands on Jenetta's waist and pulled her gently to him. Her lack of even slight resistance conveyed the message that he should continue. With his left arm around her, he bent his head forward. She put her hands on his waist as she leaned her head back to look up into his eyes and they shared a long kiss, then separated, with Zane holding Jenetta's left hand in his right.

"Thank you for a wonderful evening, Jen."

"I enjoyed it as well, Zane. Goodnight."

"Goodnight."

Lt. Commander Spence released her hand, turned, and walked away. Jenetta remained where she was and watched him go. As he reached the outer foyer, he paused and looked back. Jenetta smiled and waved. He returned her wave and then continued on until he turned into the main thoroughfare and was lost from sight. Filled with emotion as she turned towards the elevator, she wondered if this was what true love was like.

* * *

The flight bay observation room window offered Jenetta an unobstructed view of the shuttle from the *Vordoth* as it arrived and docked with the station. Jenetta was waiting at the bottom of the ramp as Gloria stepped out of the airlock and descended to the deck. The two women hugged like dear friends who hadn't seen each other in months, when in fact it hadn't even been a week. At five feet, nine inches, Gloria was presently taller than Jenetta. The slender, athletically trim brunette had an easy way of carrying herself and a quick smile that made her face glow. Her smile was, without question, her most defining physical attribute.

When the *Vordoth's* captain was lost during an attack by Raiders, Gloria, in her official capacity as first officer, asked Jenetta to assume the role of captain. Although just an ensign at the time, Jenetta was the only Space Command officer on board the freighter. She had been trained at the Academy to command a ship under attack by hostile forces and the freighter crew desperately needed a leader with that skill just then. The unique tactics Jenetta employed as their captain successfully defended the ship, saving the freighter, its crew, and its cargo.

The women spent the remainder of the morning and a substantial part of the afternoon browsing in the shops lining the concourse walkways, pausing only long enough to eat a light lunch at one of the many quick-food restaurants. Just after 1600 hours, they walked to Jenetta's quarters so she could drop off her packages before they boarded the shuttle to the *Vordoth*.

Gravity in Operations Bay Two was slowly increased as the small craft entered the bay on the *Vordoth* and settled to the deck. Three walls made of a transparent material had previously folded down from the upper deck to form an airtight space not much larger than the shuttle so the air could be evacuated. As the enormous exterior hatch closed and sealed, Gloria engaged the magnetic skids to hold the craft firmly in place during pressurization. Once the gauges had moved to green, the surrounding walls returned to their previous positions against the upper deck. Gloria released the skid's hold on the deck and flew it to a parking position where the skids were re-engaged to hold the small ship in place should gravity in the bay have to be decreased for emergency operations.

Rebecca Erikson, Charley Moresby, Leah Brewster, and Gunny Rondell watched impatiently from the observation room until the shuttle had come to a complete stop and its engines were shut down. When the bay airlock opened, they hurried in to welcome Jenetta as she emerged from the shuttle. She was immediately overwhelmed by their heartfelt congratulations for her promotion and medal honors. As a group, they all walked to the officers' lounge where they talked and laughed, as good friends do, until dinner was ready in the officers' mess.

Anthony, the gaunt officers' mess attendant with sandy hair and a permanent smile, had outdone himself with a combination of fresh and synthesized food, and the meal was almost as good as that served at Gregory's. After taking receipt of the nearly hijacked shipment of wine from the Sebastian colony, the grateful merchant had given Gloria several cases of the beverage and she brought out two bottles for the party. Jenetta limited herself to one glass at dinner and one later in the lounge. She didn't want to risk being inflicted with the slightest impairment when she reported aboard the *Prometheus* in the morning. Mikel Arneu, the Raider commandant of the base where Jenetta's DNA had been altered, had told her she would become increasingly impervious to the effects of alcohol, but this wasn't the time to test his statement.

"I wish we could attend the medal ceremony," Gloria said as they relaxed in the officers' lounge following their meal.

"I'd love for you to be there so you could share the moment with me," Jenetta said, smiling, "but I know you can't take eight months or more off just to come to Earth to see me get a small chunk of metal pinned on my chest. I'm sure the ceremony will be covered by the press."

"You can be damn sure of that," Gunny said. With his close-cropped haircut, Gunny Rondell, a retired Space Marine Gunnery Sergeant who had just celebrated his fifty-seventh birthday, looked like the stereotypical Marine NCO. Standing about six feet, four inches, he was still able to handle any three ordinary men stupid enough to take him on.

"It's been about twenty-seven years since the last MOH was awarded," Gunny said. "I was just a PFC at the time, but I remember seeing the event on the ship's closed circuit vid. The Marine, I can't recall his name— Stephen something, risked his life to save a dozen of his fellows after their assault transport crashed on a planet in the Centrasia system during a training exercise. He had lost part of a hand in the crash and been terribly disfigured by fire, but he kept running back into the small ship and dragging other Marines out until the fire got so bad that he couldn't get in anymore."

"That's *true* heroism," Jenetta said somberly. "Your story makes me feel guilty about getting the medal."

"Don't be *ridiculous!*" Leah said emphatically. Just twenty-seven years old, Leah Brewster looked like a profess-ional model. Six feet tall with a glossy black mane of hair that fell almost to her waist, she exuded sexiness. She was also hopelessly in love with Gunny. "He only saved a dozen. You saved fifty of us. I'd be on my way to a slave brothel right now if you hadn't rescued me. And the others would be headed there too, or to slave labor camps on some miserable mining planet. You deserve that medal as much or more than anyone who has ever received it."

"And thanks to your efforts," Rebecca, the ship's doctor, said, "Raider activity in this part of space has all but disappeared. Thousands, tens of thousands, of people are now traveling in safety." The attractive thirty-six-year-old brunette had been the one who awakened Jenetta after her life pod was recovered by the *Vordoth* crew.

"And the Galactic Alliance recouped the two battleships stolen from the Mars shipyard just days before they were to be turned over to Space Command," Charlie said. "I shudder to think what destruction those ships would have wrought in the hands of the Raiders." Charlie Moresby, at forty, was the Chief Engineer aboard the *Vordoth*. Of average height, with rugged good looks, he was that special person in Rebecca Erikson's life.

"And let's not forget that Jen saved both the *Vordoth and* a Nordakian convoy on a desperate mercy mission to Obotymot," Gloria said. "Without those supplies, many thousands of Nordakians would have died before another convoy could be sent. Just because you weren't injured doesn't mean you deserve the medal any less than any other recipient, even those to whom it was awarded posthumously."

"But Jen *was* injured," Rebecca said. "She suffered a broken arm while retaking the *Prometheus*. And then there was the torture and near starvation she endured at the hands of sadistic guards in the Raider Detention Center. And we can't forget the extremely painful DNA alterations that were performed on her and which are still giving her problems."

"That's right!" Gloria said firmly. "So let's not hear any more of this foolishness that you don't deserve the medals and other honors simply because you didn't repeatedly rush into a burning transport ship."

Jenetta smiled. "Forget the medal. The best thing I've gotten out of all this is five wonderful friends."

At 2200 hours, Gloria and Jenetta made the trip back to the space station, a *Vordoth* crewman piloting the shuttle because Gloria had imbibed sufficient wine to make her flying skills unsure.

The massive space station was a beautiful sight. Easily visible to the naked eye from the planet below, the station resembled an oval-cut, blue opal gemstone surrounded by a sixty-kilometer-long silver necklace. The necklace was the docking ring, of course, where dozens of massive ships could be docked with the station simultaneously. Roadway tunnels connecting the station to the docking ring appeared like spokes in a wheel.

The standard method of appending loaded cargo link sections to the rear of a freighter obviated the need for it to dock directly with a station. Although cargo was always accessible for inspection, it couldn't easily be offloaded through a freighter, except for the small, single-hull ships or the gargantuan Space Command Quartermaster vessels, so space around the station was currently dotted with dozens of commercial freighters of various lengths. A few, those who had either just arrived or were preparing to depart, were maxed out at the legal length of ten kilometers, but most were either having their cargo sections assembled or disassembled in preparation for their next run. Several enormous cargo 'farms,' filled with link sections containing cargo in transit, floated a few hundred kilometers from the station, and some captains parked their vessels near one of them while loading or unloading, but most preferred to position vessels near the station so crewmembers could enjoy liberty time within easy commuting distance. An entire ten-kilometer-long cargo section could be assembled at one of the farms and then towed to the freighter as one piece by company employees permanently stationed in civilian quarters aboard the station or on lodging barges, so the main ship need never travel until it was time to depart the area.

Once inside the station, Gloria and Jenetta said their good-byes, hugging and promising to keep in touch. Jenetta watched until Gloria's shuttle disappeared from view, then returned sadly to the BOQ. She wondered when, or even if, she would see Gloria and her other friends aboard the *Vordoth* again.

A life in space is so difficult on both romances and friend-ships, she thought.

She wouldn't have much time to dwell on it though. Tomorrow she would report for her new posting as second officer of the GSC battleship *Prometheus*.

Chapter Three
~ February 22nd, 2268 ~

At 0600 hours, Jenetta released the handle of her packed spacechest and allowed it to settle gently to the deck just inside the entrance of her BOQ quarters. Her smaller cases were stacked on top. The 'oh-gee' capacity of the large space-chest was more than adequate to lift anything she had to move. Base Housing would see that her possessions were picked up and delivered to the ship sometime during the day.

She remembered to call the base hospital and leave a message for Doctor Freidlander informing him that she was shipping out. She thanked him for making the arrangements to grow skin for a graft that would cover the indelible, tattoo-like 'Pleasure Slave' mark imprinted on her chest by her Raider captors and apologized for the wasted effort. While the skin graft was important, nothing in the galaxy was more important to her than being aboard the *Prometheus* when it departed Higgins Space Command Base.

After enjoying a satiating breakfast at the officers' mess, Jenetta headed for the docking pier where the *Prometheus* was moored.

Two armed Space Marine sentries at the airlock entrance to the forward cargo hold braced sharply to attention as Jenetta approached. Word of her new posting had obviously preceded her. Her current celebrity meant that the OD, a young lieutenant(jg), didn't have to ask what business she had aboard ship as he gave permission for her to cross the airlock threshold. Nor did he feel compelled to see proof of identification. Her face would be immediately recognized by anyone at the space station.

As she entered the ship, it felt like she was coming home. The recycled and odorless air of the forward cargo bay could never smell more invigorating to anyone and Jenetta took a deep breath. Her months as captain aboard this incredibly powerful warship had instilled deep feelings in her. She couldn't think of a single posting in the entire galaxy she would rather have, unless it was either as first officer or captain of the *Prometheus*.

After being cleared, she headed directly for the bridge. Two Marine sentries, a PFC at the entrance to the bridge corridor and a Lance Corporal outside the Captain's Quarters smartened their stance as she approached and passed them. Neither challenged her as she proceeded towards the entrance of the bridge.

As she moved within range of the portal activation sensor, the double doors slid open to reveal the ship's fourteen-meter by twelve-meter command center. The presence of only four individuals immediately reminded Jenetta of the day she had seized control of this ship at the Raider base. She paused briefly to glance at the commissioning plaque on the wall just inside the entrance and saw, to her great delight, that 'Jenetta Alicia Carver, Ensign' had been inscribed as the first captain of the ship. In grateful appreciation for her recovery of this vessel and its sister ship, the *Chiron*, she would forever be officially recognized as the first captain of the *Prometheus*. It was an incredible honor. In the entire history of the service, no other ensign, indeed no officer below the rank of commander, had captained an active duty battleship. Immediately beneath her name had been inscribed the name of the warship's *new* commanding officer, 'Lawrence Frederick Gavin, Captain.'

An old tradition aboard ships, harking back to the days when sailing ships had wooden decks, designated all crewmembers aboard ship at the time it was commissioned as 'Plank Owners.' This would mean that Jenetta was the only plank owner aboard the *Prometheus*. In later times, however, crewmembers aboard a ship during a re-commissioning ceremony were also designated as plank owners. Once the ship arrived at Earth and the launching ceremony was held, everyone currently aboard would be a plank owner.

Mesmerized by the plaque, Jenetta didn't hear the approaching lieutenant until he said, "Welcome aboard, Commander Carver."

The spoken words brought Jenetta out of her reverie. Turning to face the young officer, she smiled and said, "Thank you, Lieutenant..." She paused for just a fraction of a second as her eyes fell to the name plate on his tunic, "...Kerrey. I'm delighted to be aboard. Is the Captain here?"

"Yes ma'am. He's in his briefing room."

"Thank you," she said as she took one more furtive glance over her shoulder at the commissioning plaque.

As she had done hundreds of times before, Jenetta crossed to the Captain's enormous briefing room on the larboard side of the bridge, but this time the doors didn't open automatically as she approached. Instead, after satisfactorily identifying her by polling her CT, the computer announced her presence to the Captain. The doors opened to admit her only when he said, "Come," from inside the room. The command, spoken to the computer interface, was broadcast to Jenetta via her CT.

Jenetta entered, continued over to a wooden desk that seemed large enough to alternate as a landing pad for a space tug, and braced to attention. "Lt. Commander Jenetta Alicia Carver reporting for duty, sir," she said to the officer who occupied the floating 'oh-gee' chair behind the enormous desk.

Captain Gavin, now in his early sixties, had dark brown hair with just a touch of grey at the temples. It was difficult to be sure while he was seated, but Jenetta guessed from the appearance of his torso that he was just a bit shy of the six-foot mark. He had a strong face with good features and a fit body. Five golden pips and one red one adorned the area next to his left collar insignia. The pips indicated that the *Prometheus* was Gavin's sixth warship appointment during his career in Space Command. The normal progression of warship command from destroyer to frigate, to cruiser, then battleship, would indicate that the *Prometheus* was his third battleship, although there were intermediate steps possible with light destroyer or light cruiser commands. Though uncommon, it was even possible for an officer to have multiple commands in the same group of lesser warships, but Gavin's renown as a battleship commander was well established.

A SimWindow, presently displaying a live exterior view of a docking ring section at Higgins, filled a sizable portion of the wall behind him. Not made from the synthetic products that only simulated wood, the walls of this four-meter-square room were finished with real oak veneer in a light honey color. A long, comfortable-looking sofa, covered in the same deliciously soft dark brown leather used for the room's three 'oh-gee' chairs, sat against one wall as if patiently awaiting occupants, and the topaz carpeting gave the impression of being ten centimeters deep.

As Gavin looked up from the report he was reading on a portable viewpad, he fixed his dark-grey eyes acutely upon her face. "Ah, Carver," he said lightly. "You're early."

As second officer, Jenetta was not required to report aboard until just before her watch began at midnight.

"Yes, sir," she responded. "I guess I was anxious to be aboard. Here are my orders, sir."

Gavin took the data ring and placed it on his desk, already as familiar with the orders as she was. "Stand easy. Welcome aboard, Commander."

"Thank you, Captain," Jenetta said as she relaxed her stance slightly.

"Lieutenant Kerrey can show you to your quarters. As soon as you're settled in, you may assume your duties."

"Thank you, sir, but I needn't bother Lieutenant Kerrey. I know every square meter of the *Prometheus*."

The Captain gazed intently at Jenetta's face. "Of course, Commander, of course. My new First Officer, Commander Genevieve LaSalle, will be joining us when we reach Earth. Until that time, you'll fill in for her as Acting First."

Jenetta's heart quickened considerably, but she didn't allow any indication of her excitement to show on her face, nor did she take the deep breath her lungs screamed for. "Aye, Captain," was all she said.

"Does that cause you any concern?" he asked, watching her reaction closely.

"None at all, Captain. I'll be delighted to fill in as Acting First Officer."

Gavin continued to stare at her face closely for several seconds. She was as calm as if he'd just told her the officers' mess would be serving chicken for dinner rather than relaying the fact that she would have, without question, the most difficult job aboard ship. The First Officer, often referred to as the Exec, for Executive Officer, or simply the XO, was responsible for overseeing most day-to-day operations aboard ship. As second in command, he or she functioned as the captain's right arm in most matters related to interaction with the crew, leaving the captain free to concentrate on the ship's mission. In addition to these administrative chores, Jenetta would be the senior officer on the second watch. Her combined duties would require her to work more hours than anyone else on board. To Gavin's trained eye, Jenetta had a look of confidence with no outward signs of arrogance, the mark of a good first officer.

As cognizant as every other officer in Space Command that she'd had a stupendous six months, Gavin freely acknowledged that as a result of her efforts the Raiders had been rocked back on their heels in this deca-sector. But he was also painfully aware that she had, until several days ago, been just an ensign who'd spent most of the past decade in stasis. Since graduation from the Academy, she'd been asleep for all but fifteen months, and during three months of *that* short time she was alone in a life pod.

Like most officers in Space Command, Gavin had monitored the court-martial broadcasts. When he'd learned that Jenetta would be his second officer, he'd reviewed a number of the court sessions again, paying particularly close attention to her comport while she testified. Although she appeared intelligent and self-confident, he worried about her general appearance, specifically her apparent age. She might be thirty-two years old chronologically and wearing the bars of a Lt. Commander, but outwardly she looked like a still-wet-behind-the-ears ensign. Some crewmen and NCOs might be hesitant to trust her judgment or take her seriously. He wondered if she had developed an officer persona strong enough to overcome their resistance and earn their respect.

Gavin had argued strenuously with Admiral Holt over having her as his first officer on this most important voyage. He'd contended that the demands of establishing a command structure on a newly commissioned battleship called for the talents of an executive officer with decades of command experience aboard ship. If the task was handled improperly, it could take a seasoned officer months to undo the damage and restore a proper command structure. Admiral Holt had dismissed his arguments out of hand and told him the decision was final, reminding him that a seasoned first officer would be waiting for him at Earth Station Two when the ship docked.

Though opposed to what he was considering the *Admiral's little experiment*, Gavin was a senior officer in Space Command with over forty years of service and knew both the futility and career risks of further argument with a flag officer. He decided to make the best of it for the short cruise and keep a very close eye on Carver. Perhaps she would foul up so badly before they even left port that he could get a last minute replacement for the trip to Earth.

"Carry on, XO," he said.

"Aye, Captain."

Jenetta braced to attention, turned on her heel, and left the Captain's briefing room. She had been delighted to see they hadn't removed the furnishings. It still appeared to be the most sumptuous briefing room in the fleet, appropriate for the best ship in the fleet.

Lieutenant Kerrey intercepted Jenetta again as she crossed the bridge. The curly-haired officer seemed determined to ingratiate himself. Or perhaps it was only a form of hero worship.

"Is there anything that I can help you with, Commander Carver?"

"All I need at present is to know which quarters I've been assigned?

"Your permanent assignment is A-155-02-L, ma'am, but since you'll be the acting first officer you may move into A-155-01-L until Commander LaSalle arrives aboard ship."

"A-155-02-L will be fine. Please notify the housing officer of such."

"Yes, ma'am. Shall I show you the way?"

"That's not necessary, Lieutenant. I know my way around the *Prometheus*."

Lieutenant Kerrey blinked his smiling, chestnut-colored eyes twice and then said, "Of course, ma'am. I'm sorry."

"There's nothing to apologize for, Lieutenant. I'm going to my quarters for a few minutes and then I'll return to begin my duties."

"Yes ma'am," Lieutenant Kerrey said as he watched her walk away. It was funny, but she seemed much taller than her five-foot, six-inch height.

The sentry outside the Captain's quarters again stood a little straighter as she approached and passed him on the way to her assigned quarters across from, and just beyond, the Captain's. On Space Command vessels, the four senior line officers were always billeted off the corridor leading to the bridge. Located along corridor 0, the center-line passageway on all ships, the location of the four suites made it possible for senior officers to be on the bridge in seconds in the event of an emergency. And, being close to the center axis of the ship, their accommodations were, like the bridge itself, as protected as possible. Although each of the four quarters had an official designation consistent with compartment-naming conventions aboard all ships (Deck Number, Frame Number, Position relative to the centerline, and Compartment Use) the quarters of the four senior command officers were always simply referred to as A-01, A-02, A-03, and A-04. She didn't need to pass the Space Marine PFC at the far end of the corridor, but he smartened his stance as she reached the entrance to her quarters.

All officers aboard ship have an office attached to their quarters, the size of which varies with rank and duties. Except for the captain, a separate entrance off the corridor is provided so visitors need not pass through the officers' sitting room to reach his or her office. The captain normally conducted most ship business from the briefing room on the bridge, and although the office in his or her quarters was large enough for a small conference, it was mainly intended as a more private work space. Lack of a separate door to the office also augmented security for the ship's commanding officer.

Jenetta's new quarters had the requisite two entrances off the corridor; one led into her office and the other into her generous sitting room. At least four meters by six, the bedroom sat beyond both rooms, with a large, centrally-situated bathroom that could be entered from either the sitting room or the bedroom. The office was also accessible from the sitting room. The Captain and the first officer had larger quarters, but this space was more than adequate for her needs.

After using the bathroom to wash her hands, she went into her office to call up her duty list, a prioritized compilation of notes from the Captain and requests or messages from officers and crew now under her command. As it began to scroll up in response to the spoken command, her eyes widened and she drew in her breath sharply. The length of the list far exceeded anything she'd expected. She studied it for about ten minutes before leaving to begin what promised to be an exceedingly long workday.

Battleships represented just five percent of the Space Command warship fleet. They performed all the functions that an aircraft carrier, battleship, and small troop transport traditionally performed in one of Earth's wet fleets.

Normally, crews for newly constructed warships assembled at the Mars shipbuilding facility. There, they received fundamental training about the new vessel before assuming their duties. The ship remained at Mars until the new command was coordinated and functioning efficiently, and then conducted its space trials. Once all major, and most minor, problems were resolved, the ship was dispatched on a final shakedown cruise to a designated homeport where it would begin regular patrol operations. But having been recently recovered in space, months from Mars, this would be impossible for the *Prometheus* and *Chiron*.

Members of their new crews were being assembled on Earth, but the ships couldn't remain at Higgins for an annual or longer, unstaffed and inactive, until the crews were assembled and transported. So crews just large enough to handle most situations which would arise during a voyage to Earth were being assembled either by promotion or by transfer from the other ships docked at Higgins, or from those GSC warships expected into port before the *Prometheus* and *Chiron* were scheduled to leave. Being the two largest and newest warships in the fleet, it was a special honor to be named as a member of their crews. The paucity of available experienced personnel at Higgins meant that individuals who might otherwise not have been selected for the crew were being handed their dream. The less than five hundred crewmembers aboard each ship for the journey would be a far cry from the normal complement of three thousand, five hundred.

Returning to the bridge of the almost two-kilometer-long vessel, Jenetta took a few minutes to talk with each of the crewmembers there. When she was done she at least knew their name, rank, current job assignment, and previous posting. She would learn the rest later as she studied the personnel files in the computer.

Jenetta spent the remainder of the day preparing the ship for its journey to Earth. She worked with the officers in each section to ensure that all necessary supplies were on board and stowed properly, that all equipment was functioning properly, and that crewmember duty schedules were coordinated so all primary ship functions would be covered every minute of every day. From the moment she began work,

Jenetta became the person every officer turned to with a problem and she didn't call it a day until the second watch ended at midnight. As she went off duty, Jenetta left orders that she wasn't to be disturbed until 0800 unless it was an emergency and that problems were not to be brought to the Captain.

A quick stop at the officers' mess before proceeding to her quarters netted her a fresh chef's salad and an orange. She ate the salad in her quarters but was so exhausted that sleep won out over hunger and she never got to the orange. Still dressed, she climbed onto the bed and was asleep almost immediately.

* * *

Up and showered by 0700 the following morning, Jenetta dressed and spent ten minutes stowing the things delivered to the ship from her room at the Bachelor Office Quarters. As always, the animated picture of her family, taken at the Academy on the day her eldest brother graduated, went immediately onto her dresser. In the image that morphed to the beginning every thirty-seconds, Jenetta and her mother were the only ones not in uniform. Although her brothers were all cadets at the Academy, Jenetta had still been in high school at the time. Her father, a Captain in Space Command, had recently turned over command of his destroyer and was preparing to take command of the *Cromwell*, GSC-F839, a new frigate nearing completion at the Mars shipyard. For the picture, Quinton Carver and his wife Annette had sat on a stone bench in a small park-like setting on the Academy grounds with their children arrayed behind them. The four boys stood together with their arms on each other's back while the bushes behind them swayed ever so gently from a slight breeze. Jenetta had been shuffled off to the right in the image. Because of her clothing and detached position, it almost appeared as if she wasn't part of the group. Halfway through the image playback, Richie raised his enormous left hand and placed it on her small shoulder, finally making it seem like she might be a part of the family after all.

The animated picture of Zane Spence and herself taken recently at Gregory's went next to the family portrait on her dresser. When she had each properly positioned, she pressed the tiny button that activated the small vacuum pump in each. The suction along the bottom edge of the frame would hold it firmly in place if the ship were suddenly subjected to violent motion.

Still making it to the officers' mess by 0745, she had time for a quick bowl of cereal and a cup of coffee before the start of the first watch at 0800. She took several pieces of fruit to eat while she worked, hoping they would quell the hunger pangs she was already feeling as she returned to her office.

If she'd had any hopes that the new day might be easier, they were dashed as her duty list scrolled up on the computer. It appeared that every officer aboard ship had left several new messages since she'd gone off duty late last evening.

Jenetta intuitively knew of the difficulties involved in an entirely new command structure where routines and procedures had yet to be established. Subordinates would feel their way along uncertainly as they tried to learn what was expected of them and what authority they had to make decisions. Until they knew, they tended to be too quick to pass on problems to their senior officer. It was doubly difficult where both supervising officer and subordinates hadn't previously been posted together. The situation represented a potential logistical nightmare for an executive officer in a new command.

She knew her main job now was to make each officer understand what she expected of him or her, or she would be plagued with minor problems all the way to Earth. Instead of handling every problem that came her way on the second day, she passed many of them back to the originating officer and told him or her to resolve it and inform her of their solution.

* * *

Chief Petty Officer Filip 'Flip' Byrne entered the crowded quarters of CPO Edward Lindsey and dropped his tall frame tiredly into the only unoccupied chair of the five arranged around the table.

"You're late," CPO Lindsey said.

"Yeah, tell me about it," Flip said with disgust.

"The watch ended an hour ago."

"Just deal me in and don't give me any crap, Eddie." Flip sighed loudly. "We had to completely empty and reload cargo hold 12-420-6-A. We just finished. The LT said it would be done before we quit for the day if we had to work until third watch."

Holding his hand up to cover his eyes in pretense of a seer having an omnipotent vision, the stocky CPO Lindsey said in an eerie voice, "I see the hand of our child XO in this."

"I told you not to call her that!" CPO Byrne said angrily. "She graduated from NHSA in '56, so she's only ten years younger than you." Calming, he added, "But you're right about her being involved. She came down to inspect the hold just after we finished stacking and securing everything. One of the new knuckleheaded loader operators in my group put food synthesizer chemicals in the cage where the emergency medical stores are supposed to be stockpiled. Another knucklehead, unable to store the medical stuff properly, just dumped it in the common area. Then stuff got piled on top of it and it was buried. The XO spotted the screw-up right off. When she asked where the medical stores were, the Lieutenant couldn't answer. I expected her to cut into him like a plasma torch through aluminum, but all she did was make a sad comment about how she'd hate to be waiting for medical treatment in sickbay while they searched the entire hold for the supplies needed to treat her injuries. Then she got this sort of strange expression on her face as she looked at him. It was like the look my mother would always give me when I'd done something that *really* disappointed her. I hated that look. It made me feel about two centimeters tall. I always wished she would just smack me upside my head instead. I really felt for the LT. Anyway, after she left, he ripped into us for making him look bad in front of the XO. He swore that if anything like that ever happened again, we'd all regret the day we were posted to the *Prometheus*."

"So you got chewed out and wound up with extra duty because of the XO, the officer you keep defending."

"Hey, she was absolutely right, Eddie. How'd *you* like to be waiting for medical treatment while they hunted through an entire hold looking for the supplies they needed to treat *you*? The extra duty was because of the two knuckleheads, and I'll make damn sure they pull so many extra details for screwing up that they never do it again. I know you don't care for the XO, but she's first-rate in my book."

"It isn't that I don't like her, Flip, it's just that I don't subscribe to all the hero worship she receives. In spite of what some people think, *Jenetta Carver doesn't walk on water*."

"We were both on the *Thor* during her court-martial and I remember you always making a point of being in the vid theatre or near a monitor when the live broadcasts were on. I also remember you cheering like a madman when the verdict of not guilty was announced."

"So, I don't like to see anyone being dumped on unfairly by the brass, even officers. She done good by destroying that Raider base."

"And by recovering these two battleships?"

"And by recovering these two battleships," Lindsey admitted.

"And in saving all those people the Raiders intended as slaves?"

"And in saving all those people the Raiders intended as slaves," Lindsey admitted also.

"But?" CPO Byrne asked.

"But— I still don't think that entitles her to become the XO aboard the *Prometheus*. She's far too young and inexperienced."

"She's not the XO, Eddie. She's only acting as XO until we reach Earth."

"Acting or not, she's the XO. Our *lives* are in her hands, her very *young* hands."

"What about the Captain? Gavin's one of the most respected officers in the fleet."

"He's the *only* reason I haven't requested a transfer back off this ship."

"Are you serious? You'd give up one of the choicest postings in the fleet because a young officer is occupying a temporary position?"

"Only if she'd been made temporary captain. There's no way I'd serve under a captain who looks like she's fresh out of the academy. There's just something— *unnatural*— about it."

"Since the minute she arrived you've been searching for something to hold against her. Name one mistake she's made as XO, just one."

"That's not the point."

"That's exactly the point, Eddie. You're upset because she's doing the job as good as anyone with thirty years experience." Glancing around at the faces of the other three chief petty officers, all of whom had been sitting quietly but listening intently to the conversation, Byrne said, "Oh hell, just deal the damn cards will you, Eddie?"

* * *

By the end of the week, Jenetta's workload had been pared by ninety percent and normal shipboard routines had begun to develop. Most of the expected crew had reported aboard as other ships arrived at the spaceport. Gavin summoned Jenetta to his briefing room a little after 1100 hours.

"Stand easy, Commander," Gavin said as she entered and braced to attention. "How are the preparations for departure proceeding?"

"Very well, Captain. Armament is complete and victualing is *nearly* complete. The ship will be ready on time, but I'm not sure if all crewmembers will be aboard. A few haven't yet checked in because their ships haven't reached Higgins."

"That can't be helped. We leave as scheduled and Space Command HQ will have to figure out how to get the crew members to us."

"Aye, Captain."

"Commander, I've been keeping a very close eye on your activity during the past week."

"You have, sir?" Jenetta asked apprehensively.

"I wanted to see how you would meet the demands of an extremely difficult administrative situation, so I purposely didn't help out. I admit I was more than a little concerned about having an ensign who had just been advanced three grades functioning as my acting first officer. In fact, for two days before you reported aboard I intentionally let problems accumulate so you'd have a real mess to unravel."

"Things did seem a bit backed up at first, sir."

"Well, I'm not going to be watching you so closely anymore. You've proven that your administrative skills are just as good as your reputed tactical skills. You have everything running like a shipboard chronometer."

"Thank you, sir. I learned quite a bit during the months I functioned as captain of the *Prometheus*."

"No doubt," he said, letting his eyes drop momentarily to the gold pip on her collar. "I've noted your superior administrative performance in handling the difficult task of preparing a new command in your file. I no longer have any reservations about you being my acting first for the trip ahead. Good work, Commander. That's all."

"Aye, sir. Thank you, sir."

Jenetta returned to her duties with a slight smile on her face and felt good for the rest of the day. The Captain's involvement in the ship's preparations had been conspicuously absent during the week. Even her access to him had been severely limited. Now she understood why. It wasn't personal, as she'd begun to fear; he was only testing her ability to handle the job.

* * *

As the *Prometheus'* bridge crew made final preparations to depart the spaceport at 1300 hours Sunday, a call came from the deck officer in the forward cargo bay. The lieutenant responsible for securing the airlock reported that a large, unexpected group of Space Command personnel had just arrived. The officer in charge was requesting to be admitted. Jenetta told the deck officer she'd be right down and hurried out after turning over bridge responsibility to the next most senior command officer.

When she arrived at the cargo bay, she found a group consisting of four GSC officers and some twenty-five NCOs and crewmen already standing inside. Jenetta immediately recognized Commander Keith Kanes of SCI, who stepped forward as she approached. The five-foot-eleven-inch intelligence officer with brown hair and piercing steel-grey eyes saluted and spoke up first.

"Permission to come aboard, Commander?"

"Granted," Jenetta said after returning the salute. "Welcome aboard, Commander. What is this? We're about to get underway."

"I've brought you some passengers for the trip to Earth. And I have special orders for the Captain."

"Passengers?"

"Yes, including one for your brig."

Jenetta's gaze flew to the group and she scanned the faces. Her eyes opened a little wider when she recognized Commander Pretorious, the Raider officer who had been in command of the *Prometheus* when she led the assault to recover it. As tall as Kanes, but with curly black hair and dark bushy eyebrows that gave him a certain comical look, he was manacled with prisoner transport chains.

"Can you accommodate us?" Commander Kanes asked.

"I'm sure we can, sir. Is this your entire party?"

"Yes."

"Will you be traveling with us, sir?"

"I will."

Turning to the officer of the deck, she said, "Lieutenant, seal the airlock so the ship can get underway, then contact Lieutenant Shelton and have her arrange for four quarters in 'O' country and suitable quarters for the NCOs and ratings. You will personally take charge of the prisoner, with adequate Marine guard, and ensure he is securely quartered in the brig. High security while he's aboard."

"Aye, Commander."

The Lieutenant moved to a control console and initiated the process that would seal the enormous outer and inner doors of the bay's airlock. Jenetta remained until both hatches had been closed, locked, and certified as being sealed by the computer. She then turned to Kanes.

"This way to the bridge, Commander. Your people are in good hands."

"As am I. Thank you, Commander." As they walked, Kanes said, "You seem to be getting on quite well."

"Yes, sir. I've been very happy. This is where I want to be, where I've dreamed of being for as long as I can remember. There was a time when I believed I'd never make it."

"When you were adrift in the escape pod after the *Hokyuu* exploded?"

"Long before that, sir. I was designated as a science officer because they felt I didn't have the aptitude for command. I was sure I'd *never* have a chance for a posting like this."

Commander Kane, intimately familiar with Jenetta's file, looked at her appraisingly. In his twenty-two years as an Intelligence officer in Space Command, he'd never met anyone quite so enigmatic as the young woman next to him and she intrigued him. "It's funny how situations change."

Captain Gavin was sitting in his command chair facing the full wall monitor at the front of the bridge when the two officers entered from the corridor behind him. It was his watch and he had relieved the officer Jenetta had left in charge of the bridge when she went to resolve the issue of last minute arrivals.

As Jenetta reached Gavin's side, she said, "Captain, Commander Kanes, accompanied by twenty-five officers and men, plus one prisoner, have just come aboard. Appropriate berthing is being assigned and Commander Kanes has accompanied me to the bridge."

Gavin scowled slightly as he turned in his chair to look over his shoulder at Kanes, who had been standing behind and out of the way as Jenetta reported him coming aboard ship. It was a breach of military protocol for Gavin not to have been notified in advance of the pending arrival. Gavin turned back to Jenetta and asked, "Is everything secured below, Commander?"

"Aye, Captain. The airlock is sealed and all is ready for departure."

"Excellent. Take us out."

"Aye, sir," Jenetta said, as she climbed into the first officer's bridge chair. "Astrogation, have we received clearance for maneuvering and departure?"

"We've received clearance and the space is open, ma'am."

"Helm, has the airlock ramp been vacated and the station airlock door secured?"

"Aye, Commander. The ramp is empty and the station airlock control indicates red. The station dock master has approved our request to undock."

"Tactical, is the ship sealed?"

"Aye, ma'am. The computer reports that all access hatches are closed, locked, and sealed."

"Helm, depressurize the starboard airlock ramp at the forward cargo bay."

The faint sounds of rushing air could be heard by the crewmen and NCOs standing by to handle any problem in the forward cargo hold as pumps were engaged and the atmosphere evacuated into onboard storage bottles. After about thirty seconds, the helmsman said, "The starboard airlock ramp at the forward cargo bay is fully depressurized, ma'am."

"Release all docking clamps."

"Docking clamps released— airlock ramp is retracting— airlock ramp is retracted. The ship is floating free and clear of all obstructions."

"Reverse thrusters, twenty ticks."

"All reverse thrusters operating, twenty ticks."

The display screen at the front of the bridge, which had shown the space station appearing to move away, shifted to show the view from the stern. A small inset image near the top right of the screen now showed the view in front as the ship backed slowly away from the dock.

As the nearly two-kilometer-long ship came clear of the docking pier and other docked ships, Jenetta said, "Starboard bow thrusters, ten ticks."

"Starboard bow thrusters operating, ten ticks," the helmsman repeated.

The ship began to revolve slowly in a counter-clockwise motion. As it achieved rotational apogee, Jenetta said, "Larboard bow thrusters, five ticks."

"Larboard bow thrusters operating, five ticks."

The ship stopped turning but was still moving away from the space port dock when Jenetta said, "Helm, sub-light engines at minimum power until we clear all station traffic. Engage sub-light engines."

"Aye, Commander, engaging sub-light engines, power at minimum."

The enormous ship began to glide forward slowly, reaching ten meters per second as the helmsman maneuvered around traffic in the port. In addition to the docked ships, there were numerous ships in planetary orbit or in close proximity to the station. Once clear, the helmsman called out, "Clear of all vessels, Commander."

"Astrogation, is our course laid in and our heading correct?"

"Aye, Commander."

"Tactical, what's the status of the AutoTect grid?"

"The AutoTect grid is green, Commander. The board is clear."

The sizeable tactical station aboard the *Prometheus* was designed to accommodate no less than seven tac officers. The lead tactician, usually a commander, or at least a lieutenant commander, sat amid an almost complete circle of displays and electronic control consoles. Facing him or her on the outside of the circle were six stations for the rest of the tac team, although most seats were normally only occupied during general quarters. A bevy of holo-screens hung suspended over the encircling hardware so the lead could see exactly what each tac team member was seeing.

The ship's ACS, or anti-collision system, had the potential to detect another vessel that was hours away, even when both ships were proceeding at top FTL speed towards one another, *if* both vessels were transmitting a proper AutoTect code. The signals traveled on an Inter-Dimensional Band in hyperspace at a speed of point-zero-five-one-three light-years per minute. Green meant that no other ships are reporting a course that intersected with *Prometheus'* projected course in such a way as to present a real threat. Until recently, all use of AutoTect systems had been discontinued because the Raiders could use it to identify plump targets. As a result of Jenetta having discovered and destroyed the Raider base operating in this deca-sector, Space Command was once again requiring its use by all vessels in transit.

"And the status of the DeTect grid?"

"The DeTect grid is also green, Commander."

The ship's DeTect equipment used a special frequency in hyperspace to detect everything within four billion kilometers of a ship, much as radar and lidar served planetary vessels. The quality of the image wasn't especially good, but the computers could identify the movement of any ships, extraterrestrial bodies, or miscellany that posed a danger to the ship's navigation.

"Tactical, is the *Chiron* out of port traffic?"

"She's just clearing the port now, Commander," the lead tactical officer said.

"Helm, disengage the sub-light engines and build our temporal envelope."

After two minutes the helmsman said, "Envelope complete, Commander."

"The *Chiron* reports that their envelope is complete," the com operator said.

"Helm, engage the Light Drive to Light-375."

"Aye, Commander. Light-375 engaged."

The viewscreen showed the ship moving forward with steadily increasing speed while the small inset showed the *Chiron* to be starboard and aft. The helmsman called out the speed variations as the ship accelerated gradually to its top speed. Although capable of almost instant acceleration to the maximum rated speed of the ship, standard operating procedure was to accelerate very slowly for the first minutes whenever leaving a space station, planetary orbit, or any RP where other ships were assembled. The temporal envelope eliminated the need to engage the gravitative inertial compensator required when accelerating or decelerating in normal space.

Jenetta turned to the Captain. "We're away, Captain."

The Captain had witnessed the entire procedure, but it was traditional to report the departure when the Captain wasn't handling it.

"Thank you, Commander."

"Aye, sir.

"Commander Kanes, come into my briefing room," Gavin said as he climbed down from his chair. To Jenetta, he said, "You have the bridge, Commander."

"Aye, sir," Jenetta said. "I have the bridge." She watched as the two men disappeared into the briefing room. With the ship now under way, there was little to do, so Jenetta called the housing officer.

"Lieutenant Shelton," the lieutenant responded when the call went through.

"This is Commander Carver. Have our guests been accommodated, Lieutenant?"

"Aye, Commander. All have been shown to available quarters and we have suitable VIP quarters prepared for Commander Kanes when he's ready."

"Very good, Lieutenant. Carry on."

"Aye, Commander."

Jenetta leaned fully back in the first officer's chair, took a deep breath, and relaxed. Relative to the workload she'd had during the past week, there should be little to do during the next few months as they made their way to Earth. On a personal note, she was looking forward to finally having enough time during meals to sate her runaway appetite so she wouldn't have to spend the day snacking on fruit. Within a couple of days, they should settle into a placid routine that would continue until the end of the voyage. Of course, the arrival of the senior Intelligence officer assigned to Higgins SCB with twenty-five personnel in tow just minutes before departure was more than a little unusual. Although she appeared to be innocently staring at the front viewscreen, she was actually thinking about the rank insignia and shoulder flashes of the ratings and NCOs who had come aboard with the intelligence officer. Virtually all were weapon specialists.

Chapter Four
~ February 29th, 2268 ~

Following recovery of the two battleships from the Raiders, all ship's systems were restored to shipyard specifications. Then Space Command databases with asynchronous update capability were installed in the main computer so the cranial transducer of every officer and the ID chip of every Space Command NCO and crewman on active duty would now be recognized when they were aboard. An officer's CT offered two-way communications, while an ID chip was receive only. The computer could also instantly locate anyone with a CT or ID aboard ship by emitting a high-pitched signal far above the range of human hearing on the individual's carrier frequency and triangulating the echo with shipboard sensors.

Subcutaneously implanted against the exterior of the skull just behind the left ear, the chips created the impression when receiving a message that someone was whispering directly into the ear. A soft, chime-like noise preceded the transmission so the recipient would know the 'voice' was a transmission and not someone standing behind them. Every chip was assigned a unique address so that in a room full of Space Command personnel only the intended recipient would hear the computer-forwarded message. A minute electrical charge produced by the host's body powered the unit, but was insufficient to generate a signal of sufficient strength for transmission with CTs, so they relied on the ship's main computer to establish the carrier wave for the delivery of messages. To transmit a message, an officer need only lightly press thumb or forefinger to the face of their Space Command ring. This action generated a signal to the central transceiver, which then established a carrier wave for the officer's communication.

Although limited to receive-only mode, the ID chip could also be used by the ship's computer for allowing entrance to secure areas or unlocking equipment without further identification. High security areas and certain specialized equipment, such as weapons consoles, still required retinal image, voice identification, and/or handprint verification.

Jenetta was lost in thought when she received a CT message from the Captain. "Join us in my briefing room, Commander," she heard in her left ear.

Touching the Space Command ring on her right hand with her left forefinger, Jenetta said, "Aye, Captain. Carver out."

As she climbed down from her chair, she said to the helmsman, "Lt. Kerrey, I'll be in the Captain's briefing room. You have the bridge in my absence."

"Aye, Commander," he said. "I have the bridge." Since she would only be twenty meters away, he remained at the helm console.

Jenetta paused at the briefing room door as the computer identified her and notified the Captain of her presence. When the doors opened to admit her, she crossed the room to where the two men were sitting at the Captain's desk. She immediately spotted the data ring sitting in front of the Captain on the pristine, highly polished surface, and knew that Commander Kanes had apparently delivered his orders to Gavin.

"Yes, Captain?"

"Have a seat, Commander."

Jenetta settled into the soft comfort of the only available chair that faced the desk. Commander Kanes floated in the other overstuffed, 'opposed gravity' chair.

"Commander Kanes, would you be so good as to enlighten Commander Carver with the information you've related to me regarding your mission?"

"Yes, sir," he said. Turning slightly towards Jenetta, he said, "Commander, prior to your court-martial you told us about Commander Pretorious' attempts to secure his release in exchange for certain information?"

"Yes, sir."

"After learning that, I had several long conversations with him. He desperately wants his freedom and we've agreed to release him if his information is accurate. That's why you were prohibited from testifying about the meeting during the court-martial."

"Commander, he's a senior line officer in the Raider organization and presents a serious threat to the safety of our ships and citizens. Do you really think he's going to give us accurate information?"

"The Kinesthesian Truth Analyzer indicated he was telling the truth while making his statements and he doesn't get his freedom until after the information is verified. Additionally, data found in the computer files retrieved by you at the Raider spaceport support his statements."

"Did he give you the location of any of the other Raider spaceports?"

"No, he refused that and said he wouldn't divulge them under any circumstances. Our deal was only for this one piece of information."

"I wouldn't trust him as far as I could throw Space Command Supreme HQ, but it's your call, Commander. What does this have to do with me?"

"According to Commander Pretorious, the Raiders will purportedly attack a freighter underway from the planet Mawcett to the planet Anthius."

"All that Raider preparation and firepower for a single freighter?"

"It's being escorted by a dozen destroyers from Peabody Protection Services. As I'm sure you're aware, they're each equivalent to one of Space Command's light destroyers."

"A dozen warships protecting one freighter? What's the cargo?"

"Ancient artifacts. About ten years ago, an archeological expedition unearthed evidence that an advanced culture existed on Mawcett some twenty thousand years ago. That's about the time Earth's last Great Ice Age peaked and began to decline. So far, it's the oldest evidence of an advanced civilization uncovered in this galaxy. The planet's entire population appears to have died out while our Paleolithic ancestors on Earth were still gathering nuts and berries in forests, chasing down small animals for meat, and painting crude pictures on cave walls. Fearful of having the ship fall victim to the Raiders, the scientists on Mawcett have held off shipping any artifacts, but this past year they decided they couldn't wait any longer because they also fear the planet itself will be assaulted and the warehouses looted as the collection grows. They contracted with Peabody for protection services and prepared everything so far unearthed for shipment. The date and route are supposed to be the most closely guarded secrets in the universe, but it appears the Raiders have learned this information, probably from an inside source. The Raiders reportedly pay handsomely for information like this and I imagine that someone, maybe several someones, at Peabody or the Mawcett Archeological Expedition Headquarters have earned enough to retire. I'd put my money on an informant inside Peabody because, while MAE may have the date of the shipment, only Peabody should know the exact route."

"I take it the artifacts are valuable?"

"Extremely. Some private collectors would be willing to give their own children to own some of these old— relics. The entire shipment has been valued at twenty-eight trillion credits."

Jenetta's eyebrows rose in surprise. "That's a *lot* of incentive, sir."

"It's enough for the Raiders to pull out all the stops and attack with an overwhelming force."

"But surely the Raiders wouldn't be able to sell the artifacts as genuine?"

"There are always collectors willing to ignore the fact that the object they desire above all else is stolen merchandise. But there's another avenue as well. The shipment is insured by a large pool of insurance companies and if the Raiders don't wish to spend decades searching out unscrupulous collectors, they can always sell the stolen artifacts back to the insurance providers. Insurance companies will normally pay a ten percent finder's fee, no questions asked, for the recovery of insured goods. That's almost three trillion credits if the Raiders take the quick route. They could build and equip several new hidden asteroid bases with that much available cash."

Jenetta grimaced at the thought. "How many Space Command vessels are included in the escort?"

"None."

Jenetta couldn't believe her ears. "None, sir?"

"Peabody flatly refused to tell us when the shipment was to leave Mawcett because they feared a security leak in Space Command. I suppose that's understandable given the culpability of certain Space Command officers involved with the Raider theft of the two battleships. We naturally couldn't leave ships waiting over Mawcett indefinitely, so no ships were assigned. We weren't even aware the convoy had left orbit until two days ago. It had been sitting idle over the planet for more than six months."

"So now you know the convoy is under way. And I take it Commander Pretorious has told you the route and where the ambush will occur."

"Yes, and we can calculate approximately when they'll reach the interception point. We've stationed a small science vessel near the edge of an uninhabited solar system along the convoy's expected course. They've deployed numerous small satellites to give them extended DeTect capability across the projected path. If a convoy passes within four billion kilometers of any satellite, the vessel will be alerted and they'll notify us of the exact course and time of passage. We'll then have verification of the timetable."

"I assume that next you're going to tell me we're altering course to intercept."

"Not until twenty-one days from now. We want everyone to believe our only destination is Earth. The Raiders have spies and 'watchers' everywhere. We'll probably be watched for days until they believe we're proceeding according to your former orders. We don't believe for a second they have anything that can keep up with us, but we feel confident that small spotter ships posted along the normal space lanes are watching for our passage. Fortunately for us, the space lanes between Higgins and Earth pass within five light years of the expected ambush point."

"One battleship isn't going to make much of a difference if the convoy is attacked by double the number of warships scheduled to leave the Raider-One space port."

"We're not the only one altering course to intercept. The *Chiron* will be coming with us, for one, and a number of other ships have received orders to proceed to Earth, ostensibly to participate in the launching ceremonies of the *Prometheus* and *Chiron*. They'll all be altering course in time to intercept the convoy at the ambush point, but not before all the Raider 'watchers' believe Earth is the real destination. The crews won't be told until we're almost ready to go into battle to eliminate the risk of messages home revealing the mission, and the information about our role isn't to go beyond this room until we hold a briefing for officers a couple of days before the expected attack."

"Why even tell *me* before we need to change course?"

"Three reasons. One, you're Acting First Officer. As such you need to know because you're automatically in command should something happen to the captain. Two, you'll have to get your people up to speed on the weapon systems on this ship. I know regular weapons training is SOP, but knowing we're going into this type of battle means you should devote extra time to it *without* alerting the crew to the upcoming action. And three, you deserve it because it all traces back to you. Without the prisoner and computer files you brought back, we wouldn't have this opportunity."

"Opportunity? Sir, as I see it, we're about to fly into a major engagement against overwhelming odds with a crew complement smaller than that normally found even on a light destroyer."

"That's why I brought you some help, but they aren't to be included in weapons practice until after we alter course. Each is already an accomplished weapons specialist on temporary loan from the ships assigned to protect Higgins or from my own staff on the station. The *Chiron* received an equal number of experienced temporary personnel in the form of passengers. I use the term *opportunity* because it's the first time we've had a chance to surprise the Raiders by being somewhere, in force, where they don't expect us to be."

"How long before we reach the ambush point?"

"Twenty-five days."

"Will we be ready?" Gavin asked Jenetta.

"We'll be ready, sir."

Commander Kanes nodded.

"That's all, Commander," Gavin said to Jenetta.

"Aye, sir."

Jenetta stood and left the briefing room. Walking to the first officer's chair on the bridge, she climbed up and relaxed. Although she appeared to be idly watching the front view-screen, she was actually deep in thought. Her mind was filled with the details of establishing an accelerated weapons training schedule and the excuses she'd give when her officers asked why they were devoting so much extra time to the task.

* * *

If being the individual mainly responsible for discovering and rectifying the mistakes and shortcomings of everyone on board and then being required to make recommendations for the appropriate level of discipline hadn't already made her the most detested person on the ship, Jenetta felt the actions she took the next day would surely qualify her for that distinction. Working with her officers, each crewman aboard the ship, including those brought aboard by Captain Kanes, was assigned a specific post in the event of a call to general quarters. At various times over the next couple of days, usually in the middle of the night while most personnel were off-duty, unscheduled drills were conducted. GQ drills at such hours were highly unusual, but Jenetta felt they were necessary given the threat they were facing. The central computer polled everyone's CT or ID chip repeatedly during the drill to determine how long it took them to reach their assigned post. The drills continued until every officer and crewman could quickly reach their assigned post, even when awakened from a sound sleep. Jenetta temporarily disengaged the Captain's CT and the alert devices in his quarters just before each drill to ensure that he wasn't disturbed, but no one else was exempted from the clamorous cacophony.

With a CT and ID volume level practically guaranteed to 'rouse the dead,' no one could manage to sleep through an alert. Although the repeated drills, especially those conducted in the dead of night to the accompaniment of loud curses and oaths, didn't endear the acting XO with the crew, at least everyone understood their necessity. Once she was satisfied with the response, Jenetta reduced the unannounced alert drills to just once per week.

During the same period, weapons practice intensified significantly and the dozen fire control centers located along the center axis of the ship were rarely empty. Like the bridge itself, and the Auxiliary Command & Control center, massive bulkheads of tritanium armor and radiation shielding protected each of the weapon centers. They were also compartmentalized to protect crewmen in the event that surrounding areas were breached.

The ship's weapon systems included such realistic simulation programs that it was impossible to tell them from real combat, except that the lasers never fired real bursts and torpedoes never left the ship. The number of available fire control stations, combined with the limited crew size and pending engagement, made it both practical and necessary to train all crew members, even mess attendants and stores clerks, in the use of the phased array lasers and torpedo guidance consoles. Each laser weapon team consisted of one experienced gunner and one trainee. The experienced man actually pinpointed the target and fired the weapon, while the new man was busy searching for the next target. In torpedo guidance, the specialist continuously 'flew' the assigned torpedo to the target using video telemetry with the torpedo once a tactical officer on the bridge had identified the target and launched the weapon.

Jenetta spent as much time as possible in the fire control centers giving tips to the new gunners and guidance specialists, and encouraging them to keep working to improve their skills. The simulations actually came to be treated like recreational video games, with betting involved as the days wore on. Jenetta was aware of the gambling but looked the other way and told her officers to do the same as long as the betting didn't appear in the open. The gambling increased the incentive of each gunner and specialist to improve. Given the lack of qualified personnel, Jenetta would use every edge available.

Other than the drills and weapons practice, things did finally settle into a quiet routine. The workload Jenetta had initially found heaped on her shoulders eventually filtered down through her officers and settled onto the shoulders of the warrant officers and petty officers where it had belonged all along. Any NCO, and any officer willing to admit the truth, would confess who really kept the ships and bases operating. Jenetta was able to spend time catching up on the history of the past eleven years and begin her study of the Nordakian culture. Interestingly, she kept running into Commander Kanes when she wasn't on the bridge. He consistently dropped into the officers' mess right after she arrived or was working out in the gym each day when she was able to schedule time. He would always engage her in conversation and try to get her to talk about herself. Jenetta didn't know if this was his normal personality or an adopted practice he couldn't turn off, or if he was just trying to learn something in particular.

The absence of first and third officers made proper coverage of bridge watches difficult, so from her second day aboard ship the Captain had approved Jenetta's request to appoint Lieutenant Kerrey as Acting Second Officer. He was assigned to third watch and Jenetta was able to get enough sleep. Since the senior bridge officers' quarters were all located on the bridge deck, she could be on the bridge in less than two minutes if a problem developed.

* * *

On the twenty-first day out of Higgins Space Port, Jenetta ordered a radical course change after first notifying the *Chiron* and coordinating the turn. The astrogator looked at her questioningly but she didn't offer any further information. Finally, he asked, "How long do we maintain this new course, Commander?"

"Until the Captain or I tell you otherwise, Lieutenant," she said quietly. "And you're not to mention this change of course to anyone. Do you understand, Lieutenant? Not anyone."

"Aye, ma'am, not anyone."

Jenetta also went to the helmsman and gave the same sotto voce instructions about secrecy. He too offered a quizzical look but verified that he understood.

Just after the course change, the Captain ordered a ban on all outbound com traffic except for military communications from himself or Lt. Commander Carver.

* * *

On the twenty-fifth day out of Vinnia, all Space Command officers with the rank of lieutenant and above were ordered to the ship's largest conference room. During a presentation by Captain Gavin, they were informed of the pending action. They had already understood something major was in the works because of the communications blackout.

"We know a little about how these Raiders operate," Gavin said as the conference began. "They have an incredible intelligence network, and when they know the flight path of a freighter, they position a few cargo containers filled with electronics that can generate a plane of false contact inform- ation for tens of thousands of kilometers across the path. Collision avoidance systems sense the electronic 'debris field' and shut down the ship's Light Speed drive. While the freighter's bridge crew looks for a clear path through or around the nonexistent debris, the Raiders strike. They try to incapacitate the freighter's temporal field generator so it can't escape into FTL, and then they demand its surrender. If the freighter captain refuses to capitulate, they destroy the main ship, killing everyone on board, although there are sometimes survivors in airtight sections.

"In the case of escort vessels, they don't even ask for surrender; they just attack to keep them from putting up a fight and then repair them later, if economically feasible, and place them in service for themselves. They do a pretty good job of cleaning up afterwards, so we only know of their tactics because Commander Carver was able to defeat two of their attack ships and capture about a thousand Raider crewmembers. Planners at the Space Command War College expect the Raiders to follow an attack strategy consistent with their modus operandi two days from now. Computer, display the holo image 'WC 03 — Stage 1.'"

The large table in the center of the conference room was actually a holo-platform, and a detailed holographic image immediately appeared above it. An inordinately large group of tiny ships seemed to be hovering there, as they would in space. A few were larger than others, but the majority of ships were fairly uniform in size. Regardless of size, there was no doubt that all were warships because of their exterior configurations.

"We expect them to deploy their ships in a loose 'U' formation, as you see here," Gavin continued, "and then close to a circle when they move in once the convoy is halted. Computer, advance the image to Stage 2."

Twelve small warships, arranged in cuneal form around a lengthy freighter, appeared and moved into the center of the previously displayed group of ships before coming to a stop.

"Raider fighters will deploy from every ship while the main ships circle the convoy and remain out of easy laser weapon range at a thousand kilometers distance. Computer, advance the image to Stage 3."

Hundreds of miniscule ships seemed to emerge from the Raider warships as the twelve escort destroyers moved to surround the freighter protectively. The fighters proceeded quickly to the center of the holographic image where they began to attack the escort ships like a swarm of angry wasps.

"We'll hold off well beyond extended DeTect sensor range," Gavin said, "until they've stopped the convoy and begun their attack. Then we'll move in and ambush the ambushers while the *Chiron* and our other ships do the same. It should be pretty crazy for a while, so make sure your gunners are careful not to hit any 'friendlies.' The weapons computers of all GSC ships will be synchronized with the 'Alpha-Thirty-Six' rotating frequency ship protection code so the guns won't lock or fire on our own ships, but we need to be careful about the Peabody destroyers and the freighter.

"The hull on this new ship is comprised of three layers of reinforced tritanium armor with self-sealing membranes between each instead of the usual two layers with one membrane, so it will take a really serious hit to hurt us, but we're certainly not invulnerable. All airtight sections will be sealed off prior to our attack in case we're damaged. If anyone must travel through the ship during the fight, use Corridor 0 on any deck between five and eighteen. The airtight emergency doors in those corridors should respond to local keypad commands unless a hull breach has caused pressure to drop in the corridor or if some other hazard exists. If the door doesn't respond to commands, coordinate your passage with Damage Control Central. Are there any questions?"

"How many enemy ships are you expecting, sir?" Lieutenant Kerrey asked.

"This is the single largest operation ever attempted by the Raiders. There were twenty-three large warships at the Raider-One space port designated to participate in the attack, and they were tasked to join an equally large complement of ships from a different Raider base. With the destruction of Raider-One and its full complement of ships, we expect that ships from a third Raider base have been sent to replace them, so we're still anticipating between forty and fifty. Knowing what we do of the Raider fleet, most will probably be destroyers, but there will undoubtedly be some frigates or cruisers, and perhaps even a battleship or two."

The conference room went silent, even more than it had been. It was as if everyone had suddenly stopped breathing.

"Uh— and how many GSC ships will be there, sir?" Lieutenant Kerrey asked.

"Ten ships have been tasked to this operation, but I'm not sure how many will reach the rendezvous point by the time the shooting begins. The timetable is being governed by the speed of the convoy. We can definitely count on three ships being there—the *Chiron*, the *Song*, and ourselves. The rest are still underway to the RP at their top speed. Since all of our ships must remain outside the DeTect range of any possible Raider picket ships lest we frighten off the Raiders before they engage the convoy, the War College Planners have designated a location near the planet Vauzlee as our RP. We'll wait there until the Raiders actually launch their fighters and commence their attack. We'll then deploy all available resources at the top speed of the slowest ship so we arrive in force. Any of our destroyers that haven't yet reached the RP will proceed directly to the ambush site, and upon their arrival, join the battle if we're still engaged."

"That means we could be outnumbered possibly fifteen to one," Lieutenant Kerrey said more to himself than to the staff at the table, "—at least initially." Everyone had computed the odds long before he stated them.

"Don't forget the twelve Peabody light destroyers. They're going to be throwing everything they've got at their Raider attackers. They'll be handicapped in that they'll have to remain in fixed position around the freighter to protect it, but they'll make a considerable difference. If all our ships make it to the battle on time, we'll only be outnumbered about two to one. This is the first time we've ever had an opportunity to engage the Raiders in a real fight. If they show, then I'm willing to allow them the advantage in numbers. Raider ships usually operate singly or in very small groups. I'm counting on command and control problems because they're not adequately trained in group tactics. I'm also counting on the fact that they had to bring half their fleet from some distance away and that the change in fleet composition means they haven't had any time to train together for this operation. We have the advantage in training, skill, and ship construction. Their Uthlaro-built warships only have titanium armor. Granted, it's especially thick, but it's still just a titanium alloy. Thanks to Commander Carver, the Raiders don't have any GSC tritanium-armored battleships to throw against us, but *we* have these two new battleships to use against *them*."

"I don't mean to sound defeatist, sir," Lt. Algolwin, one of three weapons officers who had come aboard with Kanes, said, "but Commander Carver has shown everyone that even a tramp freighter with torpedoes can destroy warships."

Jenetta started ever so slightly at the use of the descriptive term 'tramp,' but she maintained a staid expression because she was aware that every pair of eyes in the room had turned in her direction. The *Vordoth* had been her first command, and as such, it occupied a very special place in her heart, even if it was more than fifty years old.

Lt. Algolwin, unaware of the veiled reaction that his choice of adjectives had evoked, continued with his statement. "Since the Raiders had possession of this ship for a while, they must have studied it for weaknesses and will be attempting to exploit that knowledge during any engagements. Do we at least have construction specs on any of the Raider ships so we can determine *their* most vulnerable points?"

"Everything we have is available in the enemy profile database. As I've indicated, we believe the heaviest concentration of Raider ships come from the Uthlaro. Those mercenary bastards will sell to anyone with sufficient credits, but we also believe that some of the Raider ships are made by the Tsgardi. From what we know, or at least suspect, the Tsgardi ships are the most poorly constructed warships in the quadrant. We can only hope that most of the ships we encounter will be made by them. We've also heard rumors that the Raiders have secured ships from the Aguspod, the Clidepp, and the Kweedee, but we have no solid evidence of that."

"SCI doesn't put much faith in those rumors," Kanes said. "The Clidepp are totally occupied with the rebels trying to take over their territory so all of their ship construction is needed for their own civil war. The Aguspod have been fighting the Raiders for at least half as long as we have so they wouldn't be selling any ships to Raiders, and the Kweedee Aggregate isn't interested in trading with anyone from outside their systems. They barely tolerate diplomatic missions. So if the Raiders have any ships of Clidepp, Aguspod, or Kweedee construction, they're ships that were salvaged after a battle and repaired, or possibly that were sold to the Raiders by deserters. You should concentrate your planning on Uthlaro construction."

"When can we pass this information on to the NCOs and crewmen, sir?" Lieutenant Brewster asked the Captain.

"As soon as this meeting is over, but— I think we should keep the enemy numbers to ourselves."

"Yes, sir."

After a minute of silence, Gavin said, "Are there any more questions?" When no one spoke up, he added, "then you're dismissed."

The officers filed out of the room in silence, each wrapped up in his or her thoughts. There would be a great many 'final messages to home' recorded tonight, just in case, even though they couldn't be transmitted yet.

As the Captain prepared to leave, he said, "Commander Carver, would you join Commander Kanes and me in my briefing room."

"Aye, Captain."

Chapter Five
~ March 24th, 2268 ~

Upon entering his briefing room, Gavin said to the two officers accompanying him, "Fix yourself a beverage, Commanders, and have a seat." All three officers had a marked preference for different blends of coffee, but the beverage synthesizer was equally adept at preparing everything from ice water to latte to non-alcoholic ale. Jenetta's preference was Colombian, a mild Arabica coffee, served black with one sugar per eight ounces, while Kanes ordered a Robusta. Gavin selected a strong espresso.

As they settled into the overstuffed 'oh-gee' chairs around the enormous desk, Gavin said, "Commander Carver, tell me about the strategies you employed against the Raiders in your engagements."

Jenetta had described her actions repeatedly at the court-martial and in such detail that her presentation now seemed to have the polish of rehearsal. She spent the next twenty minutes describing the way she had handled the three engagements, beginning with the initial attack on the *Vordoth* by fighters.

The Captain interrupted to ask a number of questions as she talked. When she finished, he asked, "How would you handle this upcoming attack?"

Although she'd spent a not insignificant amount of time thinking about the upcoming engagement since learning of it on the day they left Higgins, Jenetta hadn't really prepared any sort of presentation. She thought for a few seconds before speaking and tried to organize her thoughts as she took a sip of coffee.

Jenetta took a deep breath and began. "We're in an area of space that contains little or nothing of military or commercial value, so the Raiders would hardly expect to find even a lone Space Command vessel here, much less a task force. If our ruse has been successful, their intelligence network will have assured them that no one is going to suddenly drop by to spoil their little soirée. Since no reasonably safe means of attacking ships traveling faster than light has yet been devised, the Raiders will have to stop the convoy as you've suggested. Assuming they'll be lying doggo without any energy signatures to betray them, the DeTect system aboard the convoy ships will simply record them as naturally-occurring celestial matter, and if their position doesn't present a threat to the navigation of the convoy, the DeTect system won't even call their presence to the attention of the convoy's tactical officers. So the Raider ships probably won't move until after the convoy's anti-collision systems have canceled their envelopes. A freighter can't outrun warships, so I don't expect them to make a break for it using their sub-light engines. They'd be better off remaining behind the protection screen offered by the Peabody destroyers.

"It's reasonable, and even likely, that the Raider force will surround the convoy as your holographic projections show. But since they have the Peabody ships outnumbered by at least four to one and believe they have all the time in the world, they might simply demand the surrender of the freighter and destroyers before commencing their attack. They're more interested in preserving the artifacts than anything else, and they'd probably also like to take the destroyers intact to use them in their own operations."

"Thanks to you," Commander Kanes said, grinning, "they're probably a little short of warships these days, so I'm sure they'd love to pick up twelve light destroyers in excellent condition."

Jenetta returned the grin and then continued. "Of course, I don't expect the Peabody personnel to simply give up without a fight. That's where the Raider policy of never releasing anyone bites them on their own arse. The Peabody employees all know that capture means either death or a life of slavery for every one of them, so I anticipate they'll immediately unleash a barrage of torpedoes with the intention of fighting to the death. It would be nice if they kept the Raiders busy talking while we're rushing to assist, but that's not going to happen since they don't know of our presence nearby."

"Headquarters made that decision to ensure that word of our ambush didn't leak to the Raiders," Kanes said. "The Raiders must have someone in their pocket who's highly placed in the Peabody organization or they would never have learned of the convoy route. Peabody even put their own astrogator on the freighter so the freighter crew wouldn't have pre-flight access to course information."

"So," Jenetta continued, "with the expectation that a battle will be raging when we arrive, and that we'll have an element of surprise since the Raiders probably won't be paying much attention to the DeTect system while they're busy dodging torpedoes, not to mention that proximity warning buzzers and imminent threat alarms will be going off continuously on their bridges, it's possible we can be in the fray before they know we're there.

"But I totally disagree with the military planners at the War College who believe the Raiders will send in fighters to attack the convoy. I realize it's been their modus operandi in every attack to date that we've been able to document, but those attacks were mainly against helpless freighters and passenger liners."

"But they used fighters in their attack on the Nordakian convoy," Gavin said, "and were able to defeat the destroyer escort. If you hadn't arrived when you did, the convoy would have been lost."

"Yes, sir, but the Nordakian destroyer escort shot down dozens of fighters before being destroyed themselves. I think the Raiders will have learned from that experience. Fighters are most effective when employed in the low atmosphere of a planet. The missiles that fighters can mount are small, limited in numbers, and not terribly effective against the armor of a warship. Likewise, their energy weapons are lightweight and equally ineffective. Here, they'll be facing warships bristling with powerful laser weapons and people who know how to use them. The *Vordoth*, with no armor, demonstrated how

- 65 -

nearly useless fighters are against an armed enemy with qualified gunners.

"I believe the Raider warships will remain far enough out to be nearly impossible targets for the Peabody energy weapons, perhaps twenty to twenty-five thousand kilometers, while they pour torpedoes into the Peabody task force. The Peabody laser gunners will most likely be spending all their time on defense, trying to knock down those torpedoes, and may not even fire at the Raider ships. Of course, the Peabody torpedo gunners are going to be firing everything in their arsenal just as fast as their systems can reload. The extra distance will allow the Raider laser gunners adequate time for targeting incoming torpedoes. At just a thousand kilometers, the Peabody torpedoes would be exploding against the Raider hulls while their laser gunners were still trying to line up on the incoming weapons. Five thousand kilometers would be the minimum practical distance for proper torpedo defense, but I think they'll want extra space, as the cruiser opted for when attacking the Nordakian convoy."

"But at just a thousand kilometers," Kanes said, "the *Raiders* torpedoes would be striking the Peabody ships before the Peabody laser gunners could target the incoming missiles."

"The Raiders will believe they have overwhelming advantage in numbers and all the time in the world for their attack. Why suffer deadly torpedo strikes just to end the battle sooner? The Peabody ships, by themselves, can't hope to defeat an armada as large as the one we're expecting. I believe the Raiders will opt to protect their fleet as much as possible and beat the Peabody defense down slowly."

Gavin had said little since Jenetta began her exposition of the tactical situation facing them. He'd just sat behind his desk, staring at her placidly while nodding his head occasionally. She had just disagreed with a major point of his presentation and she looked at him now to see if he was angered by her analysis. His face was just as calm and composed as she had ever seen it and she took his silence as tacit authorization that she should continue.

"Rather than attacking in force, as the War College planners suggest, I would have us arrive in staggered formation. We should be the first of the GSC ships to arrive. I'd approach the battle zone at an oblique angle so the DeTect equipment of the Raiders doesn't issue any special alerts about a possible collision, and then circle around just outside the ring of Raider ships like the indians did with the wagon trains, picking off as many as possible before they figure out what's going on. The *Chiron* should follow thirty seconds behind and do as we do. From five thousand kilometers outside the circling Raiders, our powerful laser weapons will be highly effective against their armor and we'll have enough time to pick off most torpedoes coming our way. An undulating track will help keep the Raiders penned in during the engagement, much as they're doing to the convoy. Any additional arriving ships should fall into line behind the nearest circling ship and open fire on the Raiders immediately."

"Indians?" Gavin said quizzically.

"Native Americans, sir," Jenetta said, grinning. "One of my brothers was into twentieth century video dramas called 'westerns.' They were fictionalized accounts of encounters between Native Americans and cowboys or settlers in the western United States during the nineteenth century."

"I've heard of them, but how are their encounters applicable here?"

"The indians would allegedly attack wagon trains full of settlers, who would then drive their wagons into a large circle and use the cover afforded by the wooden conveyances to fight the indians while the indians circled the wagon train, firing from horseback. I agree with your holographic presentation that the Peabody destroyers will move to protect the freighter by encircling it with their ships."

"And the indians were successful?"

"Not always, usually because they only had bows and arrows while the settlers had lead projectile weapons. But like the indians, the Raiders should be concentrating all their attention inward toward the freighter and Peabody destroyers.

With so many Raider ships in the area, they probably won't even pay attention to another blip on their sensor screens, at least until we open fire. By the time they realize they've been outmaneuvered, we can already have targeted several of their most powerful ships and fired a full spread of torpedoes."

"I can't say I ever studied the tactics of cowboys and indians," Gavin said, the hint of a smile on his face.

"The closest parallel involving European or Asian armies or navies that I can think of, sir," Jenetta said, "occurred in the Austro-Turkish War of 1683. The Turkish Army was sent by Mohammed IV to take Vienna. A two-hundred-thousand-man force commanded by Grand Vizier Merzifonlu Kara Mustafa Pasha laid siege to the city. Count Ernst Rudiger von Starhemberg, with a defensive force of only ten thousand, managed to keep the Turks from breaching the city's walls for two months. The Turks then attempted to tunnel into the city, but before they could complete their efforts, John III Sobiski of Poland and Charles V, Duke of Lorraine, arrived with an army of seventy thousand men and attacked the perimeter of the Turkish lines, then consisting of one hundred thirty-eight thousand soldiers. Fifteen thousand Turks were killed and the rest, uh— strategically retreated— without orders and in complete disarray. Sobiski and Charles V lost a combined total of four thousand. The battle proved to be the turning point in the three-hundred-year struggle between Central European kingdoms and the Ottoman Empire."

"So, like the Europeans and the Turks, we'll have the attackers caught in a deadly crossfire between the Peabody destroyers and ourselves?" Kanes asked rhetorically.

"Of course, a certain amount of damage to the Peabody destroyers becomes a foregone conclusion once the decision is made to allow the convoy to be the bait in this operation," Jenetta said.

"It sounds like a good plan, Commander," Gavin said positively. "In fact, I think I like it better than the response suggested by the War College. They suggest launching as many fighters as we can man and then attacking the circling Raider ships with a full frontal assault by all ships. The fighters would follow us in after we clear a path through the outer perimeter of Raider ships and take on the Raider fighters attacking the convoy. But you have an excellent point that there may not be any fighters for them to take on. The War College's suggested divide-and-conquer strategy would, however, split the Raider ships into groups and cause great confusion while giving torpedo gunners and laser gunners on both sides of the ships a crack at them. After a few passes, we would be in a position to take on individual ships."

"That's true, sir, but I can see a number of weaknesses in that strategy," Jenetta said. "One, slowing and turning around after each pass through the circle of Raiders ships would take us away from the battle at a time when seconds are critical and would therefore be less effective than circling. Two, twice in each pass we would find ourselves between the Raiders and the Peabody ships. If the Peabody ships don't suppress their fire, we might run into their torpedoes. Of course, having them suppress their fire reduces the overall effectiveness of our combined forces. Three, even assuming that the Raiders send in fighters, our Marine fighter pilots would be far more effective remaining aboard to function as gunnery crews since we currently don't have adequate gun crews to man all our mounted weapons. Four, passing through the center of the battle zone would require us to man the guns on both sides of the ship. Even with the fighter pilots remaining aboard to function as gun crews, we'll only have half enough. By circling, every single weapon on the *Prometheus* and *Chiron* that faces the enemy can be fully manned while exposing a significantly smaller area of our hull to the Raider energy weapons and torpedoes. And lastly, the fighters we were able to get at SCB Higgins before our departure are not in the best of condition. I've had our small contingent of mechanics doing their best to get them marginally effective, but they're all retreads that were turned in for replacements. Most of our mechanics feel their greatest value would be as a source of emergency parts. The fighters the Raiders placed aboard before we reacquired the *Prometheus* are in better shape, but their design and armor are poor and our pilots aren't trained to fly them."

Gavin nodded thoughtfully. "Yes, there's definite merit in what you say, Commander."

"And I might also add that although the Raiders will probably be using high-explosive warheads because they look to salvage the ships of their victims, then repair and use them, I'd consider arming oùr torpedoes with fusion warheads. As much as I dislike their use, we're going to be severely out-numbered at the engagement."

"Thank you, Commander. I'll think it over and decide which tactics we'll use in the engagement. That'll be all."

"Aye, sir," Jenetta said as she stood to leave.

After she was gone, Gavin looked at Kanes soberly. "Indians," he said simply.

Kanes grinned and then chuckled aloud. "It's a real shame she never had an opportunity to attend the Warship Command Institute after completing her studies at the Academy. I'm sure she would have amused her instructors to no end with her unusual tactical scenarios."

"They do sound amusing on the surface, mainly because of her analogies to fictionalized western dramas, but tactically her ideas are brilliant. They have a novel simplicity about them that makes you shake your head and wonder why *you* didn't think of them. Although she didn't attend the WCI, there's no doubt she has a thorough knowledge and under-standing of the tactics of both ancient and modern warfare. The account she just gave of the 1683 Turkish attack on Vienna proves that. From my recollection, she was absolutely correct in every detail, and on the spur of the moment, I certainly couldn't have provided the specifics of that engagement as she did. She must have studied on her own because, while they do teach ancient battle strategies at the WCI, I know for a fact they don't teach them at the Academy. Perhaps it's better that she didn't attend the WCI; she's not saddled with the regimented thinking that seems to prevent the rest of us from developing such innovative strategies. If she had been sent to the WCI, I have no doubt she would have been among the ten percent selected to receive the intensive twelve-week course in tactics taught by visiting officers from the War College. And I predict she'll be the youngest-looking Commander or Captain at the War College when she's selected to attend that institution."

"It sounds like you're giving serious consideration to using her suggested tactics rather than the attack plan recommended by the War College planners," Kanes said.

"It's a captain's prerogative when he has better information than the planners. Keith, my XO was just an ensign when a freighter crew asked her to take command of their ship following an attack by raiders."

"I'm aware of that, sir. I spent an entire day grilling her after she arrived at Higgins with the *Prometheus*, *Chiron*, and *Vordoth*."

"So you're also well aware that she had only lightweight energy weapons and an ancient torpedo system employing four tubes with inferior ordnance when she fought both a Raider destroyer and Raider medium cruiser in separate engagements."

"Yes, I am," Kanes said, again grinning and chuckling. "Apparently no one ever informed Commander Carver that old freighters don't stand a chance in hell of winning an engagement against a modern warship, so, in her ignorance, she went ahead and disproved that postulation— twice."

"You can make light of it if you wish, but I know I certainly wouldn't care to find myself facing a Raider warship while I was in command of a freighter."

"She admits she was lucky, Captain."

"You can get lucky once in a situation like that, but twice? She destroyed both Raider vessels while suffering almost no damage to her own ship. I think you have to pay serious attention to someone who has had the degree of success in battle that she has."

"And you're willing to risk this ship and the entire task force by employing this— unique— strategy of hers?"

"She's right about one thing so far; the fighters we picked up at Higgins almost aren't worth the effort to dump them over the side. The War College is only seeing models and numbers, and is probably not aware of their mechanical condition. I've seen the maintenance reports and I'm not too keen on sending our boys and girls out in crates that reduce their chances for survival before the first laser shot is fired. I've been groping for an alternative."

"And you think Carver's *peculiar* plan is it? Captain, she's just been lucky."

"I know you graduated from the Warship Command Institute, even though you later decided to pursue a career in Intelligence and so never attended the War College. Do you remember Professor Leinsdorf?"

"Yes. I think I heard he retired recently. He taught an 'ancient weapons' course,' didn't he?"

Gavin nodded. "I remember he was quite fond of saying, 'Luck is what occurs when opportunity meets preparation.' Whenever I hear someone say that someone was lucky, I remember his words. Keith, I *know* my XO has a lot more going for her than pure random chance."

* * *

"We're all gonna die," Chief Edward Lindsey lamented strongly as he dealt the cards to the other four Chief Petty Officers at the card table in his quarters. "I just know we're all gonna die. I knew I shouldn't have left the *Thor*. She's sitting safely back at Higgins."

"Jeezz, Eddie, you're depressing me," CPO Flip Byrne said.

"*I'm* depressing you? It was the *LT* who told us we're going into combat against a Raider battle group."

"Fighting Raiders is a fact of life out here. Remember that Raider destroyer the *Thor* encountered about four years ago? As soon as he saw us coming, he turned tail and ran. That's probably what'll happen this time as well. They don't have the stomach for taking on a GSC battleship."

"But we're not taking on just one lone destroyer. We're going up against seventy-five Raider warships."

"What? Where did you hear that?"

"One of my guys overheard two officers talking in a cargo hold."

"They were talking about that in front of a crewman?"

"Nah, they didn't know he was there. I have my guys spread out in hiding places all over that deck so the officers don't see them sitting around with nothing to do during duty hours and the computers don't see them congregating when they shouldn't be, but I know where each of them is in case I need them for something. Anyway, my guy was up on top of a pile of shipping containers where no one could see him. He's got a couple of blankets up there and he spends most of the watch outta sight."

"So what else is new? We all hide our guys. To avoid make-work details, chiefs have been stashing their guys away from the eyes of officers since the square rigger days."

"So these two weapons officers, the ones who came aboard just before we left Higgins, come into the hold and close the hatch to the corridor. They were probably looking for a place where they could talk in private. My guy over-hears them talking about which gunners they intend to place where and why. Then one of them asks the other if he's prepared his final message to home yet. The second one says he did that right after the Captain's briefing. He says that even though they'll be in a fire control center, just about the most protected part of the ship, he doesn't expect to survive the battle. He said that fifteen-to-one odds are just too great, even in a battleship as powerful as this one."

"Fifteen to one?"

"Yeah."

"So where did you get seventy-five from? The LT just told us we were heading into a fight with Raiders."

"Use your head. We left Higgins with the *Chiron* on our six, right?"

"Yeah."

"And I've learned that the *Song* is supposed to rendezvous with us as soon as we stop. If the three of us are going to take on a Raider battle group, you can be damned sure that at least a couple of tin cans will be joining us. With the odds fifteen to one, that means we're facing seventy-five Raider warships. The Raiders must be figuring on retaking control in this deca-sector. We're all dead."

"There's no way they'd send just five ships to fight seventy-five," Flip said.

"Why not? We have the child XO on board after all. They probably figure she could take them on all by herself, in just a fighter."

"I told you not to call her that. Commander Carver deserves our respect for what she's done."

"Has it occurred to you that if anything happens to Gavin during the battle, she'll be in command? Captain Powers can't assign a new commanding officer over here while we're fighting." He moaned again and said, "We're all gonna die."

"I'm plenty glad she's on board *and* second in command if we're going into battle. I can tell you for a fact that the *old man* respects her."

"Whadda you mean?"

Looking towards one of the other chiefs, Flip said, "Tell him, Nera."

CPO Nera Caligara looked up from her cards. "Leave me outta this."

"Come on. Tell him what you told me."

Nera sighed. "Okay. I served as a bridge communications chief on the *Hermes* when Captain Gavin commanded her, so I guess I know him pretty well by now. The XO on the *Hermes* was an okay sort, but not exactly the brightest bulb in the executive officer lamp, if you know what I mean. I could tell Gavin liked him personally, but I could also tell he didn't value his judgment on really important matters. Since I've been aboard the *Prometheus*, I've overheard the Captain conferring with the XO a number of times on the bridge. She always defers to him, as First Officers are supposed to do with their Captain even when playing devil's advocate, but he always seeks out her honest opinion. And when *she* speaks, he listens. I mean he *really* listens. You can take that however you will, but me, I respect somebody who has the respect of somebody I respect. And I do respect the Captain. So I stand behind the XO all the way."

"Well, Eddie?" Flip asked.

"Well, what?"

Flip scowled at him. "Oh, never mind. What's your bid?"

*　*　*

The *Prometheus* and *Chiron* canceled their temporal envelopes as they reached the vicinity of the planet Vauzlee where they would wait for the distress call to come. An inhospitable ice planet on the outer edge of a small inhospitable solar system with a Type M3 MMK Class V red dwarf star, Vauzlee was uninhabited, as were the other two planets in the system, so there was virtually no likelihood of them being spotted. To further reduce the chances of alerting the Raiders to their presence, ships arriving at the RP would only communicate via directed, narrow-beam laser com signal.

It was now March 26th, 2268. Twenty-six days had passed since they had left Higgins Space Station and all was ready. Gunners and guidance specialists had been running fire control simulations almost without stop during the past two days and the crew was confident, although naturally nervous about the conflict ahead. Scuttlebutt presently had the enemy fleet at over a hundred fifty ships. Everyone now understood the reason for all the GQ drills and intensive weapons training, and their feelings toward their XO had changed considerably.

As Jenetta sat in the first officer's chair on the bridge during her watch, she thought about the imminent battle ahead and again wondered if they were doing the right thing by not alerting the convoy about the ambush so they could simply change course. But it wasn't her place to challenge either policy or strategy developed by Space Command Headquarters. They would just have to make sure the damage to the convoy was as light as possible. Unfortunately, the only way to do that was to engage the Raiders as quickly as possible and offer their hull as a substitute target.

The hours passed slowly as the entire ship waited for the distress call to come. The usual routine was forgotten and gun crews actually stayed close to the fire control centers, with just one member of each two-man crew going for coffee and sandwiches as first lunch and then dinner hours arrived and passed.

* * *

"Commander," the helmsman aboard the light-destroyer *Peabody Clarice* suddenly cried out, "The ACS has shut down our Light Drive. We've lost our envelope."

"What! Why?" Commander Kyle Schwann asked.

"There are hard contacts ahead," the lieutenant at the tactical station said. "I'm seeing hundreds spread across our bow."

"Hundreds? Out here? Impossible!"

"The DeTect system sees them clearly, sir."

"Helm, deactivate the collision avoidance control for these contacts and reengage the Light Drive."

"I've tried, sir. It won't reengage. The objects aren't stationary. In fact, they seem to be moving at random. With each vector change, the system immediately shuts down again."

"This might be a precursor to an attack, sir," the tactical officer offered.

"Sir," the com operator said, "the other ships are calling for instructions."

"Com, tell them I expect an attack to be imminent. All ships should initiate GQ and man their weapons. Then notify Commodore Blosset."

* * *

Commodore Andre Blosset was already out of bed and hunting for his slippers in response to the GQ alert when his bedside com sounded. He listened to the com operator and slammed the cover down without even responding. Less than thirty seconds later, he entered the bridge in his pajamas. He'd found his slippers but left his quarters without his robe.

"Talk to me, Kyle," Commodore Blosset said loudly.

"The ACS shut down our Light Drive. We can't reengage it."

"Sirs," the tactical officer said, "We have numerous warships taking up positions all around us."

"How many and where, dammit?" Commodore Blosset asked with annoyance. *The man should know better than to give just half the story.*

"There appears to be forty, no forty-one, warships. They're forming a circle around us about twenty-five thousand kilometers out."

"Commodore, I'm picking up a message," the com operator said. "They're demanding our immediate surrender."

"Who are *they*?"

"They didn't say, sir," the com operator replied.

"Well ask them, dammit."

"Sirs," the tactical officer said, "the computer identifies the warships as mostly destroyer-sized vessels, but some are large enough to be classified as frigates, cruisers, and even battleships."

"Battleships?"

"They have to be Raiders, sir," Commander Schwann said.

"The Raiders have battleships?"

"Nobody else would be demanding our surrender this close to the heart of Galactic Alliance space."

"Com," Commodore Blosset said, "notify all ships to move to their Protection-One positions immediately."

"Aye, Commodore."

"Kyle, what response should we give these pirates?"

"A full spread of torpedoes down their gullets, sir?"

"I agree, but let's coordinate our fire first. Com, it's— 2158. Alert all ships to fire a full spread of torpedoes at exactly 2200, then fire at will after that. As soon as they open up, send our programmed distress call. Tactical, as soon as we open fire, activate the AutoTect system. If there's any help nearby, I want them to be able to find us."

"Aye, Commodore," both men said.

"You're a real optimist, sir," Commander Schwann said. "There's not much chance of us finding help out here."

"Kyle, you're probably right," Commodore Blosset said as he climbed up into his bridge chair and fastened his seat belt, "but you just never know who's out there listening. It worked for the Nordakians last year. Their convoy hollered for help and that Space Command ensign came rushing to their rescue." The affable smile that usually covered the seventy-four-year-old's pudgy lower face was gone, replaced with a look of grim determination and purpose.

Commander Schwann looked at his commanding officer with skepticism. "We're twenty-four light years from Higgins, sir. Jenetta Carver isn't coming to *our* rescue."

"I know, but maybe we'll find our own Jenetta Carver."

"I hope *our* Jenetta Carver is coming in a GSC battleship instead of an old freighter."

* * *

It was exactly 2200:18 hours when the com station operator cupped his left ear to block any extraneous noise and sat up straighter in his chair. "Captain, distress call coming in from the Peabody convoy," he announced.

Almost immediately, Lieutenant Kerrey, manning the lead tactical station said, "The signal is coming from the expected area, Captain."

"This is it," Gavin said. "Sound GQ alert for ten seconds. Com, send the prepared message to all task force ships. Helm, take us there at Light-375, drop out of Light at one hundred thousand kilometers from the outer ring of ships and come to Sub-Light-10."

"Aye, Captain. Light-375 and then Sub-Light-10 at one hundred thousand km."

"Engage as soon as the envelope is formed," Gavin said as he pulled the seat belt around his waist and slid the end into the locking mechanism. There was naturally no sensation of movement while the ship was traveling faster than light, but when the envelope dissolved, the ship would accelerate in normal space. Although the gravitative inertial compensators would prevent most motion from being felt, there was usually a sudden lurch when the enormous engines were first engaged. And during battle the ship might be subjected to sudden violent movement when struck by torpedoes.

"Engaged, Captain."

"The *Chiron* and *Song* are building their envelopes, sir," the tactical officer said.

"Com, put me on ship-wide speakers."

"You're on ship-wide, Captain."

"Attention crew of the *Prometheus*. We've received a distress call from a convoy under attack by Raiders and we're proceeding there at top speed. ETA is eleven minutes. Clear for action."

The dozen fire control centers located along the center axis of the ship came alive as the specialists rushed in and manned their consoles. The placement of the console had nothing to do with the location of the weapon each laser array team would control. The weapons control computer would assign an array based on the simulation scores of each team once they had taken their places at a console and the computer had polled their IDs. The system would alternate a good team with one that wasn't quite as good, meaning that a poor team would have a much better team on either side. This overlap of the weapons fire meant that the chances of a torpedo getting through were therefore much less likely than if several teams with low sim scores happened to be located together.

Chapter Six
~ March 26th, 2268 ~

"The *Janice* just took a serious hit, Commodore," the com operator announced nervously. "It knocked out two of her larboard tubes. Twelve crewmen are missing— either vaporized or possibly sucked out the hole made by the torpedo."

"Damn," Commodore Blosset said. He had already lost mental count of the number of dead and wounded. The casualties were mounting too quickly. There were just too many damn Raider ships.

"Perhaps it's time to consider another option, Commodore," Commander Schwann said weakly from his chair next to the Commodore, "while our temporal field generator is still intact."

Commodore Blosset saw the desperation in his eyes, and heard the hint of fear in his voice. "You mean run away?"

"We're as good as dead if we remain here, sir. Either the Raiders will kill us or they'll enslave us, which means we might as well be dead. We still have a chance to get away if we go now. We have no chance of surviving if we remain here. They're killing us, bit by bit."

"We took an oath to protect our client's property, even if it means we have to die trying."

"We're supposed to die for a load of refuse that most people wouldn't hesitate to toss down the nearest waste disposal chute? I saw some of that stuff while it was being packed. It's old belt buckles, food containers, disposable baby diapers complete with fossilized fecal matter, glass and plastic beverage bottles, bits of plastic, and anything else that hasn't rotted or corroded completely away on Mawcett in twenty thousand years."

"It's not our job to put a value on it, Kyle."

"What if the freighter captain agrees to drop his cargo and make a run for it? Chances are the Raiders won't follow us. They just want the cargo."

"The freighter isn't a Peabody ship. If they want to drop their cargo and run, they can. We'll stay here and protect the cargo to the last Peabody ship. Now get a hold of yourself."

"Aye, sir," Commander Schwann said meekly as he slumped back into his chair. The gunners and guidance people at least had something to occupy their minds. All he could do was sit there, helpless, sweating, and wringing his hands while watching the systematic destruction, waiting for his end.

* * *

At Light-375, it took the *Prometheus* slightly less than eleven minutes to traverse the seventy-two billion kilometers to the ambush area once their DATFA envelope was formed. The small, thirty-eight-centimeter monitor screen mounted on the left arm of both the command chair and the first officer's chair displayed a battle site image assembled by the DeTect system. Clarity improved as the distance lessened and sampling increased.

A hundred thousand kilometers from the outer ring of Raider ships, the helmsman canceled the envelope and brought the six gargantuan, stern-mounted sub-light engines online. The battleship seemed to buck slightly and immediately began accelerating to Sub-Light-10 at a phenomenal rate. As they moved towards the battle action, Gavin sized up the situation and made his final attack decisions. The enemy ships were deployed just as Carver had predicted, in a huge circle roughly twenty to twenty-five thousand kilometers from the freighter. The sensors at the tactical station recorded forty-one Raider warships, mostly destroyer-sized craft, but there were a couple of frigates, half a dozen cruisers, and two older battleships. The enemy profile database identified one as being of Tsgardi design, while the other was believed to be an Uthlaro-built ship. The Peabody destroyers were using their ships to shield the freighter and firing their torpedoes as fast as their tubes could be loaded.

The Raider ships were likewise filling space between the combatants with a deadly arsenal. So far, each side was doing a pretty adequate job of knocking down the other's missiles, judging from the prodigious number of heat trails and limited number of observed impacts, but that was changing slightly as the fight progressed. Each successful blow reduced defensive energy weapons, destroyed torpedo tubes, or removed gunners from the equation.

Jenetta had to admire the loyalty and tenacity of the Peabody forces. Less dedicated captains might have decided to abandon an effort that appeared doomed to such obvious failure.

Gavin, still on ship-wide broadcast, said, "Helm, attack plan Carver-One. Tactical, concentrate on the battleships and cruisers first. Laser gunners, hold your fire until I give the word."

With the mention of her name, Jenetta sat up a little straighter. Gavin had obviously decided to use the strategy she had proposed. By prepending the battle plan with her name, he was giving her full credit for the tactic. On the down side, if it didn't work as planned, everyone would know who to blame.

At five thousand kilometers outside the ring of Raider ships, the helmsman reduced speed to Sub-Light-3 and took the ship on a counter-clockwise, mildly undulating course around the outside of the battle zone. The image on the huge viewscreen at the front of the bridge remained a wide-angle view of the battle from sensors on the larboard side of the ship, with the Peabody convoy in the dead center. Torpedo heat trails could be seen radiating away from the *Prometheus'* eight larboard tubes as the first spread of missiles left the ship.

Gavin had decided to use the deadliest of their available fusion warheads on the torpedoes for this engagement. High-explosive heads were only effective when the torpedo's hardened casing was able to penetrate the opposing ship's armor. Although the high velocity of Space Command's torpedoes usually enabled them to penetrate the enemy ship, and even travel as much as fifty meters into the ship before detonating, nuclear weapons didn't need to penetrate. They were designed to detonate just outside the enemy's hull, as close as practicable. All the weapon had to do was reach the ship being targeted. The fusion warheads were significantly more powerful than fission warheads, so any torpedoes that penetrated the geyser of defensive fire issuing from the targeted ship would accomplish their mission.

As Jenetta had speculated, the *Prometheus*, moving now at just three thousand kps, managed to knock out one of the Raider battleships before the Raiders even realized she was there.

Proximity triggers are intended to detonate the weapon immediately next to the target, but the first of the four torpedoes launched at the enemy battleship had a faulty trigger. The deadly missile actually penetrated the hull of the aging Uthlaro-built battleship before detonating. In the vacuum of space, there is no fire, flame, noise, or smoke from a nuclear detonation. One only sees an incredibly bright flash for a fraction of a second, as if someone flicked a powerful spotlight on and then immediately off. When the detonation properly occurs next to the hull, the skin of the ship begins to vaporize from the heat while impulsive shock-effect crushes anything along the leading edge of the blast. X-ray radiation then courses through any direct path no longer protected by shielding. If the enemy survives the heat, the crushing effect of the blast, and the loss of atmosphere, many will die or begin the slow, painful march towards death as their bodies are irradiated by lethal doses of unseen rays. War is indeed hell.

When the first torpedo unexpectedly entered the battleship, a number of accepted conventions could be immediately discounted. There was the brilliant flash, but there was also fire and flame, if just for an instant, as the atmosphere and materials inside the ship combusted. There was no need for the other three warheads, as everyone inside the battleship died almost immediately from the concussive force, but the other torpedoes did explode just outside where the hull of the battleship should have been.

With those first detonations, Gavin ordered all laser array gunners to fire at will. The fifth, sixth, seventh, and eighth torpedoes from the *Prometheus'* larboard tubes hadn't even reached their targets before the *Prometheus'* tactical officers launched a new salvo of death.

* * *

Sir, we're under attack!" the tactical officer aboard the second Raider battleship, *Rising Star*, screamed shrilly at his captain.

"Of course we're under attack, you fool," Captain Fulker responded. "This is a battle. Did you really expect them to simply surrender?"

"No, sir. But I meant we're under attack from someone outside our perimeter."

"What?" Captain Fulker shouted. "Where? Who?"

"It's big, sir, real big. It must be a battleship. It has to be Space Command."

"That's impossible. We'd have been notified if there were any patrols in this area."

"They just destroyed the *Soul Harvester* with four torpedoes. Command of the task force has passed to you, sir."

"The *Soul Harvester* is gone?"

"Yes, sir. Annihilated with nuclear torpedoes."

"Nuclear? Com, notify all ships that a Space Command battleship has just appeared outside our perimeter. Every resource not being directed at the convoy is to be directed at that ship."

"Yes, sir."

* * *

"Commodore," the tactical officer aboard the *Peabody Clarice* said, "another ship has just appeared outside the ring of circling ships. We're now facing forty-two Raider warships. And the new one is really huge. It must be another battleship."

This just keeps getting better and better, Blosset thought. *Maybe I* should *consider a tactical withdrawal of my remaining forces.*

"Commodore!" the tactical officer shouted, bringing Blosset up out of his reverie, "One of the Raider battleships just exploded."

"Who got him?" Blosset shouted. "When we get out of this, that gunner gets an extra month's pay."

"Wait a minute. Sir, are any of our torpedoes nuclear?"

"No, of course not. Only Space Command is permitted to possess nuclear warheads. We're restricted to high explosive warheads."

"The destroyed battleship was targeted with four nuclear torpedoes. There goes another one, no, two more. Two of the Raider cruisers were just killed by nuclear torpedoes."

"Who in the hell is firing nuclear torpedoes?" Blosset shouted. "And where did they get them?"

"The ship that just arrived is squawking her Ident, sir," the com operator said. "She's the GSC Battleship *Prometheus.* She must be the one that killed the three Raider ships."

"GSC? *Prometheus*? Kyle, isn't that the name of one of the stolen GSC ships Carver recovered from the Raiders when she destroyed their base?"

"Aye, sir!" Commander Schwann said excitedly. All trace of defeat had evaporated from his eyes, replaced by unbridled optimism. "You were right, sir. We do have our own Jenetta Carver— in the form of a battleship she recovered from the Raiders."

* * *

Once the ship's presence was known, the laser gunners aboard the *Prometheus* were free to pound the fleet of Raider ships with deadly fire from their massive hundred-gigawatt phased array lasers until the Raiders began to target them with torpedoes. And, for a few minutes, they rained an incredible amount of destructive energy down upon the pirate fleet. But the two Raider cruisers had barely joined their commanding battleship in ignoble death when a torrent of

- 85 -

torpedoes began streaming towards the *Prometheus*. The laser gunners immediately halted their efforts to punch holes in the Raider ships and began targeting the horde of incoming torpedoes. Jenetta was able to take some small comfort in the fact that every torpedo fired at the *Prometheus* was one fewer available for targeting the civilian convoy, but it was a small comfort.

From the moment the *Prometheus* left Vauzlee orbit, Jenetta's presence on the bridge was otiose. She had worked tirelessly to prepare the crew for battle but now was relegated to the position of observer while all around her the bridge crew stared intensely at their monitors, assiduously manipulated controls on their consoles, or called out information to the Captain. Everyone was so busy— so occupied— so totally immersed in their tasks— while all she could do was sit there and watch. As second in command, she was naturally prepared to take over if something happened to the Captain, but at this moment she felt about as useful as a shattered coffee mug.

Even the Captain, who was in command of the ship's actions, had a limited role once the attack plan had been decided upon and activated. He sat instantly ready to issue new orders if the situation changed, but otherwise he was mainly a spectator as the skill of his torpedo gunners, guidance specialists, and laser array gunners largely determined the outcome of this particular battle.

With everyone so preoccupied with their tasks, there seemed little chance that anyone would notice her comportment, but Jenetta nonetheless struggled to maintain a perfectly imperturbable appearance, giving the distinct impression there was no question in her mind that they would both be victorious and escape the carnage unscathed. She hoped no one noticed the way she was gripping the chair arms with her hands. With little else to do, she concentrated on relaxing her fingers, thus quashing even that vestige of anxiety as she watched the battle unfold.

Meanwhile, the Raider laser weapons facing away from the convoy and not otherwise occupied on defense began to spit their pulses of coherent light at the *Prometheus*. The great ship was pounded by myriad strikes.

As the *Prometheus* neared an apoapsis relative to its entry point around the circle of Raider ships, the *Chiron* arrived and began its attack run. The Raider ships, realizing they were sitting targets in a deadly crossfire between two great battleships, started to zigzag within the confines of their assigned circular track. The second Raider battleship, the *Rising Star*, joined her sister in death as she broke in half. Two of the flurry of torpedoes fired by the *Prometheus* had weathered the storm of laser pulses and found their target points against the hull of the poorly armored Tsgardi-built vessel.

*   *   *

"Our ships report that the number of incoming torpedoes has slowed considerably, sir," the com operator reported to the Commodore.

"Of course. The Raiders have a bigger threat to worry about than us. Tell them to keep targeting the Raiders as quickly as they can load their tubes."

"Sir," the tactical officer said as he stared intently at one of his screens, "another warship has just appeared outside the ring of Raider ships. It's following the same general route as the *Prometheus*. It's another battleship, sir, with the same configuration as the *Prometheus*. It's squawking its Ident now, sir. It's the GSC Battleship *Chiron*, the other battleship Jenetta Carver recovered from the Raiders. There goes the other Raider battleship, sir!"

Blosset allowed himself a small smile. "Well, Kyle, it looks like we might survive after all."

"I hope so sir, but we're still thirty-seven to fifteen."

"Yes, but those two GSC battleships are each worth any ten of the Raider ships, so I'm beginning to feel almost confident about our chances."

*   *   *

By the time the *Prometheus* completed a second revolution around the Raider group, the circle wasn't much of a circle anymore. The Raider ships, while returning fire with abandon, had forsaken their attempt to maintain a circling course and had begun maneuvering in every direction to avoid the deadly fire from the two GSC battleships that were decimating their numbers.

As the pirate forces ignored the convoy and consolidated their deadly fire on the circling *Prometheus* and *Chiron*, the first of the other GSC ships arrived and joined the fight. Already, the two Raider battleships, three of the six Raider cruisers, one of the Raider frigates, and six of the Raider destroyers were either destroyed or all but out of the fight, and many of the remaining twenty-nine Raider ships had taken deadly laser fire that had breached their hulls in numerous places, significantly reducing their fighting effectiveness.

* * *

"Helm," Captain Corriano of the *Song* said, as the Kamakura-class heavy cruiser arrived at the battle zone, "bring us into position behind the *Chiron*, equidistant between her and the *Prometheus*. Com, put me on ship-wide."

"You're on, Captain."

"All gunners, fire at will," Corriano said. "You know what to do, people. Make me proud."

Gavin had shared the full particulars of both battle plans with the other captains. Based on observations made as they arrived at the battle zone, they would immediately know which was being followed, but he had advised them that the attack plan would most likely be the one proposed by his first officer.

Commander Harant, the *Song's* XO, sat watching the action on the front viewscreen from his first officer's chair on the bridge. Like Jenetta, his role in the fight was over unless something happened to the Captain. All he could do was watch and possibly make a few suggestions. In response to a loud murmur of voices behind him, he turned to find the source. Half a dozen second watch officers were standing near the rear bulkhead. The first watch was composed of the most experienced officers aboard ship, so when GQ was sounded, they raced to the bridge and most relieved their less experienced counterparts. First and third watch tactical officers simply joined their fellows at the tactical station. The others should have headed to Auxiliary Command and Control. The group quieted as Harant turned around. He knew the regs specified they should be at their GQ posts, so they should be chased, but this was one of the most secure places on the ship and in AC&C they would only be observing anyway. He turned back around to watch the action unfold as laser fire from the Raiders began to pound the *Song*.

As the newly arrived GSC ship joined the circling attack, a full broadside of torpedoes spewed from its tubes and its phased array lasers unleashed torrents of coherent light pulses. In response, a number of the Raider gunners began to direct their fire away from the battleships and concentrate on the *Song*.

*　*　*

While the battle raged, Jenetta discretely called up the early reports of battle damage by touching screen contact points on the monitor attached to the left arm of her chair. She didn't want to appear overly concerned, but she knew the blizzard of laser pulses from the Raider ships had grown quite severe and she wanted to keep informed on the status of her ship. She'd felt at least one serious tremor, meaning that a torpedo had gotten through their laser protection umbrella.

The *Prometheus* was beginning its twelfth circle of the area, this time making a wider loop, when two more GSC ships, the destroyers *Caracas* and *Asuncion*, arrived. Discounting the Peabody ships, the odds were now just five to one as another five Raider ships had fallen forever silent. The area was becoming littered with the twisting and wrecked corpses of dead Raider ships.

*　*　*

By the time the last of the Raider cruisers had been destroyed, two more GSC destroyers, the *Lima* and the *Vancouver* had arrived, dropping the odds of Raider ships to Space Command vessels to just two to one. The Raiders, with only a third of their ships still able to move under their own power and dumbfounded by the arrival of more and more GSC ships, decided they'd had enough. With the destruction of the Raider battleships, cruisers, and frigates, the chain of command had completely disintegrated. Without orders, the captains began breaking off their engagements and maneuvering for open space so they could employ their Light Speed engines. One Raider destroyer began accelerating to maximum sub-light speed while building its Light Speed envelope just as a GSC light destroyer, the *Delhi*, arrived. The Raider vessel collided amidship starboard with the stationary *Delhi*, slicing it almost in half as the entire front half of the Raider ship crumbled into a compressed wad of twisted metal that fused the two ships together.

* * *

Captain Corriano was flung sideways by the impact. Fortunately he was buckled into his seat at the time, so his only injury was a bruised side and a fractured wrist from his hand striking the pivotal arm of the monitor screen mounted on the right arm of his chair.

"Tactical, what was that?" the Captain said to his lead tac officer, who was still pulling himself up to the console from the deck. He hadn't been wearing his seat belt.

"We took a hit to the larboard hull, sir," the tac officer said after checking his screens. "It was exactly opposite the bridge on this deck."

"How bad?"

"I don't know sir, but the sensors indicate we're open to space, so it must be serious."

"Commander, better clear the bridge of all non-essential personnel."

"Aye, Captain," Commander Harant said. He turned to the rear bulkhead where personnel were still climbing to their feet, but before he could give the order to vacate the deck a second torpedo struck the *Song*.

Chapter Seven
~ March 26th, 2268 ~

Two Raider destroyers, attempting to build their temporal envelope and escape following the destruction of the *Delhi*, were annihilated by the *Prometheus*. Three more were felled by torpedoes from other GSC warships. Only seven severely battered Raider ships of the original forty-one in the attack force managed to escape from what would later be described as a zone of death and destruction. In barely twenty-eight minutes of fighting, the Raiders had seen their assured victory turned into a crushing defeat. The last of the ten GSC ships tasked to the operation, the destroyers *Dublin* and *Calcutta*, arrived just as the fighting ended. They took off in pursuit of two escaping Raider ships, but once the Raiders achieved FTL Speed there was little that could be done with reasonable safety except follow for a time before returning to the battle site. The Raiders would never lead them to their base and no one wished to follow them for months only to have to turn around when the Raiders passed beyond the border of GA-regulated space.

"All stop," Gavin said to the helmsman as the *Prometheus* completed two revolutions around the battle site without drawing a single laser pulse or torpedo. Turning towards Jenetta who was calmly seated in the First Officer's chair to his left, he said, "My compliments, Commander. You really called that one. Not a fighter in sight. I think a few faces at the War College will be wearing a little egg when they view the logs from this fight. Your plan of battle was excellent, by the way."

Every ear on the bridge heard the words of praise, not that there had been much doubt as to who had formulated the attack plans that bore her name. Regulations required that a full and complete copy of all ship's logs from the period one half hour before an action to one half hour after must be submitted to Supreme Headquarters for evaluation. The Captain's praise would naturally be part of the bridge logs. Gavin knew before he uttered them that his comments would not be missed by the War College analysts preparing the post-engagement analysis reports. Saying what he did, where he said it, and when he said it, made his appreciation for Jenetta's remarkable battle prospicience and strategy an unalterable part of the conflict's record.

"Thank you, sir," Jenetta said sadly. There was no elation in her heart for having killed so many, even if they were Raiders. And while it would be awhile before casualty numbers were available, she was equally sure that Peabody and Space Command losses had been heavy.

"Com," Gavin said loudly as he climbed down from his chair, "notify all sections to submit their damage reports ASAP and notify Engineering that it's safe to send out crews and robots for emergency hull repair."

"Aye, sir. Damage reports are coming in now. I've sent them to your chair's holo-tube."

The Captain lifted the holo-tube lightly from its storage holster on the chair and activated it. With Jenetta standing next to him, he said aloud, "Damage to almost every deck, but hundreds of small hull breaches have sealed automatically and are holding atmosphere. We have major breaches on Decks Two, Seven, Ten, Eleven, Fifteen, Twenty-one, and Twenty-six. The worst breach is from a single torpedo hit that took out part of the hull on Decks Ten and Eleven near Frame Sections Seven and Eight. The damaged area encompasses a torpedo room. We lost tubes five and six, and suffered a total of seventeen casualties there, eleven dead and six injured. It appears we've sustained only superficial damage to our propulsion systems. Com, contact the other ships and find out if anyone other than the *Delhi* needs emergency assistance."

"Captain," Jenetta said, "if you don't need me here I'd like to be excused to oversee Damage Control Operations."

"Of course, Commander. You're excused."

Jenetta hurried to a lift in Corridor Three and descended to Deck Fourteen, grateful to finally have something to do as she waited impatiently for a transport car to arrive.

*　*　*

Chief Edward Lindsey leaned back into his chair in 11-280-0-C, also known as Fire Control Center Two-Eighty, and released a long relaxing sigh. "We're alive. I can't believe it. We're alive."

From the console next to him, Chief Flip Byrne said, "Thank you, Commander Carver."

"Will you knock it off!" Lindsey said angrily. "Carver had nothing to do with it. We're the ones firing the weapons. We're the ones who destroyed the Raider torpedoes and ships before they could destroy us, not Carver."

"You mean you didn't sense her behind you?"

"What? What are you talking about? Carver was never behind me. She's probably on the bridge."

"She was standing right behind you the entire time, Eddie."

"You're nuts. What's in that gum you're chewing?"

"Look at your console, Eddie."

Lindsey stared down at the laser weapon console in front of him. "Yeah, what about it?"

"Look at your effectiveness ranking."

"Holy S— eighty-three?"

"Did you ever score above sixty-five while we were on the *Thor*?"

"You know I didn't. I never could shoot as good as you. Uh— what's your ranking?"

"Ninety-one."

"There must be something wrong with these consoles."

"There's nothing wrong, Eddie. It's the XO. I could hear her behind me the whole time, calmly telling me to relax, breathe evenly, make sure of my target and lock, and gently squeeze the trigger instead of just pulling it, just like she did

- 93 -

every time she was down here during sim practice. You didn't feel her presence?"

"You're losing it, Flip."

Flip chuckled. "You've just scored higher than you ever have in your service career. Do you think you would have accomplished that if the XO hadn't been pushing us to spend more time training and to put greater effort into our training time? She may not have been physically behind us during the battle, but she was there in spirit. I definitely felt her standing at my shoulder."

*   *   *

After being whisked forward through the ship in a transport car to Frame Section Seven, Jenetta took a lift to Deck Eleven. She found people rushing around as she neared the damaged section. A Marine corpsman was tending to a seriously injured rating lying on the deck. The senior engineering officer, Lt. Commander Cameron, was barking orders via his CT as he observed the commencement of exterior repair operations on a portable monitor screen that had been rolled out flat against a bulkhead wall and temporarily fastened there. The thin, lightweight material provided a meter square 3-D image similar to that of a SimWindow. Resolution was far superior to a holo-magazine tube, but there needed to be a flat surface against which to affix it; otherwise, it would keep trying to roll itself back up for storage.

Lt. Commander William 'Wild Bill' Cameron was one of the best engineering people in the military, which is why he had been posted as the new senior engineering officer aboard the *Prometheus*. If he couldn't fix it, no one could. After graduation from the Academy, he had spent several years at such prestigious engineering schools as Cornell and MIT. Space Command had hoped to use him in design, but he reveled in getting his hands dirty and didn't feel comfortable sitting behind a desk all day. At forty-six, he was at the top of his game. Of medium height, with dark brown hair and brown, hound-dog eyes, he had rugged good looks and kept himself reasonably fit. Jenetta watched the image over his shoulder for a few minutes, waiting until his attention could be distracted.

"How bad is it, Bill?"

"Bad enough, Jen," he said, as he finally became aware of her presence and stepped slightly to the side so she'd have a better view, "but we'll get it patched. We were fortunate that only one live torpedo got through. The hull outside our torpedo rooms are heavily armored, but this one sailed right on through like it had an engraved invitation. Our people in there never had a chance. On Deck Twenty-Two a torpedo penetrated the hull, but a laser gunner had already destroyed the firing electronics. Even so, the torpedo casing held together and made it halfway through the hull. Several of my guys are up there trying to remove the high-explosive warhead, but it's pretty badly damaged. There's almost no chance it can explode, but I'll feel better when there's *no* chance."

"What are you estimating for repair time here?" she asked.

Pointing to the monitor, he said, "Right now my guys are cutting away the wreckage so we can begin rebuilding the cross-members necessary for attaching the plates. My chief assistant is supervising the preparation of the replacement plates down in engineering. Ships don't carry replacement torpedo tube hatches so we'll have to weld hull plating over the areas where tubes five and six are located. The tubes themselves are scrap so that'll do us until we can reach a repair yard. I estimate thirty hours to complete the work to a point where the sections on both decks can be re-pressurized. By then we'll have the middle titanium layer intact and we'll be ready to install a new outer membrane and finally the outer plates. At the same time, we can be replacing the inner membrane and the innermost titanium plates and radiation shielding. Then it's simply a matter of building up the layers of armor, but that'll wait until all our emergency repairs have been completed."

Jenetta nodded, her face reflecting intense concentration as the chief engineer talked. "What about the other hull breaches?" she asked when he had finished.

"At last count the bots have located about three hundred forty-three holes, and they're still finding them. Based on that, I estimate the count could go as high as six hundred. Most are tiny and self-sealed, so we never lost atmosphere in those sections, but they still have to be examined closely and patched. We have five major breaches where we lost atmosphere, but the structural integrity will be fully restored by replacing the plates. Those areas were fortunately empty during the battle and have been sealed off until repairs are completed."

"What's your best estimate of time for all emergency repairs?"

"Two days minimum and maybe as many as four. That's working around the clock just to get the torpedo damage patched and plug the major breaches where we're losing 'atmo.' I can't be any more precise than that at the moment, but we could continue the fight right now if need be. Our wounds are serious but certainly not disabling."

"Thank you, Bill. Carry on."

"Aye, ma'am."

While they were talking, the wounded man had been taken to sickbay, Jenetta's next destination.

Medical personnel engaged in triage activity were scurrying about when Jenetta entered the outer waiting area of the sickbay. The room was filled with moaning crewmen waiting for attention on temporary 'oh-gee' stretchers. Jenetta tried not to let the sadness she was feeling show on her face as she walked through the area and into the ward, but she was far from successful. She found Lt. Commander Hong, the ship's acting chief medical officer, putting a cast on a crewman's arm.

"Doctor, I was led to believe there were only a half dozen injuries?"

"There were only a half dozen *life-threatening* injuries, Commander. All have been attended to. Surgical nano-bots have been administered and the crewmen are expected to recover. Now my people are treating the broken bones, concussions, lacerations, and contusions. Most of the more serious injuries occurred in the torpedo rooms adjacent to the room that was destroyed. The shock from the explosion pitched everyone not belted down into whatever solid objects were nearby."

"Is there anything you need? Replacement supplies or anything?"

"No, we're fine here. The supply officer has already delivered the extra supplies we requested from our medical stores locker."

"Has the death toll changed?"

Lt. Commander Hong shook his head. "Just the eleven in the original count. Most were working in the torpedo room that took the hit. I understand they haven't yet recovered the bodies of two crewmen who were sucked out when the hull there was breached?"

"Yes. Thank you, Doctor."

"*Thank you*, Commander."

"For what, Doctor?"

"For caring enough about our crewmen to come here less than a half hour after the battle ended."

Jenetta looked sadly around again before saying, "It's little enough. It's been my great privilege to command these brave men and women. I know they're in excellent hands. Carry on, Doctor."

"Aye, Commander."

Returning to the bridge after visiting each of the locations requiring emergency response measures, Jenetta made her report. "Captain, repairs are underway and everything is under control. Commander Cameron estimates three or four days before emergency repairs are complete, but Frame Sections Seven and Eight might be re-pressurized in as little as thirty hours. The ship is not disabled and could continue fighting if necessary."

"Thank you, Commander. As senior officer at this engagement, I've assumed command of our forces. The *Chiron* fared about as well as we did, and damage is light on most of the ships that arrived later in the engagement, but we have one ship destroyed and three with crippling damage. In addition to numerous hull punctures, the hatch cover on the *Caracas'* temporal field generator repository was severely damaged and its generator can't be extended for examination. The *Asuncion* lost her starboard sub-light engine in addition to her numerous hull punctures. But the most seriously wounded of the three is the *Song*. It suffered a massive torpedo strike that killed all senior bridge officers. Things appear to be falling apart over there. They weren't even sure who the ranking officer is." Glancing down at the gold command pip on her collar, he said, "Commander, I'd like *you* to shuttle over and assume command. Assess the damage and determine if it can be repaired here or if the crew should be offloaded and the ship towed to a repair facility."

"Aye, sir, I'm on my way."

"It's just after 2400 hours. Call me with a status report by 1200 hours, Commander."

"Aye, sir."

Jenetta hurried out and down to Flight Operations Bay Six. Within fifteen minutes, she and a shuttle pilot were on their way to the *Song*. Pronounced 'sung,' the ship's name refers not to a melody but to the Imperial Chinese Dynasty that ruled from 960 to 1279, noted for its art, literature, and philosophy. At nine hundred eighty meters, the vessel was only half the length of the *Chiron* and *Prometheus*. And with just a two-hundred-thirty-six-meter beam, the hull encompassed only a third the interior space of the battleships, but was a formidable vessel in its own right. Since it carried significantly more than half the number of crewmen who would eventually be aboard either of the two great battleships, living quarters, flight decks, and available cargo space on its nineteen decks was considerably more limited.

*   *   *

"Captain," the com operator said to Gavin, "the senior officer of the Peabody Fleet would like to speak with you. He's identified himself as Commodore Andre Blosset."

"Put him on my CT, chief. And put his image on my right-hand viewscreen."

"Aye, Captain."

A second later, the image of a slightly heavyset man wearing the light blue uniform of Peabody Protection Services appeared on the small monitor attached to the command chair. He looked to be in his mid-seventies and his lower face was sheathed in an affable smile, but his eyes told a different story. They were filled with sadness, no doubt over having lost so many of his people. A single star on each shoulder denoted his rank. Sitting next to him was a much younger officer wearing rank insignia that indicated he was a commander; his face was anything but composed, and the strain and agonies of the past hour were etched in fine detail. In the background was the bridge aboard the destroyer *Peabody Clarice*.

"Commodore Blosset," Gavin said, "I'm Captain Gavin, commanding officer of the *Prometheus* and the senior officer of the GSC ships at this battle site."

"I've heard of you, Captain, although I don't believe we've ever met. We are deeply in your debt for your actions here today. On behalf of myself, my crews, Peabody Protection Services, and the Mawcett Archeological Expedition, I most sincerely thank you for saving our convoy from the Raiders."

"You're welcome, Commodore. I'm pleased we were able to arrive here before they managed to overcome your excellent resistance."

"It was close, sir. My list of casualties is extensive, and our ships have been heavily damaged. It might take weeks to make them ready to continue our voyage."

"That's true for us as well. It appears none of us will be going anywhere soon. If any of your people are injured beyond the capabilities of your medical people or resources in your medical facilities, we'll take them aboard one of our ships and do what we can."

"Thank you, Captain. I'll inform our doctors of your offer."

"Now, if there's nothing pressing, I have to see to our emergency repairs."

"Yes, of course. You know," the commodore said, smiling more widely, "your arrival was so fortuitous that I half expected to see Jenetta Carver on your bridge."

"Commander Carver was here until a few minutes ago. I've sent her over to take command of the *Song*. Its bridge crew was killed in the engagement."

"I grieve for your losses, sir, but I was referring to *Ensign* Jenetta Carver."

"Yes, I understood. Ensign Jenetta Carver is now Lt. Commander Jenetta Carver."

"Are you serious?" Commodore Blosset asked with obvious astonishment.

"Perfectly. Commander Carver is my second officer and has been acting as my XO in the absence of a first officer in this new command."

"Uh— I was just joking about her being on your bridge."

"I'm not, Commodore. Now, I really must go. We'll talk again when time isn't so critical."

As the connection ended, Commodore Blosset looked over at Commander Schwann, whose jaw was hanging open after hearing both sides of the conversation. "Imagine that," was all Commodore Blosset said as he leaned back in his chair and stared enigmatically up at the exterior image of the *Prometheus* that was currently being displayed on the large monitor at the front of the bridge.

* * *

As the *Prometheus* shuttle approached the *Song*, Jenetta ordered the pilot to make several slow passes around the ship. A steady tapping on thruster controls produced a helical orbit around the massive vessel. They were close enough to visually identify tiny maintenance bots crawling over the entire surface of the ship as they hunted for damage and punctures in a coordinated search procedure. Just forward of amidships, near A Deck, damage from the torpedo strike responsible for killing the bridge staff was gruesome. The gaping black hole in the ship's scarred armor looked almost as large as a flight bay doorway. Several other torpedo strikes had inflected serious wounds as well, but none so severe as the damage near the bridge.

Satisfied with her exterior inspection, she told the pilot to enter the open door at Flight Operations Bay One.

The pilot deftly maneuvered the shuttle into the bay and they felt the craft settle as gravity in the bay increased while the outer door closed. As soon as indicators showed outside air pressure and quality entering the green range, Jenetta opened the hatch on the shuttle, jumped down, and headed for the bay entrance. She was slowed temporarily as transparent walls that formed an airlock inside the hull door folded back up to the upper deck.

A young officer opening the bay entrance door just as she reached it recognized her instantly. Ensign Jassan Willis jumped back, startled, and braced to attention. He couldn't believe that just nine months after graduating from the Academy he was face to face with the most famous officer in all of Space Command. He stood at least five inches taller than Jenetta, but felt incredibly insignificant just then.

"Lt. Commander Carver requesting permission to come aboard," she said quietly as she saluted a young officer who seemed to be about the same age as her own appearance indicated.

"Uh, permission granted, ma'am," he said, his nervousness obvious in both voice and actions as he returned her salute.

"Who's in charge here, Ensign?"

"Um, I'm not sure, ma'am. As far as I know, the most senior officers left are the chief engineer, Lt. Commander Rodriguez, and the chief medical officer, Lt. Commander O'Neil. But since neither medical officers nor engineers are line officers and can't technically command a warship, I don't believe either has announced he's temporarily assuming command."

"And Lt. Commander Rodriguez is where, right now?"

"I just heard that he's up on A Deck examining the damage to the bridge. I can't be any more specific than that because the ship's internal sensor system suffered some damage and is still down. We can't presently track individuals using their CTs or IDs, but the com system is operational again. Should I call him?"

"No, just show me the way. I'm unfamiliar with the layout of this vessel class."

"Aye, Commander."

Willis escorted Jenetta to a lift that would take them up to Deck Five. They rode in silence, the ensign stealing furtive glances every so often as if he expected Jenetta to disappear if he looked away too long. On Deck Five, they took a transport car forward through the ship until they reached Section One-Forty-Eight. Another lift delivered them up to A Deck Corridor 0, where a Space Marine sergeant standing in front of an emergency bulkhead blocked their way. It had slid into position to seal off the corridor when pressure was lost on the bridge. The sergeant's eyes opened wide and his jaw dropped slightly as he recognized Jenetta. He closed his mouth and snapped to attention as she approached him.

Jenetta returned his salute and told him to stand easy.

"I'm sorry, Commander," the sergeant said as he relaxed slightly, "it's not safe to proceed beyond this point. Commander Rodriguez has ordered me to stop anyone not suited up in EVA gear from trying to venture further, for their own safety."

"Where is Commander Rodriguez, Sergeant?"

"He's on the bridge, ma'am, assessing the damage so repairs can commence."

"I was told the bridge was destroyed."

"No ma'am, not destroyed. I understand the hull was breached and most of the bulkheads between open space and the bridge were destroyed or seriously damaged. Everyone on the bridge died when the atmosphere was evacuated, but the bridge itself is mostly intact. Commander Rodriguez is suited up, trying to assess the situation so repairs can commence."

"What about the rest of the ship?"

"I only know we have serious hull breaches on at least four decks and lesser hull damage in some hundred-seventy or hundred-eighty other places. We lost eighteen of our people when the bridge was breached and at least thirty more in breaches from other torpedo strikes."

"At least?"

"That was the last figure I heard, ma'am. Lieutenant Ashraf, the ship's second watch helmsman, is collecting casualty and damage information. I'm sure she has more up-to-date information than I'm able to provide."

"Is Lieutenant Ashraf currently the senior line officer?"

"I expect so, ma'am."

"Where do you think she'd be right now?"

"You should be able to find her down in Auxiliary Control & Communications, ma'am."

"Carry on, Sergeant. Ensign, show me the way to the AC&C."

Following the ensign down two decks, then five sections towards the stern, Jenetta was escorted to a room that resembled a slightly more compact version of the ship's bridge. The AC&C could handle most bridge functions in the event of an emergency such as this one. Placed almost in the dead center of the ship, the AC&C was heavily shielded and protected from most damage by outside hostile forces. For that matter, the bridge itself was extremely well protected by having eight deck levels above it and ten below. Several compartments, all with reinforced tritanium bulkhead walls and radiation shielding, were situated between the bridge and the outer hull on A Deck. It was only called A Deck because it contained the ship's bridge, not because of its relative position within the ship. Only an extremely destructive torpedo strike could have penetrated far enough into the ship to breach the bridge's extremely protective shell.

Lieutenant Ashraf, sitting in the command chair with her back to the door, was talking to Commander Rodriguez on the com as Jenetta and Willis entered the AC&C center. A head-and-shoulders image of Rodriguez filled the monitor at the front of the room. Image resolution was low and the picture shaky, meaning it was most likely coming from a helmet cam. Rodriguez, presently speaking, probably wasn't receiving a reciprocal image.

"...It's a real mess up here, Lori. There are bodies everywhere. The first torpedo penetrated the hull and blasted away a large section of hull armor and a couple of interior bulkheads. The hole opened the first corridor on the larboard side of A Deck to space, but emergency bulkheads closed to preserve the 'atmo' in the rest of the ship. The damage was severe but not life-threatening at that point. But then a second torpedo must have come straight into the new opening and wiped out everything that remained between the hull and the bridge. The bridge's reinforced tritanium walls were breached behind the control panels near the tactical station. The hole is large enough to have evacuated the air supply within seconds. It appears that everyone managed to reach an emergency air mask, but they didn't have EVA suits, so the sub-zero temperature of space got them before they could override emergency controls and force open the bridge doors.

"It looks like a two-hour job to seal this breach once we have the new plates prepared. Most of the bridge equipment is intact but we'll have to wait and see how the decompression and sudden drop in temperature affected the electronics."

"Okay, Paul, thanks. The *Prometheus* has notified us that they're sending over their hot-shot XO to take command, so I'm just trying to hold things together until he gets here."

"Roger, Lori. Rodriguez out."

The link went blank for a second and then the viewscreen changed to show the ship's logo. Ashraf immediately turned her attention to a growing holo-tube list of battle damages.

Willis had been shifting his weight nervously from leg to leg, trying to figure out how to alert his fellow officer to the Commander's presence without interrupting the communication while Jenetta had been content just to listen to the conversation. When Ashraf made the comment about a hotshot XO coming over, the ensign closed his eyes and wished he were somewhere else. He finally coughed when she turned to the holo-tube, then said, "Excuse me, Lieutenant. Commander Carver has arrived."

Without turning away from the holo-tube she was concentrating on, Lieutenant Ashraf said, "Have him brought up here, Ensign Willis."

"Um— *she's* up already, ma'am."

Ashraf turned around in her chair with a shocked expression on her face.

Jenetta said somberly, "The hot-shot is aboard."

Ashraf shot up out of the chair as if the seat had suddenly become electrified and came to rigid attention less than a meter from Jenetta. The olive-skinned officer with almond-shaped eyes and collar-length raven-colored hair was taller, so she didn't see Jenetta's face as she stared straight ahead. "Commander, I'm terribly sorry for that remark," she said. "It was rude and almost borders on insubordination. I apologize."

"Relax, Lieutenant," Jenetta said calmly as she suppressed a smile. "Let's just put it down as the result of battle stress and forget about it."

"Yes ma'am, thank you, ma'am," Ashraf said as she relaxed her stance slightly and let her gaze fall to Jenetta's face. The relief reflected in her face lasted just two seconds before her expression suddenly turned to one of surprise. Her chestnut eyes narrowed slightly as they took in Jenetta's rank insignia on her shoulders and then the gold pip on her collar. There couldn't be more than one line officer below the rank of captain in all of Space Command who was permitted to wear a collar pip. "Excuse me, ma'am, but are you *Jenetta* Carver?" she asked.

"Yes, I am."

For Lori Ashraf, it was the first bright spot in an otherwise horrible day. Her eyes widened and she stood a little straighter again as she said, "It's a real honor to meet you, ma'am. I'm one of your biggest fans."

"Nice recovery effort, Lieutenant," Jenetta said. This time she couldn't suppress the amused grin.

"No, I mean it, ma'am. I didn't know you were the one being sent over. I didn't even know you were a lieutenant commander. You were just an ensign during the court-martial. I watched every minute of the trial and we all cheered like crazy when you were acquitted."

"I was passed over by the promotions board for eleven years because they believed I was dead. Space Command and the Galactic Alliance Council decided to make up for those lost years."

"I'm happy to see Space Command has rewarded your incredible accomplishments after putting you through that god-awful court-martial. What are your orders, Captain?"

Jenetta was momentarily taken aback by Ashraf's use of the title, although she didn't let her surprise show on her face. She knew she was there to reestablish the command structure and turn chaos and confusion into order and control, but she hadn't really thought of herself as the captain of the ship. That's exactly what she was though, albeit a temporary position. The lives of every one of the two thousand, two hundred crewmembers aboard the heavy cruiser were now her personal responsibility, and until relieved, she was the highest authority aboard ship. She inhaled deeply and expelled it. "Let me see a list of our damages," she said.

"Here you are, ma'am," Ashraf said as she handed Jenetta the holo-tube she had been studying.

As Jenetta scrolled through the reports, she asked, "How complete is this list?"

"I believe it to be about ninety percent complete, although it covers one hundred percent of the *major* damage. Engineering bots are crawling over every square centimeter of the exterior and interior hulls trying to identify damage points, however minor, and Commander Rodriguez has a dozen men suited up and performing more detailed assessments of the serious hull breaches where we took torpedo hits."

"So, according to this the sub-light engines and temporal field generator are fully operational."

"That's correct. The temporal field generator repository suffered no damage at all and the sub-light engines have been certified fully operational by our engineering department despite a few energy weapon punctures of the larboard engine nacelle housing. We terminated our attack only because the main bridge was severely damaged and all senior command officers were lost. Nearly all of the enemy ships had stopped firing by then. I was down here with most of the command personnel who weren't on duty when the GQ alarm was sounded. Until the bridge was lost, we were functioning as Damage Control Central. We lost the com system at the same time we lost the bridge, so I sent a messenger to the Maintenance Operations Center in the stern instructing them to assume our DCC duties. At that point we focused on command and control of the ship."

"And who assumed command at that time?"

"Neither Commander Watabi nor Lieutenant Commander Brunesky had reported in following the sounding of GQ, so, as the most senior officer in AC&C, I took responsibility, ma'am."

"I see. Well, first things first. Our injured personnel are our top priority. They must be taken to sickbay to receive treatment."

"Done or being done as we speak."

"Good. Next, let's designate an area to serve as a temporary morgue. Where would you suggest?"

"Um, we have an empty cargo hold."

"That'll do. Have all bodies brought there. Is the Engineering section manufacturing new plates for the hull?"

"I— guess they will as soon as Commander Rodriguez finishes his inspection."

"Get me Commander Rodriguez on the com."

Ashraf walked to the communications console and pressed several contact points. When an image of Rodriguez appeared on the com screen, she said, "Commander Rodriguez? Stand by for Commander Carver. Here he is, ma'am."

Jenetta suspected Rodriguez wouldn't be able to see her, so she didn't bother to look into the lens on the com unit. "Commander Rodriguez, this is Lt. Commander Jenetta Carver. I've been placed in temporary command of the *Song* by Captain Lawrence Gavin, commander of this task force. Are new bulkhead plates being manufactured to repair the breach on the bridge deck?"

"Not yet, Commander. I'm still on A Deck, forward of the bridge."

"Was your chief assistant killed or injured in the battle?"

"No, ma'am"

"Isn't he able to operate without your direct supervision?"

"Normally, yes, but this isn't normal. He's not experienced in titanium bulkhead plate manufacturing."

"Then I strongly suggest you get your donkey off A Deck and down to engineering if they need *you* to commence the most critical repairs on this ship. And in the future make sure your assistants get the training they need to ensure this ship isn't lost if you're injured or killed."

"Aye, Commander."

"This is a war zone. I expect the bulkhead walls on the bridge compartment to be completely repaired and the bridge re-pressurized and ready for use within six hours."

"Yes ma'am."

"Carver out. Lieutenant, see to setting up that temporary morgue. And tell the mess halls to get lots of coffee and sandwiches ready. It's going to be a very long night. The ensign here is going to take me on a tour of the damaged areas."

"Aye, Captain."

Checking the portable holo-tube again, Jenetta said, "Ensign Willis, escort me to Deck Three, Frame Section Two-Fourteen."

"Yes ma'am."

As the com link went dead, Commander Rodriquez turned to the EVA-suited lieutenant next to him. "It sounded like she said her name was *Jenetta* Carver. You don't suppose she could be…"

*　*　*

Jenetta had barely arrived aboard the damaged warship before scuttlebutt about her appointment began to ripple through the crew. In spite of their preoccupation with matters related to rescuing crewmembers trapped in airtight compartments, the recovery of bodies, and the sealing and re-pressurizing of the ship, the news seemed to spread with the speed of a DeTect beam.

On Deck Four, Petty Officer 1st/c Serge Kaliskov dropped to the deck next to Petty Officer 2nd/c Patrick O'Malley for a moment of rest after searching a damaged section for survivors or bodies. There were quite a few crewmembers still unaccounted for. Battle damage to the ship's sensor systems had kept them from locating the missing crewmen by triangulating on signals sent to their CTs or ID chips.

"She's really here," Serge said. "I just heard it from a buddy who heard it directly from Sergeant Korby, the Marine detailed to stop anyone from trying to enter Corridor 0 up on A Deck."

"What are you talking about? Who's here?"

"Who? Haven't you heard? The *Prometheus* sent over their XO to replace the Captain."

"Oh. Yeah, I knew someone was coming. So?"

"Well, it's not just someone; it's her, Jenetta Carver. *The* Jenetta Carver. The Ice Queen herself."

"It can't be. Carver's just an ensign. Perhaps the most beautiful and deadly ensign in the service, but still just an ensign."

"She *was* just an ensign, but not anymore. She's a Lieutenant Commander now, and the XO on the *Prometheus*. Or at least she was. Now she's our new Captain."

"I'll believe that when I see it with my own baby blues and not before. Space Command doesn't just promote ensigns directly to lieutenant commander and then make them the XO on one of the most powerful warships ever built."

"But most ensigns haven't fought the Raiders on three separate occasions and kicked their asses up between their shoulder blades every time. Most ensigns haven't taken on a destroyer and a medium cruiser while commanding an old bucket of a freighter and left the Raider ships in pieces, if they were lucky. Most ensigns haven't single-handedly destroyed a Raider base, killing tens of thousands of the enemy and destroying dozens of Raider warships in the bargain. And most ensigns haven't captained one of the most powerful warships ever built. Carver has."

"Yeah, I saw the court-martial too. Um, you're sure it's her? It's really *Jenetta* Carver?"

"I heard Sergeant Korby is as sure of that as he is that he can't just duck outside the ship for a quick smoke wherever he feels the urge."

Chapter Eight
~ March 27th, 2268 ~

With Ensign Willis leading the way through the unfamiliar ship, Jenetta visited each of the areas where the hull had been seriously breached. They used the ship's transit tubes to traverse the length of the ship, and the lifts and local corridors to reach the specific locations. In each damaged area, they passed groups pushing 'oh-gee' stretchers with body bags. Along the way they passed crewmen posted to keep people from entering non-pressurized areas. Portable monitor screens were rolled out on bulkheads near each breach location so she was able to see the damage and observe initial repair efforts.

Although the act of saluting aboard ship was only required when entering or leaving the vessel, on occasions when flag officers were aboard, or when being called before the captain and leaving his or her presence on that same occasion, every rating and non-com Jenetta encountered stepped back out of her way, came briskly to attention, and held their salute until acknowledged. She returned the salute casually but definitively, and mumbled, "As you were," as she passed each. Only about half the officers actually saluted but all stepped back out of her way and braced to attention until she had passed.

"Is this level of formality usual aboard this ship, Ensign?" Jenetta asked Ensign Willis. "Did Captain Corriano require such behavior?"

"No, ma'am, not at all. The Captain actually preferred a pretty relaxed environment most of the time."

"I see," Jenetta said before relapsing into silence. Although the crew of the *Prometheus* had become used to seeing her on a daily basis, she had to remember that she was still probably a bit of a celebrity here. She knew they'd get over it soon.

After visiting each damage site and receiving a personal assessment of damage to the hull and repair progress by the engineering officer or NCO in charge of overseeing the repair effort there, Jenetta had Willis show her the way to the sickbay. It was like the sickbay on the *Prometheus*, but much busier. The waiting area was filled with crewmen with minor injuries who were sitting, standing, or lying, depending upon the extent of their injury, while the more seriously injured were receiving care in the treatment rooms. Lastly, they visited the temporary morgue. Bodies in black cadaver bags were already laid out in two long rows, and those from the bridge hadn't even been recovered yet.

In the next cargo bay, hull plates were being manufactured. A machine cut out the proper shape from huge, flat plates of Tritanium according to specifications already in the computer, then heated it until it glowed white hot. After being sculpted in an enormous press, it was cooled in the new shape. Jenetta didn't understand why Lt. Cmdr Rodriguez' assistant couldn't handle the process since it appeared to be done completely by machine once the exact location of the correct plate had been determined, but this wasn't the time to raise such an issue.

Within four hours, new tritanium bulkhead plates had been welded into place around the bridge and the radiation shielding replaced. Once the bridge was pressurized, the bodies of Captain Corriano, Commander Harant, Commander Watabi, Lt. Cmdr. Brunesky and fourteen other officers and NCOs could finally be recovered and taken to the temporary morgue. Then it was just a matter of cleaning up.

Jenetta had shaken her head sadly as the bodies were carried past her vantage point near the bridge entrance because someone had really dropped the ball. There had been far too many senior officers on the bridge when the incident occurred. Jenetta could think of no valid reason why they all should have been congregated there. At the very least, Watabi and Brunesky should have been at their GQ posts in AC&C. It would have been more cramped down there and the room didn't have the larger monitors the bridge had, but when the bridge perimeter was breached, a proper command structure would have remained in place and the ship wouldn't have had to quit the battle in confusion.

Once the bodies were removed and the bridge cleaned, the electronic technicians moved in and started performing diagnostic checks on every system. Within two hours they certified the bridge to be fully operational with the exception of the control panel where the wall had been breached. For that, they removed all the damaged electronics and began replacing them. By 0800 hours, the replacement panel was ready for use, completing the bridge repairs. It was impossible to tell there had ever been a problem on the bridge. The ship's hull beyond the bridge was still open to space, but the bridge was fully functional.

As Jenetta approached the captain's briefing room, a smaller, more austere version of the one aboard the *Prometheus*, the doors opened automatically. Someone, most likely Lieutenant Ashraf, had apprised the computer system of Jenetta's appointment as captain of the ship and it recognized her as such now.

Captain Corriano's personal effects in the briefing room had already been itemized by the ship's stores officer, boxed up, and moved to storage. The stores officer had the unenviable job of doing that for every officer, NCO, and crewmember killed in the battle. He and two crewmen had been at it for hours, and many more hours of such work faced them.

From the com station on her desk, Jenetta summoned the ship's personnel officer to the briefing room. The assistance of Lieutenant Sammarco proved invaluable. Jenetta was able to quickly appoint three temporary bridge crews. The Lieutenant would contact each of the individuals and have them report to the bridge.

Ashraf was the first to arrive. The briefing room's computer interface softly announced, "Lieutenant Ashraf is at the door, Captain," when the lieutenant moved into sensor range outside the room.

"You wanted to see me, Captain?" Ashraf said a little hesitantly as she approached the desk, sure she was about to be severely reprimanded for her earlier remark now that they had some privacy.

"Yes, Lieutenant. I've put together the temporary bridge crews and I've designated you as Acting First Officer."

Ashraf stiffened in surprise. All she could say was, "Me, ma'am?"

"I don't know how long the duty will last. Captain Gavin may have other ideas about assignments once things are sorted out and may transfer other officers to the *Song* to fill the senior positions, but for today, you're it."

"Yes, ma'am. Thank you, ma'am."

"The rest of the bridge crew for this watch will be reporting to you as soon as Lieutenant Sammarco contacts them. Here's the list," Jenetta said as she held out a portable viewpad. "Your first priority is to ensure that every crewman on each watch is familiar with his or her duties and responsibilities."

"Aye, Captain."

"Questions?"

"Will you be remaining aboard as Captain until we reach port?"

"I expect to be returning to my duties as XO aboard the *Prometheus* within twenty-four hours. By then Captain Gavin will probably have found a qualified replacement with the rank of full commander, or at least someone with more time in grade than myself. But I fully intend to have the command structure aboard this ship back in good order and the repairs proceeding efficiently when I turn over command."

"Yes ma'am."

"If there's nothing else, you're dismissed."

"Aye, Captain."

As soon as Ashraf had gone, Jenetta called up the damage reports on the desk console. She observed that the work appeared to be progressing well. Lt. Commander Rodriguez might be a micro-manager, but he was an efficient one. Two of the larger hull breaches were already repaired, at least to the extent that a first layer of new exterior plating allowed the areas to be pressurized. Installation of the self-sealing membrane and interior plating was just beginning. Applying the additional outer layers of plating that formed the ship's armor in those areas would wait until all emergency repairs were complete and the engineers had an opportunity to reforge the damaged plates by melting tritanium scrap to fill holes and then shape the reconstructed plate. All other damaged tritanium plates would be reforged, reshaped as flat sheets, and then stored until needed after some future engagement.

As much as she would have preferred to be doing something physical, there was 'electronic' paperwork and a growing queue of messages to attend to, so she dove into it. Her first order of business was to prepare a complete report on the state of the ship based on her earliest observations. She listed what she had found when she arrived and the actions she had taken to restore a command structure, along with an estimate of the time required before the ship would be able to function normally. She knew the report would most likely make it to the highest levels in Supreme Headquarters, so she took great pains to craft a document that was accurate, organized, and complete. She signed the finished document as 'Lt. Commander Jenetta A. Carver, Captain, GSC Heavy Cruiser *Song* GSC-CH502'. She'd debated with herself whether to include 'Acting' before the title of Captain, then decided against it. It was normally used where a senior officer was absent from duty for any of a variety of reasons, including death or injury, and a subordinate temporarily takes over in their stead. While her appointment by Gavin was a temporary one and would never be confirmed as a permanent appointment by Supreme Headquarters, a battlefield appointment by the senior officer at the engagement was nevertheless an official appointment.

She appended a copy of the ship's imaging logs from one half hour before the battle to one half after and marked them for immediate transmission. Gavin would file a report from the *Prometheus* that covered his ship's performance, as well as a full report of the action in his role as task force commander, but the captain of every ship involved in an 'incident' was required to make their own full report directly to Supreme Headquarters within twenty-four hours. Since Captain Corriano was deceased, the duty requirement fell to Jenetta. The ban on outgoing communications was still in effect, but that didn't extend to reports to SHQ and other such official communications.

The requests from her officers took the most time to handle. Each one had to be read and responded to individually. Most were requests for temporary personnel reassignments to handle specific problems not normally handled by a particular crewman's class or grade, or requisitions for supplies and equipment from emergency stores. They were the sort of requests ordinarily handled by the XO, but there hadn't been an executive officer when the messages were queued, so they were routed to her. She would have passed them on to Lieutenant Ashraf, but the acting XO would have her hands full for quite a while just getting the new command staff organized and the requests couldn't wait.

At noon, Jenetta called the *Prometheus* from her briefing room. "Commander Carver here. Put me through to the Captain."

A few seconds later, Gavin's image filled the screen. "How are you making out, Carver. Need help?"

"Negative, sir. We have eighty-nine dead, fourteen critically injured, and three still 'missing and presumed lost,' but we're coping. The bridge is fully operational again and I've appointed temporary bridge crews to replace those killed in action. All major hull breaches, with the exception of the acute torpedo damage on A Deck, should be sealed within twenty-four hours. Due to the extensive hull damage on A Deck, we'll require as long as fourteen days of intensive repair effort to seal that part of the ship. We also have over two hundred minor hull punctures. The repair crews will begin to tackle them after they get some needed rest. The good news is that the *Song* will be able to continue on to Earth under its own power and with its current crew. As temporary captain of the ship, I've forwarded the logs from the time of the battle and my initial assessment of the ship's condition to SHQ."

"That's excellent, Commander. You've really pulled things together over there."

"If you've selected someone to replace me as captain, I can turn over command of the ship and return to the *Prometheus* at any time, sir."

"I haven't given it much thought yet. I've been too busy with the cleanup efforts. We're using our tugs and tugs from the freighter to pull all the Raider ships together. The Marines and engineers from the *Dublin* and *Calcutta* are busy rescuing survivors from airtight compartments in the *Delhi*. When that's complete, we'll have to do the same in each of the thirty-four Raider ships. Naturally, that's our top priority now and will probably take several days. Stay where you are until all repairs have been completed. I expect we'll all be here for at least two weeks, and likely a bit longer."

"Aye, Captain. I'll need some clothes if I'm going to remain here for a while."

"I'll have someone pack a bag for you and bring it over next time a shuttle goes out."

"Thank you, sir."

"*Prometheus* out."

"*Song* out."

Jenetta leaned tiredly against the back of the comfortable 'oh-gee' chair. She was anxious to get back to the *Prometheus* and oversee the repairs to *her* ship, but she would have to remain here to oversee the effort until Gavin recalled her. It was probably just as well. She would have felt guilty about relinquishing command of the *Song* to someone else while things here were still in such a state of confusion. She shook off her disappointment and returned to her paperwork.

Rising from the chair behind her desk two hours later, Jenetta went to the beverage synthesizer where she ordered a sixteen ounce mug of Colombian coffee with two sugars. It tasted slightly different from the synthesized blend she was used to on the *Prometheus*—not bad, just a little different. It still had the wonderful taste of recently roasted and freshly ground Colombian coffee beans. Taking the coffee over to the couch against the sidewall, she laid down. It had been more than thirty strenuous hours since she'd slept and she needed some rest.

*   *   *

Jenetta awoke to the sound of the computer announcing Lieutenant Ashraf's presence outside the door. "Come," she said.

Ashraf entered, and not seeing Jenetta behind the desk, scanned the room. When she realized Jenetta was lying on the couch, she said, "Sorry to disturb you, Captain. I didn't know you were resting."

Jenetta sat up and put her feet on the floor. "That's okay, Lieutenant. What do you need?"

"I wanted to inform you that all major breaches of the hull, except for the damage on A Deck, have been sealed and are holding pressure. I've told the hull repair crews to get eight hours rest before they commence work on the A Deck hull, complete the self-sealing membrane and inner plate work in the other damaged areas, and begin work on the smaller punctures. I have cleanup crews working a rotating schedule to get the ship back into shape. Uh, the *Prometheus* sent over a spacechest and several other cases for you."

"Yes, Captain Gavin has ordered me to remain in command here until the task force completes its repairs."

"Wonderful, Captain! I had your things brought to the Captain's quarters in case that might be the situation. House-keeping bots changed the bed linens and cleaned the suite after Captain Corriano's personal effects were removed. You should get some rest, ma'am."

Jenetta glanced at the wall chronometer. It was 1608 hours GST. "Yes, I could use a couple more hours if there's nothing pressing. You look exhausted. You'd better get some sleep also."

"I'm leaving now, ma'am. I was just relieved by Lt. Elizi, who's come back on duty after having six hours off."

"Okay, Lieutenant, thank you. I'll see you on the next watch."

"Aye, Captain."

Jenetta stood up and stretched after Ashraf left. The four hours she had slept only left her wanting more. She rubbed her eyes, straightened her tunic, and walked out of the briefing room. A crew of semi-familiar faces she'd only seen as she prepared the bridge crew list from the computer files was manning their stations on the bridge. The twenty-nine-year-old lieutenant with short black hair and dark-chocolate brown eyes who had just taken the command watch, Lieutenant Elizi, smiled benignly in greeting from the command chair as Jenetta walked towards the door leading to the corridor. As she returned the smile, Jenetta speculated that the woman must, like Lt. Ashraf, be of Eastern Mediterranean lineage.

The informal designation for the captain's quarters on all GSC ships was A-1, although officially the quarters on this ship was designated as A-112-01-L. Since the quarters were located in the corridor just outside the bridge, Jenetta located her new housing easily. The computer opened the door for her as she approached. She was surprised that no Marine guard was posted either outside the captain's quarters or at the entrance of the corridor that led to the bridge. She made a mental note to discuss it with the Marine in charge of security when she had a chance.

Standing just inside the entrance, she glanced around the enormous sitting room as the lighting came on in response to her instruction. Although slightly smaller than the captain's sitting room on the *Prometheus*, it was still impressive. Two sofas and half a dozen chairs were available for visitors since the captain was expected to entertain staff and visiting dignitaries on occasion. An open door on the rear wall revealed a half-bath, provided so visitors wouldn't have to use the private bath in the captain's bedroom. The door on the wall to Jenetta's left was open and offered a view of the captain's office. It contained a large desk with an abutted conference table capable of seating eleven. Of the two other doors in the room, she imagined the closed door on the rear wall would lead to her bedroom, so she moved to the closed door on her left.

As she neared it, the door opened. She stopped instantly and then took a quick step backward, assuming a defensive stance as a looming figure appeared in the darkened room in front of her.

"Good afternoon, Captain," the figure said softly as it moved forward far enough to be illuminated by the sitting room lighting. "Would you like something to eat or drink?"

"Uh, good afternoon. What are doing in here, Chief?"

"I'm the captain's steward, ma'am, your steward now. I'm Chief Steward Casell. I'm sorry if I startled you."

Jenetta relaxed and lowered her arms. She had forgotten that the captains of all frigates and larger ships have a full-time steward. It was a luxury and a status symbol that the captains of lesser ships aspired to attain for themselves. Although they didn't have private galleys attached to their quarters and weren't officially assigned a fulltime steward, destroyer captains usually designated one mess steward to see to the preparation of all their meals and deliver them either to their quarters or their briefing room at meal time. Captain Gavin's steward would be joining the *Prometheus* when it reached Earth. For now his meals were brought to him from the officers' mess.

Chief Casell had a kindly face and an unremarkable body. His hair was sort of an auburn color and as full as it had ever been. He appeared to be about forty years of age, so Jenetta assumed the NCO might have been acting as Captain's Corriano's steward for some time. It wasn't uncommon for a captain to bring his steward from a previous command as he moved to a new ship if he was satisfied with the steward's service and food preparation.

"Not a problem, Chief. I was just exploring. Why are you standing in the dark?"

"I'd just stepped into this room from the galley, ma'am, when I heard the door annunciator. I'm so familiar with the captain's suite that I don't always put the lights on when I'm passing through a room." Stepping back out of the way, Chief Casell said, "Lights on," then, "This is your dining room, Captain. The door on your immediate right leads to the galley and the door on the far right leads to my quarters. Uh, ma'am, Captain Corriano always addressed me by my given name of Woodrow."

Jenetta smiled. That was something else she had forgotten. The life of a chief steward revolves around his or her captain, 24/7, and they had minimal contact with the rest of the crew. Through long Space Command tradition, their captain usually addressed them by their given names rather than their rank. Jenetta supposed it was some sort of status symbol to be addressed in that personal way by the ship's commander, or perhaps it just made them feel closer to the one person they were devoting most of their waking hours to serving. "Of course, Woodrow. I need a few hours of sleep right now and I prefer not sleeping on a full stomach. I'll eat when I awake at 1900. Bring sufficient food for three from the officers' mess."

"Uh— I normally prepare most of the Captain's food right here in the galley, ma'am."

"Very well. Prepare chicken fillets, mashed potatoes, and mixed vegetables. For dessert, I'd like apple pie. For a beverage, coffee, Columbian, black, one sugar per eight ounces."

"Aye, Captain."

Jenetta turned towards what she believed to be her bedroom door, then stopped after a few paces and turned. Woodrow was immediately behind her. Looking up at him she asked, "Was there something else, Woodrow?"

"No, ma'am. I'm just following you to help you get settled in."

"I think I can take it from here."

"As you wish, Captain."

Jenetta entered her bedroom and smiled. It was going to take some getting used to, having a personal steward. It might be nice to have a personal chef, but she drew the line at having a male steward help her dress and undress.

Before preparing for bed, she wanted to unpack her things so they wouldn't get too wrinkled, but her cases were nowhere in sight. Opening the closet door, she found all her uniforms already hanging from the clothes bar, clean and pressed. Her cases were on the closet floor, empty, and her footwear was neatly arranged. Crossing to the dresser, she found her other clothes neatly folded and organized in the drawers. The animated picture of her family had been placed prominently on the dresser and the picture of her and Zane was on the nightstand next to her bed. She released the suction that held the frame in place and positioned it more to her liking, then locked it down again.

It appeared that whoever had been tasked with packing her things on the *Prometheus* had sent everything she owned. She wasn't sure if she was more upset by that, or that Woodrow had apparently unpacked everything for her without permission. That was his job though, so she couldn't fault him for executing his duties with due diligence. Yes, having a personal steward was going to take some getting used to.

The need for sleep was still uppermost in her mind, so Jenetta undressed, established the wakeup time with the computer, and climbed onto the large bed after telling the computer to set the bed's grav control to one-sixth normal. The thin, gravity-shielding material that lined the bottom of the gelatin-filled mattress would block most of the ship's one-g gravity, allowing her to practically float on its surface. Even at her much reduced weight, the mattress of the gel-comfort bed was a little too firm for her tastes, so she told the computer to reduce the gel pressure by ten percent and increase the gel temperature by five degrees. In seconds, the mattress had changed to conform to her requirements. It felt like she was resting on a cloud. The room's computer interface would now immediately apply the new specifications whenever she prepared for bed. Infinitely more comfortable than the couch in the briefing room, it felt so soft, warm, and wonderful that she was asleep in minutes.

* * *

Jenetta awoke as the first words of her wakeup call echoed in her head. One advantage of the CT was that no one else was disturbed by such a call, while a major disadvantage was that she couldn't simply block the voice by pulling the pillow over her head.

"Okay, computer, I'm awake. Cancel message. Carver out."

A glance up at the wall chronometer confirmed that it was 1900 hours, although she needn't have bothered. She had never yet been awakened at the wrong time and it was doubtful she ever would if she lived to be 5,000, which just might happen if Arneu was right about the age prolongation process that had been performed on her while she was a Raider captive. She shook off the memory and returned to the present but still felt tired and would love to roll over and go back to sleep. As Captain of the Ship, she was the one person aboard who could sleep in if she wanted to, but as the Captain of the Ship, duty called, and there was still so much to do. It would probably take several days to get back into a reasonable sleep schedule where she felt rested when she awoke and there would be plenty of time for extra sleep once they were again on their way to Earth.

She showered, dressed, and was about to head for the officers' mess when wonderful cooking aromas assailed her nostrils. They reminded her that she had a steward now and that Woodrow probably had her food prepared. The door opened as she approached her dining room and she saw that three places had been set at the table. She wasn't sure how to alert Woodrow that she was ready to be served and was considering knocking on the closed galley door when it opened and Woodrow appeared.

"Do you wish to be served now, Captain, or would you prefer to wait until the others arrive?"

"Others?"

"Your two guests, Captain."

"I'll be dining alone today, Woodrow."

He nodded respectfully, then reappeared a few seconds later with a plate of food and a steaming mug that he placed in front of Jenetta as she sat down at the head of the table. The food portion was about what a hungry woman of her size would normally consume and she dug in as Woodrow removed the other two place settings.

Jenetta hadn't eaten since before the battle and she felt hollow inside. She polished off the first serving of filleted chicken, mashed potatoes, and mixed vegetables, and then asked for a second full helping. When she had finished that, she asked for a third. Woodrow's eyes grew considerably larger, but he didn't dare comment. Beginning to feel somewhat sated after the three food portions, Jenetta nonetheless had room for two healthy slices of apple pie with whipped cream. It wasn't like the pie that Mom synthesized, but Jenetta complimented Woodrow before heading for the bridge. As she left her quarters, Woodrow could only stare after her and wonder how she remained so trim. He turned to the empty food pans in the galley, still shaking his head.

Lieutenant Elizi was still on duty. After listening to her brief report on the status of the ship, Jenetta relieved her so she could get something to eat. Elizi smiled and climbed down from the bridge command chair, then quickly headed for the corridor. Jenetta climbed into the vacated chair and relaxed as she turned her thoughts to the day ahead.

There really wasn't any need for a full bridge crew except that Space Command regulations required a ship's bridge be manned 24/7, even when in port. Although they were still in hostile territory, it was most unlikely that the Raiders were in any position to launch a counter-attack against the nine armed and ready Space Command vessels plus the twelve Peabody light destroyers. In fact, given their losses here and at Raider-One, it seemed highly unlikely that the Raiders would be launching any more attacks in this deca-sector of space for some time. It would be wonderful to enjoy a period of peace like the decades Jenetta had known before being awakened from stasis sleep into this nightmare of constant vigilance and life-or-death conflicts.

Jenetta checked the list of battle damages and saw that items were disappearing quickly now that hull repair teams were back at work replacing the thick, self-sealing membrane packs and inner plates, and repairing the minor hull punctures. Precisely formed pieces of tritanium were being welded over every perforation, no matter how small, when full replacement plates weren't justified.

When Lieutenant Elizi returned from dinner to complete her duty shift, Jenetta left for the sickbay. She waited patiently until the senior doctor on duty was free.

"What's your situation here, Doctor?"

"All injuries have been treated and we're just tending the more seriously injured while the surgical nano-bots assist in their recovery. The others have been released, Captain, and will be treated on an outpatient basis until fully recovered and allowed to return to active duty."

"How many do you have in the ward?"

"Ten in this ward, with sixteen more in a nearby conference room we temporarily appropriated for use as a second ward. The critical cases are all in here, of course."

"Has someone completed the required post-mortem examinations and prepared the death certificates?"

"Lt. Commander O'Neil, the chief medical officer, will begin addressing that when he comes back on duty. The living are our first priority."

"Of course. Can these crewmen receive visitors?"

"Yes, but a few are under heavy sedation and all need their rest."

"I won't disturb them for very long. I thought they might wish to know the outcome of the battle. I know I certainly would, were I in their place."

Accompanied by the doctor, Jenetta visited each patient who was awake and alert, telling him or her that she was proud of the way the *Song* had flown into the battle and joined the *Prometheus* and *Chiron* in crushing the Raider attackers. She said that everyone on board was a hero and would receive recognition as such when they reached Earth. She told them the task force had dealt a critical blow to the Raiders, destroying thirty-four Raider ships while losing only one, the *Delhi*. After visiting each of the ten beds in the sickbay, they visited the sixteen patients in the secondary ward.

Jenetta next re-visited each of the places that had suffered major hull breaches. The repair work was of the same high quality as on the bridge. Satisfied with the repairs, she returned to the bridge. Lieutenant Ashraf was there now, along with Lieutenant Elizi, whose command watch would be from midnight to 0800 once a normal duty schedule was established two days hence.

Before settling in at her briefing room desk to handle the growing list of 'electronic' paperwork, Jenetta took another look at the battle damage list. A dozen more holes had been patched and removed from the list. It appeared that at the rate the engineers were progressing, most of the hull damage repairs would be completed within twelve more hours.

As Jenetta replaced the holo-tube on her desk, a tiny cardboard box on the desktop grabbed her attention. Opening it, Jenetta found a red pip. Lt. Ashraf must have left the box there since no one else could have entered the office while Jenetta was out unless there was an emergency condition.

Jenetta walked to the small lavatory that was part of her office and used the mirror there to position the pip next to the gold one she wore. The pips showed that she'd now received two official warship commands, with one being currently active. She was smiling as she returned to her desk to work.

A number of medal and commendation recommendations from NCOs and officers for their subordinates who had performed 'above and beyond' during the battle had been forwarded to her after being reviewed and approved by Lieutenant Ashraf. After reading each report, she added her signature and forwarded them to SHQ. She spent the next several hours studying the crew personnel files. If she was going to be posted here for at least the next two weeks, she felt it was a good idea to become familiar with the backgrounds of the people for whom she was responsible.

* * *

The Peabody Protection Services destroyers were also making good progress getting their hulls sealed and pressurized. They estimated they could continue their journey within three weeks.

Following his report of their repair progress to Captain Gavin, Commodore Blosset said, "Captain, I've been thinking about your timely arrival here. We're grateful, you understand, but I can't help but wonder about it. Were you conducting maneuvers near here?"

"No, Commodore. We left Higgins Space Command Base a month ago to attend the official launching ceremony of this ship and its sister ship, the *Chiron*, at Earth. Just after departing the station, I was notified about a possible assemblage of Raider ships in this area of space. A rendezvous point was established at Vauzlee for all available ships in this deca-sector and we altered course. The *Prometheus* and the *Chiron* were at the RP awaiting the arrival of the other ships when we intercepted your call for help. Only the *Song* had so far arrived and we responded as quickly as we could. It was fortunate the other ships were nearly to the RP. They locked onto your AutoTect signal and came directly here."

"I see. Then you didn't know of the attack in advance?"

"As far as I know, Peabody didn't trust Space Command with information regarding your course and transit schedule. Why do you suppose that was, Commodore?"

"You know why," Commodore Blosset said defensively. "It was top secret. We couldn't afford to trust anyone outside our company with that information."

"If you had trusted Space Command, we would have been happy to provide an escort. Chances are that the Raiders never would have tried to hijack the cargo if Space Command was involved. They've shown a marked preference for avoiding contact with us. That's beside the point, though. It appears that someone within your company leaked the information to the Raiders. It would be wise for your superiors to investigate the finances of everyone in your firm who could possibly have known about the course and timetable. Of course, I suggest you use an independent investigation team since all your security people probably knew the route."

The commodore nodded sourly and broke off the communication link.

Gavin smiled at the blank screen. He hadn't lied to Commodore Blosset; he'd just sidestepped the question of whether or not he knew of the ambush in advance. If Peabody wished to pursue the issue further, they would have to do it with SHQ.

Chapter Nine
~ April 2nd, 2268 ~

Admiral Platt was panting like a long distance runner who had just completed a race. It had been two decades since she'd last commanded a warship, and never one in combat, but her palms were moist with sweat and her heart was beating wildly in her chest. The re-creation of the Battle of Vauzlee was so incredibly vivid that she felt as if she was there in the thick of battle with the task force.

The open area in the center of the large horseshoe-shaped table in the great hall where the Admiralty Board held their regular sessions was in fact a holo-platform. The War College's computers had created a magnificent blend of real images and computer simulations from the logs of the ships involved in the action. The final product was so incredibly detailed that one could observe everything far better than actual eyewitnesses to the event. The action could be viewed from any angle, even zoomed in and slowed to watch torpedoes and energy weapon pulses as they struck individual ships. Positioning a laser pointer on any SC ship instantly changed the projected image to a view of the ship's bridge. Special holo-monitors lowered from the ceiling and projected the bridge images, time-synchronized with the exterior action being shown on the platform. Since bridge logs were recorded from four points, the recreated holo-images allowed a view of the bridge activity in 3-D from any angle.

The ten admirals of the Admiralty Board sat transfixed at this first showing of the re-creation. In the days ahead, War College analysts would examine every second of the battle in excruciating detail.

The Board watched the battle several times before moving inside first the *Prometheus*, then the *Chiron*, the *Song*, and lastly the *Delhi*. The bridge officers of the *Delhi* never even knew of their imminent destruction as the Raider warship crushed them, along with that entire part of the ship, in a heartbeat.

"This re-creation will be available in the holo-theater downstairs to any member of the board following today's session," Admiral Moore said. "Does anyone wish to see any more before we open discussion?" Looking at each member of the Board until they either verbally or silently acknowledged his question, he said, "Since no one wishes further review at this time, we're open to discussion of what we've seen."

"The courage exhibited by our people as they entered battle against such overwhelming odds is stirring," Admiral Platt, the Director of Fleet Operations said. "Captain Gavin should be especially commended for his tactics and for his leadership."

"It was foolhardy," Admiral Hubera immediately countered. "I'm surprised by Gavin's presumption. He should have waited until his task group was consolidated and then attacked as one force, as the War College planners outlined. And he should have followed the complete plan developed by the War College instead of this half-baked tactic. It could have cost us the entire task force instead of just the *Delhi*."

"They couldn't wait, Donald," Admiral Bradlee said. "The convoy was under fire before most of our ships had reached the RP and they needed to enter the battle as soon as possible to take heat off the Peabody ships."

"The rapid attrition of the Raider forces and disruption of their chain of command was owed solely to the fact that they believed they were facing a minimal SC force," Admiral Hillaire said. "We're not talking about another military. We're talking about a criminal organization that will cut and run as soon as they believe they might get severely hurt. The tactic was brilliant, Donald, not half-baked."

"It cost us the *Delhi*, didn't it?" Hubera said.

"It most certainly did not!" Admiral Platt responded strongly. "The *Delhi* was lost because a Raider captain tried to run away without waiting until he was far enough from the battle zone to be reasonably confident that he had open space ahead of him."

"Despite the loss of the *Delhi* and crewmembers on most of the other ships involved in this action," Admiral Moore said, "we can't look upon this as anything other than an outstanding success. To have destroyed thirty-four Raider warships in one battle is second only to the blow inflicted upon them by the destruction of Raider-One."

"And for this blow," Admiral Plimley said, "like that one, we find Lt. Commander Carver with her hand firmly on the hammer."

"I saw Carver sitting on the bridge of the *Prometheus*," Admiral Burke said, "but her role was only as XO to Captain Gavin. Surely she had no active role in the battle."

"You must not have viewed the report Captain Gavin filed immediately following the battle," Admiral Plimley said. "He credited Lt. Commander Carver with developing the tactics used in this engagement. He believed in the potential of her plan so much that he made the decision to use her tactics instead of those proposed by the War College, which would have required him to launch fighters to combat the predicted force of Raider fighters. As you saw in the re-creation, the Raiders employed no fighters. Given the *Prometheus'* under-strength crew complement, the ship's fighting effectiveness would have been severely comprised by following the War College plan."

"Carver conceived the tactics Gavin followed?" Admiral Hubera said. "I should have recognized her involvement in this. We should never have taken her out of that Science Officer posting. It's where she belongs, someplace where she can't do any damage."

"Lt. Commander Carver *has* been placed where she belongs," Admiral Hillaire said, "on the bridge of a warship. If ever an officer deserved such a posting, it's she. And I'm delighted to see the wisdom of this Board's decision in that regard proven so quickly and so affirmatively."

"And now Gavin has placed her in command of the *Song*. Carver is too young and immature for such a posting. Mark my words, this will end badly."

"Donald, calm down," Admiral Moore said. "The battle is over. We won. Commander Carver is fully capable of overseeing repair efforts until a new commanding officer can be assigned to the *Song*."

* * *

The imposed blackout on personal communications was lifted on the seventh day following the battle. The brief suspension had given Supreme Headquarters adequate time to notify the next of kin of those who had made the ultimate sacrifice in service to the Galactic Alliance. It also gave the War College the time it needed to review the submitted logs and prepare statements to the press before someone learned of the battle through communication with a serving member in Space Command or the Space Marine Corps.

Jenetta sent prepared messages to her parents and brothers as soon the ban was lifted. She knew her mother, especially, would have begun to worry when word of the battle was announced and she hadn't heard from Jenetta. She told them in her messages that her arrival at Earth would be delayed by a month but that she was fine and hadn't been injured in the battle.

In the messages to her brothers, she signed off as 'Lt. Commander Jenetta Alicia Carver, Captain of the *Song*, GSC-CH502.' She knew they couldn't help but notice it and there was some small personal amusement in knowing they would be shocked by the news. When they'd been children, she'd always fought for recognition from her siblings but rarely received any. Now, already the most famous officer in Space Command, she had stolen another march on them. She was the first of the Carvers since her great-grandfather to be appointed captain of a warship as large as a heavy cruiser. She didn't use the title or say anything about it in the message to her parents because her father had only risen to command the *Cromwell*, a frigate. At one time, back in the wet navy days, frigates had been small ships that functioned as destroyer escorts. But as the decades and centuries passed, the duties of the small ships changed, and they had actually become almost as large as destroyers. When Space Command was formed, it was decided that Frigates should fill the gap between destroyers and cruisers. Larger than a destroyer at six hundred meters in length and three hundred five thousand tons, the *Cromwell*, GSC-F839, had a ship's complement of eleven-hundred and was about a third smaller in size and weight than the Kamakura-class heavy cruisers.

Jenetta was delighted when she returned to her quarters several evenings later and found three personal messages waiting for her. She played the one from her mother first.

"Hi, honey," the smiling face of her mother said, "I'm glad you're fine and so thankful you weren't injured in that battle. News of it has been playing on all vid channels for the past several days. Space Command created a reenactment of the battle from the logs submitted by the captain of each ship and gave it to the media. I was horrified when I saw your ship, the *Prometheus*, arrive where the convoy was being attacked and take on all forty-one enemy warships by itself. Whoever came up with that battle plan should be relieved of their position immediately. I never heard of such a thing."

Jenetta smiled and wondered if she should tell her mother it was her plan.

"I was so thankful when the *Chiron* and the others began to arrive to help you out. It's a miracle you weren't all injured, or even killed. And I certainly don't understand how you wind up in the middle of every fight. Don't they have anybody else out there? Your father just laughed when I asked him that. Anyway, I'm glad you're safe. Knowing that makes it easier to wait the extra month until you arrive home. Everybody on the base is just dying to see you again. All your friends from high school have been calling to ask when you'll arrive and many of the girls from the Academy have been messaging me for news. I think you're going to be pretty busy when you get home, but be sure to reserve enough time for your family. Oh, there's the timer. I have to go. Your father is preparing his own message in the study so it will probably arrive about the same time as this one. Take care of yourself, honey. I love you. Bye."

Jenetta smiled and played the one from her father next.

"Hello, *Captain.* You neglected to mention that little fact in your message, but word has already spread around the base that the entire senior staff of the *Song* was killed in the battle and that Captain Gavin, as task force commander, appointed you to take command of the stricken ship. I guess you never were one for tooting your own horn and these days you don't have to. There seem to be many people anxious to toot it for you. I know the appointment is just temporary since you're only a Lt. Commander, but the fact that Gavin chose you over everyone else in the ten-ship task force to handle the job of getting the ship reorganized after the tragedy that befell it speaks volumes. It shows the confidence and trust he has in you. Among the ten ships in the task force, there have to be at least thirty command officers with more seniority in rank or time in grade than yourself. That *you* were appointed as captain is quite a compliment, honey.

"I must say I was at first stunned by the audacity of the attack plan Gavin chose, but I certainly can't argue its success. You took out the command ship and two of the cruisers before the Raiders even began to target you. On reflection, if you had attacked in force they would certainly have noticed your approach long before you could have targeted any of their ships. And if they had known how many ships were in the task force, they might have broken off their attack and run for the safety of FTL before you had an opportunity to damage them seriously. Overall, I have to say the plan was— inspired. Gavin is to be commended for his innovative battle strategy. Since we've never fought a major enemy in space, I suppose most of the tactics taught at the War College are inadequate for such encounters and simply rely on our having overwhelming force in vessel numbers and weapon strength. Gavin's tactics are sure to be added to the curriculum. You're indeed fortunate to have him as a commanding officer. Watch him closely, sweetheart, and you'll learn a lot. There's the timer so I have to go. Give'em hell, honey. I love you. Out."

Jenetta smiled. Now she *knew* she couldn't tell her parents it was her battle plan. If her dad knew, he'd be embarrassed after the way he had just praised Gavin for it. It didn't really matter if he never learned. She knew he loved her and was proud of her for the things she had accomplished. That was enough.

The last of the three messages was from her brother Richie. Of her four brothers, she had always felt closest to him. Billy was the eldest and seemed to feel that he had to set an example for the others, which seemed to keep him a bit aloof. Andy and Jimmy, the twins, had each other for close companionship. Richie had fought for his own recognition but had never felt that he had to be a role model, and he had always watched over Jenetta a little more vigilantly than the others, all of whom would have ground into pulp anyone who hurt her. In the animated image of her family that could always be found on her dresser, Richie was the one standing next to her, the one who'd had the presence of mind to put his large hand on her small shoulder halfway through the images and make her appear more like a member of the family.

"Hi sis," the image of a very serious Lt. Commander Richard Charles Carver said as the message played. "Don't you think it's about time you slowed down a little? You're making the rest of us Carvers look bad." But Richie couldn't hold the serious expression any longer than that and his face lit up with a wide smile. "I mean, after all, the rest of us want a chance with the Raiders too. I know you were asleep for eleven years, but you don't have to make up for that entire time in just one year, do you? And now you're the captain of a heavy cruiser? My shipmates keep asking me to have you reassign us to a more forward area once you make Admiral next year."

Richie chuckled. "Seriously, sis, I'm happy for you, and proud of my little sister. You've done some incredible things and you deserve all the praise that's being heaped upon you." Faking a stern and serious expression again as he waggled his right index finger at her, he said, "But don't think you're going to make Commander before I do. There's more than one Carver who wants to take names and kick Raider ass in this galaxy. They'd better be prepared for all out war by the Carvers now that you've set the bar."

Smiling again, he said, "Take care of yourself, Jen. And don't let all the adulation go to your head. I can still beat you at Annihilator X-006 any time you want to take the gloves off and sit down at a console with me."

Jenetta smiled as she thought of the thousands of times she had played the vid game with Richie when they were young. They must have played five hundred games before she got her first win.

The messages wiped away most of the strain she'd been feeling and left only bone-weary tiredness. As she slipped into bed, she was still thinking about the messages and wearing the smile that had adorned her face since her mom's image first filled her com screen.

* * *

The section of the *Song* hull where two torpedoes had dealt the ship such a devastating blow was finally sealed on the twelfth day following the battle. Work would continue in that area until several more layers of tritanium plating were added to complete the ship's armor requirements, but the *Song*'s hull was once again fully sealed and pressurized, and the ship would soon be capable of returning to active service. The considerable internal damage to bulkheads, decks, plumbing, and electronics, other than emergency repairs, would have to wait until the ship reached a repair dockyard.

When the last of the armor plating was in place, Jenetta loaned half of the *Song*'s engineering crew to other ships still making emergency repairs while the remainder continued to work on important, but lower priority, repairs such as the replacement of damaged sensors on the hull's exterior.

On the twentieth day following the battle, Gavin announced that the damaged ships would continue on to Earth four days hence. By then, he estimated, all GSC ships would have their hulls pressurized and their engines capable of sustained travel at the ship's rated speed. The repair docks at Mars, already stockpiling necessary parts and equipment from damage lists prepared by the chief engineer of each ship, were making preparations to receive the seven heavily battered ships as soon as they arrived.

The two GSC destroyers that had arrived at the battle last, the *Dublin* and the *Calcutta*, hadn't suffered any battle damage. They would wait for the GSC salvage group dispatched to the site and then accompany them back to the reclamation depot with the *Delhi* and the thirty-four destroyed Raider vessels in tow. This was necessary to keep the Raiders from returning to salvage them. The holds of the two destroyers were filled with rescued Raider prisoners. In all, search and recovery teams had recovered one thousand, eight hundred seventy-seven Raiders discovered in air-tight compartments. The military justice courts would be busy for quite a few months as the prisoners were tried and transported to a penal colony.

Of the seven hundred forty-nine officers, NCOs, and crewmen aboard the *Delhi*, only two hundred eighty-seven were found alive. It was the worst loss aboard a Space Command vessel in over a hundred years, but considering the condition of the destroyer, it seemed like a miracle even that many had survived.

* * *

Chairman Gagarin, his face mottled with rage, stopped sputtering just long enough to catch his breath before continuing.

"Councilman Strauss, you said that this Carver was posted to an insignificant position in an obscure area of the Science Section at Higgins. You said she presented no further threat to us. Now we find out that not only is she not on Higgins, but she's been promoted to Lt. Commander and assigned as the captain of a heavy cruiser at a battle site where we've just had our head handed to us."

"The information about the posting on Higgins came from a normally reliable source and has been confirmed as accurate at the time the report was filed. He did inform us of Carver's promotion and reposting when it occurred."

"But you didn't bother to communicate that information to the rest of us?"

"What difference would it have made? I knew it would only upset you and she was temporarily out of your reach. We already have plans in place to take care of her when she reaches Earth."

"You have no idea how far my reach extends. You think I couldn't have her killed just because she's aboard a Spacc warship?"

"I think that to do so would seriously damage our intelligence infrastructure. It's incredibly difficult to turn Spaccs and we can't throw away a valuable resource on petty revenge that returns no profit."

"Petty!" Gagarin screamed. "Do you know how much this escaped slave has cost us?"

"I'm aware of the losses we suffered from the destruction of Raider-One and of the ships and personnel she destroyed."

"Then you know there's nothing petty about it."

Strauss just looked down at the table. There was no point in arguing with Gagarin when he got like this. The man was a fool. He should never have been appointed to the Lower Council, much less named to chair it. He was a lot like Mikel Arneu, another man who consistently let his emotions cloud his reason.

Development of the age prolongation process had been an outstanding achievement for Arneu. He had proposed it, pushed until he got funding, and then supervised the effort until the scientists produced results that they guaranteed would at least double life expectancy, and possibly increase it by as much as thirty to forty times normal, depending upon the age of the subject when it was administered. The incredible success of that project might even have earned Arneu a seat on the Lower Council. Strauss remembered how Arneu would practically salivate whenever he dangled the idea in front of him. But if Strauss had anything to say about it, Arneu would never sit on the Lower Council. He was useful and effective as a base commandant, but that's as high as

Strauss felt he should ever ascend in the organization. The enticement of a position on the Lower Council was just a ploy, a carrot on a stick to dangle in front of Arneu to keep him dedicated and working diligently.

When the age prolongation process was lost with the destruction of Raider-One, it proved Strauss's point of Arneu's unsuitability for a seat on the Lower Council. In the 'interest of security,' he hadn't allowed detailed documentation regarding development of the new processes and formulas to be sent to another base, or even to headquarters. If Gagarin had been able to get his hands on Arneu the day after Raider-One was destroyed, he would have throttled him on the spot. And if getting their hands on Carver would have allowed them to reverse-engineer the process, they would have spared no expense or effort to do so. But their scientists said it wasn't possible. The entire process would have to be developed again from scratch. At least they now knew that it *was* possible. Carver was a constant reminder that the human body can be remolded into whatever form they chose. And not just through careful gene manipulation prior to birth, or in the so-called 'formative' years. Changes could be inaugurated from any point in the subject's lifecycle.

"Did Carver have any part in our defeat at Vauzlee?" Gagarin demanded of Strauss.

"How could she? She wasn't sent to take command of the cruiser until *after* the battle."

"I don't know how; that's why I asked! You're supposed to know such things. Your department is charged with gathering intelligence about everything the Spaccs do and why they do it."

"It's too early to know why she was sent to the *Song*. It takes time to gather intelligence. There was a blackout on personal communications from the ships that fought at Vauzlee until a few days ago. We've only just heard from our contact aboard the *Song*. There hasn't been time for a full briefing or reassignment of tasks."

"You have somebody on the ship?" Gagarin asked, his face reflecting a malevolent eagerness.

"Yes."

"Are they capable of assassinating Carver?"

"The individual would have no reservations about it, but it's difficult to get close enough to a captain aboard their own ship, commit the act, and get away clean. Our people are in it for the money, not the cause, so we can't expect martyrdom."

"Promise your person anything. I want Carver dead."

"Anything?"

"Up to a million credits."

"A million credits? Just for killing one little girl? Wait five months until they reach Earth and the deed will be accomplished for no more than ten thousand."

"I waited once before and look where it's brought us. You promised she couldn't hurt us again, yet she shows up in a command position at a place where we again suffered severe losses. I can feel it in my bones that she had a hand in that defeat. I want her killed with all possible haste. I'll pay the million credits from my own slush account. I want her DEAD before our big operation commences. Do you understand? DEAD-DEAD-DEAD!"

"Very well. I'll pass the order along to our contact aboard the *Song*."

* * *

On the day prior to the scheduled departure, Jenetta still hadn't been relieved of command aboard the *Song*. She fretted about it all morning and then finally called the *Prometheus* just after 1400 hours to speak with Gavin.

"Captain, I've received no contact from my relief as yet."

"Are you having problems, Commander?"

"No problems, sir. It's just that the *Prometheus* is preparing to leave for Earth."

"Yes, most of the task force is preparing to leave for Earth. We'll depart just after the Peabody convoy leaves at 2100 hours tomorrow."

"Yes, sir, but I'm still attached to the *Song*."

"I realize that, Commander, and you've done an excellent job over there. Rather than changing things around now, just remain where you are until we get to Earth. In a few months when the *Song* goes into the Mars facility for repair, you'll report back to the *Prometheus*."

"Aye, Captain."

"*Prometheus*, out."

"*Song*, out."

Jenetta stood and paced around the room for several minutes while biting on her lower lip. After she had worked off most of her angst, she activated her CT by pressing her thumb onto the top of her Space Command ring. When the carrier was activated, she summoned Lieutenant Ashraf to the briefing room.

"Yes, Captain?" Ashraf queried when she entered.

"How are preparations for our departure proceeding?"

"Here's a report on the state of the ship, ma'am," Ashraf said as she held a viewpad out to Jenetta. "We'll be ready to leave at the scheduled time, assuming our new captain has arrived."

After glancing at the information on the viewpad, Jenetta said, "I've just been informed by Captain Gavin that I'm to remain in command until we reach Earth."

Ashraf smiled widely. "That's wonderful news, Captain. I'll inform the senior staff."

As the doors closed behind Ashraf, Jenetta began pacing around the office again, this time slapping the viewpad against her leg. It wasn't that she was displeased to be in command of the *Song*; it was just that she thought of the *Prometheus* as *her* ship, even if she wasn't its captain. Before being posted to the *Prometheus*, she would have delighted in being even a minor member of the *Song* crew, but that was before. This would be the first time since being commissioned that the *Prometheus* embarked without her.

*   *   *

Awakened from a sound sleep by the buzzing of his bedside com unit, Gavin glanced up at the wall chronometer. It was 0246. He grunted a couple of small expletives as he first rubbed his eyes, then rolled over and positioned himself to lift the com cover. As the small monitor activated, the face of Lieutenant Kerrey filled the screen. The captain's bedside com unit was set for blackout, so on the command chair's right-hand monitor Kerrey would only see an animated image of the captain sitting in his office. The word 'simulation' was printed at the bottom of the screen.

"What it is, Ensign?" the Captain mumbled.

"It's Lieutenant Kerrey, sir."

"I'll decide that when I know why you've bothered me at 0300 hours."

Kerrey hesitated, swallowed nervously, and then said with a hint of desperation, "I'm sorry, Captain. I tried to put him off, but Commander Kanes is demanding to speak with you immediately. He won't tell me what it's about, but he threatened to have me arrested and *court-martialed* if I didn't wake you."

Gavin mumbled something and then said, "Put him on, Lieutenant."

"He's not here, sir. He said he'll be waiting outside the door of your quarters."

"Outside my door?" Gavin asked, suddenly much more alert.

"Yes, sir."

"Very well, Lieutenant," the Captain said as he pushed the cover of the com unit down.

Ten seconds later, wearing a robe over his pajamas, Gavin admitted Kanes to his sitting room.

"I assume this is most urgent, Keith?"

"Yes, Captain. *Most* urgent! As you're well aware, the first ship targeted by the *Prometheus* when we arrived here was a battleship. We've since learned that that ship, named the *Soul Harvester*, served as the command vessel for this operation. Among the bodies found in recovered pieces of the *Soul*

Harvester was that of the ship's captain. His seared remains were in a section that contained the ship's bridge. There was little left of his body, but a personal log ring he was wearing was functional. We've been working tirelessly to decode the encrypted files it contains. One of my people has just decrypted a message that you should see immediately."

Taking the proffered viewpad, Gavin read the message on the unit's display.

"Good God!" Gavin said as he quickly lowered the view-pad. "Are you sure this was decrypted correctly?"

"I verified it personally before I made the decision to disturb you at this unholy hour."

"Send a copy of this to Captain Powers aboard the *Chiron* immediately. Priority-One. Tell Powers to contact me as soon as he's read it. I'll get dressed and meet you in my briefing room in four minutes."

"Aye, Captain.

Chapter Ten
~ April 19th, 2268 ~

Awakened from a sound sleep by Lieutenant Elizi, the bridge commander on third watch, Jenetta looked up sleepily at the dimly glowing wall chronometer before lifting the cover on the tiny com unit next to her bed. It was 0344 hours.

"What is it, Lieutenant?" she asked the projected face of the young officer. Her bedside com was in blackout mode.

"We've just received a Priority-One message from the *Prometheus*, Captain. A second later they and the *Chiron* departed the area at Light-375."

Jenetta was instantly awake. No Space Command officer would dare wake their captain in the middle of the night without good cause. A Priority-One was just such a cause. It was to be delivered to the commanding officer immediately regardless of the hour received and how the officer was otherwise occupied. News that the *Prometheus* had left the area at its maximum FTL speed with the *Chiron* was likewise good cause to wake the captain. Plans had called for the *Prometheus* and *Chiron* to depart for Earth as part of the task force in just a few hours at an established convoy speed of Light-262. And no ship left an RP at its top speed except in emergency circumstances. It built up speed gradually until it was well away from all other ships. With DATFA temporal envelope travel there were no physical limitations to instantly engaging top speed, it was just SOP that it was never done where ships were gathering or assembled. Something serious must have occurred to change plans without prior notice and induce the two battleships to depart as they had.

"Forward the message to my queue," Jenetta said, the urgency in her voice obvious.

"Already done, Captain. Uh, should I alert anyone?"

"Notify all senior officers to be in my cabin office by 0400 hours."

"Aye, Captain."

Jenetta shoved the com panel down and flung the blanket off. "Lights," she said as she swung her feet over the edge of the bed and jumped up. Seconds later she was standing in her office dressed only in her pajamas as the image of Captain Gavin leapt onto the large wall monitor in response to her uttered command of 'play Priority-One message.'

"This message is being sent to the captains of all ships at the Vauzlee battle site," the image of Gavin said. "Additional messages will follow in a few hours. Our intelligence officers have decrypted a communication found on the personal log ring of the dead Raider captain who commanded the attack force. That message contained information about a second planned attack. There is no specific timeframe mentioned, but most of the ships involved in the action here were ordered to proceed immediately to a new rendezvous point once the Peabody ships were neutralized and the freighter's cargo secured. Four of what we believe to be their oldest, slowest, and most vulnerable warships were tasked to escort the cargo to an undisclosed location referred to only as GR, while the more powerful vessels would join a group already assembling at a location referred to as AH. We have no idea how many ships are involved in this second operation, but I suspect they might be numerous.

"Since the *Caracas* and *Asuncion* haven't fully tested their sub-light engine and temporal envelope generator repairs, they will remain behind at the battle site to await the ships from the reclamation center. All other ships should depart as soon as possible at their maximum speed. The *Dublin* and *Calcutta* should, naturally, transfer all Raider prisoners in their holds to the *Caracas* and *Asuncion* before their departure. Additional orders to follow. The target of the new Raider threat is Higgins Space Command Base.

"Captain Lawrence Gavin, Captain of the *Prometheus*, message complete."

Until the message ended, Jenetta didn't realize she hadn't taken a breath since it began. When Gavin said 'Higgins,' she sucked in sharply, then released it and breathed again. She glanced up at the office chronometer before running back to her bedroom to dress.

As Jenetta left her bedroom, she found Woodrow standing beside the doorway.

"Is there anything I can assist you with, Captain?" he asked.

"Uh, what are you doing up, Woodrow?"

"After passing Lt. Elizi through to your com unit, I got up to prepare a mug of coffee for you. I've served the officers who have arrived for your meeting."

"You passed Lt. Elizi through?"

"Yes, Captain. When the captain is in her quarters, all com calls go through her steward so she's not disturbed for trivial matters. During third watch, even CT access to the captain is restricted. The XO and watch commander *can* contact you directly, but even their calls are routed through me unless they tell the computer to override the normal routing or if the ship is in danger."

"Yes, of course. Well, I'm sorry you were awakened." Reaching for the mug of coffee he was holding, she added, "Thank you for the coffee."

"Would you care for something to eat?"

At the mere mention of food, Jenetta's stomach grumbled loudly, her body's way of expressing a desire to be fed yet again.

"No time just now, Woodrow. You go back to bed. I'll eat at my regular time despite what my stomach is demanding."

"Very good, Captain."

The ship's young senior staff was seated in her office when she entered. The conference table that abutted her desk sat eleven so, with her chair behind the desk, there was more than enough room. The circumstances of the meeting were so unusual that everyone was alert and anxious to learn what was going on. The concerned faces of her officers watched her anxiously as she took her seat behind her desk and she didn't waste any time with formalities.

"My information is sketchy so I know you'll have questions when I'm done. I can't guarantee that I'll be able to answer them. I just received a message from Captain Gavin. Some of you probably already know that both the *Prometheus* and *Chiron* have departed the area at top speed. We're ordered to depart as well and as soon as possible. An encrypted message, discovered on the personal log ring of a dead Raider officer, spoke of an imminent attack on Higgins. The Raider ships at this engagement had orders to leave as soon as they had completed their mission here and rendezvous with another force assembling for the attack on Higgins."

She paused for a couple of seconds as shock and surprise registered on the faces of the other officers.

"I suppose I can speculate a little and say that they probably intended this attack to serve two purposes. One was undoubtedly to acquire the convoy's cargo and the second might have been to function as a diversion, figuring that it would draw every available GSC ship in the deca-sector. And while we were out here, weeks from Higgins, scouring the sector in a search for the ships that took the Mawcett relics, they'd have an almost clear shot at the station. A force as large as the one that attacked the convoy would most likely overwhelm the five ships comprising the standard defense for Higgins. The base at Higgins has been the only thing keeping the Raiders from controlling this entire deca-sector of space for years, so it's surprising they haven't tried to destroy it before now. I imagine they know just how dear their cost will be. But if we lose the station, the Raiders might be able to regain a significant foothold here before we can reestablish control. We can't allow that to happen. Other than Earth, our next nearest Stat-Com-1 base is two hundred light years away.

"All ships except the *Caracas* and the *Asuncion* have been ordered to proceed to Higgins at maximum speed. We will not travel together as a task force because the smaller ships would slow us down, just as we would have slowed the *Prometheus* and *Chiron*. I need your best time estimates for getting underway. Commander Rodriguez, how long will it take you to get the ship sealed and ready for departure?"

"Ten minutes, Captain, perhaps less. When I was awakened and informed that the battleships had departed the area, I asked if anyone was outside the ship. I learned there was a work party adjusting a sensor on the keel. I gave orders to immediately bring them inside the ship and prepare for departure."

"Good thinking, Commander. Does anyone else need more than ten minutes to prepare for our departure?" When no one spoke up, Jenetta said, "Good. Questions?"

"Since we destroyed thirty-four ships here," Lieutenant Elizi asked, "is it possible the Raiders will cancel their planned attack?"

"That possibility exists, but we can't rely on it. We must treat this threat seriously. Anything else?" When no further questions were asked, Jenetta said, "Okay. We'll be underway ten minutes from now, perhaps less. Dismissed."

As the officers left the conference room, all began using their CTs to issue orders to their juniors.

Seven minutes later the *Song* maneuvered for open space as it built its envelope and then disappeared from sight in an instant. With a top speed of Light-322, it was faster than any of the destroyers and should be the third ship from the battle site to arrive at Higgins.

* * *

"Good morning, Commander," the image of Captain Gavin said. The message had been received just seconds earlier while Jenetta was enjoying the first sips of morning coffee in her briefing room. The mug of steaming black elixir was just the first of many she would enjoy throughout this day. "I'm sure you understand why we didn't have the luxury of a face-to-face meeting to plan our departure and travel to Higgins. Since we're unaware of the Raider timetable, it was necessary that we return to Higgins with all due haste. Minutes might be critical. By now the Raider hierarchy must know their attempt to purloin the artifacts has failed. Logic would tell them that we had advance information about their attack and pre-positioned our forces in the area. Taking that one step further, they might deduce that we have advance information of their planned attack on Higgins. They might still hope to catch us unaware if they advance the original timetable. We have no idea how many ships they've assembled for this attack, but I'm sure they can name every ship we have in this deca-sector.

"You've done an excellent job of pulling that command together and getting the ship repaired and ready for travel, but in the event we're once more called to battle we can't afford to have you dependent upon a staff composed entirely of inexperienced junior officers. A more experienced staff will be waiting and ready to take command of the *Song* when you arrive at Higgins. I hadn't taken such action already because with the battle over I felt the current crew was quite able to handle the simple chore of bringing the ship to Earth as part of a task force. Space Command Headquarters would then have arranged for the permanent replacement of lost officers. You, naturally, will transfer back here to the *Prometheus* as soon as we meet up at Higgins.

"The *Prometheus* and *Chiron* should make the trip in twenty-four days. The slightly older design of your Light Speed drive and smaller energy plant means it will take you an extra four days. The destroyers should arrive six days after the *Song*, assuming all are able to make a hasty departure. We stripped the deca-sector clean of available ships for this last operation so we can't expect any more help beyond the five ships presently at Higgins and whichever of us arrives before the attack commences.

"There's nothing to do now except keep our fingers crossed that we reach Higgins before the Raiders.

"Captain Lawrence Gavin, Captain of the *Prometheus*, message complete."

Jenetta leaned back and soaked up the comfort of the chair while she thought. She knew that the command officers of the *Song*, although young, were competent and fully capable of getting the ship to Higgins without incident, but she didn't know how they would weather the pressures of a life-or-death situation. Who would remain calm and who would panic was something that couldn't be known until the person was under fire. During the Vauzlee engagement they had been busy performing routine Damage Control duties, so they hadn't really been tested.

Jenetta knew she had to start drilling her officers un-mercifully if they were to be prepared to handle their responsibilities calmly during battle. Training wasn't a substitute for experience, but it was the next best thing. The officers would at least know what was required of them during an emergency, as well as the options available. It also built confidence in their ability to handle any situation. And the training wouldn't be wasted if a more senior crew did take command of the ship when it reached Higgins.

Her thoughts were interrupted by a call on her CT.

"Captain, this is Lt. Ashraf," Jenetta heard.

Activating her carrier, Jenetta said, "Yes, Lieutenant. What is it?"

"We have a serious problem, ma'am. Could you come down to storage locker 7-222-1-Alpha?"

"I'm quite busy. What's the problem?"

"We've found a body."

"I thought everyone had been accounted for?"

"No, Captain, it isn't a fatality from the battle. It's Petty Officer Nichols. He didn't report for his watch this morning and he wasn't in his quarters, so we initiated a search by triangulating on his ID chip. He's just been located. It appears he was murdered sometime last night. I've sent for a medical team."

"I'll be right there."

It took Jenetta just six minutes to reach Corridor One of Frame Section Two-Twenty-Two on Deck Seven. At least a dozen crewmen were milling around the door to a storage locker, but the throng immediately parted to let their captain through. Jenetta saw the thin form of Lt. Commander Michael O'Neil, the chief medical officer, bent over the body inside the room. Lieutenant Ashraf and the ship's chief security officer, Marine Captain Russell Galont, hovered over him. Scattered on the floor around the corpse was what appeared to be a deck of playing cards. Jenetta waited patiently in the doorway until the doctor had completed his examination and stood up. The forty-eight-year-old physician turned and addressed the three officers.

"I'll have to conduct a full autopsy, of course, but my initial assessment is blunt force trauma to the head at the hands of person or persons unknown."

"You're quite sure it's murder, Doctor?" Jenetta asked.

"Quite sure, Captain. His jaw is smashed and his neck broken. It's not the sort of damage that could occur from a fall. The striations on the neck indicate that Petty Officer Nichols was facing his attacker, who is probably left-handed. When he was struck, the body reacted to the mass of the weapon and it slid slightly, causing the scratches in addition to the bruise. Nichols' right arm is broken, indicating that he might have successfully warded off a first killing blow."

Jenetta shook her head. "I didn't know him well, but he seemed like a likable crewman. Who could have done this? When was he killed, Doctor?"

"The autopsy will give us a more precise time, but current body temperature suggests he died no more than nine hours ago and probably closer to eight."

Jenetta nodded and looked at the Marine officer. "Major Galont?" Aboard ship, only Space Command officers holding that official rank, or the commanding officer of the ship, could be acknowledged as 'Captain.' Marine officers with the rank of Captain were referred to as Major as a matter of etiquette to avoid confusion.

All GSC warships carried Space Marine forces as part of their normal ship's company. In addition to their primary function of providing an armed landing force prepared to handle whatever hostile situation they were sent into, they handled security aboard ship. They posted sentries at all points of ingress and egress whenever the ship was docked at stations, or with other ships, and maintained roving patrols on a 24/7 basis. They ran the security office and responded to reports of fights, theft, and anything criminal occurring aboard ship. Marine Captain Galont had majored in criminology at the Academy. The tall, good-looking officer felt confident of his ability to handle this case.

"Yes, Captain?" Galont responded.

"As Chief of Security, you have primary responsibility for finding Petty Officer Nichols' killer."

"Yes, Captain. I'll find whoever did this."

"Very good. I want you to keep me informed of any developments through Lieutenant Ashraf."

"Aye, Captain."

Jenetta nodded, turned, and began the passage back to her briefing room on the bridge, but she couldn't get the image of Petty Officer Nichols' broken body out of her mind. Killing during time of war, or to protect one's own life, she could understand, but to take another life because of a poker game was— irrational.

* * *

It was just after noon, Galactic System Time, at Higgins Space Command Base when Admiral Brian Devon Holt's senior aide interrupted the two-star admiral's lunch to notify him of a Priority-One message from Captain Gavin. The seventy-one-year-old officer dropped the salad fork he was using and gulped down the antipasto already in his mouth. Jumping up from the table in his private dining room like an officer half his age, he rushed back to his office and selected the communication from among the prioritized list of messages that scrolled up on his desktop com unit. He watched intently as the image of the most respected captain in his command filled the viewscreen.

By the time the message had finished, Holt's color had paled appreciably. He immediately summoned his senior aide.

"Willem, activate the Combat Information Center. I'm raising the Station Defense status to War Active. Notify the captains of all GSC warships in port that there will be a CIC vidConference in thirty minutes. Prepare a message to all private and commercial traffic in the port that an attack from Raiders is imminent. We strongly recommend that all civilian ships depart as soon as possible and not attempt to return until the outcome is known. Prepare another to notify all inbound traffic that Higgins is presently closed and they should not approach closer than ten day's travel time until we meet this threat. But don't send either until I've approved them. I'll be in the CIC."

"Aye, Admiral," his aide said as he began keying in commands on his com unit. In seconds, crewmen around the station were racing towards the CIC, while others were notifying their captains of the station's upgraded defense status and the vidConference timetable. All off-duty personnel were immediately summoned to their duty posts aboard ship or on the station via emergency recall messages delivered through their CT or ID. Base personnel had never been summoned in such a manner and none wasted time trying to confirm the orders or offer explanations for their hasty departures. Unenlightened merchants on the concourse were left staring open-mouthed at empty chairs in restaurants and empty aisles in retail stores as shopping areas evacuated in mere seconds.

The CIC was illuminated and gearing up quickly when Admiral Holt arrived. NCOs and crewmen were busy removing protective covers from seldom-used equipment, flipping power switches, and performing perfunctory tests. The room had never been used for a real crisis during Admiral Holt's tour of duty, but every piece of equipment was tested and certified by engineering techs each month.

The base commander's station was among the first activated and Admiral Holt climbed into the comfortable chair, settling his imposing frame as he organized his thoughts and waited for the vidConference time. He knew Gavin would never have sent that Priority-One message unless he was damned sure of his facts and he was painfully aware that the station's protection was at minimal strength right now. The final decision to pull eight ships from their normal patrol duties and send them off for participation in the attack on the Raiders attempting to hijack the relics from Mawcett had been his alone.

As the vidConference time neared, the captains of the five warships currently serving as protection for Higgins Space Command Base logged in. A head-and-shoulders image of each commanding officer sitting in his or her briefing room aboard their ship joined the others on the huge monitor at the front of the CIC's main room until all ships were represented. Each ship would be receiving a similar display, which showed all other commanding officers participating in the vid discussion. Text beneath each image identified other, unseen senior officers presently in the captain's briefing room to receive the news. At the very least, each ship's XO was present to learn the situation. The CIC was fully populated by the officers and specialists assigned to staff the center during a crises when Admiral Holt began to speak.

"Welcome, Captains," the admiral said as the last to log in joined the vidConference. "I've received the gravest of news today. You've all been briefed with details of the recent battle that took place between our forces and the Raiders near the planet Vauzlee. While examining encrypted documents found on the body of a dead Raider officer, our people have uncovered plans outlining an imminent and massive attack on Higgins."

Captain William E. Payton of the battleship *Thor* was the first to speak. The fifty-nine-year-old senior officer appeared deceptively calm as he gazed through limpid blue eyes and asked, "How massive, Admiral?"

"Most of the Raider ships participating in that attack on the convoy of relics had orders to depart as soon as the shipment was secured. They were to travel to an undisclosed rendezvous location where they would join another force assembling for the assault on this station. We know forty-one ships attacked the freighter and convoy protection ships, but we have no idea how many other Raider ships have been assigned to this planned attack. I doubt the Raiders would underestimate our resolve to defend this base. I wish I could give you a number, but without additional intel it would just be the wildest of guesses."

"Admiral," Captain Payton said, "Considering their monumental losses at that recent battle, are we sure there's even going to be an attack?"

"An excellent question. We're sure of nothing right now, Bill, except that the Raiders apparently *were* planning to attack us. To what degree their plans will be affected by the near total destruction of their convoy attack force, I can't say. Only seven ships of the forty-one involved in that conflict managed to escape from the battle zone, but we must assume they rendezvoused with whatever force has been tasked to attack us and are now on their way here."

"What preparations are being made to protect the civilians in and around the station, Admiral?" Captain Simon H. Pope of the destroyer *Geneva* asked.

"Within the hour, all commercial traffic that has identified Higgins as a stop or final destination on their flight plans will be advised to find a place along their course where they can halt their vessel and await the outcome of the attack. All freighters and passenger liners in orbit around the base will be advised to depart as soon as possible and seek a place of relative safety. All cargo farms will be transported to a more distant location so the area around the station is clear for battle. Civilians currently housed in the station will be offered transportation down to the planet with non-essential military personnel. I haven't yet spoken to the officials on Vinnia but I'm sure they'll help as much as possible in finding temporary living quarters for the displaced civilians and military personnel if the resources of our ground base at Wytrell are incapable of housing everyone."

"How many other ships can we depend upon to bolster our forces here?" Captain Beverly P. Wong of the *Buenos Aires* asked.

"Captain Gavin learned of the intended attack around 0300 this morning. He immediately had Captain Powers awakened. Following a brief vidConference, both the *Prometheus* and *Chiron* departed for Higgins. Just before they left the site of the battle, Captain Gavin sent Priority-One messages to the other ships' captains. Those messages instructed the captains of five ships to get underway for Higgins just as quickly as they could secure for travel. Two ships that had not yet fully tested their repaired systems were ordered to remain and secure the battle zone until the reclamation ships arrive. The ships coming to assist us are the heavy cruiser *Song*, and destroyers *Lima*, *Vancouver*, *Dublin*, and *Calcutta*. All ships on patrol in this deca-sector will also drop everything and return to the base, but none may be close enough to join us before the Raiders strike."

"Excuse me, sir," Captain Wong said, "but wasn't it stated in the battle briefing that the *Song* suffered severe structural damage and had lost her entire senior staff?"

"Yes, that's correct, Bev."

"Then what kind of shape is she in? Is she even battle worthy? And perhaps even more importantly, who's in command of the ship now, sir?"

"Captain Gavin, in his capacity as senior officer at the conflict, appointed Lt. Commander Carver to serve as Captain of the *Song* on a pro tempore basis."

"Lt. Commander Carver? Jenetta Carver?"

"Yes."

"She's been appointed Captain of the *Song*? But she was just an ensign until two months ago!"

"Following her promotion to Lt. Commander, she was posted as second officer aboard the *Prometheus*. Since the battleship was without a first officer until Commander

Genevieve LaSalle reports aboard when it reaches Earth, she was serving as acting XO. With the deaths of the *Song's* entire senior staff, Captain Gavin needed someone to immediately take command of the cruiser, determine the condition of the ship, restore a proper command structure, and commence repairs. Commander Carver was the only available officer with warship command experience."

"Command experience, sir? Surely her being named as the first commanding officer of the *Prometheus* was merely an honorific for having recovered the ship."

"True," Admiral Holt said, nodding. "But the fact remains that she did captain the ship for almost five months. During that time she also functioned as the convoy leader for the Terran and Nordakian freighters, and the other battleship. I realize her crew size was extremely limited on that voyage, but she's done a wonderful job as acting XO on board the *Prometheus* since reporting aboard. And within twelve hours of taking command of the severely damaged *Song*, she had restored order, assembled a complete bridge staff, and begun systematic repair of the damage. Because she did so well, Captain Gavin made the decision to have her remain in command of the *Song* until it reached Earth. When information regarding the planned attack on this base came to his attention, there wasn't time to make other arrangements."

"But she's *just* a Lt. Commander, sir, and a recently appointed one at that. She's not experienced enough to command a heavy cruiser in a battle such as the one we might now be facing."

Admiral Holt's once jet-black hair may have turned prematurely grey, but he was physically fit and still as sharp as they come. Holt felt he knew the real reason for Captain Wong's concern. Newly promoted line officer captains in Space Command normally received a destroyer for their first command. Based on their evaluated performance in that capacity, they might then be advanced to successively more responsible commands as ships became available. The normal advancement was to frigate, then cruiser, then battleship if such commands opened up before they reached mandatory space retirement age or retired from the service, but once they had received their first command, they could possibly skip command levels. Beverly Wong was currently the most senior destroyer Captain in Space Command and had been named by COAC to move up to a more responsible command when a ship became available. But the overwhelming percentage of warships in the Space Command fleet were destroyers, making such advancement agonizingly slow for ambitious officers. While Lt. Commander Carver was captaining a cruiser, Captain Wong was prevented from advancing, even if her advancement was only to a frigate after the frigate captain at the top of the COAC list for upgrade moved up to the *Song*.

"Beverly, Commander Carver was the only line officer with command experience available at the engagement who didn't presently have a command, so she was the logical choice for appointment to Captain the *Song*. She's now fought in four engagements with the Raiders, not counting her escape from, and destruction of, a Raider base. I'm sure I don't have to remind you that her combat record includes more engagements with enemy vessels while functioning as the ship's commanding officer than any of the distinguished Captains present. The crew of the *Vordoth* nicknamed her the 'Ice Queen' for her supreme coolness under fire. Don't underestimate her ability and capacity for command just because she doesn't yet have four gold bars on each shoulder. But— for your information, Captain Gavin has already informed Commander Carver that an experienced senior staff will be waiting to take command of the ship as soon as the *Song* arrives here and that she'll transfer back to the *Prometheus* at that time. Does that ease your mind?"

Admiral Holt knew it wouldn't, not really. Whether the temporary commanding officer of the *Song* was a commander or a lieutenant commander made no difference in the ultimate ship assignment rotation. Given the imminence of the expected attack, a change in the command structure that could adversely affect the performance of *two* crews during a critical time would not even be contemplated, so Beverly Wong would *not* be given command of the *Song* when it arrived, temporary appointment or not. Until Supreme HQ confirmed a permanent appointment recommendation by COAC, Beverly wouldn't move up.

"Uh, yes, sir." Senior officers didn't reach senior rank by being insensitive to the tone of responses from commanding officers. Captain Wong suspected the Admiral might be feeling some slight irritation over what could be perceived as personal interests in her question, although she firmly believed her main concern was the competency of fellow officers during a critical time. She decided that an apology of sorts was in order. "I didn't mean to question your judgment regarding temporary field appointments, sir."

"I understand and appreciate your concerns, Beverly. Although I agree with Captain Gavin's recommendation that a new senior staff assume command as soon as the ship arrives, I personally have full confidence in Commander Carver's ability to command a ship in battle. If she had an experienced senior staff aboard, I might even be tempted to let her remain in command until the Commanding Officer Appointment Committee names the *Song*'s new captain. I tend to prefer a known quantity over an unknown under circumstances as grave as we now face."

"How soon do you expect to have your defense plans ready, sir?" Captain Hoyt asked.

"The facts, as we know them, dictate that we use Station Defense Plan Echo-Three as our opening stratagem. All ships will align in an arc formation between the station and the attackers fifty thousand kilometers out once we pick up their movements on our long-range sensor net. We'll hold position until the Raiders advance and then engage them as soon as they're in range. As the Raiders press their attack, our ships will fall back and protect that segment of the station assigned to them to the best of their ability. We're far from helpless here, but the designers of this station didn't make provisions for defending it against a full battle armada. With our great size, and having no mobility to speak of, we'll be relying on you to help knock down torpedoes directed at us. The docking ring will naturally be evacuated as soon as the

Raiders are spotted and all airtight doors in the station will be closed. Since the CIC is located in the heart of the station and we're surrounded by several bulkheads of reinforced tritanium, we should be able to remain in communication to the end."

"Whose end?" Captain Payton asked rhetorically.

"That's the question that'll keep a lot of us awake tonight, Bill," Admiral Holt responded.

*   *   *

Marine Captain Galont sat in the small conference room adjoining his office in the *Song's* security center listening to the reports from his officers. To this point, his people had mainly been concentrating on finding the murder weapon used to kill Petty Officer Nichols. They hadn't had any luck in that endeavor and Galont was taking the failure personally. He had told the Captain he would find the killer and he felt like he was letting her down.

Galont was a Marine's Marine, gung ho from the soles of his titanium-toed boots to the tips of his closely cropped light brown hair. Plenty of time spent in the ship's gym and weight room gave his six-foot-one-inch body the muscular look of a professional body-builder. His rugged good looks had always made him popular with the ladies and at thirty-eight years of age he was still in top form. One intense look from his jade-green eyes had always been all it took to stir interest in many a potential sexual partner.

Like virtually everyone else on board, Galont had watched the court-martial of Lt. Commander, then Ensign, Jenetta Carver from beginning to end. He hadn't believed for a second that such a tiny officer, and a female at that, could have done even half the incredible things being credited to her by the newsies prior to the trial. He'd decided early on that it was all hype designed to sell more newspapers or magazines, thus increasing their market share and bringing in more advertising revenue. But his mind was slowly changed as he watched the prosecution's poor attempts to tear down Ensign Carver's story. His enlightenment hadn't occurred merely because the prosecutor seemed to be badgering a beautiful and seemingly helpless young woman forced to sit in prisoner transport chains during the early hours of the trial. His mindset had changed as he listened closely to the testimony— testimony repeated endlessly owing to almost constant objections by the prosecution. When Ensign Carver was finally allowed to step down from the witness stand after twenty-two grueling days of testimony and cross-examination, Galont was firmly convinced the charges against her were absurd. She should never, ever, have been formally charged. And before any of the other witnesses had even been called he was absolutely certain she had done every one of the incredible things with which she was being credited. The image logs from the *Vordoth*, while showing her expert leadership during battle with the two Raider ships, highlighted her coolness under fire. The image logs from the *Prometheus* that showed the explosion of the Raider base had even the most intransigent critics cheering like madmen for the young Ensign.

When eyewitnesses testified to the veracity of the accounts offered by Ensign Carver in the courtroom, Galont had watched their faces closely. He *knew* those people weren't lying. They meant every word they said and no face ever projected greater respect for another person than when they looked over at Carver sitting at the defense table. By the end of the trial, Galont was sure Ensign Carver wasn't a beautiful, helpless young woman caught up in a series of events that seemed to stretch the boundaries of credulity. She was a beautiful, highly competent young GSC officer with the intelligence and force of will to accomplish the jobs she tackled and the innate ability to garner the loyalty and respect of those around her while inspiring them to do more and do it better than they ever thought they could. All too often, Space Marines were commanded by senior GSC officers who discharged their duties like effete dilettantes. They had climbed through the ranks during times of peace and prosperity, their battle skills untested. Few were strong, charismatic leaders of fighting forces. Carver was different. She knew judo and kick-boxing, and despite her diminutive size, had killed an enemy guard in unarmed combat. She could have been a Marine officer. She was the type of gung-ho Space Command officer every Marine hopes to have as their ship commander but so seldom does. It was unfortunate she was merely an Ensign.

And then, suddenly, Ensign Jenetta Carver reported aboard the *Song* to take command of the ship. But now she was Lt. Commander Jenetta Carver. Galont could hardly believe the news when Sergeant Korby reported seeing her on A Deck. His first act was to contact the *Prometheus* and speak to the Marine officer in charge of security there. He learned that, yes, this was the same officer who had been court-martialed, and yes, she had been advanced three grades, and yes, she was the second officer and acting XO on the *Prometheus*. Captain Gavin had sent her to the *Song* to restore the command structure aboard the stricken ship.

"Don't get any ideas about her remaining aboard," Major Adrian Visconti had told him, jokingly. "We need her here. We don't have either a first, second, *or* third officer aboard now. She's only there to bail your sorry asses out of a serious jam and then we want her back."

But Carver hadn't returned to the *Prometheus*. She had remained aboard the *Song* until emergency repairs were completed and then was ordered to take the ship to Earth, which meant she would be aboard for months. Galont didn't know if it was owed to her presence or the fact that the entire command structure aboard ship had been shaken up, but he knew there was a new vitality in the crew. Part of it was no doubt due to the new responsibilities heaped upon the shoulders of junior officers. They were being given a chance to show what they could do and they were busting their back-sides to impress their commanding officer with their abilities. But even the rest of the crew had shaped up.

Carver had driven everyone hard to get the ship repaired, back into fighting trim, and ready for the return to Earth, but nobody was complaining. She hadn't held them to any higher standard than the one she held for herself. She was out of her quarters by 0700 every morning and rarely returned, except for meals, before midnight. She might not know the name of every crewman on board, but she certainly knew both the first and last names of all her officers and NCOs. She'd spent her days during the repair time learning every square meter of the ship through her inspections and had even suited up several times to inspect the exterior hull while it was being patched. Galont had never even *heard* of another commanding officer who had done that. It wasn't that Carver didn't trust the engineers to do a proper job; she had proven time and time again that she did. No, Galont believed she wanted her people to know there was no place she would send them that she was unprepared to go herself and nothing she would ask them to do that she wasn't prepared to do herself. Galont had no intention of letting her down by not finding Nichols' killer.

"...and, of the hundreds of items found that are the approximate size, shape, and weight of the murder weapon, all have been discounted after laboratory analysis," Marine First Lt. Baccaron said as he wrapped up his report. "We've sealed the containers we've searched so nothing new can be added to them until we find the weapon."

Galont leaned back in his chair and stared at the overhead for a minute. Following the example of the Captain, he had recently donned a tox-suit and respirator and climbed into the garbage with his people to show he wasn't asking anything of them that he wasn't prepared to do himself. It seemed to him that he had seen a greater respect in their eyes since then. "I suppose it would have been too easy to find the murder weapon in the waste disposal system, but I can't believe the murderer would hang onto a piece of evidence that could send him or her to a penal colony for life. I'm sure the Old Lady won't let us tear apart the quarters of any crewmember unless we have a reasonable suspicion he's our man, so we'll tear apart everything else aboard this ship instead. I want to make sure the only place the killer could have hidden his weapon was among his personal effects. And when we find him, he'd better still have it if we don't."

Chapter Eleven
~ April 24th, 2268 ~

Knowing significant personnel reassignments were intended once the ship reached Higgins didn't stop Jenetta from proceeding with a vigorous training schedule for the officers and crew of the *Song*. She immediately established an aggressive program of unannounced GQ drills and kept the *Song* crew at it until every crewmember could find his or her way to their newly assigned battle station while still half asleep.

At the same time, she worked to see that everyone on board qualified as a laser gunner. Not everyone would qualify as 'Expert,' but any cook or stores clerk could jump in and take over for an injured gunner if absolutely necessary. No one was exempted except the medical staff, which would probably have more than enough to do during a fight. However, she even allowed *them* to participate in the training schedule on a limited basis if they really desired to 'get the feel' for the weapons that brought them so much work during a battle. Although it was always expected that some torpedoes would get through in a major engagement, she intended to raise the gunnery skills to such a level as to make the defensive perimeter as impenetrable as possible. The recent battle had shown that the skills of the *Song* gunners were lacking. Five torpedoes had struck the ship, compared to just two having struck the *Prometheus*. Granted, the *Prometheus* had more defensive weapons, but it also presented a much larger target and was in the battle for a longer time. The *Song* was fortunate the strikes had occurred in areas with the heaviest armor plating. It was just inauspicious fortune that a second torpedo struck at almost the precise location as one that had previously ripped away armor on A Deck.

The third phase of Jenetta's training effort was directed specifically towards the command officers on the ship. Although it was rarely employed for that purpose, the Auxiliary Control & Communications center could be utilized for bridge simulation activities, either to recreate an incident under investigation or to train command officers in much the same way they were trained at the Academy, WCI, and the War College. It was generally felt by most ships' captains that junior officers had already received all the training they needed and that actually working their watches on the bridge would give them the practical knowledge they'd need for ascent to command. Jenetta felt a continuous program of emergency and battle training should be a regular part of every bridge officer's duty schedule, just as the Marine fighter pilots were required to complete an established number of hours each month in a flight simulator. The simulations also provided her with an opportunity to evaluate the people in her command, enabling her to learn their strengths and weaknesses. Lieutenant Ashraf and Lieutenant Elizi supervised the training for all command officers, as well as each other.

"I saw the results of your simulation from yesterday, Lori," Jenetta mentioned to Lieutenant Ashraf as they held their regular daily meeting in Jenetta's briefing room.

"Katherine laid it on pretty thick," Ashraf said, grinning. "When the uncharted asteroid didn't faze me and I managed to suppress the fire in the cargo hold, she hit me with a level-one containment failure aboard an unoccupied shuttle parked in Flight Operations Bay Two. I had just twenty seconds to remotely tap into the shuttle's control systems and disengage the magnetic skid locks, cut the gravity in the bay, open the doors, and hope the shuttle floated out from the decompression."

"But it didn't."

"No, it didn't. The shuttle jammed sideways in the entranceway and a huge section of my ship was destroyed. What would you have done, Captain?"

"The same thing," Jenetta said, smiling. "You have to remember that not all simulation scenarios can be resolved satisfactorily. None of us enjoy losing our ship in a simulation, but even problems without a satisfactory solution teach us valuable lessons. They make us think and prepare us for almost any eventuality. Along the way we learn to remain calm in the face of danger. Losing your calm, whether to anger or fear, is the absolute worst thing you can let happen because your ability to reason clearly and objectively is lost along with it."

"Yes, Captain."

"Has Major Galont made any progress with his investigation into the death of Petty Officer Nichols?"

"He's following up on leads."

"Does that imply he has no suspects yet?"

"I'm afraid so. He hasn't even found a motive for the killing. Petty Officer Nichols was apparently very well liked. His only vice was gambling. He'd gamble on almost anything at the drop of a hat—sports, cards, dice, lottery, racing—it made no difference. Galont is trying to find out if Nichols owed anyone enough for them to kill him or if anyone owed him enough to try to avoid paying up. Galont says most murders can be solved by concentrating on the three basic issues of MOM."

"Mom?"

"Motive, Opportunity, and Means. The doctor pegged the time of death at 2345 hours, give or take five minutes. Galont suspects Nichols might have been gambling with someone who had to report for third watch duty and an argument broke out over credits owed, or perhaps it was a dispute over who won the game. The storage room where Nichols' body was found is reputed to have been a favored gambling spot of his. The location is remote enough that crewmembers could go there with little fear of being seen entering or leaving. Since there's nothing of significant value or danger stored there, the door is never locked."

"So Opportunity is wide open," Jenetta said. "Practically everyone on board had an opportunity to be there alone with Nichols."

"Essentially. As to Means, Major Galont hasn't found the murder weapon yet. Suspecting it might have been disposed of in a waste chute, he's had all his Marines sifting through the contents of the waste containers looking for anything that could have been used."

"Yuck. I certainly don't envy them that job."

"Nor do I. When they didn't find anything there, they sealed the inspected containers and began a systematic search of every escape pod, storeroom, cargo hold, locker, closet, and tool box. They've removed vent covers and put bots inside to crawl around and search for anything that might have been used as the weapon, then hidden. All engineering spaces and access tunnels have been thoroughly searched. Galont wants to solve this in the worst way. It turns out he knows Nichols' family. They grew up on the same GSC base and their fathers are friends. Nichols didn't get into the Academy because of truancy problems in high school. He reportedly headed to the racetrack whenever he could sneak away. And he should have made CPO long ago, but his gambling addiction kept him on Captain Corriano's bad side."

"Captain Corriano may have feared putting too much trust in someone who might let him down in a pinch. Addictions of any sort tend to make people undependable. And gambling debt can make a person untrustworthy. Space Command will downgrade the security clearance of anyone who owes a lot of money, even for legitimate reasons, because they might be tempted to sell information or perform traitorous tasks for our enemies."

"Nichols had the gambling sickness alright, but I never knew it to affect his performance. While on duty, he was all business. His finances weren't the best, but he had a decent balance in his credits account. Galont checked that early on. There have been no large deposits or withdrawals recently."

"Did anyone leave the ship between the time Nichols was killed and the time we departed for Higgins?"

"No, ma'am. Major Galont checked that immediately. The killer has to still be aboard. Three engineers did go outside to work on a sensor but all returned when ordered by Cmdr. Rodriguez. Witnesses state that none of the engineers were carrying anything that could have been the murder weapon, so it wasn't disposed of while they were outside. Airlock vid logs confirm that."

"I assume he checked for fingerprints and had the room vacuumed for evidence?"

"Yes. A housekeeping bot had cleaned the room that morning, so all the collected material had to be from the day of the murder. Galont said they found skin flecks, hairs, or fingerprints for eight individuals besides Nichols himself and the doctor. That's not conclusive though. He didn't find any from you or I, and we were both there following the murder. Each of the eight crewmembers had a valid reason for entering the storage room during their watch that day."

"So we're still at square one," Jenetta said. "Any of the twenty-one hundred crewmen on board could be the guilty party."

"I'm afraid so, Captain."

*　*　*

Admiral Bradlee took a deep breath and expelled it quickly and loudly. "This is extremely distressing news," he said to the other nine admirals seated at the large horseshoe-shaped table in the Admiralty Board Meeting Hall at Supreme Head-quarters on Earth. They had just viewed the initial report filed by Captain Gavin in which he apprised them of the recently discovered message about a planned attack on Higgins.

"Especially coming on the heels of such a great victory over the Raiders," Admiral Ressler said.

"Great victory? We lost an entire ship and most of its crew," Admiral Hubera said. Then added, "Thanks to Ensign Carver."

"Donald, we've already discussed that at length," Admiral Hillaire said. "There is no way a case can be made for laying *any* blame at the feet of *Lt. Commander* Carver."

Using his right index finger to pointedly poke the table in front of him for emphasis as he spoke, Hubera said, "Captain Gavin ignored a first-rate attack plan developed by our best minds at the War College and followed one that he credited Carver with developing, didn't he, Arnold?"

"Yes, he did," Admiral Hillaire admitted as he leaned comfortably back in his chair. "And the strategy was brilliant. The proof is that we saved the convoy while destroying thirty-four Raider warships. The *Delhi* was not lost in battle, Donald. It was lost following the battle when a frightened Raider captain tried to run away and engaged his sub-light engines before checking to see if he had clear space ahead. That could have occurred no matter whose battle plan was being followed."

"Peabody lost over five hundred crewmen and we lost nine hundred twenty-seven," Admiral Hubera said doggedly.

"We, *this board*, made the decision to allow the convoy to be bait for the Raiders, not Lt. Commander Carver. And the Raider fleet lost fifteen thousand, six hundred seventy-one crew members, most of whom were killed in battle."

"And now Captain Gavin has appointed Carver to captain the *Song*," Hubera persisted.

"He's following his orders," Admiral Hillaire said. "After this board decided to promote Carver and place her aboard the *Prometheus* as the second officer, I contacted Admiral Holt and asked him to see that Carver had opportunities to show what she's capable of. He passed that request on to Captain Gavin, who appointed Carver as Captain of the *Song* because of her command experience. I also requested that the senior SCI officer in that deca-sector, Commander Kanes, prepare a full evaluation of Commander Carver's time since graduation from NHSA. You probably recall that he worked with the JAG office to develop the prosecution's case for the Carver court-martial.

"I admit that having Carver become Captain of the *Song* is a bit beyond what I had intended, but according to Captain Gavin's reports she's done an outstanding job aboard the *Prometheus* as acting XO, and now she's done an excellent job of getting the *Song*'s command reorganized after the entire senior staff was killed. She's even managed to get the ship fully operational again after it withdrew from battle before the fight was over as the result of a crippling torpedo onslaught."

Admiral Hubera was listening with keen interest, but saying nothing.

"Why did you make such a request of Admiral Holt, Arnold?" Admiral Moore asked.

"Instead of establishing a career path for Carver that would first see her attend the Warship Command Institute and then have her posted to a line officer position, we at the Academy steered her into becoming an astrophysicist. While I sincerely hope Carver is the only officer whom we've failed to evaluate properly, I can't help but wonder if there were other superior command officers who were directed away from that career path because of our misjudgment. Oh, we all knew Carver was a brilliant student at the Academy; she has a particular genius for mathematics and science. On IQ tests that didn't require rapid response, she always scored in the genius range. She would excel at almost any task assigned her. But we misconstrued just how much her superior intelligence affected her performance in command and control exercises. What we perceived as indecisiveness was apparently a natural tendency to evaluate every detail in the extreme. She was over-analyzing every scenario. We should have been teaching her how to proceed with her first instincts, but instead, we simply gave up on her and directed her to a career path in astrophysics that allowed her as much deliberation as she desired. Fortunately for us, she somehow gleaned the ability to make the split-second decisions required of a command officer on her own. I was hoping that by closely monitoring her performance I could determine what it was that made her change so remarkably."

"And have you learned what you sought?"

"I believe so. We're convinced that finding herself in real danger was responsible for the metamorphosis. As real as our command and control simulations at the Academy are, they never impart a sense of real danger— the belief that anyone's life is truly on the line. You might feel a sense of anxiety or nervousness but never real fear. We've been discussing the creation of a special testing program for individuals of superior intelligence who appear indecisive. During their third year they would participate in an off-world exercise that would lead to them realistically being cut-off from command. Of course, we would be monitoring them constantly, but they wouldn't know we were watching or realize they were in no real danger. They would believe they were really facing death. Then we would evaluate their efforts to survive."

"Is there any further need for Gavin to extend special opportunities to Carver?" Admiral Moore asked.

"No, none. I've thanked Admiral Holt for his assistance and informed him that I don't require further special considerations for Carver. We'll continue to monitor her performance closely though. She's an exceptional young officer and bears watching."

"What are we going to do about her right now?" Admiral Platt asked. "She's still in command of a heavy cruiser. I can't help but wonder what effect that's going to have on senior officers looking to advance their careers through progressively responsible command opportunities."

"More importantly," Admiral Hubera said, "she's now taking the *Song* into battle as the ship's captain. She's too inexperienced and too immature for such an important role."

"I'm sure our senior officers will recognize the temporary nature of her command and the valid reasons for her appointment," Admiral Moore said. "And, as Captain Gavin said in his report, a new senior staff will be waiting to take command of the *Song* as soon as it reaches Higgins."

"If it reaches Higgins," Admiral Hubera said.

"What do you mean by that?" Admiral Hillaire asked.

"The last time she captained a ship headed for Higgins, she decided to take a few side trips first."

"Now Donald," Admiral Platt said, "those deviations from course were necessary and justified. She saved the Nordakian convoy, didn't she?"

"Evelyn, she merely surprised the crew of a Raider cruiser and destroyed them before they even knew she was attacking."

"Making maximum use of the element of surprise against a declared enemy," Admiral Moore said, "has always been, and will always be, a fundamental part of sound military strategy. I think we've belabored this topic enough, Donald. We have a great deal more to discuss. Lt. Commander Carver will be replaced by a more seasoned officer as soon as she reaches Higgins, and I feel confident she won't deviate from her course. She knows the importance of getting her ship there as expeditiously as possible. Now, what are we going to do about defending Higgins?"

"I'm sure Admiral Holt will use his forces to their best advantage," Admiral Hillaire said. "The seven ships from the recent battle will bolster their strength considerably when they arrive."

"The point I was attempting to make before we again got sidetracked onto a discussion about Commander Carver," Admiral Bradlee said, "was that an attack like this on a Space Command StratCom-1 base has to mean the Raiders intend to reassert themselves in that deca-sector in a major way. They've never attacked a base before and they wouldn't be taking such an aggressive stance now if they weren't confident in their ability to achieve dominance there. We can't forget that both the *Prometheus* and *Chiron* have only a minimal fighting force on board. Their new crews are still assembling here at Earth. Their present fighting effectiveness is less than one half what it should be. But that's only a concern if they arrive in time. If the Raiders attack within the next twenty days, there may not be a Higgins base to defend when they arrive."

"Our nearest warship," Admiral Platt said, "excluding the seven from the site of the recent battle, is forty-nine days away at maximum speed. Captain Gavin's message to all warships within the deca-sector will have caused them to drop everything and proceed to Higgins at top speed. There's nothing more we can do. Everything might hinge on how many ships the Raiders are able to muster for this operation."

"Given the time they've had to plan and prepare for this attack," Admiral Bradlee said, "and understanding the importance to them of its successful conclusion, I believe they'll throw every fighting vessel at us they can muster. I pray to God our forces will be victorious, but we should begin making plans to retake and hold the sector if they're not. How many ships can we pull from other sectors to replace those we'll lose at Higgins, and what resources can we commit for constructing a replacement station?"

"I think that's a little premature, Roger," Admiral Ahmed said.

"We must have contingency plans in place, Raihana," he said, "much as I wish it wasn't necessary."

"Roger is correct," Admiral Moore said. "Although we desperately hope they won't be needed, we must have contingency plans in place." Turning to his aide, he gave a couple of quick instructions, then turned back to the officers at the table. "While we're waiting for Admiral Acheson of the Corps of Engineers, let's finish up the rest of our business. We must make a final decision on the proposed expansion of the administrative center on Hawking Space Command Base. All in favor?"

*   *   *

"Admiral Nazeer is seeking confirmation that we wish to proceed with the attack," Councilwoman Overgaard said as she read the next item on the Lower Council's meeting agenda, "given the fact that his forces will be thirty ships short of the expected task force size and that the Spaccs seem to have learned of the planned attack."

"Of course I want him to proceed," Chairman Gagarin said angrily. "Our agent on the base reports that it's being guarded by just five Spacc ships, just as I planned. We know the other ships are weeks away, still licking their wounds at the site of the battle. Even without the ships that were destroyed, his task force is more than adequate to destroy the base and bring that deca-sector completely under our control. How much of an edge does he want?"

"I'm sure he feels confident in his ability to crush the Spacc forces," she said. "He just wants to confirm his orders in light of the changes in tactical asset availability and Higgins' preparedness."

"Just how many ships does he need to crush the minimal force at Higgins?" Gagarin shouted.

Overgaard ignored the rhetorical question and took a sip of tea. She knew Gagarin was feeling pressure from the Upper Council, and he was becoming more and more irrational with each passing day. He'd had operational responsibility for the attack on the convoy and now the attack on Higgins. Another sensational failure might forever end his steady climb through the ranks and his goal of ascension to the Upper Council. The powerful people who sat on the Upper Council weren't the sort to forgive and forget.

"Strauss, what's happening with your plan to assassinate Carver?" Gagarin asked.

"We've made contact with our operative on the ship. In exchange for the credits and a few other minor consider- ations, we've been assured Carver's death will be the dramatic and violent event you seek."

"But *when* is it going to happen?"

"Just as soon as our operative can arrange it. I remind you that you can't spend a million credits if you're sitting in a penal colony for the rest of your life. There must be an escape route open before the attempt is made. Be patient and it will happen."

"It had better happen soon, for your sake."

* * *

"Captain," Jenetta heard through her desktop com unit when she lifted the cover and saw the image of Lieutenant Risco, "Major Galont would like to speak with you." Risco, as acting third officer, was senior officer on the bridge whenever Jenetta was working in her briefing room.

"Send him in, Lieutenant."

A moment later the computer announced Galont's presence at the door.

"Come," Jenetta said as she finished reading a report and placed the holo-tube down on her desk.

"Good afternoon, Captain," the Marine officer said as he braced to attention in front of her desk.

"Good afternoon, Major. Stand easy. Do you have something new to report regarding your investigation?"

"Not exactly, ma'am. I'm sure Lieutenant Ashraf has kept you informed of our progress."

"She has. She tells me you've made very little."

"That's true, unfortunately. Since I've been unable to develop a list of likely suspects, I'm now attempting to narrow the field a bit by developing lists of 'unlikely' and 'highly-unlikely' suspects."

"What criteria are you using?"

"Anyone who was on duty at the time of the murder and whose presence can be corroborated by at least two other crewmen is being placed on the highly-unlikely list. Anyone whose presence on duty can only be corroborated by one person is being placed on the unlikely list. The same holds true for anyone who was off-duty and whose presence is corroborated by at least two others. Almost everyone else remains on the suspect list."

"That sounds like a sensible plan."

"From an investigation standpoint, it was fortunate the murder occurred during the second watch. The number of personnel on third watch drops precipitously."

"Yes. And now you're here to hear my alibi?"

"Uh— yes, Captain."

"I was in my quarters. But since I was alone, I have no one to corroborate my presence there. However, my steward keeps pretty good track of my movements when I'm there, so he might vouch for my assumed presence."

"Yes, I've already spoken to him, and he did." Galont knew he was treading dangerous ground. He couldn't make even the slightest suggestion that the ship's captain was involved unless he had solid proof that she was. His questioning of her was a mere formality anyway. He knew she could never have gone to the location where the murder was committed without someone seeing her along the way. Other crewmembers could wander the corridors at night without anyone paying them much attention, but the passage of the ship's captain anywhere but on A Deck at that hour would be remembered. And her steward should have known if she'd left her quarters. "Did you know Petty Officer Nichols, Captain?"

"I encountered him several times during my inspections of the ship. I only spoke with him once, though. He seemed personable and intelligent. Naturally I viewed his personnel record when I took command, as I did for every other member of the crew."

"Had you ever met him before boarding the *Song*, heard about him, or read anything about him?"

"No. Not to the best of my recollection."

"Thank you, Captain. Since your steward corroborates your alibi and you've only been aboard the ship for a short time, an incredibly busy time at that, I'm placing you on the 'highly unlikely' list."

"How many crewmembers do you have on the 'unlikely' and 'highly-unlikely' lists?"

"Thirteen hundred seven with your name added there."

"That's about two-thirds of the crew. You've made good progress after all, Major."

"Thank you, Captain. But it still leaves seven hundred ninety-four on the 'suspect' list, and you're the last to be interviewed. The murderer was quite clever. He didn't leave behind a single clue we could zero in on."

"Don't get discouraged. Criminals always slip up somewhere. Something will turn up."

"Aye, Captain. I just hope we catch him before he strikes again."

"Again?"

"Yes, ma'am. I originally thought the murder might have occurred because third watch was about to begin and the murderer had to leave, either before the game was over or perhaps over a dispute about credits owed when it was time to settle up."

"But you no longer think that?"

"No ma'am. I changed my opinion once I'd had time for a thorough examination of the facts. The playing cards scattered around the body made it appear that they had fallen during a struggle. But I discovered later, when his body was removed, that there were no cards beneath it, indicating they had been scattered around the body after Nichols was down. It's possible he wasn't even playing cards. And then there's the murder weapon. Nothing stored in that room could have made the wounds to Nichols' arm and head. The murderer must have brought the weapon with him. That suggests premeditation. While almost anyone can kill during a period of high emotion or stress, only someone who has come to grips with the moral aspects of cold-blooded murder can kill with premeditation. That person, having once done the deed and not gotten caught, will have less aversion to killing again."

"What's your next step?"

"Frankly, Captain, I'm not sure how to proceed from this point. We seem to have exhausted all our leads."

"Are all of the senior officers on your 'highly unlikely' list?"

"Yes, ma'am."

"Then perhaps we should have a meeting to discuss the case. I'm not trying to usurp your authority, but perhaps together we can come up with a suggestion you might find useful."

"Okay, Captain. Maybe someone will have an idea I haven't thought of."

"Good. We'll meet in the conference room on this deck at 1500 hours. I'll have Lt. Ashraf notify the senior staff while you arrange for whomever you wish to bring from your staff."

"Aye, Captain. I'll do it immediately."

After Galont left, Jenetta leaned back in her chair and thought about the crime. She had no training in criminology and didn't think for a second that she could handle the case better than the professionals could. Still, Marine Captain Galont seemed to need some help. So how does one ascertain who the killer is when there are seven hundred ninety-four suspects and no evidence?

At 1500 Jenetta welcomed the group in the conference room. In addition to Marine Captain Galont's senior staff, the meeting was attended by the XO (Lt. Ashraf), the *Song*'s second officer (Lt. Elizi), the chief engineer (Lt. Cmdr Rodriquez), and the chief medical officer (Lt. Cmdr O'Neil).

"It's now been a week since Petty Officer Nichols was murdered and we still have no evidence pointing to the identity of the killer," Jenetta said. "Our goal here today is to see if we can suggest a course of action that will lead to unmasking him or her. I invite you to speak freely, voicing any questions you have or any recommendations. Perhaps it might help if we first reviewed what we do know. Lt. Commander O'Neil, would you give us the results of the autopsy?"

"Yes, ma'am. As I suspected from the beginning, PO Nichols was struck twice with a blunt instrument by an assailant standing in front of him. Nichols must have tried to ward off the first blow and suffered a broken right arm. The second blow, the killing blow, landed here." The chief medical officer pointed to a spot on the right side of his own head. "That blow both fractured his submaxilla and shattered vertebrae in his neck. It was the killing blow." The doctor proceeded to explain in specific medical terms exactly what occurred, then continued, saying, "I place the time of death at 2345 hours, give or take a few minutes."

"Could the wound have been caused by someone's hand or foot?" Elizi asked.

"No, it was definitely a solid object. It appears to have been cylindrical, quite smooth, and about the diameter of a holo-magazine cylinder but quite heavy and solid."

"Thank you, doctor," Jenetta said. "Is there anything else you can tell us? Anything you're unsure of and so didn't include in the official record?"

"Well— I *suspect* the attacker is most likely left-handed and probably stands between five-foot-ten and six foot. It would have been much more difficult for a right-handed person, or a shorter one, to deliver the killing blow."

"What if Nichols turned away and bent over in pain after his arm was broken?" Galont asked.

"That's why I didn't put my speculations into the official report. They're only accurate if Nichols remained upright and facing his attacker. While it's unlikely, the killer could be right-handed. The blows *could* possibly have been delivered backhand or with the less dominant limb."

"Thank you, Doctor," Jenetta said. "Major, what can *you* tell us?"

"Upon discovering the body, we immediately secured the crime scene, collecting fingerprints, hair, and skin flecks. We identified all individuals represented by the evidence and determined that everyone had a valid reason for being there sometime earlier in the day. It's possible the killer didn't leave any evidence of their presence. He or she was there for less than a minute. Although the room isn't locked, the computer keeps a log of every time the door is opened. Nichols arrived at the storage room at 2338 hours and his ID was logged when he opened the door. The door was next opened at 23:44:06 and again at 23:44:51, but both times by the inside sensor, so no new ID was logged. The killer must have sidled up to the door, knocked, and been admitted by Nichols rather than moving into the area where the door's admittance sensor would scan for an ID. It appears the killer scattered a deck of cards over and around the body before he left. It's what initially made us think Nichols might have been killed because of a gambling matter. I believe now that it was done to intentionally mislead us. We know that nothing stored in the room could have made the wounds, so the killer had to have brought the weapon with him."

"Him?" Ashraf asked.

"I use that solely in the generic sense. We don't know the sex of the killer."

"Is it possible to get fingerprints from the deck of cards?" Ashraf asked.

"The deck was almost new and we only found Nichols prints on the face and backs of the cards. If we knew the precise order of the cards before they were dropped, we might be able to develop some partials from the edges, but Nichols had obviously shuffled the deck. We did have the computer attempt to reconstruct prints from the deck edges by arranging every possible permutation of their order, but the edges were just too smudged to get a decent print that matched up with anyone on board other than Nichols. One permutation gave us a partial that pointed to a senior engineering tech, but at the time of the murder he was working with a crew of eight other techs in the stern engineering room on Deck Three. It would have taken a minimum of eight minutes to travel to the storage room where Nichols was murdered and another eight minutes to return. Everyone confirmed his presence and swears that if he had been gone for more than a couple of minutes, his absence would have been glaringly obvious since he was the lead on the repair assignment."

"What about the other door sensors in the corridors?" Rodriquez asked. "Some of them had to have recorded the passage of the killer."

"They recorded Nichols' movements only. No one else passed through the corridor near the storeroom between the hours of 1854 and 0623 the following morning."

"Wait a minute," Jenetta said. "That's impossible. I'm sure you're not telling me the murder was committed by a ghost."

"The logs only show Nichols' passage through the corridor leading to the storeroom," Galont said adamantly.

"Is that possible, Commander?" Jenetta asked Rodriquez.

"If the killer used a utility tunnel to get to the storage room, it is. I'll check and see if there are any access hatchways near the storeroom."

"And if there aren't?" Ashraf asked.

"Then I would have to say it's almost impossible to approach the storeroom without being sensed and logged. The killer could have slid against the wall, keeping so low and close that he wasn't noticed by a door's motion sensor where there's only one door, but where two doors are opposite one another, there's no way he could have avoided them both. Once a sensor detects movement near a door, the computer activates additional sensors that allow it to make a determination as to whether the individual intends to enter the room by the position and stance of the body. If the person isn't stopped and facing the door, the computer logs the sensor hit but then cancels the door activation routine."

"Are there any vid cams in that corridor?" Jenetta asked.

"No, ma'am," Rodriquez said. "Vid cams inside the ship are limited to the bridge, AC&C, weapons control centers, the brig, maintenance and launch bays plus their control rooms, sensitive engineering areas, and high-security areas such as the armories and secure holds, plus transport cars, lifts, and airlocks. All conference rooms have systems for creating logs of meetings, such as the one being created presently, but those systems are only activated when a request is made at the time the room is reserved, or by someone in the room when the meeting begins."

"Assuming there are no access tunnels in that area and that the killer is flesh and blood, how could he trick the sensors so they didn't record his passing?" Jenetta asked.

"He couldn't," Rodriquez said, "unless he was wearing an EVA-type suit helmet especially lined to prevent the computer from sensing his CT or ID chip. But anyone wearing, or even carrying, such a helmet in a corridor would be grossly out of place and therefore immediately noticed by anyone he passed. Even if he was the only one to use the corridor by the storeroom, he had to have used other corridors to get there and somebody would have noticed someone carrying a helmet. Of course, the logs could have been altered after the fact to remove a record of his presence."

"Who has access to the logs?" Dr. O'Neil asked.

"The logs can be accessed only by authorized personnel on the bridge or in Engineering."

"No one else?" Jenetta asked.

"Well, our academies and schools graduate the best and the brightest. It's possible that someone of intelligence and superior computer skills could hack the system and alter the logs."

"Wouldn't that be detectable?" Ashraf asked.

"If someone erased entries in the main log there would be time sequence gaps in the records. If someone only altered entries, which is significantly more difficult, it could go undetected. We'd have to compare the main log with the transaction history logs for each sensor and try to spot any anomalies. Of course, if the killer is sufficiently adept to alter the main log, he or she could easily alter or delete the corresponding records from the transaction history logs."

"So it appears our killer either travels by access tunnel or is a highly sophisticated computer expert," Jenetta said. "Major, it appears that you and Lt. Commander Rodriquez have some investigating to do."

"Yes, ma'am. With the Commander's help, my people will start cross-checking the logs immediately."

"It'll be a simple matter to check on the access tunnels, Captain," Rodriquez said to Jenetta. "How should I proceed if there is an access point in that corridor near enough to the storage room that the killer could have used to avoid being detected by other sensors?"

"Inform Major Galont immediately and let him handle it," Jenetta said. "He's heading up this investigation. Are there any other suggestions or questions? No? Then you're dismissed. Thank you for your assistance today."

* * *

"We can't remain on War Active status, Admiral," Captain Charles E. Hoyt said from his briefing room aboard the destroyer *Calgary* during the regular morning vidConference of all commanding officers in the small protection fleet—regular only since the CIC was activated. "It's placing too much stress on our people."

"Yes, that's true, Charles," Admiral Holt said. "As soon as we've completed our preparations, such as they are, I'll lower our status to War Ready. We'll then remain at that level until the Raiders make their first move or we're reinforced by the task force ships underway for Higgins."

"I'm quite concerned about the fighting effectiveness of the *Prometheus* and *Chiron*, should they arrive in time," Captain Marie A. Simpson of the destroyer *Bonn* said. "We know they were severely under strength at the Battle of Vauzlee and that both lost crew during the battle."

"As am I, Marie. Supreme Headquarters and the Admiralty Board also share that concern. It's a shame they weren't able to pick up the crewmembers assembling for them at Earth. I think each captain here should plan to transfer ten percent of fighting personnel to the battleships as soon as they arrive. We'll need every one of their guns manned for the fight ahead."

"They already have twelve of my best gunners aboard," Captain Payton said. "Commander Kanes took them two months ago. I assume it was in preparation for the attack on the convoy."

"Yes. It was classified 'need to know only' at the time so he couldn't share the information. We borrowed people from every ship in port. All crewmen will be returned at the conclusion of this upcoming engagement."

"Assuming we survive," Captain Simpson said morbidly.

"I refuse to entertain any other possibility," Captain Simon H. Pope of the *Geneva* said.

"Ignoring the facts won't change them, Simon," Captain Simpson said.

"The Raiders have been pretty successful at avoiding confrontations with us for years," Admiral Holt said. "The Intelligence Section believes that during those years they've been stealthily building their forces in and around this deca-sector. We can guess why. They've felt the day would come when they could challenge us directly for control here."

"SCI believes the Raiders plan to wrest complete control of this deca-sector from the Galactic Alliance?" Captain Pope asked.

"It's a logical conclusion based on the facts," Captain Payton said. "They've been slowly expanding their presence throughout G.A. space for the past decade, but there's been a much heavier concentration of attacks in this deca-sector than in any other area of G.A. territory."

"The destruction of Raider-One, rather than pushing them back into the shadows, has apparently emboldened them," Captain Simpson said. "With their losses there, and now at Vauzlee, I'm sure they're becoming desperate. They have to know their chances of controlling this deca-sector are slipping away. If they attack, I expect they'll be coming with everything they have."

"I think Marie is right," Admiral Holt said, "but I don't want to hear any defeatist talk. The Raiders represent a significant threat, but we're not paid mercenaries. We're Space Command officers. We'll remain at our posts until the end. And when the laser pulses stop and the torpedoes have done their damndest, we'll still be here. I'm confident we'll be victorious."

*   *   *

Waking to the sound of an alert horn is never pleasant. Jenetta had been there too many times before. She knew she hadn't scheduled a drill for this morning so it had to be a real emergency. She glanced up at the chronometer as she leapt from her bed and grabbed her robe. It was 0438. Since there was no message being broadcast to abandon ship, she didn't take time to dress. She just slipped into her robe and carpet skimmers before darting into the corridor and running to the bridge. The crewmen there were calm, but intensely focused on their display monitors. Jenetta walked quickly to Lt. Elizi, who was sitting in the first officer's chair. Elizi was speaking to someone on her CT while focusing on the small monitor screen attached to the left arm of the chair.

"What is it, Lieutenant?" Jenetta demanded.

Jenetta waited for several seconds and then asked again, "What's the problem, Lieutenant?"

Elizi looked up, a startled expression on her face as she realized for the first time that her captain was standing in front of her, addressing her. "One second, Captain," she said, her face regaining the look of concentration it had held before Jenetta spoke up.

After several seconds, Elizi said, "Elizi out," thereby closing the CT carrier she had been using. "Captain, we have an out-of-control fire on Deck Seven, Section Eighteen."

Chapter Twelve
~ May 8th, 2268 ~

Swiveling the small monitor around so Jenetta could also see the image, Lt. Elizi pointed to a spot on the three-dimensional deck plan of Deck Seven, Section Eighteen. By touching any point on the image and moving her finger, the displayed image would revolve up, down, or sideways to see it from a different perspective. "It's here," Lt. Elizi said, pointing to a room highlighted in shades of red that indicated temperature gradients above forty degrees Celsius, "in the Corridor Five storeroom. Fire crews from Engineering are just beginning to arrive now. There weren't enough personnel on duty to initially handle the blaze, but the GQ alert has awakened everyone on the ship and more crewmen are checking in and suiting up."

"What about the fire suppression systems?"

"They've failed to operate. We don't know why, but neither the Alonn gas nor the fire suppression foam systems responded."

"What's in that storeroom?"

"It's a paint locker, which is why the blaze grew out of control so quickly. A lot of the material in there is highly flammable."

"A paint locker?" Jenetta knew that paint used onboard ship was mixed with a fire retardant as it was applied, but new paint had to be stored in its normal flammable state because the fire retardants caused the pigments to coagulate, making it unsuitable for use after a few days. "What else is in that area?"

"Other storerooms mostly. No armaments. No crew quarters. The rear bulkhead of the paint locker adjoins a large engineering section."

"What's in that engineering section?"

Lt. Elizi tapped an icon on the border of the monitor image, then touched the section in question. A list scrolled quickly up the screen. She looked up at Jenetta with a concerned expression. "It's a high security area. It contains data storage and the weapons control computers."

"Weapons control?"

"Aye, Captain." Lt. Elizi touched her Space Command ring, put her left hand up to cup her ear, and glanced away. "Watch command officer," she said. After listening for a few seconds she said, "Elizi out. Captain, the Maintenance Operations Center is sending us a live vid feed from the fire area."

Turning to the com chief, Jenetta said, "Put the vid feed on the front viewscreen. Make a general announcement to the crew that we have a fire onboard, but that there appears to be no imminent danger outside of Section Eighteen on decks six through eight."

"Aye, Captain."

An instant later, the image of a ship's corridor with a haze hanging heavily in the air appeared on the large monitor. Firefighters, fully encased in bright yellow protective suits, could be seen moving into and out of frame as they worked to attach something near the top of a corridor door. Once the large object, coupled to a large-diameter hose, was connected to the door using a special quick-setting epoxy, the firefighters pulled back. No further activity was observed for anxious minutes. Jenetta assumed the device was performing some important function and that the firefighters had pulled back to a safe area while it operated.

After what seemed like an hour to the anxious spectators but was actually only about ten minutes, a pair of firefighters again moved into frame. After squirting a liquid around the base of the device they'd attached to the door, they just stood there. A few seconds later, the device began to peel away from the door. As it fell away into the hands of the waiting firefighters, fire and smoke belched from a new twenty-five-centimeter hole in the door. Another pair of firefighters appeared at the edge of the frame with a fire hose and began shooting a stream of fire suppression liquid into the hole from several meters away. There was no panic and the firefighters moved with skill and purpose.

The firemen with the hose inched closer and closer to the storeroom's door as the flames retreated into the room. As they reached the door, they held the hose up to the hole while another firefighter appeared with a large pry bar. The bar was inserted into the narrow slit where the door met the casing and the firefighter yanked with all his strength. The door, warped somewhat from the heat, yielded only slightly. Another firefighter appeared to lend his strength to the effort, and the door slid back a dozen centimeters. Flames immediately leapt from the narrow opening, momentarily engulfing the pair and charring their protective suits a bit, but they pulled back to a safe distance, uninjured.

The pair of firefighters spraying foam into the hole shifted position and began spraying a narrowed stream of fire suppressant into the small gap where the door had been opened. As the flames there retreated, another firefighter appeared near the door with a small, thin bundle. The pair spraying suppressant gave way so the device could be slid into the narrow gap. Suddenly the device popped and extended to a full meter in length. The door was instantly pushed into the wall pocket where it normally resided when open. Flames again roared from the room and the firefighters quickly yielded as the device fell to the deck, collapsing back into the small bundle it had been only seconds before.

With the door opened wide, a second pair of firefighters with a hose appeared next to the first and also began shooting foam into the room. The flames slackened as the two teams moved ever closer to the door and then into the room. More and more firefighters joined them, some dragging hoses and some wearing portable suppressant units in backpacks.

Jenetta and the bridge crew watched until the fire was completely extinguished. The last hose was turned off at 0512.

"Lt. Commander Rodriquez reports that the fire appears to be completely extinguished, Captain," the com operator said. "He says it will take perhaps fifteen minutes for the air in that section to be purged of all smoke and fire residue. He's setting a re-flash watch as a precaution against possible re-combustion."

"Thank you. Tell him we observed the effort and his people are to be commended for a job well done. Also tell him we'll have a meeting of senior staff at 1000 hours in the conference room on this deck."

"Aye, Captain."

"Lieutenant," Jenetta said to Elizi, "you kept your cool and took the appropriate action. Well done."

Elizi smiled. "Thank you, Captain."

"I'm returning to my quarters now that the excitement is over. I'll relieve you at 0800."

"Aye, Captain."

Jenetta walked tiredly back to her quarters and lay down, but she was restless and couldn't sleep. She wanted answers immediately but knew she had to allow the engineering teams the time to investigate. She finally got up, showered, and notified Woodrow that she would like breakfast a little early. Like everyone else on board, he had been awakened by the alarm and had foreseen the possibility that Jenetta might wish to eat when the crisis was over. He brought her a steaming mug of coffee as she entered her dining room and took her customary seat. Within five minutes, he produced heaping plates of eggs, toast, breakfast sausages, hash browns, pancakes, and fruit.

At 0750, with her runaway appetite sated briefly, Jenetta left her quarters and walked the twenty meters to the bridge. Risco was already there, speaking with Elizi about the fire.

"You're relieved, Lieutenant," Jenetta said to Elizi after being briefed on the condition of the ship. "Get some breakfast. I'll expect you at the 1000 meeting. You'll be able to sleep afterwards."

"Aye, Captain."

"Lieutenant Risco, I'll be in my briefing room."

"Aye, Captain, I have the bridge."

After completing her usual morning work, which consisted chiefly of scanning reports filed by officers aboard the ship, Jenetta reviewed the logged images of the firefighting effort. The crews had done an excellent job of containing the blaze quickly. She next listened to Rodriquez' initial report. It was naturally a bit sketchy and only gave the highlights of the firefighting effort. A complete investigation should already be underway and she expected the final report to be incredibly detailed.

A few minutes before 1000 hours, Jenetta left her briefing room and walked to the conference room. Her senior officers were already gathered. They knew of her habit of always arriving a few minutes early and made a point of arriving before she did.

"Take your seats, please," Jenetta said.

Most of the officers had prepared a beverage at the synthesizer after their arrival. Ashraf had prepared a mug of coffee for Jenetta and a tea for herself.

"Commander Rodriquez, what can you tell us about the fire on Deck Seven?" Jenetta asked.

"I have some preliminary information, but we won't know the full story for some hours yet."

"Tell us what you do know," she said calmly.

"Yes ma'am. The fire started around 0419 hours. The paint locker was already fully involved when Engineering Specialist 1st Class Paul Douglass, working on Deck Eight, began checking on a faint odor of smoke. He was smart enough not to try to open the door to the paint locker after placing his hand against it and feeling intense heat. He alertly notified the bridge, who sounded GQ before also notifying the engineering duty officer in the Maintenance Operations Center about the reported blaze. My fire crew, at least those on duty, immediately suited up and raced to Deck Seven while other personnel remotely closed all airtight doors and vents in Sections Seventeen through Nineteen on Decks Six, Seven, and Eight to make sure the blaze and smoke would be contained once the paint locker door was opened. Air vents in the paint locker had sealed automatically when the blaze was detected. We evacuated air in as many surrounding compartments as possible where no life was present according to the main computer. We set air scrubber equipment operation in all adjoining areas to maximum. Additional off-duty personnel continued to arrive in support of those already on the scene. When they felt ready, they attached a McCarthy fire valve to the top of the storeroom door. The valve assembly contains a laser cutting torch that opens a hole to allow fire-fighters to ventilate the room by sucking out smoke and pumping in Alonn gas. If you simply open the door, you're re-introducing oxygen where combustion has probably ceased but where fuel gases and smoke remain at high temperature. Combustion would restart with an explosive effect. This is commonly called a backdraft. It's an extremely dangerous situation.

"Once the room was properly ventilated, we began spraying fire retardant through the McCarthy valve. The large size and shape of the storeroom prevented that effort from being totally effective so the valve was eventually removed from the door and the door opened. The explosive effect had been largely negated, but the materials in the paint locker still presented my firefighters with a horrific blaze to smother. They began spraying fire retardant into the room as fast as they could and eventually managed to quell the fire."

"We saw the effort," Jenetta said. "They did an excellent job. What I want to know is how the blaze started and why the automatic systems didn't immediately alert us and commence suppression operations."

"How it started we don't yet know. I suspect arson."

"Arson?" Jenetta repeated loudly. "On what basis?"

"The materials stored in that room are highly combustible. For this reason, every possible effort has been made to ensure that nothing in the room can initiate a blaze. Also, we've discovered that the fire notification and suppression systems on Deck Seven, Section Eighteen were intentionally deactivated just before the blaze started."

"Deactivated intentionally? Are you sure?"

"There's no question, Captain. Someone got into the computer and shut off the systems. We didn't discover it until we began our investigation after the blaze was out."

"But if they destroyed the ship, they'd risk death as well."

"I don't think they intended to destroy the ship. The other decks and sections were excluded from the tampering. Where we had evacuated the air, the flames couldn't spread, but even if we had lost control of the fire in Section Eighteen, the flames would have been stopped cold when the fire expanded into areas where the fire suppression controls were still active. But Section Eighteen on Deck Seven could have been a complete loss."

"So they don't have a death wish," Jenetta speculated rhetorically. "What other reasons could they have? Stop us from reaching Higgins in time to face the Raiders, divert our attention away from the murder investigation, or something else? I understand the weapons control computers are in an area adjoining the paint locker?"

"That's correct, Captain," Commander Rodriquez said.

"If they'd been damaged, how long would it take to repair or replace them?"

"It depends on the extent of the damage, naturally. The systems have triple redundancy, but everything is in that one section. If the fire had gotten out of control, we might not have been able to repair them. A full replacement could take a month or more. We'd have had to cobble together a system from scratch because we really just carry replacement component assemblies for those most likely to fail."

"So we could have arrived at Higgins unable to assist in its defense?"

"Yes, Captain."

"What else is in that section?" Jenetta asked.

"Our main data storage and retrieval center. The hardware containing the sensor log records Major Galont's people and mine have been searching are stored there, as well as all vid logs."

"So the murderer might have been hoping to stop our investigation cold."

"It's possible," Rodriquez said. "The perpetrator could never have gotten into that engineering section without being observed and recorded, so this might be the only way to inflict such damage while keeping his identity unknown."

"And given the degree of damage to the paint locker, there's almost no chance of finding any identifying inform-ation pointing to the arsonist," Galont said.

"It's interesting that this occurred on the same deck as the murder of Petty Officer Nichols," Jenetta said.

"Deck Seven has little traffic during the hours these crimes have been committed. That means few witnesses to the passage of our malefactor," Galont said.

"Did you prepare a list of individuals who passed through that area in the hours prior to the fire?"

"We checked the logs as soon as the fire was extinguished, but they contain no record of anyone having passed through that corridor from the end of the second watch at midnight until Specialist Douglass arrived. But the door was opened at 0412 and again at 0415."

"So, who opened the door?"

"Unknown. It's not a secure area so no special clearance was required, but since it's a fire hazard area, anyone seeking entrance must brandish their hand within centimeters of the admittance sensor. That's to keep the door from opening unintentionally if there *is* a fire inside, as when Specialist Douglass stepped in front of the door. The system should have automatically logged the ID of the person seeking entrance."

"Unless it was a cleaning bot," Elizi said.

"Cleaning bots can't open the door because of the flammable materials stored there. And the sensors *do* record a bot's ID whenever it enters a room." Rodriquez said.

Jenetta sucked in a full breath and then released it slowly while she thought. "Then it appears our saboteur was able to clear the log records while engineering was still fighting the blaze. He, or she, appears to be both intelligent and efficient, in addition to being ruthless. I want this person found and stopped before he does any more damage. Is there anything we can do that we're not already doing? What about compiling a list of the fifty most capable computer people on board and checking their alibis thoroughly?"

"We've already compiled a list of everyone with the ability and experience to potentially hack into the ship's computer systems," Marine Captain Galont said. "The main computer has sifted through all personnel records and provided us with thirty-six names. We're working our way down through the list as quickly as we can, beginning with the most capable computer experts first. We've bypassed the top individual on the list, but everyone else remains on the list until they're cleared beyond a shadow of a doubt."

"I don't want anyone skipped. Why can't you check the alibi of the first person on the list?"

"Uh, it's you, Captain."

"Oh. Well— I know I'm not the killer or saboteur."

"As do we, Captain," Galont stated. "Short of confining everyone not on duty to their quarters and having all my Marines patrolling the corridors constantly, I can't think of a thing we can do that we're not already doing."

"I will not allow this person or persons to drive us to *that* extreme," Jenetta said. "But let's increase the patrols on second and third watch, and have them specifically concentrate on areas that don't normally see much traffic during those hours, such as Deck Seven. It won't be necessary to stop anyone unless they're doing something suspicious, but all patrols should carry portable sensor equipment to record the ID of everyone they pass. If we can't rely on the central system to provide information on the movements and identities of our perpetrators, perhaps the portable systems can provide some leads."

"You think there might be more than one, Captain?" Lt. Ashraf asked.

"I admit it's hard to believe we might have both a murderer *and* a saboteur aboard this ship, but I'm trying to keep an open mind about everything at this point. It's most likely the same individual."

* * *

A couple of days later Jenetta was returning to her quarters after a grueling hour in the ship's gym, her first opportunity to work out since coming aboard, but she stopped short as she stepped from the lift into Corridor 3 on A deck. Laundry bots lined both walls of the corridor for some distance. Jenetta had never seen such a sight anywhere except outside the laundry itself, and only rarely there. As she moved into the center of the corridor, eight of the five-foot-tall bots detached themselves from the queue and prepared to enter the empty lift. Their half-meter wide by meter deep, box-like bodies with two articulated arms would completely fill the lift, so one necessarily stood patiently by until the rest were settled, then slipped into the last available position. When the doors closed, the rest of the bots in the queue advanced to fill the now vacant positions closest to the lift.

Jenetta looked at the bots suspiciously as she walked slowly towards her quarters near the entrance to the bridge in Corridor 0. There was no logical reason why they should be congregated on A Deck.

As she turned into Corridor 0, she found Lieutenant Risco standing in the hallway, staring into her quarters. So intent was the young officer that she didn't hear Jenetta come up behind her.

"Your quarters would never pass inspection at the Academy, Lieutenant," Jenetta said lightly, staring over Risco's shoulder. Risco, totally preoccupied with her thoughts, started at the sound of the unexpected voice, then immediately calmed.

"I've never seen anything like it, Captain," she said. "Laundry bots were standing in my doorway pitching dirty clothes into my sitting room. I guess there wasn't enough room to get inside by the time I arrived."

Indeed, the room was filled with dirty laundry. Mountains of the stuff covered what Jenetta guessed from the placement and contours of the piles was the underlying furniture.

"We'll have engineering clear it out right away," Jenetta said.

"I've already called it in, Captain. Right now my only concern is for my cat, Simone. She usually curls up on the sofa when I'm not here. I hope she's all right. I've been calling but she hasn't responded."

"Cats are very intelligent creatures, Lieutenant. I'm sure she headed for cover as soon as the laundry started flying."

"I hope so. She's all the family I have. I couldn't bear it if she was killed by some laundry bots run amuck."

Jenetta placed her hand lightly on Risco's shoulder and squeezed gently before moving away.

As Jenetta neared her own quarters, the doors opened as they should, but she was unable to enter. The condition of her sitting room resembled that of Risco, but if anything, the piles were even higher. A solitary figure stood forlornly in the middle of the room. Woodrow had managed to clear a spot in which to stand, but it wasn't like clearing a path through snow. The laundry piles were interleaved and the weight pressing down from above prevented some pieces from being removed.

"Woodrow," Jenetta said, grinning, "I see you've been letting your work pile up."

"I don't understand it, Captain. I was in the galley when I heard the door annunciator. When I came out, a dozen laundry bots were in the sitting room flinging dirty laundry everywhere. I tried to shut them down, but they wouldn't respond to verbal commands. When the first group had flung everything they had in their storage compartments, another group moved in and did the same. Then another and another."

Jenetta grinned again and depressed the face of her Space Command ring, then said, "Commander Rodriquez."

"Rodriquez here, Captain," she heard an exasperated voice say a couple of seconds later.

"Commander, if the laundry is full I would think you could find a better place to store the dirty laundry than my quarters or that of the other officers on A Deck."

Although Jenetta had tried to make it sound light, Rodriquez apparently wasn't in the mood for levity.

"I'm sorry, Captain. As a matter of fact, the Laundry is completely empty and the cleaning machines are sitting idle. I believe the problem lies with the Laundry Module in the computer system. It looks like someone has been tampering with it. All of the records are messed up and code has been overwritten. All the clean clothes in the Laundry at the start of the first watch were delivered to the wrong quarters. Then the bots began removing clean clothes from the quarters of various crewmembers and redistributing them to other quarters. Soiled clothes were never brought to the laundry."

"Are you saying that by tomorrow morning we're all going to be naked?"

"Well," Rodriquez said quietly, "everyone still has the clothes they're wearing now."

"I'm wearing sweats. I just came back from the gym."

"Don't worry, Captain. We'll find *your* clothes."

"That's comforting. Do you think our saboteur is behind this?"

"It would seem that way, ma'am. I can't imagine anyone else hacking into the laundry system and changing the code."

"At least it's a bit less harmful than his last effort. Keep your people on it, Commander. We can't have the routine of this entire ship upset because our people don't have clean clothes to wear."

"Aye, Captain," Rodriquez said.

"Carver out."

Jenetta stood looking at the mountains of clothes in her sitting room for several more seconds, then said, "Woodrow, I'll be in my briefing room until this matter is— sorted out."

"Aye, Captain," he said.

Chapter Thirteen
~ May 13th, 2268 ~

"Sir," the *Prometheus'* astrogator said to Gavin, "Higgins has acknowledged our imminent arrival and issued a straight-in approach clearance. They're announcing that all approach regulations have been suspended for SC warships returning to the station.

"Understood, Lieutenant," Gavin said from his command chair on the bridge.

"Uh, sir?"

"Yes, Lieutenant?"

"They're routing us directly to the docking ring."

"The docking ring? That can't be. Confirm that approach directive."

"I have, sir. They're directing us to dock at Kilo-Two. *Chiron* is being directed to dock at Lima-Two."

"Com," Gavin said, "Verbally confirm docking instructions."

"Aye, Captain," the com chief said. A few seconds later he said, "Docking instructions verbally confirmed, sir. We're to proceed directly to the Kilo-Two docking pier."

"What the devil..." Gavin muttered under his breath. "Astrogation, time to Higgins?"

"Our ETA is eighteen minutes, six seconds."

"Very well," Gavin said curtly, then sat back in his chair and stared at the front viewscreen. They were still much too far from Higgins to see the space station or even the planet Vinnia that it circled in geosynchronous orbit. Currently traveling at Light-375, the miniscule pinprick of light, a reflection from the system's star, was not yet visible to the sensors. With the approach speed limits set aside, they would come in as hot as they dared, then drop their envelope at the inner-pattern marker just ten thousand kilometers from the station instead of at the fifty-billion-kilometer point. At that time, they'd engage sub-light engines and travel the rest of the way at one hundred kps, the normal inner-pattern speed.

"New message from Higgins, Captain," the com chief said a few minutes later. "There are two hundred crewmen waiting to board when we dock. They've appended a roster."

"Forward a copy to my holo-tube, Chief," the Captain said.

"Aye, sir."

Gavin lifted the holo-tube from its storage pocket on the side of his chair and depressed the recessed activation switch. A visual image immediately leapt upward from the device. As he scrolled through the names, checking ranks and assignments, he saw that more than half were gunnery teams. The others were engineers, medical personnel, and support crew. "That explains the docking," he muttered as he deactivated the device and slipped it back into its storage holster. "Com, forward a copy of that list to the docking bay officer. Direct him to bring adequate help to verify the identities and orders of all new personnel as they board. Also send a copy to the housing officer."

"Aye, Captain."

"Preparing to drop envelope, sir," the helmsman said.

"Acknowledged."

As the enormous ship came to a stop at the leading edge of the inner-pattern and then began to move forward in n-space, picking up speed rapidly, the image on the front viewscreen rippled slightly for a fraction of a second and then stabilized. This was an indication that the ship's astrogation computer had switched over to mainly optical sensors. While traveling faster than the speed of light, the image on the viewscreen was, perforce, a non-optical representation prepared from digitized sensor data.

Deployed in positions roughly a thousand kilometers from the station, none of the five ships representing the station protection fleet presented any obstacle to the *Prometheus* or *Chiron*. Ordnance and fuel barges were standing by near the assigned docking piers waiting for the two massive ships to moor so they could move in and begin their re-supply efforts.

As the helmsman completed the dock-and-lock fifteen minutes later, Gavin jumped from his chair and hurried down to the forward cargo bay. The great airlock doors in the bay were still sliding back as he leapt through the opening, startling the Higgins dockmaster. Gavin hopped into the first parked driverless vehicle he encountered without asking to whom it was assigned and ordered it to take him to the headquarters section of the base. As it began moving through the docking ring, Gavin ordered it to exceed the limits imposed by its speed governor, using his authority as a senior SC officer to override the normal safe speed limit.

"I must see Admiral Holt immediately," Gavin said to the senior aide as he entered the Admiral's outer office.

The aide verbally repeated the request to the com unit on his desk. A second later the com unit beeped lightly as a message from the admiral appeared on the screen. "You may go in, Captain Gavin," the aide said.

The double doors to the Admiral's office slid open noiselessly as Gavin strode quickly down the short corridor. Admiral Holt was on his feet and walking briskly towards the doors as Gavin entered the office. Gavin's first impression was that the Admiral hadn't slept a wink in days. His face was haggard and drawn. Dark shadows underscored his eyes.

"Larry," the Admiral said, presenting a warm and genuine smile as he extended his hand, "thank providence you're here. You don't know how relieved I am that you've arrived before the Raiders. With the *Prometheus* and the *Chiron* bolstering our forces, perhaps we'll have a chance now."

Pumping the proffered hand, Gavin said, "Any sign of the Raider attackers, Admiral?"

"No, none. Not a peep from any of the sensors on the Distant DeTect grid."

"Let's hope it remains that way for another ten days. By then the *Song* and the four destroyers should be here. Have you assembled a senior staff to take command of the *Song* when she arrives?"

"I've prepared a list of officers. They won't actually assemble until the ship nears the station."

"Who will the Commanding Officer be?"

"Commander Harlan Acklee of the *Calgary*. He's senior on the Promotion Selection Board's list for Captain in this deca-sector. He understands the position isn't permanent and he'll just be captain for the duration of the crisis, then return to his ship."

Gavin sighed lightly. "Acklee. I've met him. He appears competent enough— but he's a bit of a stiff."

"Yes, he's a little too rigid and formal at times, and doesn't seem to have much of a sense of humor, but Hoyt says he's a good officer."

"Has he seen any action?"

"Unfortunately, no. Oh, he's been involved in some light interdiction activity, but it's all been strictly third-rate, amateur smuggler stuff. He's never come under fire."

Gavin scowled. "That's too bad. It would be nice to know how he'll bear up."

"Captains with battle experience are in very short supply. The Raiders have done a good job of avoiding contact with our warships in the past."

"I'm sure this is an all-or-nothing situation with the Raiders. They're going to be tough and I expect them to throw everything they've got at us. We can't afford to have an unseasoned captain crack under the strain of battle." Looking away as if in deep thought, Gavin said, "I don't suppose..."

After a few seconds of silence, Admiral Holt said, "Suppose what, Larry?"

Snapped out of his reverie, Gavin said, "I was trying to think of a way we might leave Commander Carver in command of the *Song* until the battle is over. As much as I'd love to have her back aboard the *Prometheus* in case something happens to me, I'd rather have a battle-seasoned officer commanding on the bridge of the *Song*. When it comes to a fight, she's as rock steady and cool as they come. Following the battle at Vauzlee I reviewed the bridge logs before I submitted my reports to SHQ. I was a little too preoccupied during the battle to notice her comportment, but in my review I discovered firsthand why the *Vordoth* crew nicknamed her the Ice Queen. Admiral, you wouldn't believe it. She just sat there in the first officer's chair on the bridge calm as could be, glancing up at the monitor occasionally and sipping her coffee. It was as if she didn't have a care in the world. You'd have thought we were running a simulation rather than fighting for our lives."

Admiral Holt chuckled. "I seem to recall a certain captain arguing with me recently, rather strenuously I might add, when informed she was to be his acting first officer for the trip to Earth."

Gavin reddened slightly. "Okay, sir, I'm a big enough man to admit I was wrong. Your assessment of her was completely accurate. If anything, she's even better than you stated."

"Well, I had an opportunity to review all the Intelligence interviews with the people she rescued and the crewmembers of the *Vordoth*. I saw the kind of loyalty she inspired in people who came under her command and protection. The statements from all the witnesses verified her accounts of the actions with the Raiders and her escape from the Raider Base. Never once did she try to embellish the account to make herself look better. If anything, she's too modest about her part in everything that happened, crediting much of it to luck. I sincerely wish I *could* leave her in command of the *Song*, Larry. And not just for the battle, but permanently. It's not up to me though. You know COAC has sole responsibility for assigning commanding officers to ships. Only the Admiralty Board can override their appointments and they've already acknowledged that Commander Carver will surrender command to a more seasoned officer as soon as the ship arrives here."

"That's just the point, Admiral. Commander Carver *is* the most seasoned combat officer we have in the entire *service*."

"I meant seasoned as in years of *command* experience, not combat experience."

"Well— at least I'll get her back," Gavin said, then looked to the Admiral apprehensively. "I *will* be getting her back, won't I?"

"Of course you will. It's where she wants to be more than anything. I'd love to have her here in command of my planning staff, but she wouldn't like it. She's a line officer through and through. She wants— no, she *needs* to be on a warship. She won't be happy anywhere else."

"Has the War College come up with any new plans for the defense of the base?"

"No, they insist that every simulation they've run shows that Station Defense Plan Echo-Three provides the best overall defensive posture. Once the Raiders move in, they recommend Foxtrot-Five, followed by Bravo-Two."

"But the Raiders must have a copy of the manual. They're probably familiar with every established battle plan in it."

"Probably."

"Damn," Gavin said, "they'll be able to predict our every move before we make it *and* they'll have prepared a counter for each tactic. I wish Carver were here now. I'd love to hear her suggestions for the defense of this base. Her prediction of the Raider attack plan at Vauzlee was one hundred percent accurate. I bet there are a lot of noses severely out of joint at the War College."

"So I read in your report. You really think her input would be that valuable?"

"Absolutely," Gavin said. "She displayed a level of insight that would make you believe she sat in on the Raider battle briefings and then developed a unique battle plan that proved to be the perfect response. I think we could use some of that uniqueness here, something the Raiders *won't* be expecting."

"Okay. There's still time, I suppose. Send her an encrypted message. Give her all the particulars and ask her for any suggestions she might have."

"Aye, Admiral," Gavin said grinning. "I will."

"I'd surely love to get some updated intel on Raider movements."

"As would I," Gavin said. "I half expected them to be here already. I kept praying we'd make it here before they attacked. Perhaps they had to wait while the seven destroyers that managed to escape the fight at Vauzlee completed their repairs. We pounded them damn hard. With the loss of so many expected ships, the senior officer of their attack force might have decided he needed every single vessel in top fighting trim."

"That's a good possibility. They know our people are dedicated and better trained, and that our ships are better armed and armored. They can only hope to defeat us through the sheer weight of numbers. They have to be able to attack us with heavier volleys of torpedoes than we can hope to shoot down."

"Since they expected so little opposition at Vauzlee, I think we should assume their better ships were held in reserve for the attack on this base."

"That, also, is a good possibility, much as I hate to admit it. Intelligence has heard repeated rumors in recent years that the Raiders have been striving to upgrade their fighting forces. Their successful raid on the Mars' shipyard where they managed to steal both the *Prometheus* and the *Chiron* would seem to bear that out. I imagine they've also been pressing the Tsgardi and Uthlaro to produce stronger, faster, and better-armored warships."

"I'm sure you're right, sir," Gavin said. "While I doubt if the Tsgardi have made many technological advances beyond what they've stolen from the Flordaryns, the Uthlaro are a different matter entirely. They're intelligent, innovative, ruthless, and openly mercenary. I predict that one day our two civilizations will clash violently."

"Perhaps, Larry. I don't know. Fortunately they're so far beyond our borders that it probably won't happen in our lifetimes."

"I don't know, sir. Our ships keep getting faster and I expect they're making similar advances. But that's of secondary import right now. I'd better get back to my ship. I want to undock as soon as possible. I don't want to be maneuvering for clearance when the Raiders arrive. I just wanted to check in with you to see if you'd heard anything new."

"I'm delighted you're here, Larry. I might actually get a little sleep now."

*   *   *

Jenetta awoke confused, unsure of where she was. She had gone to sleep in her warm, relaxing bed but now found herself lying on an ice-cold slab of plasticrete. Strangely, she still appeared to be in her bedroom.

"Lights," she said to the computer and the room illuminated.

She pushed herself up onto one arm and felt the gel-comfort mattress with the other. It was as rock hard and cold as a flight bay deck.

Thinking she might have said something during her sleep that altered the bed settings, she said, "Computer, adjust bed to my default settings."

"Unable to comply," the computer said in her CT. "No local adjustment of bed settings is permitted."

"Computer, I am the Captain of this vessel and I order you to override that command and permit local adjustments."

"Unable to comply," the computer said.

Jenetta sighed and swung her legs over the edge of the block of stone that an hour before had been a warm, comfortable sleeping platform. According to the wall chronometer it was 0212. She had just put on her robe and slippers when she heard a light knock at her bedroom door. It could only be one person.

"Come," she said, and the door slid open.

"Excuse me, Captain," Woodrow said. "Lt. Commander Rodriquez just called to apologize. He says that every bed aboard ship has suddenly become as solid as stone. He has his people working on the problem and hopes to restore local control of bed adjustments shortly."

"Our saboteur again, I suppose?"

"Yes, Captain, that's the speculation. In the meantime, might I suggest you use one of the sofas in your sitting room? It will only take me a minute to make one up as a bed."

"Thank you, Woodrow. That would be preferable to trying to sleep on a plasticrete mattress."

"Just give me one minute, Captain."

Woodrow prepared the temporary bed while Jenetta watched. He had already brought sheets and a light blanket from somewhere. It took him less than a minute.

"Where are you going to sleep, Woodrow?"

"I have a sofa in my quarters, Captain. I'll be fine."

"Very well, Woodrow. Thank you."

"Good night, Captain."

"Good night, Woodrow."

* * *

The bed problem had been resolved by the time Jenetta was awakened with a ringing sound in her head. She sat up on the sofa and cupped her left ear. The noise seemed to be originating in her CT. She pressed the face of her Space Command ring and said, "Carver out," to disengage the carrier, but the signal persisted. The wall chronometer in her sitting room indicated it was 0452. Jenetta had just risen to her feet when Woodrow entered the room.

"Commander Rodriquez just called, Captain," her steward said. "It appears the saboteur has gotten into the CT and ID systems module. Our people are trying to locate the problem and restore the proper coding."

"Damn, that could take hours. Is everyone on board affected, or only me?"

"It appears to be a system-wide problem. I'm hearing a strange ringing sound in my left ear."

"Contact Commander Rodriquez and tell him to manually disconnect the carrier signal transmitter until his people find the problem in the code. It's better to lose the system for a while than to have everyone get a splitting headache."

"Aye, Captain."

"Oh, and Woodrow, tell him to have his people check to see if any frequency was exempted. If the saboteur excluded himself, it may tell us who he is."

"Aye, Captain."

Five minutes later the ringing in her head suddenly stopped, but Jenetta was too awake to fall back asleep so she showered and dressed. Woodrow had her breakfast ready when she emerged from her bedroom.

* * *

"Captain," Jenetta heard in her CT, "we have another problem." She instantly recognized the voice of Lieutenant Risco. The CT and ID systems had been restored by 0730.

Jenetta sighed, closed the report she was reading, and pushed down the cover of her com unit. As she emerged from her briefing room, she was pleased to see that no one on the bridge appeared overly concerned. The problem couldn't be a serious one.

"What is it, Lieutenant," Jenetta asked as she reached her command chair.

Risco, presently sitting in the First Officer's chair, said, "All transport tubes and lifts have suddenly stopped operating."

"All of them?" Jenetta asked in surprise.

"Yes, ma'am. Every single one."

"Have you notified Commander Rodriquez?"

"Yes, ma'am, but he can't do anything at the moment. He's trapped in a transport tube car on Deck Five back near Section Two-Sixty-Eight."

"Does he have a theory about the problem?"

"Yes, ma'am. He says it has to be a problem with the transport system module in the main computer. Most likely it's the work of our computer saboteur again. He's dispatched people to start investigating but says it will take time for them to track down the affected code. He'll join them as quickly as possible, but that probably won't be for another twenty to thirty minutes. He has to get out of the transport car, find an access hatch, and then use zero-grav tubes to reach Engineering."

Jenetta sucked in a deep breath and then expelled it quickly to show her exasperation. "If I ever get my hands on the person responsible for all these computer problems, I'm going to personally wring his neck."

Risco suppressed a grin. Since no one had been hurt, yet, and there was no present danger to the ship with this latest problem, she could afford to be personally amused by the problem. Her cat hadn't been harmed by the erratic action of the laundry bots. Simone had simply hidden beneath the sofa until the room was cleared.

Jenetta turned towards the bridge doors and said, "I'll be in Engineering." Then she stopped, turned again and said, "Cancel that. If a serious problem occurs while the tubes and lifts are down, I may not be able to get back here in a timely manner. I'll be in my briefing room."

* * *

Since the inception of Space Command, its vessels have always employed four separate and distinct onboard computer systems. Life Support, Propulsion, and Weapons Control computers, while fully integrated with the ship, were stand-alone systems with no interfaces to each other or to the Main Computer System. Engineers tended to describe these three systems as 'simple' because most of their functions were 'burned' into circuit rods. Little remote tampering was possible.

Life Support was responsible for monitoring and adjusting air temperature heating and cooling systems, water heating and recycling functions, and air purification and regeneration. Thousands of sensors located throughout the ship constantly monitored system operations. While someone could possibly tap into a local loop and modify parameters beyond establish- ed 'comfort' settings for a specific location, the tampering would quickly become obvious. Only from within the ship's highly secure Main Engineering Section could the system, or specific locations, be deactivated or seriously affected.

The Weapons Control system, while capable of perform- ing complex computations and tasks on demand, was similar- ly tamper-proof. It had a specific job and performed its func- tions within the tightly controlled parameters of its mission. Code changes required the replacement of circuit rods with the new programming 'burned' into memory circuits.

Propulsion was the third 'simple' system. Operational access was limited to consoles on the bridge and AC&C. Like the other two systems, isolation of the circuitry made it almost invulnerable to loss of control from hacking efforts within the ship or by outside efforts.

All other shipboard functions were handled by various modules within the Main Computer. Although user 'rights' were strictly and carefully apportioned through CTs, IDs & passwords, the system was accessible by anyone with the proper user interface hardware.

* * *

Jenetta plopped down in her chair and stared at her desk's surface after leaving control of the bridge with Risco. The saboteur was stirring anger in her like the anger she'd felt when she awoke in the Raider cell and first discovered the slave imprint she still wore on her chest. Whoever the individual was, she intended to find him— if she only knew where to look.

As if by divine enlightenment, she suddenly realized where *she* should have been looking all along. She activated the large wall monitor and removed a wireless computer keyboard from her desk. The tightly furled floppy membrane resembled a holo-tube when in its storage state but instantly rolled out flat on her desktop as she removed the Velcro band and activated as soon as she simultaneously touched the proper contact spots near the top left-hand and top right-hand corners.

Jenetta knew the saboteur must be leaving some evidence of hacking in the computer. Perhaps one would point Jenetta in the proper direction. Although she was the ship's captain, high level systems access privileges had never been established for her in the main computer. Ship's captains normally either didn't have time for playing around inside computers or weren't sufficiently computer literate or inclined to do so. Jenetta Carver was both able and so inclined, but she hadn't had the time since coming aboard the *Song*.

The lack of system access privileges presented no difficulty. She had been hacking into computers since almost before she could walk, but as a 'whiter than white-hat hacker,' it was never with malicious intent. Within ten minutes she was cruising through the system modules looking for evidence of unauthorized access by the saboteur. She looked in the transport module first since that appeared to be the most recent point of attack and immediately found broken links and missing code structures. The saboteur had definitely been there. Accessing the history log that recorded all code modifications, Jenetta searched for some indication of the saboteur's identity, but his back-trail was too clean. He was too good. He wasn't able to cover his modification efforts, but he left nothing that pointed back to him. When it was obvious this was a dead end, Jenetta turned her attention to restoring the links and missing code by reversing the logged modifications. She finished the restoration and was considering where to look next when she was interrupted by a message from Lt. Risco.

"Captain, the transport systems have just come back on line. I thought you'd want to know in case you still want to go down to Engineering."

"Thank you, Lieutenant," Jenetta said almost absent-mindedly before returning her full attention to the monitor.

Jenetta then began skimming through the millions of instruction sets in the main computer, hunting for something, anything, that would point to the saboteur. The systems code of any ship's main computer was almost bulletproof by the time the newly-built ship left the Mars space dock and was, therefore, seldom modified. Unless the saboteur was a renowned computer expert, he or she had to have left a trail a mile wide. Using the transaction history logs, she reviewed all recent activity.

As her investigation intensified, she discovered the saboteur had always entered the system through an almost never used access socket. Prior to Petty Officer Nichol's death, that particular socket hadn't been accessed since the ship had been built. Jenetta checked the access registry file and discovered, to her surprise, that the socket wasn't listed there. The address hadn't been removed; it had never *been* there. Apparently, that was either the result of an oversight on the part of the original systems team or perhaps it had been intentionally left off the list to provide a permanent backdoor for maintenance programmers. This might be the break she was hoping for. Either the saboteur had stumbled across the unused socket by accident or he'd had contact with someone who worked at the Mars Shipbuilding facility when the system was installed.

With each sabotaged instruction set she located, Jenetta's ability to identify the handiwork of the saboteur, or rather the lack of it, increased. She finally came to the conclusion that the saboteur wasn't a galaxy-class computer expert at all but simply a persistent blunderer. For every successful attempt to sabotage a module, he had made a hundred or two hundred attempts that didn't succeed. She spent most of her time reversing his entries. Even if there was no apparent damage now, some minor change he made might cause a problem in the future. She finally worked out an algorithm that would reverse all the saboteur's changes by identifying them through the access socket address. After first testing it thoroughly, she activated the simple script she'd written. It tore through the computer modules undoing everything the saboteur had done in weeks of sabotage effort. In seconds it had accomplished what could have taken many weeks of manual effort to achieve.

Weary from the hours of work, Jenetta leaned back in her chair to think about the problem. Now that she had learned how to spot the work of the saboteur and could even have the computer identify it, she might be able to trap him the next time he logged in. At one time terminals and computers were hardwired to computer networks and it would have been so easy to determine the location in the ship where the saboteur was accessing the system if that was still the case. But wired networks were a thing of the far distant past, too ancient even to be considered antiques. For this reason, most computer professionals would be at a loss to locate the saboteur.

But Lt. Commander Jenetta Carver wasn't an average computer professional. She wasn't even an average computer expert. For all of her life, she'd had two passions: computers and the desire to travel among the stars. So when it came to either, she knew her stuff. She had learned things about computers that even their design teams didn't know. She would first have to write a quick subroutine that would sample the socket address once each minute throughout the day. When the computer found that particular access socket in use, the system would begin logging all keystrokes to a special file she created. Jenetta would know every module the saboteur tried to enter or affect. It wasn't enough just to undo his changes; she wanted to know what the saboteur was attempting next.

The second part of her plan would be an effort to locate the saboteur. Every key station contained standard logic circuits. If she could cause one of the timing circuits in the key station to oscillate at a given frequency above the range of human hearing when the station accessed the identified socket address, the ship's CT and ID sensors might be able to triangulate on that signal. It took her just fifteen minutes to write another quick subroutine that would do what she wanted. Then it was simply a matter of waiting for the saboteur to return to the system, and waiting was always the most difficult part of any such security action.

* * *

"Good morning, Commander," the image of Captain Gavin said as Jenetta sipped at her first mug of coffee in her briefing room. The message had arrived overnight, but since it wasn't marked Priority-One, Jenetta's sleep hadn't been disturbed. "The *Prometheus* and *Chiron* have arrived at Higgins and re-supplied in preparation for the attack. We've each received two hundred additional temporary personnel culled from the five ships forming the protection group so all our weapon stations will be manned. All commercial traffic has been cleared from the port and all civilian and non-combat personnel have been evacuated to the planet's surface.

"Admiral Holt has ordered that Station Defense Plan Echo-Three be implemented as soon as we detect the Raiders on the Distant DeTect network. After initial contact and exchange of ordnance, we're to fall back and assume a defensive posture that will allow us to protect the area of the station assigned to our ship. The War College defense plans only sanction use of offensive tactics when the defensive forces outnumber the attackers. We certainly don't expect that to be the case when the Raiders arrive. We're anticipating an enemy force of at least forty warships, while our defensive force presently consists of just seven ships.

"With expectations that we might be able to expand our response options to an attack by a force of superior numbers, the admiral has indicated a willingness to entertain proposals which might be viewed by some as being— disharmonious— with defensive postures espoused by the War College tacticians. We must do everything possible to protect the station, so maneuverability is severely limited. If we attempt to lure the Raiders away from the station, they'll probably ignore us and continue on to destroy Higgins. As you can imagine, options appear quite finite. If you have any tactical suggestions, I promise they will be given the utmost consideration.

"Captain Lawrence Gavin, Captain of the *Prometheus*, message complete."

* * *

After thinking about the problem for the best part of a day, Jenetta sent Gavin *her* thoughts on what to expect from the Raiders when they arrived, then headed for her quarters. It was after midnight and she was exhausted. Deep in thought as she walked, she slapped a small viewpad against her thigh. The third watch had just reported for duty and the bridge crew watched her curiously as she crossed the bridge and disappeared into the corridor.

Although Raider ship movement had been more or less restricted at Vauzlee, the opposite would be true at Higgins. The Raiders would be on the offensive and able to attack from any point, while Space Command would be the besieged defenders. Saddled with responsibility for knocking down any torpedoes intended for the space station, the Space Command vessels would be unable to maneuver to any significant degree. They'd be like clay ducks in a shooting gallery. The only difference there was that the ducks didn't get to shoot back.

Perhaps she was reading too much into his obviously carefully-worded communication, but she felt Gavin was asking not just for ideas to enhance Station Defense Plan Echo-Three, but for tactical plans that could *replace* that archaic defense posture. Therefore, she'd outlined several strategies the defenders might consider employing instead. The planners at the War College were excellent tacticians when Space Command had both weapons and numerical superiority but had never before fought a defensive battle where it lacked either. Relegated principally to police duties since the service had been formed, ships normally operated as separate entities. Flag officers traveled in luxurious VIP guest quarters to reach a base or return to Earth, but no admiral had ever stood on the bridge of a ship in space and directed a battle. The battle at Vauzlee had been the first ever coordinated assault on an enemy in space. As such, ships, weapons, and strategies had never been developed for the kind of enemy action they now faced.

The plans Jenetta proposed for the protection of the station employed maneuvers that would probably be scoffed at by War College tacticians, but when 'damn the torpedoes, full speed ahead' tactics were deemed totally inadequate, guile must move to the forefront. It was true that her plans entailed a certain amount of risk but certainly no more than attempting to engage in a toe-to-toe slugfest with a significantly more powerful force. The Greek soldiers who climbed into the wooden horse at the siege of Troy certainly knew the risk if they were discovered, but after attempts to storm the city's walls had proven unsuccessful, some measure of surreptitious behavior was mandated. Since her days of electronic game-playing with her brothers, sneaky battle maneuvers had always been Jenetta's forte.

Her soft-soled boots glided silently over the carpeted deck as she entered her quarters, still slapping the viewpad against her right thigh. The ragged edges of an idea for a particularly devious offensive maneuver kept brushing against her conscious mind, but she couldn't quite grasp it. Deep in thought, she didn't raise the illumination in the sitting room from its normally low level as she paced around the interior. It was several seconds before she realized Woodrow hadn't immediately emerged from his quarters to greet her and offer her food and beverage as he always did regardless of the hour. She also realized she wasn't alone. She stopped in the middle of the room, whirled, and spotted the intruder standing silently in the shadows against the wall opposite her office and dining room.

"Hello, *Captain*," he said, taking one short step forward now that his presence was known. "I see it's official this time. You do have a talent for getting back to the big chair. Ut— don't touch your ring or I shall be forced to fire."

Jenetta's left arm had been slowly inching towards the Space Command ring on her right hand. If no vocal message was received once a carrier wave was established, the security center would be notified immediately that either a medical emergency or security problem existed. "How did you get aboard this ship?" Jenetta demanded.

"It was all too simple," Commander Pretorious said smugly. "A few days after the battle, Kanes released me and gave me a shuttle loaded with food as per our prior agreement."

"Did he also give you that NCO uniform and the laser pistol you're pointing at me?"

Chapter Fourteen
~ May 16th, 2268 ~

"No, of course not," Pretorious said, grinning malevolently. "I got these on my own, and that was also amazingly easy. I just dropped by the wrecked GSC destroyer and picked them up. The armory was wide open, literally. An entire bulkhead wall had been ripped away in the collision. You wouldn't believe the incredible arsenal I've got stashed away in my shuttle. Once I get to the mining colony on Sasone, I'll make enough from the sale of those weapons to hire a ship that will take me anywhere in GA space I want to go."

"To the nearest Raider base, I assume."

"Not directly. First, I have to get to a location where I can hitch a ride with one of our spotter ships. Then I can transfer to a Raider vessel when we're far enough away from prying eyes."

"I see."

"Getting back to my story— With a Space Command uniform and a legitimate Space Command shuttle registered to the *Prometheus*, I've been able to go virtually anywhere without being questioned. Being in an isolated area of space with emergency repairs occupying everyone's mind, nobody gave a second thought to another shuttle zipping between ships. I'd heard a couple of Space Marine guards in the *Prometheus* talking about you being placed in command here, so I came over with a concocted story about being sent to pick you up for a trip back to the *Prometheus* for a meeting with Captain Gavin.

"The Petty Officer in the flight bay said he hadn't heard anything about you leaving the ship and was about to call the bridge to notify you that I was here when I spotted the deck of cards in his pocket. They saved his life because I was prepared to stop him from alerting you to my presence. I asked him if he played poker and he totally forgot about making that call. We talked poker for a while until I said I'd better report to you to find out what was going on.

"I went up to the visitor's quarters section and picked out a nice room for myself, took a nap, then returned to the flight bay to tell the Petty Officer the trip was postponed. I told him I'd been ordered to stand by on the *Song* and even assigned temporary quarters where I could wait. He invited me to play poker with him and his buddies that night if I was still around, but I told him I was too tired.

"*You* killed Nichols," Jenetta said.

"Of course," Pretorious said matter-of-factly. "I had to. I ran into him the evening before the task force was due to leave and he questioned the continued presence of a shuttle belonging to the *Prometheus*. I told him I'd received orders to return to the *Prometheus* the following morning if you didn't need me. The fool bought that and invited me to play poker again. I told him I hated penny-ante games, but I'd play if the stakes were high enough. So he invited me to play in a private game, just the two of us, and he gave me directions to a storage room he often used for such games. He said it was remote and we could play without worrying about interruption during the second or third watches."

"But you weren't there for long. We didn't find your fingerprints or any evidence of your presence."

Pretorious smiled. "Just long enough to do my chore. He opened the door when I knocked and smiled at me like I was a pigeon he was going to pluck. But when I raised the landing strut stabilizer rod I'd brought along, his expression changed and he took a quick step backward. He blocked my first swing, but when he dropped his arm in pain I swung again. I took the deck of cards from his pocket after he was down, and holding it lightly by the edges, I sprinkled them around his body to make it look like a gambling argument. Then I returned to my quarters to wait until breakfast time. I intended to enter your quarters when your breakfast was delivered, then make my escape before the task force left for Earth. No one would question my departure for return to the *Prometheus*. Once I was outside the ship, I could hide near one of the wrecked ships until most everyone was gone, then drift away quietly. The sudden departure for Higgins made me modify my plans.

Jenetta didn't mention that her breakfast wasn't delivered each morning but was fully prepared in her own galley. And there was no way Pretorious could move around the battle zone *now* without being observed. The craziness prevalent immediately following the battle was long gone. Every tac officer on duty in the task force would see the *Prometheus* shuttle leave the *Song* and question its destination. Fighters would be dispatched within minutes of the shuttle's refusal to answer the resulting hails or if Pretorious offered lame excuses and tried to escape the area. Not being equipped with FTL, a shuttle couldn't possibly elude a Marine fighter. Jenetta also refrained from saying that if she wasn't on the bridge for departure, the *Song* would never leave the area until her absence was explained. The entire task force would delay its departure while a search for the killer was conducted. She had to keep Pretorious talking and pointing out errors in his *brilliant* plan might make him reluctant to say more. "But you weren't content with just waiting," Jenetta said. "You had to harass us with fires and computer problems?"

Pretorious grinned. "Waiting in the visitor's quarters was almost as bad as being in the brig aboard the *Prometheus*. Hacking into the computer system gave me something to occupy my days. Besides, I needed information about your schedule so I could find a way to get access to you when you were alone. I also wanted to make your life as miserable as mine has been since we left Raider-One."

"Why set the fire?"

"No particular reason other than make as much mischief as I could. I left the fire suppression systems in the other sections alone so it couldn't get too far out of control."

"And the transport tube problems and laundry screw-ups?"

"The same. Those systems were the only ones I could get into or I would have done a lot more. I couldn't find any access to the Weapons Computer, but I discovered that the torpedo load and launch systems are handled by a module in the Main System. I wanted to screw up the instruction sets so that when you tried to fire your torpedoes, they jammed in the tubes. Unfortunately, that module in the computer has more firewalls than a munitions plant."

"Why did you end the mischief?"

"On the day after the transport tube shutdown, you were supposed to be plagued by a problem with bots. Every house-keeping bot on the ship would suddenly receive a priority command to vacuum the boots of every crewman while they were being worn. I was *really* looking forward to seeing that one. I figured most crewmen would spend their day lying on the deck after having tripped on bots whenever they turned around. When it didn't happen, I figured you were onto me. I dared not log into the system again in case you were waiting for me and had arranged some way to track my access point."

"You're right. We were waiting."

Pretorious smiled smugly. He was really getting off on this little game, having been unable to ostentate his cleverness with anyone during the months of isolation. Jenetta still hadn't figured a way to jump him without getting shot but was ready to take advantage of any opening that would get the pistol away from him. Her body, although appearing calm, was tensed like a coiled spring, but he had remained four meters away, far enough from her to make it impossible to reach him before he fired. He had only made one mistake so far; he hadn't made her drop the viewpad she was holding at her right side between thumb and forefinger. Perhaps he felt the small, flat device weighing only a few ounces presented no danger. Jenetta needed a diversion and was considering what she might say that would allow her to use her hands for expression. She could then flip the viewpad away from her in the hope that Pretorious' eyes would be distracted long enough to make her move. She had remembered reading something in an old detective novel when she was small where the protagonist had deliberately flipped away a lit cigarette. After subduing the killer, he'd told an associate it was almost impossible for most people not to follow the burning tobacco embers to the ground with their eyes. Perhaps the same would be true with the viewpad.

"How did you get food?" she asked.

"I snuck out each day after the third watch had started and ate in one of the mess halls. I even made a few friends from the second watch who were having dinner each morning when I came in just so I could keep abreast of the news. Then it was back to my quarters after I had eaten to relax and wait until today."

"Why today?"

"We're almost to Higgins. According to the scuttlebutt, you'll probably be returning to the *Prometheus* once we get there. Too many people aboard the *Prometheus* know my face. I'd never be able to get near you as I have here. This might be my last chance to earn a fat fee for doing what I was willing to do for free."

"A fee?"

"The million credits I've been promised for killing you."

"I had no idea my death was so important to your Raider bosses."

"You've cost them a great deal of money. They want to make sure you don't have a chance to do it again. The bounty on your head is one of the highest they've ever offered— even higher than for most heads of state they've assassinated."

"You've been in our brigs since Raider-One was destroyed. How could you possibly know what they're offering?"

"Simple. Until you blocked all outgoing com traffic on the morning we departed for Higgins, I was in touch with them through coded personal transmissions. My messages went out with the other personal communications from the ship. I've been promised a full captaincy when I get back. I'm getting the next available warship."

"Congratulations. How did you get into my quarters, by the way?"

"I got the idea while I was mucking around in your laundry bot program. I learned when laundry deliveries were made to the officers on Deck A, then simply followed a bot in when it came to bring you clean towels. I made a promise to you once and I had to keep it. The fee the company is offering simply made it imperative that I not leave until our business is conclud…"

The door annunciator system announcing Lieutenant Ashraf's presence outside the door interrupted Pretorious. As his head turned towards the corridor door, Jenetta was temporarily excluded from his main vision.

She knew it was time to act. His eyes would be off her for only a second. Although any movement might be perceived in his peripheral vision, this might be her best opportunity, her only opportunity. Instead of using the viewpad for a distraction, she decided it could best serve as a weapon. In an instant, her right arm swung backwards, then came forward again with all the power she could put into it. With a snap of her wrist, she released the viewpad. The quick fluid movement sent it spinning vertically toward Pretorious' head. The thin, rigid, twenty-six-centimeter-square device sliced through the air like a Shuriken.

Her movement did catch Pretorious' attention. His face and eyes turned back towards her just in time for the spinning viewpad to impact his nose and forehead. She'd timed it almost perfectly. Although she'd been aiming for his chin, this worked out better. His head snapped back in a reflexive action as the viewpad ricocheted off his face. A trickle of blood appeared almost immediately from a deep gash while the spinning viewpad continued on over his head to ricochet off the overhead before knocking a ceramic vase off a shelf. The force with which the viewpad struck Pretorious' face so startled him that he momentarily relaxed his grip on the pistol.

Jenetta had started moving the instant she released the viewpad. She saw the pistol tumble towards the floor as she took her second step forward, but Pretorious recovered quickly and dropped as fast as gravity would allow. The sound made by the ceramic vase as it crashed to the floor was synchronized perfectly with the fall of the pistol and it imparted a surreal quality to the scene to hear that sound as the pistol bounced.

Time seemed to slow down for Jenetta as she saw Pretorious drop to one knee and bend forward, extending his hand towards the still moving pistol as it skittered slightly away from him. She knew he'd reach the pistol before she could. She also knew Pretorious wouldn't waste any more time talking now that she had made her move. If he fumbled in the least while picking up the pistol, she could drive a fist into his face, but she couldn't depend on clumsiness. Her best chance was to disorient him with a kick to the head.

On her third bounding step forward Jenetta landed with both feet together, then launched herself with a powerful thrust of her legs while swinging her torso. The motion was a variation of a move she frequently used in kickboxing. More like an attack kick associated with tae kwon do, it caused her body to spin as it rose into the air. As she twisted, Pretorious got a grip on the pistol and began to rise, looking up just in time to see her coming at him through the air. Though the Raiders operated as a paramilitary organization, they had no academy and Pretorious was simply a bridge officer without any formal training in unarmed combat. He could plan attacks on other vessels and direct the fire of devastating weapons, but he wasn't prepared for a personal attack by someone trained in martial arts. Instead of relaxing and allowing himself to roll with the blow, as had happened with the viewpad because he hadn't had time to think about it, he foolishly stiffened, bracing himself in anticipation of the imminent contact.

With all the force her powerful limb could deliver, Jenetta's left leg snapped out and her foot made contact with the left side of his face just as Pretorious fired. His head was snapped violently sideways as he pulled the trigger. As his shot burned through her tunic, it seemed to Jenetta as if she had just kicked a tree and been kicked in return. She felt the shock of the kick from her toes to her hip, as well as the intense pain of the laser as the shot burned through her midriff.

The sickening noise of snapping bones reached Pretorious' own ears first, but Jenetta heard also. Her forward momentum carried her into him and he toppled backwards, crumpling instantly to the deck like a puppet whose strings had been cut.

From atop him, Jenetta heard him gasping frantically for air and knew his neck had been broken from the force of her desperate action. The pistol had again fallen to the floor, but there was no urgent need to retrieve it now. She dragged herself slowly off Pretorious and knelt tiredly next to him. The stench of burnt flesh and smoldering cloth reached Jenetta's nostrils as both hands clutched her midsection where she'd been shot.

Using the security override code assigned to her as acting first officer, Lieutenant Ashraf opened the door and burst into the room.

"Captain, is everything all right? I heard a crash…"

Ashraf's eyes grew as wide as saucers and she stopped talking as she spotted the deflated body of Commander Pretorious lying on the floor. She immediately ordered the computer to raise the illumination in the room.

"What's going on, Captain?" she asked anxiously.

Through clenched teeth, Jenetta grunted, "Just a visit from an old *friend*, anxious to conclude our business." She winced from the pain of her wound as she struggled to get to her feet.

Ashraf's eyes opened even wider when she spotted the burn hole in the center of Jenetta's tunic. She touched her Space Command ring and barked, "Emergency medical team to the Captain's quarters! Security to the Captain's quarters! Ashraf, out." Helping Jenetta to a nearby sofa, she said, "I was coming to tell you Major Galont has discovered there's been an unauthorized use of guest quarters." Looking at the body on the floor, Lt. Ashraf asked, "Who is he, Captain?"

"I suspect he's our unauthorized user of guest quarters. He's Commander Pretorious, a Raider officer whom I took prisoner when I commandeered the *Prometheus* for my escape from the Raider base. I suppose he was still harboring a grudge. He once told me that I was dead and he dropped by for a visit today to prove it to me." Deciding it was better that everyone not yet learn Commander Kanes had released the potential assassin, she added, "He, uh, must have escaped from the *Prometheus'* brig during the battle and stolen a shuttle during the post-battle confusion."

"He was in the brig on the *Prometheus*?"

"Yes. He was the one who divulged the information about the Raider ambush on the Mawcett convoy."

Four Marines, laser weapons at the ready, suddenly burst into the Captain's quarters just in time to hear Pretorious' last strangled gasps for air and witness his death. Lt. Commander O'Neil and a nurse followed them in as soon as the Marines determined there was no imminent danger. As the doctor dropped to one knee in front of Jenetta and lifted her tunic to examine her wound, the nurse examined Pretorious, shaking his head when Lt. Commander O'Neil glanced over. He quickly tilted his head to one side to indicate the apparent cause of death.

"The laser burned a hole through the skin and muscle across the front of your body, Captain," Lt. Commander O'Neil said. "It entered just above and slightly to the right of your navel, traveled through some twelve centimeters of abdominal muscle to your left, and exited, sealing the wound as quickly as it was made. The shot fortunately missed the stomach, and no other organs or major blood vessels appear to have been damaged. Once you've healed, you're going to have scars where the shot entered and exited, but they can be taken care of by cosmetic surgery. In the short term there'll be a considerable amount of pain from the muscle damage, so I'll administer an anodyne. The initial dosages will keep you off your feet for several days. Tomorrow we'll perform some tests to see what corrective surgery will be required."

The door to the corridor opened again and Marine Captain Galont hurried into the room. As he strode to where Jenetta was sitting, he glanced about the room and his eyes filled with horror when he saw the body on the floor.

"This NCO, on the other hand," Lt. Commander O'Neil continued, while gesturing towards Pretorious, "wasn't so fortunate. He appears to have expired immediately from a broken neck. Uh, shall we put his body into the hold we're using as a morgue freezer for the time being?"

"No. I don't want that scum put in with our brave crewmen. He's not Space Command; he's a Raider officer wearing one of our uniforms as a disguise to get close enough to assassinate me."

Galont, visibly startled by the news, yanked what appeared to be a small viewpad from a side pocket. He poked at the device lightly with his index finger a couple of times, then held it out towards the crumpled figure on the deck. Pulling it back to examine the display, he said, "That's confirmed, Captain. He has no ID chip, but he does have criminal identification marker tags in his body. He's identified as Levande Pretorious, aged 43. He was a Raider officer with the rank of Commander when he was captured on August 11th, 2267 by ..." Galont looked up in surprise before continuing, "Ensign Jenetta Carver."

"Just remove the uniform he's stolen, Doctor," Jenetta said, "and perform the mandated autopsy. Then stuff him into a body bag and put him— put him down in the Engineering locker where we store the spent deuterium canisters. It's cold enough in there that he won't start to stink."

"I'll take care of it, Captain," Ashraf said, "as soon as the doctor is finished with the body."

"Where's my steward?" Jenetta asked suddenly. "Where's Woodrow?"

The Marines were immediately alert again in case there were other assassins hiding in the suite. They started with Jenetta's office and cleared each room. One rushed back out of the dining room and signaled urgently to Lt. Commander O'Neil, who jumped up and hurried into the dining room with Marine Captain Galont right behind him.

Jenetta watched anxiously from her place on the sofa. After a few minutes, Galont emerged from the dining room door and walked to Jenetta.

"They found him in the galley, Captain. The doctor says he has a concussion but believes he'll survive. He's sent for a stretcher."

"Thank God Pretorious didn't shoot him," Jenetta said, relieved.

Two medical attendants arrived with an 'oh gee' stretcher, and in a matter of minutes, whisked Woodrow off to the sickbay. The Marines finished searching the suite and returned to pick up Pretorious' body. They unceremoniously carried him out by the arms and legs, his head dangling slackly beneath his body.

"Major," Jenetta said, "you can terminate your search for Nichols' killer. Pretorious confessed to it. He did it to keep Nichols from alerting anyone to his presence aboard this ship. If you'll check the flight bay where Nichols was assigned, you'll find a shuttle registered to the *Prometheus*. That's how Pretorious got on board. He told me he filled the shuttle with weapons stolen from an armory on the *Delhi*. He also confessed to being the saboteur causing all those computer-related problems. I'll send you a copy of the full report on this incident when I've completed it."

"Aye, Captain."

Lt. Commander O'Neil had returned to work on Jenetta after Woodrow was taken to the sick bay. He squirted an antibiotic solution into the cavity created by the laser, then sprayed a solution onto each end of the wound. The latter solvent instantly solidified into flexible bandages that sealed the openings. But when he attempted to administer the anodyne, she refused.

"No painkillers, doctor. I can't afford to be less than fully alert right now."

"Captain," Lt. Commander O'Neil said cogently in his best doctor-to-patient voice, "while not life-threatening if treated properly, your injury is extremely serious. You won't be able to function properly because the pain will be a constant distraction for your attention. You must take this medication and appoint someone to function in your stead until you've begun to recover from this wound."

"Doctor, this ship is scheduled to arrive at Higgins in a little over twenty-four hours. A Raider attack on the base there is an imminent possibility, perhaps even before we arrive. While I have the utmost confidence in my crew to handle this ship, I cannot afford to be napping while we fly into battle. I *will* be on the bridge, and I will *not* be impaired by drugs if we encounter the Raiders. You've said my injury is not life-threatening. I can promise you that in six hours I will be substantially improved and capable of performing my duties. I'm a fast healer and pain doesn't incapacitate me as it does most others."

"As chief medical officer I have the authority to relieve you of duty and order you to bed, Captain."

"And as captain of this ship I have the authority to remand anyone who interferes with the safety of this vessel or its crew to a bed in the brig— *even* chief medical officers." Softening her expression and the tone of her voice, Jenetta said, "If— tomorrow— I believe my condition will prevent me from performing at one hundred percent, I'll relieve myself."

Lt. Commander O'Neil grimaced and then nodded. He knew the best chance for the ship and crew if they flew into battle lay in having her in command on the bridge. "Very well, Captain."

"Now if everyone will excuse me, I'll get a little rest."

As the room cleared, Jenetta walked to her bedroom. Although the doctors at Space Command had tried to remove the mind conditioning she'd been subjected to while a prisoner of the Raiders, they hadn't been entirely successful. After a few minutes of severe pain, her DNA-modified body had begun to produce a neurochemical that put her into a mildly euphoric state. She was actually feeling considerably better as she laid down on her bed and was asleep almost instantly.

* * *

Marine Captain Galont returned to his quarters after leaving the Captain. He flopped tiredly onto the soft comfort of the sofa in his sitting room and stared up at the overhead.

He was a failure. He had failed to catch Nichols' killer and now he had failed to protect his captain. It didn't even seem possible that she could have survived. Pretorious had a laser pistol and the element of surprise, while she was unarmed. She should be dead! It was a tribute to her fighting skills that the assassin was dead while she was still alive after walking into that ambush, even if she had been seriously wounded. When she was feeling better, he would have to interview her so he could complete the report on the incident. Incident? It was a full blown disaster. For over a month Pretorious had the full run of the ship. He'd lived in a luxurious VIP suite and walked the decks with impunity, creating one ship-wide problem after another. And he *never* should have been able to get to into the Captain's quarters.

Space Command policy dictated that all warships have two permanent sentry posts on A Deck. One sentry was to be posted outside the captain's quarters and the other was to be posted at the beginning of the corridor leading to the bridge. This policy ensured that there were always two Space Marines between the captain and any potential assassins, except when he or she might leave A Deck. Captain Corriano had thought the rule ridiculous and ordered Maine Captain Galont to remove the sentry at his door. As ship's captain, the policy was within his power to alter. Galont had tried to convince him otherwise, but each attempt made Captain Corriano more intractable on the subject and he finally ordered that both sentries on the bridge deck be removed.

Galont should have restored those posts after Corriano was killed and Carver assumed command. The efforts to recover from the battle damage and the murder of PO Nichols had distracted him and the situation had existed for so long that he hadn't even thought about restoration of the posts. So it was his fault Pretorious had been able to get close enough to attempt an assassination.

He tried to think of what he could say to her when she was feeling better, but how does one apologize to someone for allowing them to be shot and almost killed. It seemed he was even a failure at apologizing.

Jenetta came awake instantly when the computer delivered her regular 0600 wakeup call. A twinge of pain in her left side reminded her that she had been shot less than six hours earlier, but the pain was nowhere near as bad as one would expect. She was careful not to put too much strain on the wound as she showered and prepared for the day ahead, and found that she began to feel considerably better as she moved around. Except for the occasional soreness and being ravenously hungry, she felt almost well.

Jenetta's first act after dressing was to contact the sickbay to learn what she could of Woodrow's condition.

"He's going to recover just fine, Captain," Lt. Commander O'Neil said. "He just needs a week or two of bed rest."

"Thank you, doctor. When can he receive visitors?"

"Not before tomorrow. I want him to remain perfectly calm until then. Don't worry, we're looking after him. How are *you* feeling this morning?"

"Fine. When I twist my body or bend over, I feel a slight bit of pain, but if I remain stationary it completely clears up."

"Until they heal, you'll continue to feel the pain any time you put stress on the damaged muscles. Do you still believe you can perform your duties without an anodyne?"

"As long as I don't have to fight off any assassins for a few days, I'll be fine."

"Very well, Captain. Let me know if your condition changes. As soon as we dock at Higgins, I want you to report to sickbay for a complete examination."

Jenetta nodded and pushed the viewscreen cover down on the bedside com unit. She brushed her hair quickly and prepared to walk to the officers' mess, but she heard noises coming from her dining room as she emerged from the bedroom. Walking to the door, she peered in. A mess steward, busy setting her place at the table, looked up.

"Good morning, Captain. I'm Petty Officer 1st Bartollow. Lieutenant Androsa has assigned me to be your steward in place of Chief Casell until he's ready to resume his duties. If you approve that is."

"Yes, that's fine. What's your given name?"

"Cynthia, ma'am."

"Very well, Cynthia. I'd like a mug of Columbian coffee, black, two sugars, two sectioned grapefruit halves, six eggs over easy, eight pieces of buttered toast, whole wheat, half a dozen sausages, a triple side of hash brown potatoes, and a tall stack of pancakes with maple syrup."

"Right away, ma'am," the mess steward said without even blinking. Jenetta instantly realized Woodrow must have mentioned Jenetta's unusual appetite when speaking to the other mess stewards.

When the food was served, Jenetta attacked the meal like she hadn't eaten in a week. She assumed her altered body was working overtime to repair the damage and she did her best to fuel its efforts by polishing off everything Cynthia prepared in far less time than it took to prepare it. Prior to having her DNA altered by her Raider captors, the amount she'd just consumed would have lasted her a week.

As she stepped out of her quarters on her way to the bridge, she almost walked into a Marine, who quickly braced to attention. She stopped short, expecting him to move around her and proceed down the corridor, or at least move out of her way, but he remained rooted where he was beside her doorway.

"Were you looking for me, Corporal?" she asked.

"No ma'am, Captain."

"Then why are you standing there?"

"This is my post, ma'am."

"Your post?"

"Yes, ma'am. I have your door and Lance Corporal Dwiggens has the corridor."

Jenetta turned her head and saw another Marine about thirty meters down the corridor where it branched, standing at attention. Anyone on their way to the bridge or to the quarters of the four senior command officers would have to pass him.

"How long have you been here?"

"Dwiggens and I were part of the squad that responded to the incident last night. Marine Lieutenant Schwab assigned us to your protection detail right after we carried the assassin's body to sickbay. We'll be relieved at the beginning of first watch."

"And what exactly are your orders?"

"To see that no unauthorized person or persons enters the quarters of the Captain, that of the other senior officers, or the bridge."

"I see. Very well. Please stand on the other side of the doorway or against the opposite wall in the corridor so I don't run into you every time I'm moving between my quarters and the bridge. Carry on, Corporal."

"Yes, ma'am."

It seemed a little like locking the bank after the thief had absconded with the assets, but it wasn't something she should discuss with the Corporal. He had his orders, after all, and couldn't disobey them.

Everyone on board knew of the attempted assassination by then so Jenetta received quite a few surprised looks when she entered the bridge. All eyes strained to see if she showed any sign of the damage perpetrated by the Raider assassin. Although her normally staid movements seemed to be a little more deliberate than usual, there were no signs of extreme pain, such as wincing when twisting and turning. After listening to Lt. Elizi's report and relieving her, Jenetta announced she would be in her briefing room and handed off bridge command to Lt. Risco. All eyes followed her movements until the doors to her briefing room closed behind her, then turned to silently exchange questioning looks with others on the bridge. It didn't seem reasonable that a person who had slain an assassin by herself just six hours ago, *after* being shot in the midsection, would be walking around, much less moving without evincing any pain. The legends associated with Jenetta Carver's name were sure to grow again.

Jenetta prepared a cup of steaming black Colombian coffee as soon as the doors closed behind her. Alone in the room, she permitted herself to wince slightly from the pain as she took her seat behind her desk.

"Captain, Major Galont would like to see you," Jenetta heard from her com just before noon.

"Send him in," she replied.

Galont entered the briefing room and approached the desk after being admitted. "Good morning, Captain," he said. "I was surprised to hear you were up. Do you feel able to talk about the incident?"

"Yes, Major, I do. If you hadn't come by, I would have sent for you. I want to have the matter settled and the reports filed before we reach Higgins. Have a seat. Would you care for a beverage?"

"No, thank you, Captain. I'm about caffeine'd out this morning."

"Okay, then sit back and relax while I tell you all about our assassin."

Relating everything that had occurred from the time she discovered Pretorious in her quarters until Lt. Ashraf entered the room took just eight uninterrupted minutes.

"Incredible," was all Galont said at first as he digested all she'd told him. The admiration he held for his superior officer had jumped up another notch.

"So, by Commander Pretorious' own admission, we know we have the murderer, saboteur, and potential assassin. I went into the computer a short time ago and removed the code I inserted to alert us if the saboteur accessed that socket again. We don't need the alert information anymore. I also wrote a short report for the systems people at Mars telling them about the unregistered address and what I did after I hacked into the computer. After downloading the historical logs, I'd like them to wipe the main system and reload the most recent version of certified software while the *Song* is at the space dock for repairs. That will ensure everything Pretorious mucked around with has been cleansed."

"It's incredible that Pretorious was able to move about so freely. I suppose I wasn't doing my job as security officer."

As she looked at his face and saw his downcast eyes, Jenetta realized for the first time that Galont was blaming himself for everything that happened. She should have seen it sooner, but she'd been too absorbed in other matters.

"I realize you might be feeling some responsibility for what's happened, but it was not in any way your fault. I know how hard you've worked to find Nichols' killer and our saboteur. Our systems and procedures are designed to prevent unauthorized persons from gaining access to our ships, but that effort is ordinarily only in operation while we're docked at a port. No one could have anticipated that a murderer and saboteur would arrive at a battle site wearing a legitimate Space Command uniform in a shuttle properly registered to the *Prometheus*. If there's a failure here, it's in the sensor system we use to scan ID and CT devices. We should also be scanning for those criminal marker tags you identified in Pretorious' body with the tiny device you have.

"If the sensors built into our ships cannot be adjusted to also scan for the markers, then we should at the very least have new sensors added at every possible place of entry, such as the cargo bays, flight bays, and individual airlocks. If we had had them, Pretorious would never have been able to get to Petty Officer Nichols. The system would have warned Nichols before he even opened the airlock hatch into the flight bay. He could have alerted security and had a team come to check out the situation while Pretorious was still isolated in the bay. You might want to think about including that recommendation in your report. I realize Space Command might resist a little because of the expense, but it's an important safety measure. We should also find a way to have the onboard sensors record the presence of anyone who does *not* have a CT, ID, or other identifiable marker in his or her body so security can be alerted. A warship is no place to have unauthorized people wandering around at will."

"That's an excellent suggestion, ma'am. The personnel sensor grid aboard ship should be upgraded, if possible. As you say, none of this should ever have happened. You would not have been shot and PO Nichols would still be alive. We found the murder weapon in the guest quarters Pretorious was using, by the way. It has Pretorious' fingerprints all over it and matches the striations on Nichols' body. What should we do with Pretorious' body? Eject it into space when we're near enough to a star for it to be caught in its gravity?"

"No, I have a better idea of how to dispose of his corpse. For now just leave it in the storage locker."

"Aye, Captain. As I'm sure you're aware, I've ordered that the Marine guard on your door and the bridge corridor be reinstituted. Captain Corriano ordered them off when he took command in direct noncompliance with Section Seven, Part Three, Paragraph Eighteen of the Space Command Warship Operations manual. I've kept a copy of his verbal order in case I ever needed it. I'm sorry, Captain. I should have reestablished the guard posts when you came aboard."

"It was a crazy time. I noticed the situation and meant to discuss it with you, but other events drove it from my mind so I'm just as culpable."

"We're fortunate you're so adept at defending yourself and that you'll fully recover from your wound."

"I imagine that viewpad to the face came as quite a surprise to Pretorious," she said with a slight grin. "I'm glad it's over and he's finally resting where he belongs." Jenetta paused for a second before continuing. "If you hadn't discovered that Pretorious was staying in the guest quarters, I might not be alive now. It was the distraction of Lt. Ashraf coming to my door with that information that allowed me to flip the pad at him. I've noted your diligence in your file and commended your efforts in working this case."

"Thank you, Captain," Galont said with a smile.

"Thank you, Major. Dismissed."

"Aye, Ma'am."

Galont felt substantially better after his meeting with the Captain. He still blamed himself for not restoring the sentry posts earlier, but the Old Lady wasn't blaming him and even commended his efforts in the investigation. He vowed that never again would he allow anything to happen that might make her disappointed with his actions.

* * *

"You're awfully quiet tonight, Eddie," CPO Flip Byrne said.

Chief Edward Lindsey stared at his cards for a couple of seconds before lifting his eyes to stare at Flip.

"It's the new XO," Eddie said. "What a piece a work."

"Commander Ashe is a full commander, Eddie. He's more than sixty years old and has forty-one years of service since graduating from the Academy."

"What the hell has that got to do with anything? If he was any good, he'd have made captain more than a decade ago. Damn, he's almost reached mandatory space retirement age."

"Weren't those your three complaints with our last XO? Insufficient rank, age, and experience? You should be happy. You got what you wanted—a senior officer with *decades* of experience."

"I bet Captain Novak of the *Asuncion* was glad to pawn him off on Gavin," Eddie said. "But I can't believe he might actually become the Acting Captain of the *Prometheus* if something happens to the Captain when the Raiders get here."

"Ya know, I heard the crew of the *Song* is pretty damn happy with *their* new Captain."

Eddie glowered at him. "Who told you that?"

"I've got a few friends on the *Song*. I had a chance to speak with them after things calmed down at Vauzlee. Commander Carver has the support of everyone on board and has them pulling together like never before. Of course, she had the support of *almost* everyone on board the *Prometheus* by the time she left."

"Yeah, yeah, yeah. I was wrong. Is that what you want to hear, Flip?"

"That'll do for a start. She's coming back, ya know?"

"Yeah, but maybe not soon enough. If something happens to the Captain while Ashe is still acting XO here, *he'll* become Acting Captain. Carver's official posting as second officer means she'll be under him. I can't imagine going into battle with him at the tiller. I don't have a death wish."

"You should have remembered that old saying, Eddie, before Carver left."

"What old saying?"

"Be careful what you wish for."

"Yeah, yeah, yeah. Are you going to bid or just stare at your cards all night?"

* * *

The GQ alerts sounded at 0302 aboard all seven ships in orbit around Higgins. Instantly, people were jumping out of their racks and into their uniforms. All drills had been cancelled when the CIC was activated, so everyone knew this was the real deal. The Raiders were on their way in. Possibly within minutes, every Space Command crew would be fighting for their very survival amid death and destruction on an incredible scale.

Gavin hurried to dress, but there was no panic in his movements. As he walked into the bridge he noted with satisfaction that his crew appeared almost as calm as he did. Truth be known, it was almost a relief the battle was upon them. Waiting is always the worst part of warfare because the mind is free to imagine all sorts of terrible injuries and consequences. Once the battle begins, the training takes over and all concentration is devoted to the tasks at hand.

Chapter Fifteen
~ May 18th, 2268 ~

Gavin climbed into his command chair on the bridge and turned his attention towards the large viewscreen at the front. The *Prometheus'* com operator had already logged into the CIC and the front monitor was quickly filling with the faces of other ships' captains as *they* climbed into their command chairs. While Gavin looked on, Admiral Holt arrived in the CIC and sat down at the station reserved for the base commander.

The Admiral waited until all seven Captains were seated in their command chairs before saying, "The time has arrived, my friends. The sensors have detected a large force moving this way. It can't be anything other than the Raider attack force. They jammed the Distant DeTect network signal before we could get a precise count, but we know the force is comprised of at least thirty-one ships. We won't have an exact count until we have a visual. We're sending updated information to each ship's astrogation officer. You should now move to your Station Defense Plan Echo-Three designated position and hold in preparation for meeting the enemy."

Gavin looked at his helmsman, Lieutenant Kerrey, and nodded. The ship began to move towards the position fed into the computer by the astrogator. The front view changed to an image of space ahead of the ship and the small, thirty-eight-centimeter monitor mounted on the right arm of his chair filled with the images of the other six Captains and an image of the CIC with Admiral Holt. He could speak directly with any other commanding officer via his CT simply by touching the officer's image or make a general announcement to all by touching a small icon on the bottom left side of the screen.

* * *

The buzzing of the com station on the nightstand next to her bed awoke Jenetta at around 0311. She raised the cover and looked into the face of Lt. Elizi. "What is it, Lieutenant?"

"Sorry to wake you, Captain. We've just received a message from Higgins. Their Distant DeTect network has recorded the approach of a large fleet. They believe it to be the Raider attack force."

Jenetta was instantly awake. "How far out?"

"They expect the Raiders to attack within the hour."

"What's our time to Higgins?"

"Eighty-two minutes, eighteen seconds."

"I'll be on the bridge in a few minutes."

"Should I sound GQ, Captain?"

"Not yet, let's give everyone a few more minute's sleep."

"Aye, Captain."

The screen went blank as Jenetta pushed the top down. Flipping back the bed's lightweight covers, she leapt to the floor and retrieved a uniform from her closet.

Cynthia had a mug of steaming Columbian coffee ready for her as she emerged from her bedroom. She accepted the mug, took a quick sip, and smiled at the young steward.

"Cynthia, get down to one of the Secure rooms on Deck Ten as soon as you can and get yourself seated and belted in," Jenetta said. "I won't be back here until after the battle is over and I want you to be as safe as possible in the meantime."

"Aye, Captain. Good luck."

"To all of us," Jenetta said as she walked briskly to the door, being careful not to spill her coffee.

As she emerged from her quarters, she turned to face Corporal Matthews.

"Corporal, get yourself and Dwiggens to a Secure room location."

"These are our posts, Captain. We can't leave them. Besides, there are relatively few places safer than Corridor 0 next to the Bridge."

"Very well. At least don't try to stand during the battle. Either sit or lie on the floor so you aren't knocked down."

"Aye, Captain."

A minute later, Jenetta had relieved Lt. Elizi and was climbing into her command chair on the bridge.

"Okay, Com. Let's wake everybody up. Sound GQ for fifteen seconds, then put me on ship-wide vid."

GQ alarms throughout the ship immediately began their piercing, plaintive yowl as CPO Hannigan keyed in the command. Exactly fifteen seconds later, they ceased their screams.

"Attention, crew of the *Song*," Jenetta said, looking at the vid lens on her right-hand monitor when a red dot appeared in the corner of the screen, "this is the Captain. We've just received a message from Higgins. A large group of ships believed to be the Raider attack force is fast approaching. We'll arrive at the station within sixty-seven minutes. At that time, the battle should already be underway. Everyone should be at their battle station fifteen minutes from now, ready for action. Good luck and good shooting."

Jenetta looked over at the com operator and nodded. CPO Hannigan terminated the broadcast signal as the ship's corridors came alive with hundreds of crewmembers racing for their GQ posts.

The large viewscreen at the front of the bridge was displaying a view of space in front of the ship. Jenetta stared at the screen as she thought about the battle ahead. She hadn't told her command officers they were to be replaced as soon as the ship reached Higgins and was now glad she had withheld that information. Believing themselves to be the senior staff of the ship during the upcoming battle had made them work harder to prepare. If they had thought others would be taking over and they would be pushed back into a supporting role with little responsibility, they might not have worked as hard.

For the next fifteen minutes hardly a word was spoken on the bridge. Only the communication that was absolutely necessary could be heard as officers and NCOs reported to the bridge and relieved third watch personnel, who in turn left to report to their GQ posts. Jenetta broke five minutes of complete silence when she said, "XO, is everyone at their battle station?"

"The computer reports everyone at their station except Specialist 1st/c Bowens," Lieutenant Ashraf said, looking at the small monitor mounted on the left arm of the first officer's chair.

"And where is Specialist First Bowens?"

"He's just left the sickbay, Captain. He's running for his station."

"Why was he in the sickbay?" Jenetta suspected a nervous stomach.

"According to the medical log, he tripped while jumping out of bed after the GQ alert woke him and sliced his leg on his night table. The deep cut has been bandaged and the doctor reports he's fit for duty. I have an update. The computer reports he's reached his battle station, Captain."

"Very good," Jenetta said, smiling to herself as she remembered a similar incident where *she* had displayed a bit of clumsiness after being awakened in the middle of the night by a sounded alert.

Jenetta resumed her vigil of the front viewscreen as the bridge again lapsed into total silence. At exactly 0401, CPO Hannigan at the com station said, "Captain, Higgins reports that the Raider fleet has closed to ten million kilometers. They expect to engage in seconds."

"Thank you, Chief. Can you pick up the transmissions from the CIC?"

"Negative, Captain. The base computer will only release that to ships actively engaged in the battle. We're not permitted to log in yet."

"Very well. What can we access?"

"Only the CIC General Information channel. At present it's announcing the attack is imminent and that all station personnel should get to Secure areas."

Jenetta snorted slightly. "Very well." She leaned back in her chair. They would be deaf and dumb until they were close enough to be considered part of the battle action. That probably meant about five-point-eight billion kilometers, the distance the *Song* could travel in sixty seconds at its top speed.

*   *   *

"Admiral," the lead tactical officer aboard the Raider battleship *Glorious* said loudly, "eighteen seconds to the eight million kilometer mark."

Admiral Nazeer, in command of the battle group, leaned back into his chair on the tactical bridge. "Send the message that all ships should drop their envelope at that point and engage their sub-light engines," he said.

"Aye, sir," the com operator said as he transmitted the prepared message.

"Admiral," the lead tac officer said, "the Spaccs are arrayed exactly as expected fifty thousand kilometers from the station."

Admiral Nazeer grinned. The Spaccs were always so predictable. They were following the War College's Station Defense Plan Echo-Three precisely as predicted by the Raider battle planners. Then they'd probably execute Foxtrot-Five, followed by Bravo-Two. This was going to be too easy. He didn't know how they'd learned of the pending attack, but it didn't really matter. It would have been nice to have the element of surprise, but the disparity of warship numbers was so great that the lack of an unexpected attack was inconsequential. The recurrent announcement on the station's general information com channel to civilian traffic that they should leave, or not approach, had simply cleared the area for battle. They wouldn't have to decide if a ship was a Spacc vessel or not. They could shoot at everything near the station and be assured of hitting a warship. He fully expected to take out the entire protection force with his first volley.

Gavin appeared calm and relaxed as he sat in his command chair intently watching the front viewscreen. Currently set to maximum magnification, he could see the large force of ships in the CG representation as they made their way directly towards the waiting Space Command vessels. *Perhaps that isn't exactly accurate*, Gavin thought. The truth was that the seven Space Command vessels, spread out with ten kilometers between them so that no single Raider weapon had a chance of damaging more than one ship, had moved to interpose themselves directly between the approaching Raider force and Higgins SCB. All crewmembers were at their battle stations and ready for action. In the next few minutes, the battle would begin. There were a lot of sweaty palms and dry mouths among the crew.

The sensors had noted thirty-one ships before the net was jammed, but seventy-two ships now appeared in front of the station's defenders and dropped their envelopes. It was almost a certainty the Raider torpedoes would have nuclear warheads this time around. They weren't expecting to acquire any salvageable Space Command vessels following this battle so they would be doing everything possible to obliterate the defenders. For their part, the Space Command crews felt the same way. The incredible disparity in ship numbers made it impossible for them to hold back. They would not be looking for crippling blows. They needed to destroy the Raider vessels completely. A damaged ship can still fight on and can still kill. After dropping their temporal envelopes, the seventy-two Raider ships spread out to form rows of twenty-four, arrayed in three stacked layers so every ship had a clear view of, and shot at, the station's defenders.

Less than twelve hours ago at a battle briefing with the Admiral, Gavin presented the vid from Carver in which she offered her tactical suggestions. He reflected now on the surprised expression that had come over the Admiral's face as he'd listened attentively to the unorthodox tactics proposed by Carver. The Admiral had just scowled and shaken his head as each new tactic was presented and elaborated. As the meeting ended, Holt said he would have to think about the suggested tactics before he could possibly allow them to be implemented. Gavin hoped Holt's order to array according to the War College's defense plan Echo-Three wasn't a grave misjudgment.

Gavin's calm demeanor thoroughly perplexed the crew on the bridge. At Vauzlee, they had been outnumbered two to one when the Peabody ships were factored in, but here they were facing a far more serious threat. With odds of ten to one, none seriously believed they would survive this encounter. Even if the *Song* and the three destroyers currently underway to Higgins arrived before the start of the battle, their additional strength would make little difference given the disparity in fleet sizes, yet Gavin seemed to be personally amused by something.

So far, the Raiders were behaving precisely as Commander Carver had predicted, and Gavin couldn't help but be amused by it. It was as if she had mantic powers. Looking down at his seat-mounted monitor, Gavin immediately knew by the strange expression on Holt's face that the admiral also realized the accuracy of Carver's predictions. This knowledge gave Gavin hope that they might yet survive the day.

"Multiple launches," Lieutenant Hoffmann, lead tactical officer on the *Prometheus*, said aloud. "Six hundred eighteen torpedoes inbound. ETA for lead torpedo is two-seven-zero-seconds."

All eyes not occupied elsewhere watched the front viewscreen as the wave of devastation bore down on the seven Space Command vessels. No move was made to stop or avoid the inbounds until the missiles had been traveling for one hundred twenty seconds.

"All ships, prepare to execute plan India-One," Gavin heard in his CT. It was the voice of Admiral Holt at CIC. He had thankfully decided not to follow the Foxtrot-Five tactic that would see them hold position and attempt to shoot down as many of the Raider torpedoes as possible. All officers on the bridges of the seven defending ships heard the directive. Gavin didn't have to relay instructions to his helmsman.

A temporal envelope immediately began to form around the *Prometheus*.

*   *   *

"What?" Admiral Nazeer said, "They're forming temporal envelopes? Why? You can't fire a missile through a temporal envelope."

"We do outnumber them more than ten to one, sir," his XO said. "Perhaps they're bugging out."

"No, not Space Command. They'll remain doggedly at their posts, fighting, until we crush every last breath from their broken bodies."

Until now, the Spaccs had behaved exactly as expected, as evidenced by their formation according to Strategic Station Defense Plan Echo-Three. The Raider battle planners had meticulously reviewed every plan in the Spacc's Station Defense Operations Manual and prepared a specific counter move for each, but nothing in the Spacc manual called for them to form their temporal envelopes while facing the enemy. Plan Echo-Three simply called for the Spaccs to empty their tubes at the enemy. While preventing them from firing their torpedoes because all guidance information would be scrambled in the torpedo's electronic brain as it passed through the temporal barrier, an envelope didn't offer any protection from inbound torpedoes

"Ah ha! I know what they're doing!" Admiral Nazeer said arrogantly. "We obviously have someone with a little imagination on the other side. They mean to move their ships at the last second so the torpedoes we've fired will lose their targeting as the Spacc ships accelerate away to a new position. Blast it. I *knew* we should have gotten closer before we fired our first salvo, but the planners *insisted* the Spaccs would simply stand their ground and try to knock down all our torpedoes. If we had waited until we were less than a hundred twenty seconds away we might have gotten all of them. Dammit! Com, warn all ships that the Spaccs are suddenly going to disappear and then reappear at a much reduced range, firing everything in their bow tubes. I want everyone ready to lock onto those ships and fire the next salvo the instant they reappear. Our imaginative Spacc friend is going to get a nasty surprise when he pops his head back up."

* * *

The closest Raider torpedoes were less than ten seconds away when the seven Space Command vessels engaged their Light-Speed drives. After first moving very slowly with Sub-light engines to a slightly altered position, the seven Spacc ships disappeared from visual screens, exactly as Admiral Nazeer predicted. The inbound Raider torpedoes, sensing the initial movement of their targets, used the last of their fuel to alter their flight path to new coordinates. When the ships completely disappeared a second later, the torpedoes were pointing well away from the station. They would continue on the last heading in ballistic flight until they self-detonated.

Diving down and under the incoming waves of death, the seven vessels reappeared just a thousand kilometers from the Raider fleet and dropped their envelopes so they could fire their torpedoes. Within a second of arriving at their new location, all seven ships fired a full spread. They didn't wait to target the Raider ships. They just emptied their tubes in the general direction of the enemy. In the weapons control centers located along the center axis of each ship, practiced guidance specialists waited. As each tube released its load, a specialist assumed control of the pernicious projectile and began guiding it towards a pre-selected Raider ship using fully interactive telemetry.

* * *

As the six hundred eighteen torpedoes first fired at the Spacc ships began to self-destruct so they didn't present a hazard to their own ships during the battle, imminent threat alarms began shrieking on every Raider ship. Gunners, hunched over targeting screens, strained to identify the threats on forward-looking monitors as exploding torpedoes whited out their screens momentarily, confusing their sensors and blurring their vision. Tactical officers cursed their equipment as it failed to register the approach of the Spacc missiles. Aboard the Raider destroyer *Mourning Star*, the eyes of the tac officer opened wide as he realized the torpedoes were approaching not from in front but from behind the fleet. He identified thirty-four inbound torpedoes less than nine seconds away and closing. Even though his ship hadn't been targeted, he screamed into his headset to alert other tac officers that the threat was on their stern and called for all laser gunners to open fire on the inbound torpedoes. But the stern of a warship was its weakest point. Although a freighter relied on side-mounted engines in rotating nacelles for both sub-light propulsion and maneuvering, warships used their side-mounted engines only for maneuvering quickly during battle conditions. Massive stern-mounted engines brought warships up to speed quickly, but the location of the engines restricted the placement of laser weapons on the stern and thus the coverage that could be provided.

The Raider attempt to defend against the thirty-four torpedoes was feeble at best compared to the defense they could have mounted if the attack had come at the bow or sides. They had already lost precious seconds just trying to locate the Spacc ships. Everyone aboard had been concentrating forward, waiting for the Spacc ships to reappear in front of them as Admiral Nazeer had predicted. They never expected the Space Command group to suddenly reappear just behind them.

As the few mast and keel laser gunners who *could* see the incoming torpedoes loosed a barrage of coherent light pulses in their direction, the Space Command vessels were swinging around, emptying their larboard tubes as they turned. And as their bows came to bear on the Raider fleet, they released a full salvo. Thirty-six torpedoes fired from the broadside tubes streaked towards the Raider ships, almost immediately followed by eighty-four more even before the initial salvo of thirty-four had reached the Raider fleet.

The Raider ships were left with no choice but to turn and face the onslaught of ordnance from the Space Command vessels so a greater concentration of laser weapons could provide energy defense against the assault, but in so doing they exposed their sides to the first salvo of torpedoes. The Spacc laser gunners not currently involved with defensive operations loosed a torrent of laser pulses at the exposed hulls. It can be reasonably assumed that the face of every guidance specialist and laser weapon team aboard the Space Command vessels lit up with a broad smile as the Raiders gave them targets a blind man couldn't miss.

Of the initial salvo fired from the stern tubes of the Space Command ships, eighteen were knocked down by the Raider gunners, but sixteen got through to their targets. Three Raider ships were obliterated almost immediately as secondary explosions from ruptured fuel systems or damaged fusion plants completed the job started by Space Command torpedoes, and eight more were so badly damaged that they were permanently out of the fight. Five might still be able to fight, but their offensive and defensive capability had been severely compromised.

The urgency of turning so their lasers could be used in defense of the ship had prevented the Raiders from making use of their own stern tubes, but all fifty-eight of the undamaged ships began to fire their broadside tubes as they came to bear. The Space Command laser weapon teams, busy targeting Raider energy weapons or punching holes in the sides of Raiders ships, had to stop and redirect their fire towards inbound torpedoes as space between the two forces filled with streaking death in hardened casings. The Space Command ships had begun to build their envelopes again as soon as the spread of torpedoes from their bows had left the ship.

* * *

Admiral Nazeer ground his teeth angrily as the battle damage information poured in. Eleven ships destroyed and five more in seriously bad condition, barely able to continue the fight. At least half of the others had lost energy weapons and were venting atmosphere to some degree from laser damage. The battle planners at Raider Central Command had declared with supreme confidence that the Spaccs would *never* allow the Raider fleet to get between them and the station. In fact, the Galactic Space Command Station Defense

Operations Manual clearly states that enemy ships *must* never be allowed a clear path to the defended station. But the damn Spaccs had just thrown the book away and done the inconceivable. And Nazeer, in his arrogance, had let them.

He had lost almost twenty percent of his fleet and thirty percent of his fighting effectiveness when he was suckered by that damn Spacc move. If he knew who the sneaky bastard was who'd devised that one, he'd gladly give another ten percent of his force to nail his ass.

"Okay," he mumbled to the unseen enemy who had just stolen a march on him. "You got one past me. But that's the last one you get. Prepare to die!"

Even though the Raiders were now between the station and its defenders, Nazeer couldn't use it to his advantage. If his ships turned their backs on the Spaccs to make a run on the station, the Spaccs would begin pounding their much more vulnerable sterns to space dust. Neither was Nazeer willing to surrender his heavy advantage in numbers by sending even a part of his force to attack the station while the rest engaged the Spacc ships. He needed all his lasers for a defensive umbrella. Nazeer knew that with their superiority in numbers his forces were sitting in a much better position. Eventually, the law of averages would prove out and Raider torpedoes were going to get through, reducing the already limited Spacc forces with each strike. For now the ships of both fleets continued to pound away at the other.

"Admiral," the tactical officer said after the third barrage of torpedoes from the Spacc forces ended, "they're forming their envelopes again."

"And we still haven't taken out any of their ships?"

"No, sir. I'm sure we've hurt them though. Although they've knocked down all of our birds, we've been clobbering them with our laser arrays."

Nazeer nodded. He'd known the Spaccs wouldn't remain in their position much longer. They'd only reappeared this close so his forces wouldn't have time to properly prepare their defenses for the Spacc torpedo attack. At this distance, his fleet's greater firepower would eventually overwhelm them in a bare-knuckle fight, even if the Spacc ships did have significantly better hulls and armor. But where were they going? He knew they'd never leave the area.

"Com, alert all ships to keep an extra special eye out their stern in case these bastards try another flanking maneuver like the last one."

*   *   *

The Space Command laser teams continued to fire until the order came to cease. The torpedo gunners had already ceased before the envelope formation began since torpedoes become almost useless after passing through a temporal field boundary. Upon receiving the order to execute India-Two, all seven ships seemed to disappear at once as their Light-Speed drives were engaged.

*   *   *

"Behind us," the tactical officer on the destroyer *Mourning Star* screamed into his headset and the eyes of all tac officers shifted to their aft monitors as the GSC destroyer *Buenos Aires* appeared twenty thousand kilometers behind the Raider fleet. Nervous helmsmen on every Raider ship engaged side-mounted engines and even thrusters in a desperate effort to get their ships turned to face the new direction before Spacc torpedoes could again assail their vulnerable sterns. Torpedo gunners immediately targeted the GSC ship. Four hundred sixty-four torpedoes spewed from bow tubes as they came to bear. The Raider gunners were taking a page from the Spacc handbook, and although their telemetry technology wasn't as advanced, they would attempt to lock onto targets and guide the torpedoes *after* they were in flight.

As the blizzard of torpedoes raced towards the *Buenos Aires*, imminent threat alarms began sounding at every Raider tactical station. Horrified tac officers realized that as they had been watching the *Buenos Aires*, the other six Spacc ships had returned to previous positions behind them just a thousand kilometers away and fired a full salvo of seventy-five torpedoes from their bow tubes towards the again susceptible sterns of the Raider ships.

The SC laser teams continued to provide defensive fire as the six Space Command warships formed their envelopes and again disappeared.

"Son of a...!" Admiral Nazeer screamed loudly at no one in particular as damage reports came flooding in.

Another nineteen ships had been completely destroyed and nine more seriously damaged while his people had been wasting their torpedoes firing at a wisp. The Spacc ships had been limited to stern torpedo numbers the first time, but for the second maneuver they had simply dipped under the Raider fleet and taken a quick, fifteen-second circular trip around the station's outer traffic pattern. When they returned, their bows still pointed towards the Raider fleet. The trip, lasting only as long as they estimated it would take the Raider ships to turn a hundred eighty degrees after spotting the *Buenos Aires*, had been so quick that DeTect sensors were still reporting the information as the GSC ships fired their torpedoes. No one had noticed, or at least not realized the significance of the fact, that the GSC destroyer *Buenos Aires* had never dropped her temporal envelope so she could fire torpedoes. As the massive barrage from the Raider fleet bore down on her, she simply engaged her Light-Speed drive and again disappeared from sight and targeting systems.

* * *

"That's cut them down to size," Admiral Holt said excitedly to his ship commanders as the seven ships reappeared at their original positions fifty thousand kilometers from the station. "*Thirty* of their largest and most powerful ships out of the battle and fourteen more severely damaged. Very well done! Prepare to execute India-Three as they approach the station."

* * *

"The seven Spacc ships have assumed a defensive posture fifty thousand kilometers from the base between our forces and the space station, Admiral," the tactical officer said to Admiral Nazeer. "They're back at the Echo-Three positions where they started."

"That bastard has suckered me twice, dammit. I want his hide on my office wall. I bet he has to be inside the Space Station. Enough of this damn nonsense. Com, notify all ships to execute attack plan Niagara."

*   *   *

"The Raider fleet is moving towards the station, Captain," the tac officer aboard the *Prometheus* said. "They're in two parallel formations, approaching the station like stacked waves."

"Waves?" Gavin echoed. Carver hadn't expected the Raiders to throw caution to the wind this early by committing to a direct frontal assault on the station. She had given a sixty-seven percent chance that they would attempt to circle the station, imitating the action of the Space Command forces at Vauzlee. India-Three was her response to that action.

*   *   *

"Prepare to execute India-Four," Admiral Holt bellowed. "The Raiders have advanced the script a bit."

As the Raider ships accelerated to Sub-Light-100, the bridge crews aboard the Space Command vessels kept one eye on their monitors and the other on the front viewscreen. From their last battle positions, it would take the Raider ships just over a minute to reach the station, but time seemed to slow down, the seconds passing like minutes.

The seven Space Command vessels were still mainly intact. Less powerful than Space Command's Phased Array Lasers, the Raider energy weapons had failed to penetrate the titanium hulls with most strikes, and where they had penetrated, the punctures were quickly sealed by internal membranes. Only a few holes were bleeding atmosphere.

Positioned directly between the station and the Raider fleet, the Space Command ships waited for the inevitable torpedo barrage.

*   *   *

"All ships," Admiral Nazeer said to the thirty-six Raider vessels still able to fight, "slow to Sub-Light-5 and prepare to fire all bow torpedoes on my command."

Nazeer watched the forward monitor closely as his tac officer calculated the optimum firing point. The Spaccs hadn't yet begun to build envelopes so they wouldn't be disappearing at the last second this time.

"Optimal range in eighteen seconds, Admiral," his tac officer said. "The countdown is on your left monitor.

Nazeer's eyes darted to the monitor, counting down with the timer. As it reached one second he said, "Fire torpedoes."

Two hundred ninety-eight torpedoes spewed forth from the Raider fleet.

* * *

With an average of forty-two nuclear-tipped torpedoes bearing down on each ship, it would be a miracle if none got through. Following the India-One maneuver, the defenders had managed to deflect or destroy every torpedo sent their way, but those were staggered firings coming from the Raider ships on a 'fire at will' basis as gunners got a lock on a target. This barrage had been fired as one massive salvo, relying on the ability of the guidance people to find a target after launch and 'fly' the ordnance to that point. Two hundred ninety-eight torpedoes were a serious threat, but it was less than half the six hundred eighteen the Raiders had let fly when they first arrived.

Captain Payton sat grimfaced on the bridge of the *Thor*. He wasn't anxious to die, but he knew his ships and his crew were expendable. Everything must be sacrificed to save the station.

"Okay, people," Captain Payton said, "here they come. All gunners fire at will as soon as you have a lock. If this is to be our final hour, let's ensure that it's our finest hour."

Pulses of coherent light began to fill space between the seven warships and the approaching torpedoes. Intermixed with the laser pulses was a full spread of eighty-four torpedoes from the bow tubes of the Space Command vessels.

They didn't expect to fool the Raiders, but the energy pulses might confuse the Raider defensive systems slightly.

* * *

Admiral Holt watched anxiously from the base's CIC as the horde of nuclear-tipped torpedoes approached his small protection fleet. The fifty-thousand-kilometer distance took his station's Phased Array Lasers out of the defensive picture for the present, but his weapons experts were standing by, waiting for the inevitable approach by the Raider armada.

As his ships knocked down approaching torpedoes, red lights on the threat board began to wink out, but far too many remained. As the distance closed, the red lights disappeared at an ever faster rate, but there were still so *many*.

* * *

Captain Wong, aboard the *Buenos Aires*, watched tensely, her hands gripping the arms of her command chair so tightly that she would have left fingerprints in a more pliable material. Most of the incoming torpedoes had so far been destroyed, or had had their detonation circuitry ruined by laser strikes, but it would only take one.

The threat alarms at the tac station had been bleating out danger warnings for over thirty seconds. If a torpedo was going to get through, it would happen in the next ten seconds.

Wong had just begun to think they might once more escape mostly unscathed when she was suddenly pitched violently sideways. Her seatbelt kept her from being thrown from her chair, but the powerful movement twisted her body in such a way as to cause a severe muscle spasm in her back.

"Tac, where have we been hit?" Captain Wong asked through clenched teeth as she winced in pain.

The lead tac officer, flung just as violently as everyone else, was gripping his console and trying to decipher the readouts. "We were struck amidship on the starboard side, Captain. I can't be any more precise than that. I only know the exterior hull sensor grid is damaged there."

"Com, see if engineering has any more information. Helm, can we move?"

"It appears so, Captain, but I'm getting strange readouts from the starboard sub-light engine. Our movements may be sluggish if we have to rely solely on the larboard engine and thrusters for maneuverability."

"Do the best you can. We'll be moving very shortly now."

* * *

Admiral Holt relaxed slightly and expelled the breath he'd inadvertently been holding. Only two torpedoes of the almost three hundred fired at his ships had done serious damage. The *Buenos Aires* and *Thor* were hit, but both were reporting themselves battle worthy. It was time for their next move. Since the Raider ships were still bearing down on the seven Space Command warships at five thousand kilometers per second, it seemed their intent was to plow through the defenders and attack the station directly.

"All ships execute India-Four," Holt said.

Almost as one, the seven warships turned up on end and flew perpendicular to the plane of attack established by the approaching ships. The *Buenos Aires*, an enormous fissure apparent on its larboard side just aft of its maneuvering engine, *was* just a bit slower than the others, and there was a hole in the *Thor's* bow large enough to fly a shuttle through.

* * *

"What the *devil* are they doing now?" Admiral Nazeer said as he watched the holographic image of his fleet's closure on the station. "Tac?"

"Sir?"

"Suggestions."

"I— uh, don't know, sir. There's nothing like that in the Station Defense Operations Manual. They seem to be deliberately exposing their keels to our energy weapons."

"It has to be a botched maneuver. Let's take advantage of their screw up. All laser gunners open fire. Fill their bellies with holes."

As the Raider ships saturated space with pulses of coherent light, Admiral Nazeer's tac officer suddenly screamed, "Admiral, minefield ahead."

"All ships break off," the Admiral shouted, but it was too late. Traveling at five thousand kilometers per second space normal, the front wave of eighteen ships couldn't stop or turn away in time. They plowed directly through the minefield.

Ten of the lead wave of ships encountered a fusion mine. Eight of those were almost obliterated as the mines exploded against their bows. The proximity triggers fired their mine just ahead of actual contact with the ship and the ship's speed ensured that the effects enveloped the ship from the bow to the stern. The other two ships, suffering the effects of the blast against either their larboard or starboard hulls, were so badly damaged that they were permanently out of the fight. The second wave was able to avoid the minefield completely.

"Dammit!" Admiral Nazeer screamed at his tac officer. "Where did that minefield come from? Didn't you scan the area before we began our attack run?"

"Yes, sir, Admiral," the nervous tac officer said. "Those mines definitely weren't there when we launched our torpedo strike a few minutes ago."

"Then where the hell did they come from?" he screamed.

"They must have been dropped somehow by the Spacc ships, sir."

"Dropped?!" Admiral Nazeer screamed. His face grew even angrier as he realized he had been suckered yet again. "Yes, dammit. That had to be the reason for that crazy maneuver and why they exposed their bellies to our fire. They distracted us by offering so easy a target that we never noticed them dropping the mines. Dammit," he bellowed, "I want some Spacc butt." Pressing the com control on his chair, he shouted, "All ships, attack the station. Blast it to space dust and rubble."

Admiral Nazeer leaned back in his chair and watched the action on the bridge's large monitor as his ships, now scattered all around the station, began to launch torpedoes from all operational tubes. There would be no more formations, no more coordinated attack strategies. Each captain knew that once they reached this point, they were on their own with orders to destroy the station at all costs. They were free to maneuver however they wished to accomplish their mission.

The Spacc ships had taken up positions within a few kilometers of the station. They knew there would be no more maneuvering and prepared for the final slugfest. They would hold position and do their best to knock down any and all torpedoes from the twenty-six remaining Raider ships, but at almost four to one, the numbers were still significantly in favor of the Raiders.

The Raider ships began to circle the station following unplanned and uncoordinated circular and elliptical paths. They seemed to be everywhere as they fired torpedoes from their bow, broadside, and stern torpedo tubes. The space around the station was alive with surging death. With no pattern being followed by the Raider ships, the danger of running into one of their sister ships, a Raider torpedo, or one of the remaining Spacc mines seemed to be as great as the danger from Spacc torpedoes.

Inexorably, the advantages of numerical superiority shifted the tide of battle from the series of sensational kills by the Spaccs to significant strikes by the Raiders. Even with the station's own defenses fully engaged, more and more of the Raider torpedoes began to penetrate the defensive umbrella and strike their targets. The Spacc ships began to take serious hits, each of which reduced their ability to defend themselves and the station. Nazeer had always known that, in the end, the volume of torpedoes he could fire at the station and its defenders would make all the difference.

* * *

Captain Payton sat cursing the fates under his breath. A Raider torpedo had taken out a significant area of his bow in the last barrage, leaving the area open and exposed to space. Airtight emergency doors had immediately sealed off the area, but he had lost all of his bow tubes and at least a hundred crewmen who were working in the four forward torpedo rooms involved. He'd turned his ship towards the station so he was pointed away from the circling Raiders, but Bellona-class battleships only had eight tubes mounted in the stern. That was just half the number of tubes he'd had in his bow.

His energy weapon gunners were doing a good job so far, but several torpedoes had gotten by them and struck the station, two hitting the docking ring and one striking the station itself. He felt incredibly impotent. His ship, while still firing torpedoes as fast as the tubes could be loaded, had to remain in position and take a pounding by Raider ships free to maneuver at will. On the front viewscreen, he saw a circling Raider ship suddenly obliterated by a brilliant flash of light. A torpedo from one of the defenders had scored a killing hit. A brief cheer went up on the bridge a second before Payton was flung violently sideways and everything went dark.

*　*　*

Gavin sat quietly watching the battle rage in front of him. Throughout his long and distinguished career he'd never felt so helpless. Even during the years before becoming a ship's captain when he'd had to sit by and watch his commanding officer make all the decisions he hadn't felt so ineffectual. But he knew his duty and he would do it.

The images of Captain Payton of the *Thor* and Captain Simpson of the destroyer *Bonn* had disappeared from the monitor by his right hand. He could only assume that meant their ships had been severely damaged or perhaps totally destroyed. He couldn't take the time now to check. His people needed to concentrate on the tasks at hand.

So far, the *Prometheus* had been lucky. Only three torpedoes had gotten through the invisible barrier established by the laser weapons protecting the ship, and they had all been fission-type warheads rather than fusion weapons. But tritanium armor had still been ripped away or melted, and great rents had been opened in the hull. The worst was just aft amidship, but no major systems had been compromised there. The maneuvering engines were still intact even though they weren't needed at present. Oddly enough, the worst internal damage was to the torpedo room lost during the Battle of Vauzlee. The hull had been covered over in that area because parts weren't available to repair the damaged tubes, so the area had been empty of personnel. Perhaps it was a blessing that the crew of the *Prometheus* was so nominal at present. Other than torpedo room personnel and engineers needed to handle emergencies and report damage, most everyone on board was either in one of the weapons control centers, the bridge, the AC&C, the Maintenance Operations Center in the stern, or one of the Secure rooms. All located along the center axis of the ship, these areas were the most heavily fortified and protected.

*   *   *

Admiral Holt watched the holographic representation of the furious action outside the station with rapt fascination. It reminded him of an old movie he'd once seen that attempted to recreate the craziness of a dogfight in the skies over France during Earth's First World War. That the maneuvering of modern destroyers weighing more than a hundred thousand tons each could be evocative of the choreography employed by the paper-covered kites they had flown back then was amazing. But such were the advantages of total weightlessness and massive maneuvering engines.

The *Thor* and *Bonn* were out of the fight and several minutes ago had been officially listed as destroyed. The hulls were still there, but the damage was incredible. With just five of his ships still fighting, twenty-four Raider ships still circled the station. All bore the unmistakable signs of severe battle damage, but they were still maneuvering and still firing waves of torpedoes at the station and protection fleet. The Space Command ships also bore the conspicuous signs of battle involvement. The great battleships were only still operational thanks to the incredible armor they carried. The *Chiron* had so far withstood the devastating effects of four nuclear-tipped torpedoes that would have destroyed lesser ships and the *Prometheus* had suffered three. The question now was how many more hits could these behemoths withstand and still remain in the fight? For that matter, how much longer could the severely damaged *Calgary*, *Geneva*, and *Buenos Aires* remain battle-ready? With each injury, fewer torpedoes and less laser fire came from the struck ships.

Without checking, the admiral knew personnel were being called away from Secure rooms and weapons consoles to fight fires and seal atmosphere leaks, while other personnel carried bleeding, wounded, and irradiated comrades to emergency triage centers where their injuries could be evaluated and basic medical treatment begun. The medical personnel aboard those ships were no doubt being taxed to their limits.

*   *   *

"The CIC GI channel reports that the Raider fleet has attacked the station in two massive assault waves, Captain," CPO Hannigan said aboard the *Song*. "Most of the lead ships were destroyed by mines, but the others have broken formation and are now attacking independently. The fighting is fierce and the station has already suffered great damage."

Jenetta slumped slightly in her seat before remembering she must appear unperturbed in front of the crew and she immediately reassumed the apathetic posture she always strove to project when on the bridge. She knew that independent action on the part of the Raider ships indicated the battle had entered the final stages. She began to fear the *Song* would arrive too late to be of any help in protecting the base.

"Astrogation, how long before we reach Higgins?"

"Sixteen minutes, forty-three seconds, Captain."

Jenetta clenched her jaws and stared at a front view-screen devoid of pertinent information.

"The CIC is calling, Captain. They want to know how far we are from the station."

"Astrogation?" Jenetta said.

"Approximately ninety-six billion kilometers, Captain," the astrogator said.

"Relay that, Chief," Jenetta said.

"Aye, Captain."

Several more minutes passed as Jenetta stared intently at the front viewscreen as if searching for any sign of the station, knowing all the time that it was far too distant to see yet.

"Captain, there's something strange here," CPO Hannigan, said.

"What is it, Chief?" Jenetta asked.

"I'm picking up com signals coming from an area where there shouldn't be any."

"How far away, Chief?"

"I've taken several reading over the past ten minutes to plot the position. The computer estimates they're coming from a point some fourteen billion kilometers from Higgins."

"Is the traffic heavy?"

"Extremely! That's why it caught my attention."

"Could it be a relay satellite?" Jenetta asked.

"Doubtful, Captain. The transmissions appear to be originating from that location."

"Tactical, send a plot to my right-hand monitor and send the coordinates to astrogation. Astrogator, how much additional time will we expend if we divert to that location on our way to Higgins?"

Jenetta stared at the small screen while the calculations were performed.

"Four minutes, fifty-two seconds, Captain, if we don't stop there," the astrogator said.

"Four minutes, fifty-two seconds," Jenetta whispered to herself as she stared at the plot image on her monitor. Not very much time in the normal scheme of things, but right now she knew it could be measured in lives lost.

"Captain, message from Captain Gavin," CPO Hannigan said, "He says to tell you— *the Indians have them surrounded?*"

A hint of a smile crossed her face and then was gone. "Acknowledged. Tell him the cavalry is on the way."

In the westerns her brother Richie so enjoyed as they were growing up, the cavalry almost always managed to arrive in the nick of time. She hoped they would be in time to help the besieged defenders at Higgins.

Jenetta knew losing five minutes at Higgins could be crucial. Their forces were being pounded and the firepower of the *Song* was desperately needed if they were to have even a remote chance of prevailing. The battle at Vauzlee had lasted less than thirty minutes from the time the first torpedoes had been launched and less than seventeen minutes following the arrival of the *Prometheus*. This battle had already been raging for nineteen. If she diverted and was wrong about the transmissions, her career in Space Command would be over. Not only that, many people at the station might die in that interval and she could be court-martialed for her action.

There was another consideration as well. Although FTL speed was provided using electrical energy produced by the ship's antimatter processing and the ship could effectively remain underway for up to half a century without returning to a base for refueling, the sub-light engines relied on hydrogen for propulsion. The most common element in the universe, hydrogen was normally harvested in the dense upper atmosphere of gas giants where it was most plentiful or in various nebulae where heavy concentrations were found. Huge tanker vessels with enormous scoops and collector systems spent weeks collecting hydrogen and then offloaded their supply at tank farms before heading out again. But hydrogen was also available in trace amounts in open space. Stationary warships could collect hydrogen on their own, but their processing systems were small since their needs were ordinarily limited. They normally only had to refill their tanks for the amount of fuel expended during their approach to a station or for the small amount used when maneuvering around the ships they stopped for inspection. Following extensive maneuvers, warships would always fill up from a base's supply. The *Song* had used up more than half its supply while maneuvering in sub-light during the Battle at Vauzlee and the month they'd spent at the battle site hadn't been long enough to replenish even a small part of what they'd used. And it wasn't possible to collect hydrogen while cocooned in a DATFA envelope traveling FTL.

Once it reached Higgins, the *Song* would have to quit the battle when it ran out of fuel for the sub-light engines. Deviating now would exhaust still more of the precious commodity when the *Song* reached the location of the transmissions and thus reduce the time it could participate in the fight at Higgins. The conundrum of what was behind the mysterious transmission of signals originating at a place where there should be no signals more than provoked Jenetta's curiosity, but the prudent course of action was definitely to ignore the unexplained com signals and continue on to Higgins as ordered.

"Dammit," Jenetta muttered almost silently under her breath.

Chapter Sixteen
~ May 18th, 2268 ~

"Helm," Jenetta said, after silently cursing herself a half dozen times for her folly, "make for the source of the communication signals but not directly at it. Make your heading a hundred kilometers to starboard. When the source is three hundred twenty degrees off our larboard, drop our envelope and accelerate directly towards the source at maximum sub-light. Tactical, prepare to fire a full spread from the bow tubes as soon as you have a target lock. You'll have just five seconds to identify your targets, get a lock, and fire. Target the largest ships first. Deploy a sensor buoy as we go sub-light. Helm, as soon as the torpedoes have been fired, resume course for Higgins at our fastest possible sub-light speed while you reform our envelope. Resume maximum FTL as quickly as possible."

"Aye, Captain," the helmsman and tactical officers said loudly.

Most eyes on the bridge were glued to the front view-screen as the ship, traveling at its top speed of ninety-four-point-six million kilometers per second, drew ever closer to the source of the com signals. Jenetta, her heart beating at twice normal, did her absolute best to appear composed and icy calm. To the bridge crew she appeared as cool as the surface of Vauzlee, the ice planet nearest the scene of their last battle. While others licked their lips nervously or swallowed imaginary lumps, she seemed to be calmly contemplating the color of the coffee in her ever present coffee mug.

From the corner of her left eye, Jenetta saw a face that shouldn't be on the bridge. Catching Lieutenant Ashraf's eye, she nodded her head slightly toward the third watch astrogator who was standing near the rear bulkhead. He had reported to the AC&C when relieved following the sounding of GQ, but he must have snuck back to the bridge at some point after that. Ashraf turned her head in the direction of the nod.

"Lt. Merdana," Lt. Ashraf said loudly, "what are you doing up here?"

"Uh, nothing, ma'am. I'm just observing."

"Didn't you learn anything from our last engagement? You know all officers whose GQ post is not on the bridge have no place being here when we're about to go into action. Your post is in the AC&C, so do your observing from there. Now get your donkey out of here in ten seconds or you go on report."

"Yes, ma'am," the young lieutenant(jg) said nervously as he hurried towards the corridor door.

Lt. Ashraf looked over at Jenetta and shook her head. The corners of Jenetta's mouth turned up momentarily before she turned her attention back to the front monitor.

*   *   *

The ship's DeTect system spotted the *Song* and sent a message to the ship's ACS, which caused a warning buzzer to sound on the lead tactical officer's console. He immediately stabbed at the button to silence the buzzer and checked the plot. The approaching ship was almost four minutes away in FTL. It was large and had to be either a freighter or a warship, but since it was neither coming from the direction of the space station nor heading towards it, it obviously wasn't a Space Command or Raider vessel. It had to be some fool freight hauler who hadn't heard the Space Command broadcast to avoid this area until further notice. Since its course would take it well wide of the stern, it presented no danger of collision. The lead tactical officer breathed a sigh of relief and returned his full attention to the battle.

*   *   *

Finally, the *Song* helmsman said, "Five seconds to sub-light. Three... Two... One... Sub-light."

As the ship emerged from its temporal envelope, the helmsman engaged the sub-light engines. The enormous ship leapt forward in n-space, accelerating as if shot from a catapult while the gravitative inertial compensators kicked in to keep the crew from being spattered against the rear bulkheads. At the same time, the enlarged CG image of a single battleship a thousand kilometers distant off the larboard bow filled the front viewscreen. And what a battleship! It was the largest warship anyone on the bridge had ever seen or even envisioned. The tactical computer put its length at three thousand, two hundred twenty-seven meters with a beam of four hundred twenty meters. Having an estimated mass of almost three and a half million tons, it was like a floating island in space and out-massed both the *Prometheus* and *Chiron* combined. Space Command's newest class of battleship only measured one thousand nine hundred seventy meters in length, had a beam of two hundred ninety-two meters, and massed nine hundred thirty-two thousand tons. The *Song*, at only nine hundred eighty meters in length and massing four hundred seventy-six thousand tons, was positively dwarfed by the gargantuan vessel. In fact, the Raider battleship was wider than all the destroyers in the Space Command fleet were long. The Franklin Class frigates, the largest warships before moving up to the light cruisers, were only six hundred twenty-four meters in length.

Jenetta's heart skipped a beat when she first saw the battleship, but she maintained her composure. The configuration of the ship was unlike anything she had seen before, but since it was in a battle zone and wasn't Space Command or Nordakian, the warship had to be presumed to be an enemy ship. "The bigger they are, the harder they fall," she muttered to herself.

As the *Song* continued to accelerate at a phenomenal rate, it turned directly towards the battleship. Two of her tac officers were already hunched over their equipment, painting key target points on the battleship's hull that would be stored in the electronic brains of the torpedoes. Once released, the torpedoes would be on their own since the *Song* was already late for another appointment.

Five hundred kilometers from the battleship, the *Song* eructed a full spread of torpedoes from its bow tubes. Twelve cylinders of death burst almost simultaneously from the heavy cruiser and streaked towards the enemy battleship, their heat trails visible on the front viewscreen. A second later, as the *Song*'s helmsman swung the ship to resume course for Higgins, the lead tac officer said, "The battleship has just scanned us, Captain."

* * *

As warning buzzers assaulted the ears of the lead tactical officer aboard the Raider battleship *Glorious*, he realized the ship he had chosen to ignore was not a freighter after all. "Admiral," he said loudly and nervously, "a warship has just appeared off our larboard side."

"What?" Admiral Nazeer said as his attention was distracted from the front viewscreen. "One of ours?"

"No, sir. The computer identifies it as Space Command. It's a Kamakura-class heavy cruiser."

"Impossible. The only Kamakura-class heavy cruiser in this deca-sector is the *Song*. And we know the *Song* was severely damaged at the site of the convoy attack."

"The *Prometheus* and *Chiron* are defending the space station sir. Perhaps the rest of Gavin's task force is out here searching for us. The cruiser has launched torpedoes."

"Red alert," the admiral bellowed. "Tactical, launch torpedoes as soon as you have a lock. Com, alert the fleet that we're under attack. Tell Captain Wolff to break off two destroyers and dispatch them to us immediately. Helm, get us moving."

* * *

"They've launched torpedoes, Captain," the lead tactical officer aboard the *Song* announced.

Jenetta just sat in her command chair calmly watching the forward viewscreen. She had already made her decisions and given her orders. There was no changing them now.

As ordered, the helmsman had begun to form the temporal envelope as soon as the torpedoes were away. Accelerating rapidly under the power of its straining sub-light engines, the *Song* was quickly distancing itself from the battleship. The torpedoes from the battleship were likewise accelerating rapidly as they flew in pursuit of the *Song*, but it would be several minutes before they could hope to overtake the ship.

"A day late and a credit short, I'd say," Jenetta murmured as she glanced at the chronometer in the corner of her chair's left monitor. The envelope would be formed before the torpedoes could catch them. As the *Song* disappeared from both sight and torpedo-targeting systems, she said, "Tactical, let's see the image recorded by the sensor buoy you deployed. Put it on the front viewscreen."

The images from the buoy, transmitted on the IDS Communications band, appeared a second later as the tactical officer isolated the correct azimuth and inclination to project from the collected data. When the CG images created from the buoy's sensors appeared, the *Song* could be seen moving away on a course directly towards the battleship, firing its torpedoes.

Being so far from the battle zone, most of the Raider battleship's laser gunners had wandered away from their consoles to talk and joke with their fellows. The GQ alert sent them scrambling for their stations, but only those who had conscientiously remained at their assigned posts aboard the battleship were able to rake the starboard side of the heavy cruiser as it turned towards Higgins. They then turned their fire on the inbound torpedoes. They were good and there were quite a few of them, so they managed to knock down three or four of the inbound torpedoes. If the *Song* had only fired four, if the *Song* had fired them from a greater distance, or if the laser gunners had been more disciplined, the battleship might have remained undamaged. But there were only seconds between the time the *Song* was scanned and the time the torpedoes began to explode against and inside the hull of the enemy ship. The Raider admiral had barely enough time to give orders to his com operator and his tactical officer. If he'd known just how close the *Song* was when it emerged from FTL and turned towards the battleship, perhaps he wouldn't have bothered.

The *Song* had expended all its fusion warheads at the Battle of Vauzlee, and unlike the *Prometheus* and *Chiron*, hadn't had an opportunity to resupply, so the torpedoes fired at the Raider battleship only carried high-explosive warheads. The acceleration of the ship towards the battleship, coupled with the acceleration of the torpedoes themselves, provided sufficient impact force for two of them to punch completely through the battleship's extra-thick titanium armor and explode well inside the ship, while the others only managed to rip away sections of armor plating and perhaps pierce the hull sufficiently to evacuate the air in some of the outermost sections. Two huge holes suddenly appeared in the battleship, belching fire for the briefest of seconds and then simply bleeding atmosphere as alarms sounded throughout the ship. The gargantuan ship was wounded, but neither out of the fight or even seriously damaged. And the *Song* couldn't return to fire again. It might have been suicide anyway now that the Raider crew was alerted to their presence.

That could very well have been the end of the *Song*'s attempt to disable the battleship if one of the two torpedoes that had pierced the hull hadn't fortuitously ruptured a liquid fuel storage tank supposedly protected by reinforced titanium bulkheads. Sparks from a smashed housekeeping bot working in the area when the torpedo exploded ignited the gushing fuel and a massive explosion promoted secondary explosions that began to ripple through the ship. The tiny, insignificant bot performing a self-test diagnostic routine on its damaged components had unintentionally continued the job begun by the *Song*'s massive torpedoes. As the lights from the explosions dimmed, bits of wreckage from the enemy ship could be seen radiating outward in every direction.

The torpedoes launched from the Raider battleship lost the *Song* as it disappeared at Light-322 and exhausted their fuel trying to reacquire a target long gone before entering ballistic flight and eventually self-detonating.

The *Song*'s twelve torpedoes might have seemed like over-kill initially, but there hadn't been time to wait around and fire a second or third salvo if a first salvo was shot down or failed to disable the target. There were a few light claps and small cheering noises at the damage inflicted upon the battleship, but it was fairly subdued. The crew knew the real battle was still just minutes ahead of them.

"Astrogation, time to Higgins?" Jenetta asked.

"Two minutes, sixteen seconds, Captain," he responded.

"Com, I need damage reports," Jenetta said.

"They're coming in now, Captain. I'm forwarding them to your chair's holo-tube."

Jenetta reached for the holo-tube, lifting it from its storage holster on the outside of her chair. The list of damage reports that jumped up from the tube as she activated it showed that the ship had been struck repeatedly by the powerful laser weapons of the battleship. A few dozen punctures had self-sealed, but one location was continuing to bleed atmosphere slowly, indicating severe damage to the self-sealing membrane in that part of the ship. That hull section had been sealed off and engineers were suiting up in EVA gear in preparation for rigging a temporary patch against the inside plating. The ship was still battle worthy.

All idle talk on the bridge ceased as everyone's thoughts turned to the upcoming fight.

"Captain," Chief Hannigan said, "the *Prometheus* is asking for our ETA. They desperately need any reinforcement we can offer."

"Tell them we're proceeding at one hundred percent FTL and we'll be there in two minutes, Chief. Helm, do you remember the maneuver used at the recent battle?"

"Aye, Captain. I was in AC&C. You want me to turn to starboard when we arrive and circle the area?"

"Affirmative. That was the coded message Captain Gavin sent earlier. Com, put me on ship-wide."

"You're on, Captain," the com said as he linked Jenetta's CT to the intercom system.

"Attention, crew of the *Song*. This is the Captain. In less than two minutes we'll reach Higgins where an intense battle is currently raging. Captain Gavin has ordered us to circle outside the battle as we did during our last engagement a month ago. Gunners, you have permission to open fire as soon as you get a lock on any target. Make your shots count. Let's send these Raiders where they belong."

With the completion of the message to the crew, Jenetta's role in the battle was mostly over. She would now sit calmly on the bridge and watch as the battle raged around her, ready to give new orders if and when the situation warranted them, but basically the fight would be in the hands of her crew.

Ninety seconds later, the *Song* appeared at Higgins and dropped its envelope less than a thousand kilometers from the station. Her massive sub-light engines were engaged and she surged ahead towards the battle zone. Torpedo specialists and laser weapon teams were hunched over their screens, ready for almost anything except the sight that greeted them. The battered and broken hulls of warships floated and twisted silently everywhere. Huge, gaping holes in the station and docking ring were further testament to the ferocious fighting that had just taken place here, but there wasn't the slightest sign of activity. No torpedoes flew at the *Song* and no flashes of coherent light buffeted her hull.

"Com," Jenetta said with a slight sense of urgency in her voice, "try to contact the *Prometheus*."

"The base's Combat Information Center is trying to contact us, Captain."

"Put it up on the viewscreen."

An image of Admiral Holt sitting in his chair in the CIC appeared a second later.

"Sir," Jenetta asked, "what's happened? Where are the Raiders?"

"We're still trying to work that one out ourselves, Captain. They were pinning our ears back when they suddenly broke off the engagement sixty seconds ago and left in every direction. Captain Gavin believes they might have left to regroup so they can attack again when we stand down to make emergency repairs. I've ordered all ships to remain in War Active status while we determine the situation. If they have really quit the battle, we'll need to begin making emergency repairs. Since you have the only undamaged ship, you'll have picket duty."

"Understood, sir. We only have one section that's losing atmosphere."

"What? I thought your emergency repairs were completed weeks ago."

"They were, sir. The damage I'm referring to is a new puncture received a few minutes ago during a skirmish with a Raider battleship."

"There were no Raider battleships at this action, only cruisers, frigates, and destroyers."

"Yes, sir. The battleship was located some fourteen billion kilometers from here."

"And this battleship was directly in your path?"

"Uh, no, sir. We had to deviate slightly to engage it."

"Your orders were to proceed directly to Higgins, Commander Carver."

"I felt that a slight deviation of four minutes, fifty-two seconds was warranted, sir."

"I want a full report regarding that incident by first watch."

"Yes, sir."

"How much time will you need for your emergency repairs?"

"My chief engineer is preparing a tritanium hull plate now. He estimates no more than sixty minutes to secure it in place on the outer hull if there's no damage to the cross-member supports."

"Very well. Initiate that repair immediately, but only send out the people necessary to complete the repair. Better position a shuttle outside also to pick up your people in case you have to seal up quickly and prepare to meet the enemy. When your ship is fully pressurized, you'll commence picket duty if the Raiders haven't returned."

"Aye, Admiral. Sir, our hydrogen tanks are low and our torpedo supply is almost exhausted."

Admiral Holt scowled. "I'll have the coordinates for the cargo farm transmitted to you. There are fuel and weapons barges there. Resupply after your emergency repairs are complete. Now, is there anything else that will prevent you from commencing picket duty?"

The tone in the Admiral's voice spoke volumes and Jenetta reminded herself of the pressure he'd been under for the past month. "No, sir," was all she said.

"Good. Keep this com line open so we have immediate access to each other."

"Aye, sir."

"CIC out."

"*Song* out."

Jenetta leaned back in her chair and relaxed slightly. She hadn't realized just how rigidly she had been sitting until Admiral Holt turned to other matters. She could still see the activity in the CIC and knew they could likewise see her. Although delighted to have destroyed the Raider battleship, she knew there might be hell to pay for her deviation from course. Spontaneous actions that defied standing orders and protocols, however well-intentioned and successful, had ended the careers of many officers.

"Chief Hannigan, inform Commander Rodriguez that he may commence external repairs to the hull where we're losing atmosphere. And have a shuttle launched and standing by to retrieve engineers as the Admiral ordered."

"Aye, Captain," the com operator said.

The bridge was quiet and the mood subdued as the bridge crew went about their business under the eyes of the CIC. Every person on the bridge had seen Jenetta's court-martial for destroying a massive Raider base without permission. And they had just seen the look on Admiral Holt's face and heard the tone of his voice when he learned of their course deviation. They wondered if they would soon be witnessing another court-martial of their highly respected captain— this time for destroying a mega-giant Raider battleship without permission.

"Tactical," Jenetta said, "do you have eyes on the *Prometheus*?"

"Aye, Captain. I have identified all seven of our warships."

"Put the image of the CIC on my seat's right monitor and put an image of the *Prometheus* on the forward screen."

"Aye, Captain."

A second later the large monitor at the front of the bridge lit up with a close-up view of the *Prometheus*. Jenetta's heart leapt into her throat and it took all of her self-control to suppress her emotions. Her beautiful ship was practically wrecked. *No*, she thought, *not wrecked, but very seriously damaged.* There were a dozen massive breaches in his two-kilometer-long hull and it appeared that at least half his laser arrays had been destroyed. Two-thirds of his torpedo tubes appeared to be out of commission as well. The status board still listed him as being War Active, but his fighting ability had to be just a fraction of what it had been at the start of the engagement. She felt a little sick and wished she could immediately shuttle over to help in any way she could, but she had her orders. She knew they would be so busy over there that a call from her would be a distraction, so she didn't ask Chief Hannigan to contact Captain Gavin.

Instead she said, "Tactical, show me each of the other ships, starting with the *Chiron*."

The *Chiron* looked as bad, and maybe even a little worse than the *Prometheus*. It had also been pounded by Raider forces using nuclear warheads on their torpedoes, but thanks to its heavily-armored triple hull, the brother ship of the *Prometheus* would live on to fight another day. The *Geneva* and *Buenos Aires* were still listed as being battle-ready, but after seeing the damage to their hulls and engines Jenetta wondered if they could even maneuver. Of course, their orders required them to remain in position and defend the station, so maneuvering wasn't required. The *Thor*, *Bonn*, and *Calgary* were listed on the status board as being out of action and the damage to the three ships seemed so extensive that they might have to be scrapped. Jenetta couldn't help but wonder if an earlier arrival by the *Song* could have prevented any of the damage. Sick of looking at the carnage and visualizing the death and suffering aboard each ship, she choked down her nausea and had the tactical officer replace the image on the forward monitor with the view of the pristine Combat Information Center.

Jenetta sat calmly in her chair, sipping her coffee and reading reports on the holo-tube until informed that the repair was completed and the ship fully pressurized again. The hull punctures that had self sealed would have to wait. She told Chief Hannigan to notify the CIC they were leaving to resupply before beginning picket duty. A com operator at the CIC acknowledged, but Admiral Holt never looked up from the report he was reading on a holo-tube.

Higgins Space Command Base employed a modified version of the DeTect System used by every spaceship to see anything within four billion kilometers. Homocentric rings of tiny DeTect satellites would identify any movement within their range and instantly relay that information back to the station on a dedicated IDS band. This extended network, referred to as a Distant DeTect Grid, allowed the station to 'see' any movement within a hundred billion kilometers in any direction. The *Song*'s first task was to locate, and deactivate or destroy the DDG jamming satellites dropped by the Raiders during their approach to the station. Then, in the hours and days following the engagement, they constantly crisscrossed space around the station.

As the only ship operationally capable of performing picket duty, the *Song* couldn't remain quietly in one small area watching and listening for any movement of enemy ships. Most of the *Song*'s travel was in areas beyond the range of the restored sensor net, but they were also required to respond to any detection of ship activity received by the station on the DDG, so they would sometimes cross through areas close to the station, taking the shortest route to the potential enemy vessels. With every interception, the vessel turned out to be merely a freighter on its way to Higgins— one that hadn't reported in yet because of their distance from the station. Even in cases where the freighter did report in, the station frequently wanted a visual confirmation of the ship. No one was really ready to accept either an AutoTect signal or friendly declaration of arrival while the station's protection fleet was unable to quickly respond to an attack. Either could too easily be forged, so virtually every ship was challenged and identified before being allowed to proceed.

On several occasions, the *Song* passed through the area where they had encountered the battleship. In the first days following the battle, telemetry from the small sensor buoy dropped by the *Song* showed the ship was still located where it had been when the *Song* encountered it and its continued presence in the area fueled fears that the Raider ships were regrouping to attack. The deplorable condition of the protection fleet prevented any assault on the gargantuan vessel, but continued monitoring showed no activity around the ship. It was odd that no emergency repair teams attended to the ship's obvious wounds.

Finally, the base sent out a small scout ship. Its more powerful sensors would deliver a better overall evaluation of the enemy ship's condition as the tiny craft made several high-speed passes just outside effective energy weapon range.

The results of the probe were startling. The hulk appeared dead, with only minimal life-signs present. Admiral Holt made a decision to investigate further. The scout ship made ever closer and closer passes to the battleship but never drew any fire. The close passes revealed much more extensive damage than originally believed and confirmed the fact that the ship was an almost lifeless hulk.

Additional scout ships were sent out with orders to search the wreckage and they actually found Raiders still alive, trapped in airtight sections. In total, they rescued three hundred eighty-one survivors aboard the ship and found another ninety-six floating in life pods nearby. The ship had carried a crew of just over four thousand at the time of its destruction.

Most of the small wreckage was gone, having long ago tumbled away from the explosion site, but when several large chunks were identified by the science officer aboard the *Song*, courses and speeds were logged into the navigation files to aid all ships in avoiding the wreckage in the future. At some point, reclamation ships would attempt to track down the larger pieces that had broken off and bring them to the reclamation center to keep the spaceways around the station clear of obstructions.

The *Song* continued its solo patrol of the area around the station until the first of the destroyers from the Vauzlee site arrived some six days after the battle. With the arrival of each additional ship, the arc of the patrol perimeter assigned to each picket ship lessened, allowing them to increase the depth of their coverage until the ships making repairs could be almost assured of receiving at least an hour's advance warning if the Raiders returned.

Once all four destroyers from the Vauzlee battle had joined the *Song* in patrolling the immediate area around Higgins, the status in the CIC was downgraded from War Active to War Ready. The change allowed for a much broader repair effort than had been permitted previously and the duty schedules aboard the picket ships could be relaxed enough so that crewmembers could catch up on some much-needed sleep. There had been no sign of the Raiders since they had departed so abruptly.

Woodrow had meanwhile recovered from his injuries. When he first awoke following the attack, he'd been delighted to learn that his captain was not only safe, but that she'd dealt with the assassin who had attacked them both. Jenetta visited him in the sickbay for a few minutes every day once the battle was over. She learned he had been taken completely by surprise while working in the galley. The door sensor had logged the arrival of the laundry bot, but he hadn't gone out to check on it. Since Pretorious had neither a CT nor ID chip, the computer didn't record his entry. Woodrow didn't know anything was amiss until he saw Pretorious from the corner of his eye a second before he was struck down. He returned to duty as Jenetta's steward fifteen days after the attack that had nearly taken his life.

It was while the *Song* was out on picket duty that the convoy from Mawcett finally reached Anthius. Although family members had been notified of the deaths of their relatives immediately following the Battle of Vauzlee and Space Command had released a simulation vid of the battle prepared from the warships' logs, specifics were sketchy and the media was disappointed when informed that a full report wouldn't be released until the analysis of all logs was complete, perhaps in as little as six months. But the newsies waiting to greet the convoy got a much bigger story than anything they had expected when assigned to cover the event. Every Peabody gunner had enjoyed a front row seat to the epic battle so there were suddenly hundreds of eyewitnesses to the Battle at Vauzlee who were willing to talk. The newsies descended upon them like ravenous sharks in a feeding frenzy, eager to record as many accounts as possible. Every Peabody crewman knew the first ship to arrive had been the *Prometheus* and word had quickly circulated after the battle that Lt. Commander Jenetta Carver was the XO on board the *Prometheus* when the attack began. Almost from the beginning, her name was the only one being bandied about when discussing the battle.

*　*　*

"Come," Jenetta said, when the computer announced that Lieutenant Ashraf was at the door of her briefing room. The report she'd been reading was exceedingly dull so she was thankful for a brief distraction. She pushed down the cover of the com unit and looked up as her XO entered and settled into the 'oh-gee' chair in front of her desk. Their relationship had grown a lot less formal in the months they had worked together.

"Isn't it a little early for our daily briefing, Lori?" Jenetta said quizzically.

"Yes, Captain, but I thought you'd want to see these right away," she answered, holding out two holo-magazine cylinders.

Jenetta accepted them and activated the first by depressing the recessed switch. Immediately, the holographic image of a newspaper's front page leapt upwards from the tube. The full-page headline read, 'Carver Saves Convoy.'

"My God!" Jenetta exclaimed as she saw the heading. She quickly read the story by twisting the end of the tube to scroll down and then activated the other cylinder. The headline in the second newspaper read, 'Carver Protects Artifacts.'

"I can't believe this," Jenetta said after reading the second article. "They make it sound like I was the only one at the engagement. There were almost ten thousand Space Command officers, NCOs, and crewmen at that fight. And far too many didn't survive the battle. Why are they giving me so much credit for the victory?"

"Probably because you've been the most visible Space Command officer in this war against the Raiders. You've done more during the past year by yourself than all of Space Command was able to accomplish in the decade prior. During the court-martial, your image appeared almost daily on every magazine and newspaper in Alliance space. It appears you've become the poster-girl in our war against the Raiders. I imagine that as soon as the newsies learned you were the First Officer aboard the first SC ship to arrive at Vauzlee, they knew they had their headline. And from what I've read, the Peabody crews are singing your praises and crediting *you* with their rescue."

"I was just one of thousands at the battle. It's not right."

"They couldn't very well list everyone who fought; there isn't enough room on the front page. So they took the most visible person for their story."

"You're probably right. That'll teach me to go around destroying Raider warships and their bases," Jenetta said with a sardonic grin.

Chapter Seventeen
~ June 17th, 2268 ~

Recalled to the base thirty days following the battle, the five ships that had been performing picket duties joined the eight so far returned in response to the emergency message sent by Gavin to all ships on patrol in the deca-sector. Emergency repairs to four of the ships that had fought the battle— *Prometheus*, *Chiron*, *Geneva*, and *Buenos Aires*— had been completed, and while they might be in the dockyards for months while repairs necessary to bring them back to full fighting trim were completed, they were at least sufficiently spaceworthy to travel to the Mars facility under their own power. Three ships— *Thor*, *Bonn*, and *Calgary*— were so badly damaged that they might have to be towed to the Mars facility. Crew losses had been especially heavy on those ships.

All repair efforts had so far been directed at the ships, so the docking ring and station still bore the terrible scars of battle. Huge sections had been sealed off and less than a dozen docking piers in the ring could be utilized. Quartermaster ships, filled with supplies and building materials, were already underway from Earth and half a dozen other planets. Transport ships filled with base construction crews were also on their way. Higgins was too vital to the security of its deca-sector and the economic stability of the Galactic Alliance to have it non-operational for long.

The *Song*, with a current crew size of more than twenty-one hundred, was assigned one of the few available berths on the docking ring. The others were occupied by the ships damaged in the battle. The four arriving destroyers from the battle of Vauzlee, with crew sizes of about seven hundred, were required to remain in orbit and use their shuttles for station access, but since the shopping concourse was still closed down, easy access to the station by off-duty crew-members wasn't as important as it normally was.

With the lifting of the ban on travel to Higgins, sporadic passenger and freight traffic already in transit began to appear around the station almost immediately. The destroyed Raider ships, after being searched for personnel trapped in air-tight areas, had been towed to a 'salvage farm' area guarded by security forces from the station. Over the coming months, Intelligence teams would scour the ships for any information that could provide a clue about Raider base locations and other planned or completed operations.

Of the seventy-two vessels that had assaulted the base, just sixteen were sufficiently space-worthy to flee when the *Glorious* was destroyed. The fifty-six ships lost in this fight, combined with the thirty-four lost at Vauzlee and the fifty-eight lost when Raider-One exploded, meant the Raider threat in this part of space had been pushed back to levels from which they hopefully might never recover. At the very least, travelers should be safe from pirates for several years to come.

The *Song* had no sooner completed its docking procedure than Jenetta received an order to report to Admiral Holt's office. The order called for her immediate appearance. She hurried to change her tunic and brush her hair before rushing off the ship.

Owing to the severe damage and the necessarily circuitous route required to bypass closed sections of the docking ring and station, the trip to the Headquarters Section of the base took three times longer than normal. And then she was required to sit in the Admiral's outer office for another twenty minutes before the com beeped and the Admiral's aide motioned that she should go in. She tugged on her tunic to straighten it as she stood up, then walked down the short hallway. The double doors to the Admiral's office opened before she reached them. Upon entering the large room, she walked directly to the conference table where Admiral Holt and a number of senior officers were seated. She recognized

Admiral Margolan, the senior JAG officer on Higgins, Commander Kanes of Intelligence, Captain Gavin, Captain Powers of the *Chiron*, and four of the five Captains whose ships had formed the basic protection force for the base and who had fought in the battle. A meter from the table she came to rigid attention as she faced the admiral without acknowledging the others.

"Lieutenant Commander Carver, reporting as ordered, sir," she said, staring straight ahead.

The admiral looked at her intently for a full ten seconds without saying anything. While facing his withering glare during the incredibly long scrutiny, Jenetta refused to twitch or move a single muscle, except for normal respiration.

"You were ordered to proceed directly to Higgins Space Station by Captain Gavin," he said gravely. "You chose to ignore those orders, did you not?"

"Um, no, sir, not exactly."

"What?" the admiral said, before turning to glance at Gavin, whose only response was to return the look, furrowing his brow and shrugging his shoulders almost imperceptibly.

"Those were not my precise orders, sir. Captain Gavin ordered me to depart immediately for Higgins at our maximum speed. I appended a copy of that logged message to the report I submitted immediately following the battle here. Following receipt of the orders, I held a quick meeting with my senior staff to prepare for departure and we left as soon as practicable. The *Song* was under way within twenty-four minutes of me being awakened and notified of both a Priority-One message and the departure of the *Prometheus* and *Chiron*, sir."

"And you interpreted *those* orders to mean you could then deviate from them at any point you chose?"

"I was ordered to leave immediately for Higgins and we did. Nothing in my orders specifically precluded a small deviation of four minutes and fifty-two seconds for good and valid reasons."

"Knowing the station was under attack by an enemy force of significantly greater strength and that *seconds* mattered, you felt that you had a good and valid reason for deviating from course?"

"Yes, sir."

"Explain."

"My senior communications chief discovered an inordinate amount of encrypted com traffic originating from a point some fourteen billion kilometers from the base while the battle was under way. I suspected a command ship or group might be operating from a safe location. I believed that if I could interrupt the flow of command instructions it would impede their attack by sending the enemy ships here into disarray, making it easier to overcome their remaining forces when we arrived. I ordered my ship to the source of the communications signals expecting to find a command ship and several screening vessels. We were fortunate in that there was only one ship. We dropped our envelope, fired a full spread of torpedoes from our bow tubes, then immediately resumed course for Higgins at our maximum sub-light speed while building our envelope. Sir, I knew I was stepping slightly outside the spirit of my orders, but I had already technically adhered to the *letter* of those orders."

"Have you become a *space lawyer*, Commander?" Admiral Holt asked scathingly.

"No, sir. But officers will, at times, be faced with situations that force them to closely examine the letter of their orders and make a decision as to just how much leeway they have to best accomplish the true mission as they see it."

Admiral Holt again looked intently at Jenetta for ten seconds without saying anything. He finally broke the silence by saying, "The true mission as *they* see it?"

"Yes, sir. As I saw it, my mission was to protect this base by destroying as many of the enemy as possible and ending the attack on Higgins as quickly as possible. I believed I had information not available to CIC and that taking time to await approval to divert from course would have exhausted precious seconds, or even minutes, we couldn't spare."

Admiral Holt took a deep breath and released it. "This time you get away with it, Commander. A post-analysis of the battle using our station sensor logs and information obtained from captured Raider prisoners corroborates your theory that the Raider action was being directed from that remote location. It's also the only reasonable explanation for the Raiders to jam our DDG net when they arrived. It wasn't to hide the number of ships in their fleet or the existence of a second force as we originally thought, but to hide the arrival and continued presence of the command vessel. When the ships attacking Higgins lost contact with their command ship, they must have panicked. Since they knew we had surprised them with an unknown force at Vauzlee, we believe they might have feared another unknown force was about to descend upon them. In all probability, your action saved this station and our protection force from complete destruction. I've decided you are to be officially commended for your insight, resourcefulness, and courage under fire."

Jenetta smiled slightly as relief coursed through her. "Thank you, sir."

"As you no doubt realize, assembling initial crews for the *Prometheus* and *Chiron* greatly taxed the limited personnel resources of this command. With the casualties at Vauzlee and those here at this latest engagement, we have become seriously short of senior officers in this deca-sector. Therefore, you will not rejoin the *Prometheus* as Captain Gavin had informed you— at least not yet. You will instead remain in command of the *Song* until you reach Earth as originally intended following the Vauzlee action."

"Aye, sir."

"That's all, Commander. Dismissed."

Jenetta braced to attention, turned on her heel, and walked from the room.

As the doors closed behind her, Jenetta stopped to breathe deeply and release it slowly before continuing down the hallway to the outer office.

Inside the office, Admiral Holt drew in a deep breath and expelled it quickly. As he replaced his sham scowl with a wide grin, he said, "Damn, I like that young officer. No criticism of present company is intended; you all know the esteem I hold for you, but I wish I had a dozen more just like her to form the core of the *next* generation of senior officers that will safeguard this part of space."

"She had to know she was risking her career when she deviated from course," Admiral Margolan said. "A board of inquiry might even have found her guilty of dereliction of duty if she had guessed wrong."

"Of course she knew," Gavin said, "but I doubt if it made her hesitate for more than a few seconds. Her perspicacity has never been in question. She correctly assessed the situation and took the only course of action her intelligence and sense of duty would allow."

"I'm glad your orders didn't specify that she come *directly* to Higgins," Admiral Holt said. "Her sense of duty might have forced her into following the *letter* of those orders. The Raiders were giving us a damn rough time there at the end. I doubt the *Song*'s weapons could even have made that much of a difference in the outcome, considering that with three of our seven ships completely out of the action and the other four seriously damaged and almost out of action themselves, the Raiders, with sixteen ships still able to fight, had a considerable edge in fighting effectiveness."

"We're just fortunate that so many of the Raider ships were of Tsgardi manufacture," Captain Powers of the *Chiron* said. "The Uthlaro ships, while still inferior to our own, held up substantially better. If the entire Raider fleet had been Uthlaro-built we would have been far worse off. And I shudder to think what might have happened if their ships were as tough as ours. If not for our advance knowledge of the attack at Vauzlee and our subsequent victory there, they would have outnumbered the base protection force by twenty to one. With those odds, the station would have fallen for sure. By the way, I've seen the simulation of the Battle of Vauzlee just released by Supreme HQ to the media. The victory appears all the more impressive when viewed from an outside perspective. Commander Carver should be officially commended for developing the battle strategy for that engagement."

"She deserves a lot more credit than that, Steve," Gavin said, chuckling.

"What do you mean, Larry?"

Gavin looked towards Admiral Holt to confirm it was okay to brief the group. Holt decided to answer the question himself.

"Simply that all eight of the India plans we prepared for the defense of this station were devised by Commander Carver," Holt said grinning. "Larry contacted her right after your ship and the *Prometheus* arrived here. With my approval, he relayed our situation, then subtly asked her what strategy she'd employ. Her tactics revolved around a prediction that the Raiders would most likely arrive as one force and fire a full salvo of torpedoes at our ships from a great distance rather than waiting until they got closer, believing we'd just sit on our— positions, and try to knock down all incoming torpedoes. Commander Carver's proposed response to the arrival of the Raider armada, India-One, required me to throw away the book.

"I don't mind telling you her battle plans scared the hell out of me at first. If we followed the first two, we'd be giving the Raiders a clear path to the station. But the more I thought about it, the more I realized it was the only viable solution if the Raiders did as she predicted. The number of torpedoes they initially launched at us, combined with the Echo-Three constraint that we hold position and knock down all incoming birds, would have seen our protection fleet destroyed at the very outset of the battle. Commander Carver's proposal that we align ourselves in front of the station as if we really were following Echo-Three was inspired. The Raiders no doubt believed we were following the Station Defense plan and totally wasted their first volley. And if they didn't attack as she expected, we could still follow the scripted actions of Echo-Three.

"If India-One was successful, Commander Carver gave India-Two a ninety-eight percent chance of being just as successful. As you know, those two maneuvers alone reduced the Raider force by a full *thirty* warships, with fourteen more severely damaged. That represented *half* of their strength. India-Three could have taken another one-third to half of their remaining force, but we never got to implement it because the first two maneuvers were so enormously successful. The late Admiral Nazeer of the battleship *Glorious* saw us whittling down his ships and decided to use what vessels he had left to wash over us in two large assault waves while he still had a force large enough to accomplish that. India-Four was Commander Carver's response if and when they took that action. And she knew that following that point the attack would devolve into individual ship attacks. The other four India plans were our responses in case the Raiders didn't arrive as one large force, but rather attacked initially from multiple points less than two minute's weapons distance from our ships, immediately pinning us in a defensive posture between them and the station."

"I believe," Gavin said, "that if we had followed the standard tactics developed by the War College for the defense of GSC orbiting stations, we wouldn't now be sitting here calmly discussing said tactics. They're probably perfectly adequate for defense against two or three ships, or even half a dozen, but certainly not for an attack like the one we faced."

Kanes began chuckling loudly. When the others at the table looked at him, he said, "I should have recognized Commander Carver's hand in those tactics. They're very unlike *anything* you're going to find in a Space Command battle strategy handbook. While India-One and India-Two were *spectacularly* devious, India-Four even surpassed *them*. I can't imagine where she got the idea of covering the keel of all seven warships with mines that could be released to create an instant minefield in front of an attacking enemy. It always seems that whatever she comes up with is— unique."

"Throughout this past year," Gavin said, "Carver has repeatedly proven her brilliance as a military tactician. Prior to the Battle at Vauzlee, she spoke to Commander Kanes and myself of the Austro-Turkish War of 1683, specifically mentioning the Battle of Vienna. She said that battle marked the turning point in the three-hundred-year struggle between Central European kingdoms and the Ottoman Empire. I believe the Battle for Higgins will ultimately mark the turning point in our decade-old battle with the Raiders."

"She certainly doesn't lack guts either," Captain Payton said. "I've viewed the image logs she submitted of her attack on that Raider battleship. It has to be the most formidable-looking warship I've ever seen. She just barged in there, dropped her envelope, and fired her torpedoes virtually pointblank without worrying about being outgunned twenty or thirty to one."

"I'm not trying to derogate her bravery," Captain Simpson of the destroyer *Bonn* said, "when I say she expected to be gone before they could return torpedo fire. She certainly could have found herself in a situation well beyond her control. But since she had already planned her exit, I have to admit it was a most intelligent attack strategy."

"Yes," Captain Hoyt of the destroyer *Calgary* agreed. "Carver is an intelligent young officer. But perhaps she takes too many risks. Conservative isn't a word you can apply to any of her tactical plans. I must admit it alarms me a little and I genuinely fear for the safety of the people under her command. Every plan seems to be an *all or nothing* line of attack."

"I think I know her well enough by now to say with complete confidence," Kanes said, "that you can be quite sure all risks have been calculated from every possible angle before she acts. Provided, of course, she has the *time* to consider her actions. And when she hasn't had time, her native intuition has proven uncanny. Your perception might come from the fact that she doesn't shrink from a fight. She believes in taking the battle to the enemy wherever and whenever she feels the odds are in her favor. And I happen to agree with her. We won't win this war by avoiding conflict."

"It sounds like you're a real fan, Keith." Captain Pope of the destroyer *Geneva* said. "Have you tried to recruit her for your Intelligence Section?"

"Yes, I have, as a matter of fact. The recruiters at the Academy slipped up royally by not considering her. I would love to have her in my section. Unfortunately, she has her heart set on being aboard a warship."

"She seems to have recovered well enough from her wound that she can walk without any sort of aid," Admiral Holt said.

"What wound?" Gavin asked.

"Didn't you know?" Admiral Holt replied. "She was shot in the midsection the evening before the *Song* arrived here."

"What? No, I didn't know. Her ship's been on picket duty. And since I don't currently have an XO, or at least one I can depend on to do the job properly, I've been totally involved with supervising my emergency repairs. You say she was shot in the midsection?"

"The shot narrowly missed her stomach as it entered her midsection just above her navel and plowed through twelve centimeters of abdominal muscle before exiting. The doctor reported that only skin and muscle was damaged. Although the laser sealed the wound as quickly as it was made, the doctor said in his report that the pain from the damaged muscles must have been excruciating."

"Who shot her?" Captain Powers asked. "One of her own crew?"

"No, the Raider officer who gave us the information about the attack at Vauzlee in exchange for his freedom— a Commander Pretorious. Following the battle, we released Pretorious and gave him a shuttle loaded with a year's supply of emergency food packs. Unless he screwed up his astrogation, it should have been sufficient to get him to the mining colony on Sasone where he could get a ride to wherever he wanted to go. But instead of leaving, he stayed near the battle site. During the confusion, he snuck aboard the *Delhi* and stole a Space Command uniform and laser pistol, plus a large cache of weapons he intended to sell on Sasone. Then he flew to the *Song* and docked, using the excuse that he was Commander Carver's assigned pilot. Since he was flying a shuttle registered to the *Prometheus*, the petty officer in the flight bay bought the story. I imagine things were pretty confused aboard that ship during the first couple of days following the battle."

"Did you know about this Keith?" Gavin asked Kanes.

"I received a copy of the report from the *Song*'s chief security officer after the battle here was over. According to him, after Pretorious made it aboard he located a vacant suite on the visitor's deck and moved in while he formulated a plan to assassinate Carver. We know now his scheme was to attack Carver just before the task force departed for Earth, then slip away in his shuttle. But the petty officer who'd observed his arrival questioned his continued presence on board. Pretorious feared the PO might report his suspicions to security, so he lured him to a remote location under pretext of a high-stakes card game, then killed him and tried to make it look as if the PO had been killed in a gambling dispute. When the planned attack on Higgins was uncovered, Pretorious was required to modify his own plans. It was impossible to leave the ship while it was traveling FTL. In total, he spent almost two months aboard the *Song*, hiding out in the visitor's suite during the first and second watches and then sneaking to a mess hall for food. During the days he hacked his way into the main computer system and played havoc with the code. He caused one serious ship-wide problem after another. His only mistake seems to have been sneaking into Commander Carver's quarters to carry out his assassination plot. She stopped him— permanently."

"I've been so busy that the reports have been stacking up on me," Admiral Holt said, "but I've had my senior aide reading them and alerting me to anything that required my attention. He spotted a reference to the shooting incident in Commander Carver's report, so I read the security officer's report and then Commander Carver's full report of the incident. It seems Pretorious waited until the *Song* was nearing Higgins so he'd be able to get off the ship undetected.

If he'd tried to kill her earlier, and succeeded, he'd be stuck aboard while the ship was turned upside down in a hunt for the killer. He got into her quarters by following a laundry bot and disabled her steward, then waited for her to return. She says in her report that he wanted to gloat a bit rather than killing her immediately. He was distracted for just an instant when her first officer came to her door and she was able to launch a viewpad across the room and into Pretorious' face with enough force that he dropped the pistol. She immediately charged, but he managed to recover the pistol before she reached him. She leapt up and spun, aiming a kick at his head that broke his neck just as he fired."

"Incredible!" Captain Simpson said breathlessly.

"You haven't heard the best part," Admiral Holt continued, chuckling. "According to her chief security officer, the chief medical officer tried to administer pain killers, but she refused to be treated. She said she wasn't going to be napping when the ship arrived at Higgins in case the Raiders attacked before then. He insisted to the point of threatening to relieve her of command for medical reasons as is his right under Space Command regulations when the chief medical officer believes the captain to be incapacitated. She then promised to toss him in the brig if he took any action that threatened the safety of her ship or crew. Since she seemed to be in complete control of her faculties, the doctor backed down. Marine Captain Galont said he was very relieved he didn't have to decide whose order to obey."

"It was fortunate for us," Captain Powers said, "that she was able to continue in command. I doubt anyone assuming command in her place would have deviated from course and taken out that command ship. It's not the kind of responsibility an *acting* captain would ever dare take on."

"You forget, Steven," Gavin said, "that Carver essentially *is* only an acting captain. I appointed her as captain under my authority as the senior officer at Vauzlee and subject to the provisions of battlefield appointments and promotions, but she won't be permitted to retain command once we reach Earth. Only a Space Command officer holding the rank of captain can be named as the permanent commanding officer of a heavy cruiser."

Captain Powers smiled and then chuckled. "You're right, Larry. I did forget that for a moment amid all this talk of her tactics, actions, and heroics."

"From everything I've heard and witnessed," Captain Simpson said, "I expect that if Commander Carver remains in the service, she might well become the youngest officer, by a wide margin, ever to attain the rank of Captain and command a ship of the line."

*　*　*

"Thank you, Eddie," CPO Flip Byrne said gleefully as he joined the other chiefs at the card table and took his seat. "Thank you, thank you, *thank you*."

Chief Edward Lindsey finished dealing the first hand and looked up from his cards with narrowed eyes before saying, "For what?"

"For wishing that Commander Carver be replaced on board this ship as acting XO."

"What are you talking about?"

"Your wish was granted. She was sent over to the *Song*."

"I thought you liked her?"

"You mean you haven't heard?"

"Heard what?"

"Commandeer Carver is being officially commended for saving Higgins."

"What? She wasn't even at the battle. How can they credit her with saving the station? *We* were the ones getting our asses shot off out here."

"While we were getting our asses shot off over here, she was four FTL minutes away, engaged in solo combat with the largest battleship ever *seen* in Galactic Alliance space— perhaps the largest battleship ever conceived. A reclamation vessel just dragged the hulk in and put it in the scrap farm with the rest of the Raider trash. You should see that thing; it's gigantic. It makes the other ship hulks in the farm look like minor detritus. It's at least a thousand meters longer than the *Prometheus*."

"A thousand meters *longer*? What was she doing fighting a super dreadnaught solo with just a cruiser?"

"Her job, Eddie. And it wasn't just a super dreadnaught; it was the command ship for the Raider attack forces. After Carver destroyed it, the Raiders here got spooked and bugged out. End of battle. If the Commander hadn't been assigned to the *Song*, she wouldn't have been out there to save our asses. So thank you, thank you, and thank you."

"Who says the battleship was the command ship?"

"Everybody— including Admiral Holt. He personally wrote the commendation for the Commander."

"This is genuine? Not some made up bull?"

"It's the God's honest truth. Commander Carver saved all our asses."

"Damn."

"Is that all you've got to say? You still believe she doesn't deserve the full measure of your respect?"

"Well—," Chief Lindsey said a bit sheepishly, "Damn, Flip, maybe she does walk on water."

Chapter Eighteen
~ June 19th, 2268 ~

The task force departure for Earth was scheduled for 0130. The *Song* was the second ship to go to FTL after the *Prometheus*. Once underway and settled into Light-262, the established task force speed, Jenetta turned the bridge over to Lieutenant Elizi and walked to her quarters to get some sleep. The slower speed of the task force would add a month to the normal travel time of either the *Prometheus* or *Chiron*.

Jenetta hadn't been able to get together with Commander Spence during the few days she'd had at the station after being recalled from picket duty because he was still down on Vinnia. He'd been evacuated to the surface of the planet with other non-combat personnel before the Raider force had arrived. Given the amount of damage to the station, it might be months before the evacuees were recalled to the orbiting space station. Enormous areas would necessarily remain sealed off until repairs were completed. Nor could Jenetta travel down to the planet to visit him. The station was still on elevated alert, although downgraded from War Ready, and ship commanders were barred from taking personal leave. At least Jenetta had been able to speak with him via com signal several times during the past week.

At 1000 hours the first morning following their departure, Jenetta was on the bridge when the com operator said, "Captain, you have a call from Commander Kanes aboard the *Prometheus*."

"I'll take it in my briefing room."

"Aye, Captain."

Jenetta walked into her briefing room, placed her coffee mug on the desk, and took her seat before raising the view-screen panel on the com system.

"Good morning, Commander Kanes," Jenetta said as his face filled the image area of the com screen.

"Good morning, Commander. I've received your— little present. I understand it arrived just minutes before we departed Higgins."

"I hope you liked it, sir. I've been saving it in a cold storage locker until it could be delivered. I'm sorry I didn't have time to wrap it properly, but the sentiment is sincere."

Kanes wrinkled his brow at this display of black humor, but realized he had prompted it by using the phrase 'little present.' His occupation required him to understand people and motives, and he knew that forwarding the body to him was her way of saying, 'I told you so,' without appearing insubordinate by actually coming out and *saying* 'I told you so,' to a superior officer. At first he'd been a bit incensed but then realized her assessment of Pretorious had been more accurate than his own and that perhaps he even deserved the silent rebuke.

"I was more than a little surprised by the events that transpired," he said. "I thought I had seen the last of Pretorious. I'm delighted the bastard was such a damned poor shot."

"A broken neck does tend to spoil your aim, sir. He apparently had trouble with goodbyes and just couldn't leave without visiting me one last time."

"How is your wound?"

"Pretorious was incapacitated so quickly that he released the trigger almost immediately after squeezing it, so he didn't have a chance to sweep it across my torso. The healing qualities I received as a result of the DNA modifications have mended the damage and left no sign that I was even wounded. I'm completely healthy again."

"That's good news. I, uh, understand Admiral Holt has forwarded medal recommendations in your behalf."

"Medals? For killing Pretorious?"

"The medals are for your actions and leadership at Vauzlee and then at the Battle for Higgins. I know for a fact that he's been *very* impressed by your performance. Why do you think he's letting you skipper the *Song* back to Earth?"

"He said he was short of qualified officers."

"Not so short that a full commander couldn't have been found. Commander Harlan Acklee of the *Calgary* was still available. He was the officer designated to take command of the *Song* if you'd arrived before the engagement with the Raiders. You're still in command there because of the superior job you've done over the past few months. Receiving a battlefield appointment from Captain Gavin, an appointment endorsed by and then extended by Admiral Holt, is going to look *very, very* good on your record the next time you come up for review by the promotions board."

Jenetta sighed silently, uncomfortable for not realizing the true reason why she hadn't been relieved of command. With seven ships out of service until their repairs were completed, and even with the deaths and injuries of so many Space Command personnel, there still must be a dozen or more senior officers who could be sitting in her chair right now. "Yes, sir. I expect you're right."

"Being right is my business. I'm just sorry I wasn't as right about Pretorious as you were. I thought he was more interested in freedom than petty revenge."

"There was nothing petty about it, sir. Oh, it started out that way. Pretorious did come aboard with a plan to assassinate me, but if not for the million-credit bounty placed on my head by the Raider hierarchy he might have left when he found out how difficult it is to get at the ship's captain aboard a Space Command vessel. The bounty made the risk acceptable in his mind."

"There's a million-credit bounty on your head? That changes the situation considerably. Now I can understand him taking the risk. You never mentioned the bounty."

"I didn't want it to color anyone's behavior towards me. I'll take certain precautions, but I won't let it affect my life to the point where I'm afraid to show my face. While I'm ensconced within the Space Command sphere of influence, I'm as safe as anyone could be without surrendering any of her personal freedoms. Pretorious was the exception, not the rule. I won't mourn his passing and I doubt anyone else will. I'm just happy he wanted to gloat instead of shooting me immediately. It gave me a chance to spoil his plans."

"And no one can ever say you squander your chances, Commander. That's one of the things that has consistently intrigued me. Your Academy record states you have trouble making decisions. It says you hesitate much too long when confronted by difficult choices. Although your command simulation scores were among the lowest in the class, you've changed into someone who makes split-second decisions and then acts with speed and purpose."

"Sir, there's a world of difference between pretending you're in command during a lab exercise, however realistic, and actually being in command during a life-and-death situation."

"The normal line of reasoning is that people become *more* indecisive when faced with life-and-death situations simply *because* of the possible consequences."

"Perhaps for some. But when I was confronted by my own mortality, I knew hesitation meant death. At the Academy, I was mainly worried about my grades, or about being embarrassed in front of my classmates if I made a wrong decision. Out here, my life and the lives of my crews have been on the line. I didn't have time to worry about how some professor or review board was going to grade me on every move, utterance, or simple gesture I made, or what someone was going to think about me afterwards, so I didn't try to analyze every situation fifty different ways. I went with my instincts, only concerned with whether we were going to be alive or dead at the end of the day. The old 'me' is gone now. Since being found in the escape pod, I've looked upon this as my second life— or perhaps my third after my enslavement at the hands of the Raiders."

"After seeing your grades, I was astonished the SCI recruiters let you slip through their fingers while you were at the Academy. Your math and science scores were consistently at the top of the class. That's the fertile ground they like to till."

"They may have felt my indecision would be too much of a handicap. Recruitment efforts probably wouldn't have done much good anyway; I've never wanted anything except to be aboard a ship in space."

"What is it? The excitement— the danger— the unknown?"

"All of those things, I guess," Jenetta said casually.

"You'd have the same things working in my intelligence section."

"It just wouldn't be the same. I'm happy where I am, Commander. Thank you for the offer, though."

"Okay, Commander. If you change your mind, you always know how to get in touch with me at Higgins."

"Yes, sir."

"I'll see you at the ceremony on Earth. Have a safe trip, Commander."

"You too, sir."

As the image of Kanes winked out on the com, Jenetta sat back in her chair and thought about the offer. She knew her face was too well known to allow her the freedom to move around the way an intelligence officer has to. That meant she would be stuck behind a desk doing analysis work, which didn't interest her at all right now. As people began to forget about Jenetta Carver and what she looked like, perhaps in a year or so, the situation might change.

* * *

"Does anyone wish to review the presentation again?" Admiral Moore asked of his fellow officers in the Admiralty Board Meeting Hall. They had just finished watching the special holographic vid prepared by the War College from the logs of all the ships involved in the Battle for Higgins. The logs had been individually viewed by the Board soon after the action, but the special presentation vid, with charts and a holo-graphic representation, gave a substantially better overall perspective of the event without influencing any particular viewpoint.

"I certainly don't," Admiral Platt said. "I've screened all the ship logs so many times that I can't stand to watch the deaths of our people and the destruction of our ships again."

"I feel the same," Admiral Bradlee said. "I think we all understand exactly what took place at Higgins. Our people did an incredible job against an enemy force of vastly superior strength, but there's no doubt in my mind that Lt. Commander Carver ultimately saved the station from certain annihilation when she destroyed the Raider battleship *Glorious* commanded by Raider Admiral Nazeer."

"I don't wish to see it again, either," Admiral Hubera said. "And I am sick of hearing about Carver. It's always Carver did this, Carver did that, or Carver did that other thing. There were more than eight thousand other brave Space Command officers, NCOs, and crewmen at the Battle for Higgins. Two thousand, three hundred fourteen, a full quarter of our fighting forces there, won't be returning. But all we seem to do is talk about one little girl— one lone, inexperienced JORG who acts more like a loose cannon than a disciplined officer. Approving that court-martial recommendation was the single biggest mistake this board has ever made. It turned Carver into some kind of superhero to Space Command and Space Marine personnel alike, not to mention the public at large. Now whenever anything happens the first thoughts in anyone's mind are: 'Where was Carver when this happened?' 'What did Carver do?' 'How did Carver save us this time?' I tell you, I'm sick to death of hearing about Jenetta Carver. I'm sick to death of seeing her face on every holo-magazine cover. I'm sick to death of seeing her face on every vid news broadcast. I'm sick to death of being questioned about her by the newsies. And most of all, I'm sick to death of talking about her in this chamber."

During Hubera's tirade the other admirals just looked on dispassionately. The silence lasted for several seconds after he finished.

"Donald," Admiral Moore finally said, "we all understand your frustration, but please refrain from referring to Lt. Commander Carver as a Junior Officer Requiring Guidance. The evidence clearly shows that her actions *did* save Higgins. It was her battle plan tactics that reduced the initial threat by two-thirds and gave our people a fighting chance. No one is saying she did it all by herself and no one ever meant to imply that. Our people performed heroically and that heroism will be properly recognized. But our forces were nearly destroyed, and in the end, we would most likely have lost the station if Lt. Commander Carver hadn't taken that battleship out when she did. All our analysts concur. Those facts can't be disputed."

"She violated her orders by deviating from her course," Hubera contended. "I told you she would. She was ordered to go directly to Higgins. And then—" Hubera paused for a second as if groping for a point to make, "then she tried to take full credit for the victory at Vauzlee."

"The news articles about Commander Carver's involvement at Vauzlee were written by newsies covering the arrival of the artifact convoy at Anthius," Admiral Moore said. "She had absolutely nothing to do with them. She was on picket duty around Higgins when those stories were written and filed. And we've already reviewed the allegation about her deviation. We decided she had a valid reason for ordering a minor course change that added less than five minutes to a twenty-eight-day voyage. I like to think that in her place I would have taken the same action. The issue before us this morning is Admiral Holt's recommendation that Lt. Commander Carver receive the Space Command Cross for taking decisive action that saved Higgins Space Command Base from near certain destruction. We've viewed the bridge logs from the *Song* that show the dilemma Commander Carver faced. We watched as she weighed the options and decided to deviate from her established course despite the possible repercussions and career dangers. Do you dispute that her actions were directly responsible for the survival of the station?"

"No," Admiral Hubera snapped through gritted teeth and then ground them as he slipped into silence. It pained him so much to admit it that he wouldn't even look up.

"Then all in favor of approving the medal award?"

Even Admiral Hubera raised his hand with the rest, but he still didn't look up.

"And all in favor of awarding the second Purple Heart to Commander Carver?"

That was basically a rubber-stamp vote. No one could deny Lt. Commander Carver had been shot and seriously injured by an enemy combatant while her ship was rushing to join the forces defending Higgins.

"And all in favor of approving the Bronze Comet recommended by Captain Gavin for her outstanding service at Vauzlee?"

Again Admiral Hubera raised his hand without looking up. He was hoping to get this business over and done with now.

"The medal awards proposed for Lt. Commander Jenetta Alicia Carver by her commanding officers have been unanimously approved by this Board. That concludes the medal award discussions for all personnel participating at the Battle of Vauzlee and the Battle for Higgins."

A collective sigh of relief wafted around the room. Admiral Hubera, although admitting she deserved the awards, had kept them talking about Commander Carver for hours while he tried to convince them not to award the medals because it would turn even more attention her way. They were all weary of the discussion.

"This Board has spent an inordinate amount of time discussing one young officer today and during the past year," Admiral Moore said. "We know the attacks on the Mawcett convoy and on Higgins were being planned while Lt. Commander Carver was still in stasis sleep in the *Hokyuu* life pod, and we know now that it was a fortunate day for us when she was found and awakened. No one has ever suggested the actions of Lt. Commander Carver alone have knocked the Raiders to their knees in this part of space, but neither can anyone deny that in the decade before she was awakened the situation had gotten progressively worse. There seemed to be no relief in sight. Unassisted by Space Command, she did annihilate Raider-One, and along with it, fifty-eight Raider warships and more than eighteen thousand personnel. The Raiders lost another two warships and two thousand personnel when she destroyed those two vessels while acting as captain of the *Vordoth*. A prisoner that *she* brought to Higgins provided the information that allowed us to engage the Raider forces at Vauzlee and information found *there* informed us of the attack on Higgins. Having that information prevented us from being caught totally unaware. Many of Space Command's finest men and women died in the two recent confrontations, but each engagement must still be looked upon as outstanding victories in our battle with the Raiders. The series of events set in motion by Commander Carver's actions have brought about such incredible changes that we now see freighters and passenger ships again plying the space lanes in Galactic Alliance space with little fear of attack.

"Commander Carver is due to arrive at Earth soon and the date of the Medal of Honor ceremony has been established. I'm proud I will be able to welcome this exceptional young officer back to Earth and that I will be the one to place the medal around her neck. She deserves it, as well as all the other honors we bestow upon her.

"Once Lt. Commander Carver has received her medals, including the Tawroolee Medal of Valor from the Nordakian planetary government, I expect she will slowly recede back into the fabric of the Space Command family. She has never sought publicity, and in fact, has tried to evade the newsies whenever possible. Her renown can be attributed solely to the outstanding noteworthiness of her accomplishments. She's a superior officer and will always be an invaluable asset, but with the Raiders so badly hurt they probably won't show themselves openly again, I expect there will be few opportunities for her star to ever again shine as brightly as it has this past year. She will take her rightful place as a line officer and I know she will perform her duties to the absolute best of her abilities. I fully expect she will one day rise to command a battleship and I know she is up to the task.

"Are there any other comments before we move on?"

"I'd like to say something about Carver," Admiral Hubera said.

Half of the Board members rolled their eyes while the rest simply sighed silently and closed theirs for a few seconds.

"I want to apologize to my fellow Board members," he began contritely. "I realize it must seem like I've made a personal crusade of protesting all the attention paid to Lt. Commander Carver. I did so only in what I felt were the best interests of the service. It's been my belief that I had to temper what I perceived as almost hero worship among some Board members. If I offended, I'm sorry. I agree with Richard that Lt. Commander Carver's time in the spotlight is almost over. As she functions as second officer aboard the *Prometheus* in the decades ahead, I feel confident she will develop the maturity necessary to advance in rank and fully expect that one day she might even become a warship captain. Since I'm almost eighty-five now, I don't expect that to happen within my lifetime, but I believe it might happen."

"I disagree," Admiral Hillaire said.

"You do?" Admiral Moore said in surprise. While Admiral Hubera had always appeared to oppose Commander Carver's actions, Admiral Hillaire had been a staunch supporter.

"Oh, not that Lt. Commander Carver will one day get her own warship, but that it won't happen in Donald's lifetime. If he wasn't healthy he wouldn't still be an active member of the service, which means he can probably expect to live the average lifetime of one hundred thirty to one hundred forty years. And I believe Lt. Commander Carver will get her first warship before Donald even hits the century mark."

A chuckle passed around the room as Admiral Hubera scowled and muttered something unintelligible under his breath.

Chapter Nineteen
~ October 27th, 2268 ~

The *Song* arrived at Earth Station Two just twenty-nine seconds behind the *Prometheus* after traveling to Earth at Light-262, the highest speed available to the older destroyers in the convoy.

While the *Song* was docking at her assigned docking pier, the press was lining up to greet Jenetta. She walked to her briefing room for one last review of her prepared speech once the ship was docked and the airlock seal verified by the station dock master. She had just completed reading her speech aloud when she was informed by Lt. Ashraf that she had special visitors waiting in her quarters. Knowing that neither strangers nor even dignitaries would ever be allowed into her private quarters without her advanced permission, she ran there with all the enthusiasm of the twenty-two-year-old she basically was. Space Marine Cpl. Matthews braced to attention as she approached, but she hardly glanced at him as she darted into her sitting room. Her visitors were there alone, sitting on a sofa. A tray of light snacks sat on the end table next to the sofa but the cheese, crackers, uncooked vegetables, and dips appeared untouched.

Without even giving them an opportunity to stand up, she ran to the sofa and dropped to her knees in front of her mother and father as they leaned forward to rise. All three hugged and cried for several minutes. To her parents, having lived for so many years with the report of her loss, she was returned from the dead. For Jenetta it was a reunion that during the early days in the Raider detention center she had almost forsaken hope of ever enjoying again. No one said anything for several minutes. Tears of happiness flowed freely from Jenetta and her mother, while her dad's eyes were moist and a few tears trickled down his cheeks.

Jenetta's dad, trying to get his feelings reined in after they had worked through the first of their emotions, said in a cracked voice, "Now, is this any way for the captain of a GSC Heavy Cruiser to act?"

Jenetta sniffled and wiped away her own tears of happiness as she stood up. "No, sir. I'm sorry, sir." The formality was a game they had always played at the house when sentimentality started getting the better of them.

"That's better. Now tell us all about this ship of yours, Captain."

"Well, it's not really my ship once I deliver it to the Mars shipyard, Dad. I was only placed in command to bring it here. I'll be resuming my position as second officer aboard the *Prometheus.*"

Her father looked at her and smiled. "I'm prouder of you than I can say, Jenetta. I'm proud of all my children, but for you to overcome the handicap of that incident at the Academy with then *Professor* Hubera, and then to become a Lieutenant Commander and the captain of this cruiser, albeit a temporary appointment, all by the tender age of thirty-three makes my chest swell with pride."

"Thanks, Dad," Jenetta said, feeling a lump form in her throat at this expression of admiration from her father, her own personal hero.

"Even Billy, who's a Commander now, hasn't had his own command yet, while you've had three ships."

"Only two were GSC ships, Dad. And only this ship was really an authorized posting."

"Since you're being officially recognized as the first captain of the *Prometheus*, that's an authorized posting also, even if it did occur after the fact." Touching the red pip on her collar, he said, "You know that, or you wouldn't be wearing that second pip. But whether authorized postings or not, it makes no real difference in the long run. Each was indisputably a command. And while performing as the captain of this cruiser you took your crew into battle and destroyed a Raider battleship, saving Higgins. It'll all be in your file and will weigh heavily with the Promotion Selection Board, and ultimately with COAC, when your name comes up for consideration." Lowering his voice a little to indicate it was a confidence, he added, "Secretly, I think Billy's a little worried you'll make Captain before he does."

"That's silly. He has seven more years of commissioned service and he's only one step away from Captain."

Jenetta's father laughed. "And you're just *two* steps away, and a Medal of Honor recipient after Saturday. That, combined with the Space Command Cross you'll be receiving soon, the two Purple Hearts, Bronze Comet, and the Space Command Star, makes you the most highly decorated officer on active duty in Space Command."

"It's still silly. I won't even be eligible for promotion to Commander for almost three more years. Billy will be eligible for promotion to Captain before then since he was promoted a month earlier than I was. Besides, you've always told us we shouldn't be in competition with each other. You've said you just wanted us to be ourselves."

"Billy's the eldest, honey," her mother reminded her. "It's understandable he might feel some embarrassment about possibly being surpassed by the youngest."

"And the numbers you're quoting are just the normal 'minimum years in grade' guideline," her father said. "It can be waived for officers showing exceptional leadership or meritorious service. I'd say your performance over the past year definitely puts you at the top of both categories. You've repeatedly proved your fitness for command. You only need confirmation by the Selection Board. And there are more Commander positions available each year than Captain positions. One thing is for sure, when your name comes up for consideration, the board members won't have to be reminded who Jenetta Alicia Carver is."

"But I was just promoted eight months ago."

"They only placed you where your number of years of commissioned service indicated you could be. I think it would have been a bit too much to promote you directly to Commander from Ensign, especially since you still look like a recent Academy graduate. Lieutenant Commanders, on average, have attained their rank when they've had between fourteen and eighteen years of commissioned service, but some have achieved it in as little as eleven years. You have a little more than twelve years now, even if all but a year was in stasis sleep. At the very least you would have achieved Lieutenant and been knocking on the door of Lieutenant Commander if they hadn't overlooked you during the search for *Hokyuu* survivors. I'll be surprised if they don't consider you when the Promotion Selection Board convenes next September. Up to ten percent of the officers named on the Selection List can be early promotion, you know. That would make you available for promotion by the fourth quarter of next year."

"How do Richie, Andy, and Jimmy feel about my promotion and postings?"

"They're all happy for you, sweetheart," her mother said. "Even Billy. You can't fault them for a little jealousy. Andy and Jimmy are both hoping to receive promotions to Lieutenant Commander this coming year. The GAC has made special arrangements with SC for all of them to be here for the ceremony. Billy and Richie are already in port. Andy and Jimmy are expected in before Saturday."

"I can't wait to see them. It's been so long since we were all together."

Jenetta half-turned and said, "Come," when the computer interface announced that Lieutenant Ashraf was at the door.

"Excuse me, Captain," Ashraf said as she entered the room and braced to attention. "The press is still waiting out on the dock."

"Thank you, Lieutenant. I'll be there in a few minutes."

"Yes ma'am."

Jenetta turned back to her parents as Lt. Ashraf left. "Space Command wants me to do this interview. I couldn't face the newsies when the court-martial was over so I ran away from them. Why don't you come along and when it's over I'll give you a tour of the ship."

Ten minutes later, Jenetta was stepping up to the podium on the small temporary stage erected by the spaceport's dock personnel. A Marine security detail, insisted upon by Marine Captain Galont, had cleared the way for her and now stood nearby to protect her from overzealous newsies, or perhaps them from her if they encroached too far. She read the statement she had prepared while en route to Earth and then answered questions for about an hour—not that she could really add anything that hadn't been already stated during the court-martial, but the court's video records and transcripts hadn't been released to the news services yet so the reporters were still hungry for information, and it *was* her first statement to the press. They also plied her with questions about her role in the battles of Vauzlee and Higgins, but she declined to answer, citing the fact that it would be inappropriate until the official reports were released by Space Command. As the reporters hurried away to write and file or transmit their stories, Jenetta returned to the ship with her parents. She knew her father wanted to see the *Song* and her mother just wanted to be with her and hold her hand, so both would appreciate the tour.

"That was an excellent presentation, Commander," her father said as they walked back aboard the ship.

"Thank you, sir. I've had a long time to prepare myself."

"What's this I hear about an intruder on your ship who tried to assassinate you?"

Jenetta looked at her father and asked cautiously, "Where did you hear that, Dad?" Although it had been months since Pretorious had snuck into her quarters and tried to 'conclude their business,' she didn't believe the story regarding the assassination attempt had yet been released.

"Oh, a newsie asked me to comment on it while you were answering questions from the press." Her father tried to look nonchalant but didn't fool Jenetta. So many people within Space Command knew of the event that he might have picked up information about it on the base and was offering her an opening so she could present the information to her mother on her own terms before it became public. "There're also some persistent rumors circulating that you developed the battle tactics used at both Vauzlee and Higgins," her father said.

Although Jenetta hadn't related the details of her involvement with the tactics used in the two battles to her parents, she wasn't exactly trying to hide them. She *had* purposely evaded explaining about the injury for which she was receiving the second Purple Heart, but since she seemed sound of limb with no visible scars, her mother hadn't pressed the issue. If the press really did have the story about the assassination attempt, it would shortly become common knowledge, so Jenetta decided it was better they hear the full accounts from her first. She related the whole story regarding Pretorious during the tour. Her mother clutched her arm tightly as she told them about hitting him with the viewpad and then kicking him as he fired. Her mother insisted on seeing the wound immediately and Jenetta allowed her to open her tunic and raise her blouse to see the spot where she had been shot, although it was hardly proper for a ship's captain to allow that in a corridor.

"But there's nothing here, honey," her mother said. "Not even a scar."

"I told you it healed."

"But there should be entry and exit scars if you were shot by a laser pistol and haven't received corrective surgery," her father said.

"I healed without scars. It seems to be a benefit of the DNA procedure that was performed on me. I heal exceptionally faster than most other people and the injuries mend without leaving marks or scar tissue. Even the old compound fracture scar from when I fell out of a tree when I was seven has disappeared. X-rays don't show any evidence that the leg was ever broken, nor is there any discernible evidence of a fracture from when my arm was broken during the seizure of the *Prometheus*."

"And the battle tactics rumor?" her father asked candidly.

"Alright," Jenetta said softly, smiling. "I'm guilty. I'm the one who came up with the insane plan to initiate our attack on the Raider fleet at Vauzlee with just the *Prometheus* so we could cause as much damage as possible before the Raiders knew of Space Command's presence in the area."

"That was you?" her mother said in shock.

"When one takes the time to study it closely, dear," Jenetta's father said, "they understand it wasn't insane at all. In fact, I believe I told Jenetta it was *inspired* back when I thought Gavin was responsible for developing it. Learning that my daughter was the architect fills me with— awe. And the defensive plans at Higgins? They were yours also, were they not?"

"I made some suggestions, Dad. I haven't viewed the battle logs or the recreated simulations yet, so I don't know how closely they might have followed them."

"The *inside* story I've heard is that they followed them to the letter. You've stirred up quite a controversy at the War College, honey. I understand half the instructors have branded you impulsive and reckless while the other half is insisting that your innovative tactics be immediately incorporated into a new Station Defense Operations Manual."

"I seem doomed to be at the center of controversy," Jenetta said.

"A famous showman once said there's no such thing as bad publicity," her father said, grinning. "As long as your name continues to be associated with outstanding success in battle, let the controversy reign. Admiral McGinty at the Warship Command Institute was so impressed that he asked me to drop over and see him."

"Has he offered you a teaching position?"

"Me? No. He doesn't want me, honey; he wants you. He wondered if I might be willing to help persuade you to accept a full professorship at the Institute. He'd like you to teach a course in Modern Warfare Techniques. He says he spoke to Holt, but Holt refuses to release you from his command structure unless you request a transfer. McGinty says he can promise you a promotion to full Commander within five years and to Captain within fifteen if you transfer to the War College."

"Me? A professor? I don't think so, Dad. I just got what I've worked for my entire life—a line officer posting aboard the best ship in the fleet. If I ever manage to make captain I want it to be on a ship, not in a classroom."

"I told McGinty your heart was in space, but I also promised I'd pass along his offer."

Sadly, Jenetta couldn't go planet-side with her parents following their special tour of the *Song*, but as she walked them to the Earth shuttle dock for their trip home she promised to come down as soon as possible. Her security detail had again fallen in around her as she left the *Song*. They cleared the way and kept anxious admirers from getting too close to Jenetta and her parents. She later stood at a viewing port and watched as the small ship containing her parents backed away from the airlock, remaining there until the ship was lost from sight. Her mother's perfume and her father's cologne were still fresh in her memory as she reentered the *Song* and the officer of the deck smiled at the expression of happiness that replaced the normally staid façade.

The following morning the *Song* backed slowly away from the docking pier at Earth Station Two and made the quick trip to the Mars shipyard. The *Geneva* and *Buenos Aires* had traveled overnight and were already berthed inside enclosed repair docks. The *Prometheus* and *Chiron* were scheduled to arrive at Mars later in the day.

Located in fixed orbit above the red planet, seventy of the hundred ship berths at the enormous shipyard were totally enclosed. Once the massive end doors were sealed, the berth was pressurized so workers wouldn't need EVA suits. The enclosed berths were used both for laying the keels of new ships and for repairs and refits where the hull had to be opened. Once a new or repaired ship was fully pressurized it could be moved to one of the 'open' berths for completion. They weren't completely open, of course. A skeletal structure around the vessel offered a number of advantages, such as lighting and anchor points, but workers did have to wear full EVA suits. So if enclosed berths were available, ships were kept inside. The extent of necessary repairs justified the removal of five as yet unpressurized newly-built ships from enclosed berths to make room for the five ships returning from Higgins.

As the *Song* waited for traffic in the yard to be halted so it could proceed to the appointed berth, its shuttles, tugs, and fighters were launched. The fighters proceeded down to the planet where they would be housed in an underground base for the duration, and the tugs and shuttles were flown around to the rear of the berthing structure and parked in a docking bay from which they could be launched at any time. If the small vessels weren't stored elsewhere, they would be stuck inside the enclosed berth until repairs were complete and the dock opened.

The gargantuan doors of the berthing structure were opened wide to receive the ship, but the almost kilometer-long vessel was ordered to come to a halt outside and wait. Within minutes yard tractors arrived and attached themselves to the ship. When all were secure, they took control of the ship and very slowly moved it into the enclosed space. Tether lines attached to the ship held it securely in position. It was another hour before all movement ceased.

Although every damaged hull plate would be replaced, most of the ship would remain pressurized. Even if the berth structure suddenly lost atmosphere, the ship was safe for habitation. Half the crew had already departed and would spend the next month on shore leave before returning to allow the other half to leave. Half of the Space Marine contingent would likewise remain aboard at all times to provide continued security aboard ship.

At the yard director's office, Jenetta inquired about turning over responsibility for the ship.

"I'm sorry, Commander," Mr. Quintana said, "but many regulations have changed since the Raiders were able to steal the two battleships from our yard. Now, once a ship has been commissioned, only the next commanding officer can accept responsibility for it unless the ship has first been decommissioned. I certainly can't accept it. Uh, do you know who will be relieving you?"

"I haven't been told who will be taking command of the *Song*," she said. "I was only ordered to deliver it here."

"Might I suggest that you contact Supreme Headquarters?"

"Yes, I will. Thank you, Mr. Quintana."

"In the meantime, as the ship's present commanding officer, you'll be available for regular consultation regarding the repairs and the schedule?"

"I suppose I will."

"Excellent. And, by the way, welcome home, Commander. All Earth is waiting to greet Jenetta Carver and thank you for what you've done."

"Thank you, Mr. Quintana," Jenetta said smiling. "I'm delighted to be home again."

"Captain Charles Yung of the Frigate *Roosevelt* will be the new Captain of the *Song*?" Jenetta repeated to the aide at the Admiralty Board who had finally been able to answer the question she'd been asking everyone she could reach for the past hour.

"Yes, Commander. The Admiralty Board has confirmed his COAC selection and appointment."

"And can you tell me when he'll relieve me of command?"

"He's received and acknowledged his orders. I understand he's on his way to Earth now. He should arrive here in— oh about— seven or eight months, assuming no other delays or course deviations."

"Seven or eight *months*?"

"Yes, ma'am. The *Roosevelt* has been on patrol out in deca-sector 8667-1844. Captain Yung has hitched a ride back

- 313 -

aboard the Destroyer Tokyo, but she's an older ship and it will take at least that long for her to arrive here. You're to remain in command until he relieves you."

"I see. Thank you, Commander."

"My pleasure, Commander. Welcome home."

"Thank you," Jenetta said just before pushing the com cover down. She snorted slightly. She might be technically in command of the *Song*, which prevented her return to the *Prometheus*, but that wasn't going to keep her stuck aboard ship. She touched the face of her Space Command ring and when a carrier was initiated she asked for Lieutenant Ashraf.

"Yes, Captain," she heard in her head.

"Lori, could you come into my briefing room please."

"Right away, Captain."

A few minutes later, Ashraf entered in response to Jenetta's command to the door interface.

"You wanted to see me, Captain."

"Yes, Lori. Have a seat." After she had sat down, Jenetta said to her, "It appears I shall be remaining in command longer than I expected."

"Wonderful, Captain," Ashraf said smiling.

Jenetta couldn't help but smile. Each extension of her command time aboard the *Song* had been greeted similarly by Ashraf. "But I need some time with my family. So I'm going to leave you in command out here while I enjoy some liberty time. You have adequate personnel to keep the bridge fully staffed and you can always contact me if you have any problems. My folks live just outside the base so my CT should function, but I'll bring a portable repeater with me to ensure you can always get through. Since the ship is sealed inside a space dock, I don't expect many problems here."

"No, ma'am. I can't see many problems arising while we're in space dock."

"If you have no further questions, I'm going to take a shuttle down to my parent's home."

"Have a wonderful shore leave, Captain."

"Thank you, Lori."

The commander of an SC warship enjoyed certain personal privileges not extended to most other crewmembers. One was full access to the ship's support craft. Since the square rigger days, captains have usually had a small vessel reserved for their use. Although the *Song* didn't have a shuttle reserved exclusively for the captain, there were several from which Jenetta could choose rather than waiting for one of the yard's shuttles that made regular runs to the orbiting stations. She made a decision to pilot the craft herself rather than keeping a pilot waiting around while she was on liberty. And by having her own transportation, she would also be able to return to the ship immediately if a problem arose. Her parent's home was just off-base in an area occupied exclusively by SC officers and their families. There was even a special gate onto the base from the adjoining secure housing community.

She received permission to land on the Potomac SC base without having to identify herself personally over an open communication channel. She was logged simply as a shuttle flight from the *Song*. Wanting to keep as much distance between herself and the newsies as possible, she then swore the grinning ground crew to silence about her presence once she had exited the craft. She knew her presence must be reported to the base command structure, but she hoped some overeager public relations officer didn't issue a press release.

The base commander, upon learning of her arrival, immediately rushed over to greet her personally. He invited her to share a meal with him but understood when she requested a rain check. He then placed a military 'oh-gee' vehicle at her disposal for the entire length of her stay on Earth.

As she cruised towards the home where she had spent all of her young life before entering the Academy, she breathed deeply. This was her first time dirt-side since landing on Obotymot a year earlier and she enjoyed the smells that assailed her nostrils and the sounds that reached her ears. There was the familiar fragrance of the flower gardens meticulously maintained by armies of gardener bots, the sound of happy children playing in a base schoolyard, and even the faint smell of saltwater from the not-too-distant Chesapeake. It was wonderful to have the sun on her face and arms, and the wind in her hair. The most difficult part of her drive home was keeping under the posted speed limit. She had a penchant for high speed.

Jenetta slept in her own bed that night for the first time in more than twelve years. Initially, her parents had kept everything because her body hadn't been recovered. They'd clung to a tiny sliver of hope that she'd be found alive. Later, when Space Command had listed her as officially 'missing and presumed dead,' they had just never gotten around to disposing of her things. Eventually they'd packed everything up and stored it in the attic, but after learning she'd been found alive and well they'd reassembled the room to appear as it had when she'd left. They'd even gotten the gel-comfort bed's controls set the way she liked them.

Billy and Richie arrived home the next day. There was a dynamic reunion with lots of hugging and laughing and discussions that lasted late into the night. The following days were more of the same. They had eleven years to catch up on, after all. Billy never let on that he harbored any jealousy towards Jenetta and she began to wonder if it was all in her father's imagination.

On Thursday, Andy arrived home and on Friday Jimmy showed up. Each arrival was another occasion for celebration and more long discussions. Jenetta never mentioned it, but she was dismayed by how much older everyone seemed. For them it was twelve years since she had left Earth, but to her it seemed like only a year and a half, and she neither looked nor felt much different than when she left. Her appearance actually made her feel much more like a 'kid' sister than she had even before.

Being together allowed them to discuss things they hadn't felt comfortable talking about in vidMail messages. Jenetta was shocked to learn Billy had been married. Three years after Jenetta's 'death,' he'd married a young woman he met at

Belagresue. Unfortunately, the marriage only lasted two years. She'd said she understood there would be long absences but wasn't really prepared when he didn't return home in the two years following the honeymoon. She divorced him before he received leave and he had never seen her again. He'd come to realize during their separation that the marriage hadn't been a wise one to begin with because their interests were too diverse. He was now engaged to another woman, but this time she was a Space Command 'brat.' The daughter of a Master Chief Petty Officer, she was one of three siblings. Her father had been away most of her life and was currently serving on the GSC frigate *Washington*. She claimed her life had been wonderful at the base and was both fanatically devoted to the military and fully prepared for the long absences. Her parents heartily approved of the union. Billy and Regina were to be married as soon as he could arrange leave and travel to Concordia SCB. He showed Jenetta and everyone the latest images he had of her. In one, she was sitting with her sisters. The three attractive blondes didn't stop laughing during the entire thirty seconds the animated image ran. Jenetta wished him all the happiness in the galaxy with his bride-to-be.

Richie was likewise engaged to be married. His future bride lived on the Sebastian Colony. The daughter of a vintner, they had met three years earlier and Marisa had twice traveled to meet with him when he could arrange leave on a suitable planet. They were hopelessly in love and he showed Jenetta an animated image he always carried with him. Jenetta liked the auburn-haired beauty's smiling face and she told Richie how happy she was for him. The couple planned to settle on Earth after they were married, although he would be gone more than he was home. His future wife had already met Mom and they'd hit it off right away. If he could arrange for housing in the area, his new wife would have family nearby.

Andy and Jimmy both had special people in their lives but hadn't advanced to the point of talking marriage yet. Andy's girl was a lieutenant aboard his ship. He and Linda were on the same watch, although she was a supply officer while he was a line officer. Jimmy was involved with a Lieutenant(jg) who was a nurse. Unfortunately, they were on different watches and that made their lives difficult. She was always going off watch when he was coming on. Even on the same ship, love can be difficult.

Her brothers asked Jenetta if she had met that special someone yet, but she replied that she hadn't had time. She said she'd been too busy kicking Raider butt to think about love. That drew a loud avalanche of ribbing and several jealous comments about her being out where the action was while they were stuck in *backwater* sectors where the most exciting thing to happen was a smuggler trying to evade their check-points.

*   *   *

Councilman Strauss was the last to arrive for the special meeting of the Lower Council. Rather than taking his usual place, he sat down in the chair at the head of the table that Chairman Gagarin usually occupied.

"I have an announcement," he said. "Chairman Gagarin has retired from the company. Apparently, the severe losses we've suffered while he headed the Lower Council have led the Upper Council to institute a few changes. I have been named as his successor."

"Surely the Upper Council doesn't hold us responsible for the losses at Vauzlee and Higgins?" Councilman Blosworth asked.

"Us? No. Chairman Gagarin had complete operational leadership in both debacles. He alone has been singled out for censure."

"What about Captain Wolff?" Councilwoman Overgaard asked. "He made the decision to quit the battle at Higgins just when we were about to overcome the Spaccs."

"We've reviewed the message log from his ship and decided he shouldn't be held accountable. He was only following orders from Admiral Nazeer. The last orders he received from the com operator aboard the *Glorious* were, and I quote, 'Admiral Nazeer states that the *Glorious* is under attack by a Spacc force. He orders you to break off.'"

"Break off?"

"That was the order Wolff received. Then the com channel went dead. Following that, only encrypted signals on a Space Command frequency were received from the area where the battleship had been positioned. We've confirmed the authenticity of the message by also checking the logs of several other ships that survived the attack. We may never know why Admiral Nazeer gave such an order; perhaps he panicked. When Space Command encrypted messages were detected coming from the area where the command vessel had been stationed, Wolff naturally feared that an unexpected Spacc task force was about to descend upon them as happened at Vauzlee. By that time, our remaining task force was too badly damaged to take on a fresh Spacc assault force. He immediately ordered all ships to break off, as ordered, and head in different directions before proceeding to the Raider Four base when they were sure they weren't being trailed."

"But there wasn't any other Spacc task force," Councilman Blosworth said. "It was just Carver with her heavy cruiser."

"Yes," Strauss said with a single chuckle, "just one mid-level officer with a severe stomach wound. Pretorious' aim was apparently a little off."

"Are you going to increase the bounty?" Councilwoman Overgaard asked.

"No. In fact, I've lowered it. I've felt the amount was excessive from the moment Gagarin set it. I've reduced it to ten thousand credits."

"No professional assassin is going to attack a highly visible Spacc officer for a mere ten thousand credits," Councilman Kelleher said as he scratched his bearded chin. "An assassin would have to be pretty desperate or hopped up on narcotics to attempt such a mission. Killing a Spacc officer is always a risky business. It's not like killing a mere business leader or politician. If Space Command identified the assassin, he'd suddenly find he had a million Spaccs looking for him with murder in their eyes."

"That's perfectly acceptable. I've never approved of this kind of revenge anyway. I'm only offering the ten thousand because Upper Councilman Stengel is upset with Carver for destroying the pretty new battleship they'd planned to use as a temporary base in that deca-sector after Higgins was obliterated. In a few months when he's calmed down, I'll try again to convince him to drop the bounty altogether. I agree we must keep Carver under close observation, but I've cancelled the *accident* I'd arranged at Gagarin's behest."

"I support that position," Councilwoman Overgaard said. "We cannot allow ourselves to get caught up in ridiculous revenge operations. This is a business."

Chairman Strauss nodded. "Unless anyone has anything more to add, this meeting is ended. Oh, one last thing. If anyone cares to attend, there will be a brief graveside ceremony this Friday for Chairman Gagarin. That's all. Goodnight."

*　*　*

On Saturday, the 7th of November, 2268, the entire Carver family traveled together to the Galactic Alliance Headquarters Complex in Nebraska for the Medal of Honor ceremony. Nary a cloud was visible in a clear sky of deep majestic blue. Although the overnight air temperature had dipped slightly below the predicted fourteen degrees centigrade, bright sunlight was rapidly warming the countryside to comfortable levels. A massive raised stage sat on the edge of the parade ground within three concave, semi-circular rings of tall flagpoles, each bearing the cloth emblem of a member planet in the Galactic Alliance. Two thousand folding chairs erected to seat the expected attendees filled the field in front of the stage.

Upon their arrival, Jenetta was immediately directed to a structure beneath the stage where officials were assembling in preparation for going up top. Her family was meanwhile escorted to front row seating. All heads in the room swiveled in her direction as Jenetta entered and was intercepted by Admiral Moore's chief aide. Captain Knott then escorted her around the room, introducing her to people in their order of importance, beginning with the Chairman of the Galactic Alliance Council.

"It's a distinct honor to meet the officer who has played such a key role in making travel on the spaceways once again safe for the citizens of our nation," Chairman Neville Oscar Rainey said obstreperously as he smiled and extended his hand. Naughty Nev, as he was known in the media for the frequent rumors of successful seductions among both single and married women, had been a professional politician for all of his life. A tall, handsome man, he had a soft speaking voice when he wasn't trying to be the center of attention. Like all other successful politicians, he had the gift of making people feel like his best friend in the world, even when he found it necessary or desirable to twist the knife he had just shoved into their back. "You've rekindled hope that we will one day wipe out the scourge that has menaced our peoples for so many years. My office door will always be open to you, Commander. If there's ever anything I can do, please call on me."

"Thank you, Mr. Chairman," Jenetta said.

Fearful Jenetta might be so politically naïve as to actually believe a politician meant it when he used the old 'call on me if you ever need anything' cliché, Captain Knott dragged her away before she had a chance to actually ask for something.

As each of the political officials welcomed her home to Earth and thanked her for her service to the Alliance, Jenetta smiled and thanked them for the honor they had chosen to bestow upon her. Admiral Moore's aide kept her moving through the crowd so she would have a chance to meet everyone before they had to go onstage. There had been so few such occasions in recent decades that every politician who could wangle a seat on the stage had come here to be seen. Someone had even taken pity on the President of the United States, who was currently involved in a hotly contested bid for reelection, and allowed him a seat in the back row. No other representatives of Earth countries had been granted such a privilege because there were too many GA politicians who wanted seats and who had pulled every string and called in every favor owed to get one.

After being introduced to all of the political officials present, even the U.S. President, Jenetta was introduced to the Space Command Officers in the room, beginning with Admiral Moore.

"I can't tell you how pleased I am to meet you at last, Commander," the eighty-year-old Admiral said, "and to welcome you home to Earth. You've done a spectacular job for the Galactic Alliance and for Space Command. You're really just beginning your career, but what a beginning it has been. Few military officers throughout history have enjoyed the overwhelming success in a lifetime of service that you've had at such a young age."

"Thank you, sir. I'm delighted to once again stand on the planet of my birth. I've admired you for a long time and it's a particular honor for me to meet you today."

Admiral Moore smiled kindly as Jenetta was pulled away to be introduced to the other members of the Admiralty Board. All had come to meet the young woman except Admiral Hubera, who maintained he'd already had the *honor* of her acquaintance for an entire semester at the Academy.

With the help of Admiral Moore's aide, Jenetta managed to meet everyone present before it was time for the ceremony to begin. Captain Knott, previously anxious about what Jenetta might inadvertently say and fully prepared to cover any solecism unwittingly wrought by her political naïveté, was delighted she had weathered the session like an experienced political campaigner.

* * *

Flags undulated proudly in the freshening breeze as political officials and military officers climbed the steps to the stage. The grass of the parade ground had begun to adopt a sickly brown color recently as the vegetation made its annual preparation for the bleak winter months ahead, but grounds-keepers had sprayed a chlorophyll-based dye that made the parade grounds appear as green as they had in late spring.

A full regiment of meticulously groomed Space Marines wearing their striking medium-blue and dark-blue dress uniforms launched the ceremony. Led by the renowned Space Marine Marching Band to the strains of a John Philip Sousa inspirational tune, they paraded through the narrow area between stage and guest seating, then continued around the field to the open area behind the guest seating where they formed up their ranks, remaining at attention until ordered to adopt a Parade Rest stance.

Rather than permitting dozens of vid teams from the various news organizations to run rampant during the ceremony, the event was being filmed by Space Command Public Relations personnel. From the main PR building, the SCPR cameramen controlled vidcams that floated inconspicuously at a dozen prime vantage points around the grounds. Housed in the same kind of camouflage battle armor that allow Marines to completely blend into the background, the 'oh-gee' vidcams were almost impossible to spot without performing an electronic sweep. The newsies were permitted to tap into the signal feeds being relayed to a vid center in the main PR building. Those few actually in attendance at the parade grounds were required to remain in their seats until the ceremony was complete under threat of permanent expulsion from any and all GA and SC events.

So many years had passed since the last ceremony to award a Medal of Honor that the politicians were determined to exploit it to the maximum. Despite half-hearted attempts by Space Command to limit the time exhausted by key political figures, a series of long-winded speeches about Space Command and what it meant to the citizens of the Galactic Alliance was inevitable.

Jenetta sat stiffly between Captain Gavin and Commander Kanes in the front row on stage while her family watched from the reserved front row guest seating. As a young girl, she had scorned skirts and dresses, but following her enslavement by the Raiders an increased predisposition for such garments in formal situations had developed. Space Command gave female officers the right to wear either trousers or a skirt as part of their dress uniform and Jenetta had chosen the latter for the ceremony. Her mother was delighted to see her daughter exhibiting signs of increasing feminine behavior and the hundreds of male attendees who spent the hours ogling her gorgeous legs appreciated her choice of uniform as well.

At long last Jenetta was called to center stage. She stood, took two steps forward, and turned sharply to face the podium before marching to confront the most senior officer in Space Command. As she stood at attention before Richard E. Moore, Space Command's Admiral of the Fleet, he read the official citation.

"Lt. Commander Jenetta Alicia Carver, Galactic Space Command, has distinguished herself by actions above and beyond the call of duty. On 20 July 2267 through 11 August 2267, then *Ensign* Carver, cut-off from Space Command supervision and on her own initiative, undertook to infiltrate a Raider stronghold for the purpose of gathering intelligence information…"

Jenetta's mind wandered as the admiral's voice droned on in praise of her accomplishments. She thought about the *Vordoth*, the Nordakians, the fearful enemy actions, the dangerous yet exciting penetration into Raider-One, and her escape from the detention center, trying, unsuccessfully, to forget her time spent as a prisoner of the Raiders. She came back to reality as the admiral neared completion in his reading of the citation.

"…where she remanded her prisoners to Space Marine custody and relinquished command of the two recovered battleships to the Space Command senior staff at the base. Lt. Commander Carver's extraordinary heroism and devotion to duty have been in keeping with the highest standards of military service and reflect great credit upon her and the Galactic Space Command."

Finally, Admiral Moore lifted the wide blue ribbon bearing the medal from the open case being held by his aide and placed it around Jenetta's neck, where he clasped the two ends. He then came to attention, took one step back, and saluted Jenetta. She returned the salute sharply, performed an about-face, and returned to her seat as the audience applauded and cheered. As she stood in front of her chair until the audience's exuberance began to wane, she wondered facetiously how much was out of gratitude that she wasn't going to make a speech also. The Chairman of the Galactic Alliance Council gave a 'brief' twenty-minute address in praise of Jenetta's accomplishments and then closed the ceremony.

A large assembly of people remained behind to personally congratulate Jenetta after the Space Marine divisions had marched proudly from the field and the politicians had moved through the crowd, glad-handing the electorate. Most of the officers of the *Song* and *Prometheus* were among those waiting to personally congratulate her, as were many of the Academy classmates who had attended her funeral service following the disaster that befell the *Hokyuu*. Jenetta spent about an hour smiling and accepting congratulations before the crowd started to disperse. She recorded the contact information from a number of her former classmates and promised to be in touch when she had time.

As Jenetta approached her family afterwards, her father and brothers, all in full dress uniform, lined up. They came to rigid attention and saluted her while her mother looked on proudly. As she faced them and returned the salute, Jenetta choked up. Tears stung the corners of her eyes. She had worked so hard for so many years to gain the same respect she had always felt towards them and this simple gesture on their part was more precious to her than all the awards Space Command could possibly bestow in a lifetime. A newsie who had hung around after all the rest had gone to file their stories had seen her approach her family and quickly shot a vid that captured the entire tender scene. A frame from it appeared as a front page news lead around Galactic Alliance space in the following days. Anyone viewing that image would *never* have the impression that the youngest member of the Carver family was any less loved and respected than any other.

Perhaps it was time to change the old image in the 20x30 centimeter black anodized frame she always kept on her bedroom dresser.

~ finis ~

Jenetta's epic adventures continue in:

*** **The Clones of Mawcett** ***

Appendix

This chart is offered to assist readers who may be unfamiliar with military rank and the reporting structure. Newly commissioned officers begin at either ensign or second lieutenant rank.

Space Command	Space Marine Corps
Admiral of the Fleet	
Admiral	General
Vice-Admiral	Lieutenant General
Rear Admiral - Upper	Major General
Rear Admiral - Lower	Brigadier General
Captain	Colonel
Commander	Lieutenant Colonel
Lieutenant Commander	Major
Lieutenant	Captain
Lieutenant(jg) "Junior Grade"	First Lieutenant
Ensign	Second Lieutenant

The commanding officer on a ship is always referred to as Captain, regardless of his or her official military rank. Even an Ensign could be a Captain of the Ship, although that would only occur as the result of an unusual situation or emergency where no senior officers survived.

On Space Command ships and bases, time is measured according to a twenty-four-hour clock, normally referred to as military time. For example, 8:42 PM would be referred to as 2042 hours. Chronometers are always set to agree with the date and time at Space Command Supreme Headquarters on Earth. This is known as GST, or Galactic System Time.

Admiralty Board:

Moore, Richard E.	Admiral of the Fleet
Platt, Evelyn S.	Admiral - Director of Fleet Operations
Bradlee, Roger T.	Admiral - Director of Intelligence (SCI)
Ressler, Shana E.	Admiral - Director of Budget & Accounting
Hillaire, Arnold H.	Admiral - Director of Academies
Burke, Raymond A.	Vice-Admiral - Director of GSC Base Management
Ahmed, Raihana L.	Vice-Admiral - Dir. of Quartermaster Supply
Woo, Lon C.	Vice-Admiral - Dir. of Scientific & Expeditionary Forces
Plimley, Loretta J.	Rear-Admiral, (U) - Dir. of Weapons R&D
Hubera, Donald M.	Rear-Admiral, (U) - Dir. of Academy Curricula

Ship Speed Terminology	*Speed*
Plus-1	1 kps
Sub-Light-1	1,000 kps
Light-1 (*c*) (speed of light in a vacuum)	299,792.458 kps
Light-150 or **150 c**	150 times the speed of light

Hyper-Space Factors	
IDS Communications Band	.0513 light years each minute (8.09 billion kps)
DeTect Range	4 billion kilometers

Strat Com Desig	Mission Description for Strategic Command Bases
1	Base - Location establishes it as a critical component of Space Command Operations - Serves as home-port to multiple warships that also serve in base's defense. All sections of Space Command maintain an active office at the base. Base Commander establishes all patrol routes and is authorized to override SHQ orders to ships within the sector(s) designated part of the base's operating territory. Recommended rank of Commanding Officer: **Rear Admiral (U)**
2	Base - Location establishes it as a crucial component of Space Command Operations - Serves as home-port to multiple warships that also serve in base's defense. All sections of Space Command maintain an active office at the base. Patrol routes established by SHQ. Recommended rank of Commanding Officer: **Rear Admiral (L)**
3	Base - Location establishes it as an important component of Space Command Operations - Serves as homeport to multiple warships that also serve in base's defense. Patrol routes established by SHQ. Recommended rank of Commanding Officer: **Captain**
4	Station - Location establishes it as an important terminal for Space Command personnel engaged in travel to/from postings, and for re-supply of vessels and outposts. Recommended rank of Commanding Officer: **Commander**
5	Outpost - Location makes it important for observation purposes and collection of information. Recommended rank of Commanding Officer: **Lt. Commander**

Sample Distances

Earth to Mars (Mean)	78 million kilometers
Nearest star to our Sun	4 light-years (Proxima Centauri)
Milky Way Galaxy diameter	100,000 light-years
Thickness of M'Way at Sun	2,000 light-years
Stars in Milky Way	200 billion (est.)
Nearest galaxy (Andromeda)	2 million light-years from M'Way
A light-year (in a vacuum)	9,460,730,472,580.8 kilometers
A light-second (in vacuum)	299,792.458 km
Grid Unit	1,000 Light Yrs² (1,000,000 Sq. LY)
Deca-Sector	100 Light Years² (10,000 Sq. LY)
Sector	10 Light Years² (100 Sq. LY)
Section	94,607,304,725 km²
Sub-section	946,073,047 km²

The following two-dimensional representation is offered to provide the reader with a feel for the spatial relationships between bases, systems, and celestial events referenced in the first three novels of this series. The mean distance from Earth to Higgins Space Command Base has been calculated as 90.1538 light-years. The thousands of stars, planets, and moons in this small part of G.A. space would only confuse, and therefore have been omitted from the image.

Should the map be unreadable, or should you desire additional imagery, .jpg and .pdf versions of all maps are avail-able for free downloading at:

www.deprima.com/ancillary/agu.html

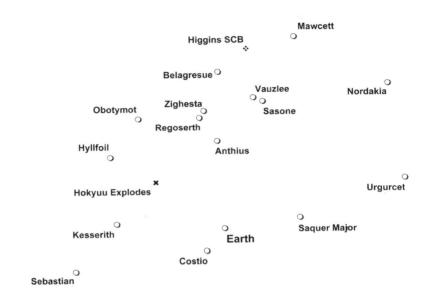

Lazziter ○

Mawcett ○

Higgins SCB ❖

Belagresue ○

Vauzlee ○ ○

Nordakia ○

Obotymot ○

Zighesta ○

Sasone

Regoserth

Hyllfoil ○

Anthius ○

×
Hokyuu Explodes

Urgurcet ○

Kesserith ○

Saquer Major ○

Earth ○

Costio ○

Sebastian ○

❖ Ethridge SCB

Made in the USA
Lexington, KY
22 April 2013